"What?" I snap[...] were staring into [...] chest heaving with short, rapid breaths.

"Bayta?" I asked, dropping down on the bed beside her and taking her hand. It was icy cold. "Bayta, what is it?"

"They killed him," she whispered, her voice shaking. "They killed one of the Spiders."

"Who did?" I asked, a creepy feeling running up my back.

"The crowd, the mob. All of them. They're attacking the Spiders," she murmured, her eyes still blank, "and they're going to kill them all."

She closed her eyes. "And then they're going to kill us."

* * *

"Tim Zahn's *Night Train to Rigel* is SF adventure in the classic mode. Have fun!"
—*Analog Magazine*

BOOKS BY TIMOTHY ZAHN

*Denotes a Tor Book
†Denotes forthcoming

Night Train to Rigel

TIMOTHY ZAHN

A TOM DOHERTY ASSOCIATES BOOK
NEW YORK

This is a work of fiction. All the characters and events portrayed in this book are either products of the author's imagination or are used fictitiously.

NIGHT TRAIN TO RIGEL

Copyright © 2005 by Timothy Zahn

All rights reserved, including the right to reproduce this book, or portions thereof, in any form.

Edited by James Frenkel

A Tor Book
Published by Tom Doherty Associates, LLC
175 Fifth Avenue
New York, NY 10010

www.tor.com

Tor® is a registered trademark of Tom Doherty Associates, LLC.

ISBN-13: 978-0-765-34644-5
ISBN-10: 0-765-34644-3

First edition: October 2005
First mass market edition: October 2006

Printed in the United States of America

0 9 8 7 6 5 4 3 2 1

For
Pastor Rick House—
who has helped keep me
on the rails

Night Train to RIGEL

ONE :

He was leaning against the side of an autocab by the curb as I walked through the door and atmosphere curtain of the New Pallas Towers into the chilly Manhattan night air. He was short and thin, with no facial hair, and wore a dark brown overcoat with a lighter brown shirt and slacks beneath it. Probably no more than seventeen or eighteen years old, I estimated, the sort of person you wouldn't normally give a second look to if you passed him on the walkway.

Which was why I gave him a very careful second look as I headed down the imported Belldic marble steps toward street level. I had no doubt there were plenty of nondescript people wandering the streets of New York this December evening, but their proper place was the nondescript parts of the city, not here in the habitats of the rich and powerful. There was already one person out of his proper social position in this neighborhood—me—and it would be unreasonable to expect two such exceptions at the same place at the same time.

He watched me silently from beneath droopy eyelids, his arms folded across his chest, his hands hidden from view. A beggar or mugger should be moving toward me at this point, I knew, while an honest citizen would be politely stepping out of my way. This character was doing neither. I found myself studying those folded arms, wondering what he might have in his hands and wishing mightily that Western Alliance Intelligence hadn't revoked my carry permit when they'd cashiered me fourteen months earlier.

I was within three steps of the kid when he finally stirred, his half-lidded eyes opening, his forehead creasing in concentration. "Frank Compton," he said in a gravelly voice.

It had been a statement, not a question. "That's right," I confirmed. "Do I know you?"

A half smile touched his lips as he unfolded his arms. I tensed, but both hands were empty. His left hand dropped limply to his side; his right floundered a bit and then found its way into his overcoat's side pocket.

It was still there as he slid almost leisurely off the side of the autocab and crumpled into a heap on the sidewalk, his eyes staring unseeingly into the night sky.

And with the streetlights now shining more directly on him, I could see that his coat was wet in half a dozen places.

I dropped to a crouch beside the body and looked around. A kid with this many holes in him couldn't have traveled very far, and whoever had done this to him might be waiting to add a second trophy to the evening's hit list. But there were no loitering pedestrians or suspicious parked vehicles that I could see. Trying not to think about rooftop assassins with hypersonic rifles and electronic targeting systems, I turned my attention to the kid himself.

Three of the bloodstains were over the pinprick-sized holes of snoozer loads, the kind used by police and private security services when they want to stop someone without using deadly force. The remaining wounds were the much larger caliber of thudwumpers, the next tier of seriousness in the modern urban hunter's arsenal.

The tier beyond that would have been military-class shredders. I was just as glad the attacker hadn't made it to that level.

Carefully, I reached past his limp hand into his overcoat pocket and poked around. There was nothing there but a thin plastic folder of the sort used for carrying credit tags or cash sticks. I pulled it out, angled it toward the marquee light from the New Pallas behind me, and flipped it open.

There was a single item inside: a shimmery copper-edged ticket for a seat on Trans-Galactic Quadrail Number 339216, due to depart Terra Station at 7:55 P.M. on December 27, 2084, seven days away. The travel designation was third class, the seat listed was number twenty-two in car fifteen.

The destination was the Rigel star system and the Earth colony of Yandro.

Yandro, the fourth and final colony in the United Nations Directorate's grand scheme to turn humanity into a true interstellar species and bring us into social equality with the eleven genuine empires stretching across the galaxy. Yandro, a planet that had been a complete and utter drain on Sol's resources ever since the first colonists had set out ten years ago with the kind of media whoop usually reserved for pop culture stars.

Yandro, the reason I'd been kicked out of Western Alliance Intelligence in the first place.

I looked at the dead face still pointed skyward. I have a pretty good memory for faces, but this one still wasn't ringing any bells. Shifting my attention back to the ticket, I skipped down to the passenger information section at the bottom.

And found myself looking at a digitized photo of myself.

I stared at it, the back of my neck starting to tingle. The photo was mine, the name and ID number printed below it were mine, and if the thumbprint wasn't mine it was a damn close copy.

Long experience had taught me that it wasn't a good idea to be caught in the vicinity of a dead body, especially one as freshly dead as this. I took a minute anyway to go through the kid's other pockets.

It was a waste of a perfectly good minute. He had no ID, no credit tags, no handkerchief, no pocketknife, no unpaid bills, no letters from home. Besides the ticket folder, all he had was a single cash stick with a hundred ninety dollars left on it.

From behind me came the sound of chattering voices, and I turned to see a party of four impeccably dressed young people emerging from the New Pallas for a night on the town. Casually, I stood up and stepped past the crumpled figure, heading down the street as quickly as I could without looking obvious about it. The movers and shakers who lived in this part of the city did occasionally have to deal with the distasteful business of death, but it was always done in the most genteel and civilized manner, which meant they had genteel and civilized thugs on the payroll to do it for them. I doubted that any of the theater-bound party tripping lightly down the steps had ever even seen a dead body before, and they were likely to make a serious commotion when they finally spotted him. I intended to be well on my way to elsewhere when that happened.

I'd made it to the end of the block, and had turned the corner, when something made me pause and look back.

There was a figure standing in front of the body. A slim, nondescript figure, his shoulders hunched and his head forward, clearly leaning over for a close look at the dearly departed. With the distance and the restless shadows thrown by the streetlights, I couldn't make out his face. But his body language wasn't that of someone horribly shocked or panicked. Apparently, dead bodies weren't anything new to him.

And as I watched, he straightened up and turned to look in my direction.

With a supreme act of will, I forced my feet not to break into a full-fledged sprint, but to continue with my original brisk stroll. The man made no move toward me, but merely watched until I'd moved out of sight around the side of the corner building.

I walked two more blocks, just to be on the safe side. Then, as the wail of sirens began to burn through the night, I flagged down an autocab.

"Good evening," the computerized voice said as I climbed in. "Destination, please?"

I looked at the folder still gripped in my hand. Seven days until the train listed on the ticket. Slightly less than a seven-day flight from Earth to the Quadrail station sitting in the outer solar system near Jupiter's orbit. If I was going to catch that train, I was going to have to leave right now.

Awkward, and very spur-of-the-moment. But in some ways, it could actually work out to my advantage. I'd been planning on taking the Quadrail out into the galaxy sometime in the next couple of weeks anyway, buying my ticket with the brand-new credit tag in my pocket. This way, I could at least begin the trip on someone else's dollar.

Only I hadn't intended on heading out quite this soon. And I hadn't intended on beginning my journey at any of Earth's pitiful handful of frontierland colony worlds.

I certainly hadn't intended to leave with a dead body behind me.

But someone had gone to a great deal of trouble and expense to buy me a ticket to Yandro. Someone else had given his life to get that ticket into my hands.

And someone else had apparently been equally determined to prevent that ticket from reaching me.

"Destination, please?"

I dropped the folder into my pocket and pulled out my cash stick, wishing I'd taken the dead kid's stick when I'd had the chance. My credit tag contained an embarrassment of riches, but tag transactions were traceable. Cash stick ones weren't. "Grand and Mercer," I told the cab, plugging the stick into the payment jack. Fifteen minutes at my apartment to get packed, another autocab ride to Sutherlin Skyport, and I should be able to catch the next flight for Luna and the Quadrail station. If the torchliners were running on time this week, I should make it with a few hours to spare.

"Thank you," the cab said, and pulled smoothly away into the traffic flow.

The moonroof was open, and as we headed south along Seventh Avenue I found myself gazing at the few stars I could see through the glow of the city lights. I found the distinctive trio of Orion's belt and lowered my gaze to the star Rigel at the Hunter's knee, wondering if our own sun was even visible from Yandro.

I didn't know. But it looked like I was going to have the chance to find out.

TWO :

"Attention, please," the soothing voice called over the restaurant loudspeakers. "Quadrail Number 339216 will be arriving from Helvanti and the Bellidosh Estates-General in one hour. All passengers for New Tigris, Yandro, the Jurian Collective, and the Cimmal Republic please assemble in the Green debarkation lounge. Attention please . . ."

The voice ran through the message once more in English, then switched over to Juric and then Mahee. Finishing the last two bites of my burger, I wiped my hands and poked my cash stick into the jack on the bar in front of me. Most of the restaurant's other customers were staying put, I noted, apparently booked on later trains. Sliding off my stool, I activated the leash button fastened inside my coat and my two ancient carrybags rolled out from beneath the counter.

They'd made it about two meters when one of the motors in the larger one seized up and started it rolling in circles. Swearing under my breath, I shut off the leash and scooped the bags up by their handles, hoping no one had noticed. There were few things more ridiculous looking than misfiring luggage, and few things more pathetic than an owner too lazy or too poor to get it fixed. Slinging the larger bag's strap over my shoulder, trying to look like I was just carrying them for the exercise, I headed for the door.

I was halfway there when I saw The Girl get up from one of the booths and join the trickle of exiting patrons, her own single carrybag trailing obediently behind her.

I'd first spotted her at Sutherlin Skyport as we'd gotten on the Luna flight together, her third-class seat five rows up from mine. She'd been hovering at the edges of my attention ever since, through three separate flights and two different transfer stations.

Now, it seemed, she was also going to be traveling on my Quadrail.

The fact that we'd spent a week on the same space vessels was no big deal in and of itself, of course. There was only one practical set of scheduled flight connections between the Atlantic side of the Western Alliance and the Quadrail transfer station. Anyone who had decided to take a trip to the stars within a three- or four-day window had no choice but to fly with me.

My problem was that The Girl didn't seem to fit any of the standard passenger profiles. I hadn't seen her mingle with any of the other travelers, or even speak to the attendants except on business. Space travel had its share of the shy and the aloof and the just plain oblivious, but most of those eventually gravitated to one activity or another aboard ship, even if it was just to wrap themselves in a cocoon of stargazing silence in one of the observation lounges. I'd made it a point to periodically wander through all the public areas of the torchliner, and I'd never seen The Girl outside her cabin except during meals or an occasional visit to one of the shops. She hadn't even shown up for the shipboard Christmas celebration.

I gazed at her back now as we walked down the corridor toward the debarkation lounge, watching the light glint off her short, dark brown hair. She was about twenty-two, a decade younger than I was, with eyes that matched the color of her hair and the slender, trim figure of someone who exercised to keep in shape, as opposed to someone who did hard physical labor for a living. Her face was pretty enough, but there was a strange sort of distance to her eyes that was more than a little disconcerting. Possibly one reason I'd never seen anyone aboard the torchliner approach her more than once.

And there was one other peculiarity I'd noted during our flight: Never had I seen her pay for anything with a credit tag. With her, apparently, it was strictly cash sticks.

Of course, I wasn't using anything but cash sticks, either. But I had good reasons for not wanting anyone to trace my recent movements. Not with the body I'd left back at the New Pallas Towers.

I wondered what reasons The Girl had.

The shuttle was already loading when our restaurant contingent arrived. I made my way inside, found a seat, and threw my bags up onto the safety-webbed conveyer that would carry them up to the roof luggage hatchway. Fifteen minutes later we undocked. Passing beneath the guns and missile ports of the Terran Confederation battle platform floating overhead like a brooding predator, we started across the final fifty-kilometer leg of our journey to the Quadrail station.

I gazed out the window as we approached, half listening to the murmurs and twitterings from the first-timers among us. The Quadrail Tube lay across the starscape straight ahead, a shiny metal cylinder stretching seemingly to infinity in both directions. Despite its sheen, it was strangely difficult to see until you were practically on top of it, which was probably why a hundred years of outer-system probes had drifted through the space around Jupiter without ever noticing this thing sitting just beyond its orbit.

The ends of the Tube were even harder to see, fading away in both directions as the whole thing receded into the strange hyperspace where most of it lay. There had been a few attempts to follow the cylinder out to those vanishing points, but no matter how far you went, the Tube seemed perfectly solid the whole way. A trans-optical illusion, the experts called it, a fancy way of saying they didn't have the foggiest idea how it worked.

But then, as far as I knew, none of the other alien races who traveled the Quadrail knew how it worked, either. The Spiders who ran the system were the only ones in on the secret, and they weren't talking.

The station itself was an extra-wide spot in the Tube, five kilometers long and two in diameter, with hatches of various sizes set in neat rows around its surface. Current theory held that it had to be built wider than the rest of the Tube in order to bring it more solidly into normal space. The more cynical view was that the Spiders had to do *something* to justify the trillion-dollar fee they charged to put a Quadrail station into a solar system.

Two of the smaller hatchways had passenger shuttles like ours already snugged up to them, ready to pick up incoming passengers. Another ten or twelve of the cargo hatches were similarly occupied, which meant there must be at least one freight train arriving soon as well. Cargo was the true economic backbone of the operation, of course, given that the Quadrail carried every gram of trade that passed among the galaxy's thousands of inhabited star systems. Passenger transport was nice to have, but in the larger scheme of things I suspected all of us together barely registered as a footnote on the Spiders' balance sheet.

Our shuttle eased past a drifting maintenance skiff and zeroed in on a hatch marked with bright lavender lights, rolling over to press its upper surface against the alien metal. There was a click of lockseals, and the shuttle's dorsal hatch slid open. Sensing the presence of air against it, the station's hatch irised open in response, and the passengers unfastened their restraints and floated their way into a civilized line at the ladder.

The information cards everyone received with their tickets emphasized the fact that, unlike the transfer station's rotational pseudogravity or the Shorshic-style vectored force thrusters that everyone else in the galaxy used, the Tube's system of artificial gravity began right at the inner edge of the entrance hatch. But there was always one idiot per shuttle who hadn't bothered to read the directions. Ours was six people ahead of me, floating with brisk confidence up alongside the ladder and then abruptly changing direction as his head poked through the hatch and the Tube's gravity grabbed him and shoved him straight back down again. On his next try, he made sure to hang on to the ladder the whole way up like he was supposed to.

And a minute later, for the first time in over two years, I was standing inside the greatest engineering feat the universe had ever known.

The station's general layout was prosaic enough, and aside from the fact that it was built into the inside of a huge cylinder, it would have felt right at home beside any Earthbound train or monorail yard. There were thirty sets of four-railed tracks spaced evenly around the surface, with groups of elegantly designed buildings set between them that functioned as service centers, maintenance facilities, restaurants, and waiting rooms for passengers transferring between different lines.

Why four rails were needed per track was one more mystery in the Quadrail's stack of unanswered questions. Two rails this size were required for physical stability, and a third could be explained if power was being run to the trains from an external source. But no one could figure out why the system needed a fourth.

Most people probably never even wondered about it. In fact, at this point in their journey, most people didn't even know the tracks were there. The first thing *everyone* noticed when they first entered the Tube was the Coreline.

The official rundown on the Quadrail described the Coreline as an optically coruscating pipe inside the Quadrail Tube of unknown composition and purpose, which was rather like describing a bird of paradise as a flying thing with colors. Ten meters in diameter, glowing and sparkling and flashing with every color in the spectrum—including deep infrared and ultraviolet—the Coreline was like a light show on caffeine overdose. At apparently random intervals the pattern changes increased in speed and intensity, and most people swore they could see the thing writhing like an overtensioned wire getting ready to snap. The loose wire meshwork that encased the Coreline another dozen meters out added to the illusion, looking like a protective safety screen put there to protect passengers from shrapnel if and when the thing finally blew.

Fortunately, sensor measurements had long since proved that the writhing was just another optical illusion. Those same measurements had also confirmed that the aptly named Coreline did indeed run along the exact geometric center of the Tube.

And that was *all* the sensors revealed. Most of the experts agreed that the Coreline was the key to how the Quadrail system operated—all except those who insisted it was the fourth rail, of course—but that was as far as anyone had ever gotten. No scanning equipment compact enough to fit through the Tube's hatches had enough power to penetrate the Coreline's outer skin to see what kind of equipment was tucked away inside, and the more powerful warship-class sensors couldn't penetrate the outer wall of the Tube itself. Information stalemate, in other words, which was exactly how the Spiders liked it.

"Welcome, traveler," a flat voice said in my ear.

Speak of the devils. Adjusting my expression to neutral, I turned around.

A Spider was standing behind me, a gray half-meter-diameter sphere hanging beneath an arching crown of seven segmented legs, the whole thing softly reflecting the Coreline's ongoing light show. The whole thing was about twice my height, with the sphere hanging half a meter above my eye level, which marked this particular Spider as a maintenance drudge. That alone was noteworthy; usually it was the smaller conductors who did whatever communicating the Spiders deemed necessary. "Welcome yourself," I replied wittily. "What can I do for you?"

"Where is your luggage?" it asked.

I looked back at the mass of bags being ferried up from

the shuttle, some of them starting to roll away as their owners keyed their leashes. "Over there somewhere," I said, pointing. "Why?"

"Please bring it here," the Spider said. "It must be inspected."

I felt my stomach tightening. In all my previous trips aboard the Quadrail the only times I'd seen anyone's luggage pulled for inspection was when the Spiders' unobtrusive sensor array had already decided there was something inside that violated their contraband rules. "Certainly," I said, trying to sound calm as I tapped the leash button, hoping fervently that the bags wouldn't embarrass me by dying halfway.

For a wonder they didn't, successfully maneuvering their way around the rest of the luggage to where the Spider and I waited. "Shall I open them?" I asked.

"No." The Spider stepped over them and shifted to a five-legged stance, deftly inserting the ends of its other two legs into the handles and lifting the bags into the air like a weight lifter doing bending bicep curls. "They will be returned," it added, and strode off toward one of the buildings beside the track where my Quadrail was scheduled to arrive.

I watched it go, wondering like everyone else in the galaxy what the devil was inside those dangling globes. But the Spiders' metallic skin was just as effective at blocking sensor scans as the Coreline was. They could be robots, androids, trained ducks, or something so weird that no one had even thought of it yet. It disappeared into the building, and with a sudden premonition, I spun around.

The Girl was standing over by the pile of luggage, her carrybag at her feet, watching me. For a second we held each other's gaze across the distance. Then, as if she'd just realized that I was looking back at her, she lowered her eyes.

Scowling, I turned and headed for the platform. If the Quadrail was on time—and I'd never heard of one being late—it would pull into the station exactly eight minutes from now. Thirty minutes after that, it would pull out again, with me on board.

The Spiders had until then to return my luggage, or there was going to be hell to pay.

Seven minutes later, far down the Tube, the telltale red glow of our Quadrail appeared.

The rest of the passengers had gathered on the platform, and once again I could hear the amazed and slightly nervous twitterings of the first-timers. The train approached rapidly, the red glow resolving into a pair of brilliant laserlike beams flashing between the engine's oversized front bumper and the Coreline overhead. In the spots where the beams touched it, the Coreline's own light show became even more agitated, and I amused myself by watching out of the corner of my eye as several of the uninitiated eased a few steps backward. The lasers winked out, and the dark mass resolved into a shiny silver engine pulling a line of equally shiny silver cars, the whole thing decelerating rapidly as it neared the platform. The engine and first few cars rolled past us, and with a squeal of brakes the Quadrail came to a halt.

There were sixteen cars in this particular train, each with a single door near the front. The doors irised open simultaneously and each disgorged a conductor Spider, a more or less Human-sized version of the drudge who'd made off earlier with my luggage. The conductors moved to the sides of the doors and stood there like Buckingham Palace sentries as lines of Humans and aliens maneuvered their carrybags out onto the platform and headed for either the waiting rooms or the glowing hatchways marking the spots where shuttles were waiting. At the rear, drudges were busily removing larger pieces of luggage from the baggage car for transfer to the shuttles, while on the far side of the train I knew other drudges would be doing likewise with the various undercar storage compartments.

I looked toward the front of the train, where a pair of drudges had reached the engine. One of them set its feet into a line of embedded rings and climbed partially up the side to a slightly lumpy box set into the engine's roof just behind a compact dish antenna. Two of the spindly legs reached up and popped the box lid open, delicately removing a flattened message cylinder and handing it down to the other drudge waiting below. The second Spider accepted the cylinder and passed up one of its own, which the first then replaced in the box. Deceptively compact, those cylinders were packed with the most current news from around the galaxy, along with private electronic messages and encrypted data of all sorts.

Passengers, cargo, and mail, the ultimate hat trick of any civilization. All of it running via the Quadrail.

All of it under the control of the Spiders.

A few minutes later the outward flow of passengers ended, and the line of conductors took a multilegged step forward. "All aboard Trans-Galactic Quadrail 339216, to New Tigris, Yandro, the Jurian Collective, the Cimmal Republic, and intermediate transfer nodes," they announced in unison, verbalizing the information that was also being given by a multilanguage holodisplay suspended over the train. "Departure in twenty-three minutes."

The crowd surged forward as the Spiders repeated the announcement in Juric and Mahee, rather a waste of time since there weren't any Juriani or Cimmaheem waiting for this particular Quadrail. But procedure was procedure, as I'd learned during my years of government service, and not to be trifled with merely because it didn't happen to make sense. Circling around the back of the crowd, I headed for Car Fifteen, the last one before the baggage car.

My ticket had come edged in copper, which had already indicated it was one of the lower-class seats. But it wasn't until I climbed through the door and stepped past a stack of safety-webbed cargo crates into the aisle that I realized just how far down the food chain I actually was. Car Fifteen was a hybrid: basically a baggage carrier, stacked three-deep on both sides with secured cargo crates, with a single column of thirty seats shoehorned like an afterthought between the aisle and the wall of boxes to the right.

A half dozen nonhumans were already seated: Cimmaheem, Juriani, and a lone Bellido, none of them paying any attention to me as I worked my way down the aisle. The Juriani, looking like upright iguanas with hawk beaks and three-toed clawed feet, had the unpolished scales of commoners, while the pear-shaped Cimmaheem wore their shaggy yarnlike hair loose instead of in the elaborate braids of the higher social classes.

I paid particular attention to the Bellido as I approached him, checking for the prominently displayed shoulder holsters and handguns that typically conveyed status in their culture. Actual weapons weren't allowed inside the Tube, but the Bellidos had adapted to the Spiders' rules by replacing their real guns with soft plastic imitations when they traveled.

To me, the aliens always came off looking rather ridiculous, like tiger-striped, chipmunk-faced children playing soldier with toy guns. Given that outside the Quadrail their guns were real, I'd made it a point to keep such opinions to myself.

But this particular Bellido's shoulders were unadorned, which was again pretty much as I'd expected. Interstellar steerage, the whole lot of us. Whoever my unknown benefactor was, he was apparently pretty tight with a dollar.

Still, this car would get me to Yandro as fast as the first-class seats up front. And for once, at least, I wouldn't have to worry about a seatmate of excessive width or questionable personal hygiene.

And then, as I passed the Bellido, he gave me a look.

It wasn't much of a look, as looks go: a casual flick upward of his eyes, and an equally casual flick back down again. But there was something about it, or about him, that sent a brief tingle across the back of my neck.

But it was nothing I could put my finger on, and he made no comment or move, and I continued on back to my seat. Thirteen minutes later I heard a series of faint thuds as the brakes were released. A few seconds after that, with a small jolt, the train began moving forward. A rhythmic clicking began from beneath me as the wheels hit the expansion gaps in the railing, a rhythm whose tempo steadily increased as the train picked up speed. My inner ear caught the slight upward slope as we left the station area and angled up into the narrower part of the main Tube. A moment later we leveled out again, and were on our way to Yandro. A total of eight hundred twenty light-years, a nice little overnight train ride away.

Which was, of course, the part that *really* drove the experts crazy. Nowhere along our journey would the Quadrail ever top a hundred kilometers per hour relative to the Tube itself. That much had been proved with accelerometers and laser Doppler measurements off the Tube wall.

Yet when we pulled into Yandro Station some fourteen hours from now, we would find that our speed relative to the rest of the galaxy had actually been almost exactly one light-year per minute.

No one knew how it worked, not even the six races who claimed to have been with the Quadrail since its inception seven hundred years ago. They couldn't even agree on whether speeds in this strange hyperspace were accelerated or whether it was the distances themselves that were somehow shortened.

In the past, I'd always thought the argument mostly a waste of effort. The system worked, the Spiders kept it running on time, and up to now that was all that had mattered.

But that had been before everything that had happened at the New Pallas Towers a week ago.

And, of course, before the Spiders had lost my carrybags. I could only hope they'd ended up somewhere else aboard the train and that I would find them waiting when I got off at Yandro.

Tilting my chair back, I pulled out my reader and one of the book chips from my pocket. A little reading while everyone got settled, and then I would take a trip through the rest of the third-class coaches to the second/third-class dining car. There was a chance my unknown benefactor was aboard the train with me, planning to make contact once we got off, and it would be a good idea to run as many of the passengers as I could through my mental mug file.

But even as I started in on my book, I found my vision wavering. It had been a long trip from Earth, and I was suddenly feeling very tired. A quick nap, I decided, and I'd be in better shape to go wandering off memorizing faces. Tucking my reader away, I set my watch alarm for an hour. With one final look at the back of the Bellido's head, I snuggled back as best I could into my seat and closed my eyes.

I awoke with a start, my head aching, my body heavy with the weight of too much sleep, my skin tingling with the sense that something was wrong.

I kept my eyes shut, my ears straining for clues, my nose sifting the air for odd scents, my face and hands alert for the telltale brush of a breeze that would indicate someone or something was moving near me.

Nothing. So what was it that had set off my mental alarms?

And then, suddenly, I had it. The steady rhythm of the clacking rails beneath me was changing, gradually slowing down. The Quadrail was coming into station.

I opened my eyes to slits. My chin was resting against my breastbone, my arms folded across my chest with my watch visible on my wrist. Two hours had passed since our departure from Terra Station: an hour longer than I should have slept, three hours less than it took to get to New Tigris.

So why—and where—were we stopping?

Carefully, I lifted my head and opened my eyes all the way. When I'd gone to sleep there had been six other passengers besides me in the car. All six had disappeared.

Or perhaps not. No one was visible, but in front of the stack of crates on my right, in the narrow space leading to the exit, I caught a slight movement of shadow. Someone, apparently, was standing by the car's door.

The Bellido?

I slid sideways out of my seat, my heartbeat doing a nice syncopation with the click-clack of the wheels, and started forward. Theoretically, the Spiders didn't permit weapons aboard passenger Quadrails. But theoretically, there weren't any stops between Earth and New Tigris, either.

I'd covered about half the distance to the door when, with the usual muffled squeal of brakes, we rolled to a halt. The shadow shifted again, and I crouched down behind the nearest seat as the figure stepped into view.

It wasn't the Bellido. It was The Girl.

"Hello, Mr. Compton," she said. "Would you come with me, please?"

"Come with you where?" I asked carefully.

"Outside," she replied, gesturing to the door beside her. "The Spiders would like to speak with you."

THREE :

The door opened, and because I doubted I really had a choice, I followed her out onto the platform.

At first glance it seemed to be your standard, plain-vanilla Quadrail station. But the second glance showed that there was not, in fact, anything standard about it.

For one thing, there were only four sets of tracks spaced around the inside of the cylinder instead of the usual thirty. The station itself was far shorter than usual, too, probably only a single kilometer long. Finally, instead of the standard mix of maintenance and passenger-support buildings, the spaces between the tracks were filled with purely functional structures, ranging in size from small office-type buildings to monstrosities the size of airplane hangars, with whole mazes of extra track leading between them and the main lines.

"This way," The Girl said, setting off toward one of the smaller buildings.

I watched her go, my feet momentarily refusing to move. I could think of only one reason the Spiders would possibly want to talk to me, and it wasn't a particularly pleasant thought.

And for them to have been willing to stop a whole train to

do so made it that much worse. I glanced back over my shoulder, wondering what they were going to tell the rest of the passengers.

They weren't going to tell the rest of the passengers anything for the simple fact that there weren't any other passengers. The rest of the Quadrail had vanished. My car, conveniently emptied of all its occupants except me, plus the baggage car behind it, stood together on the track in front of another engine that had apparently pushed us here.

"Mr. Compton?"

I turned back. The Girl had reached the building and was standing expectantly beside the door. "Right," I said, forcing my feet to move. She waited until I caught up with her, and together we went inside.

Beyond the door was a small room as drably functional as the building's exterior, its furnishings consisting entirely of three chairs set in a triangle arrangement facing each other. One of the seats was already occupied by an amazingly fat middle-aged man dressed in shades of blue and sporting a contrasting skullcap of gray hair. Standing behind him was a Spider midway in size between a conductor and a drudge. A stationmaster, possibly, though this one seemed slightly bigger and didn't carry the usual identifying pattern of white dots across its sphere.

"Good day, Mr. Compton," the man greeted me gravely. His voice carried an oddly bubbling quality, as if he were talking half underwater. "My name is Hermod. Please, sit down."

"Thank you," I said, stepping forward and settling into one of the two remaining chairs as The Girl took the third. "Do I get to know where I am?"

"You're in a maintenance and storage facility off the main Tube," he said. "Its actual location is not important."

"I thought all maintenance work was done in the stations themselves."

Hermod's massive shoulders shrugged slightly. "Most of it is," he said. "The Spiders don't advertise the existence of these other facilities."

"Well, this should certainly make up for that," I pointed out. "Or don't you think New Tigris is going to wonder when their incoming Quadrail comes up two cars short?"

"Give the Spiders a little more credit than that," Hermod said dryly. "They would hardly have gone to all this trouble to speak privately with you and then let something so obvious ruin it. No, you'll be rejoining the rest of the train well before it reaches New Tigris."

"Ah," I said, making a conscious effort to sit back in my chair as if I were feeling all relaxed, which I definitely was not. So not only did the Spiders want a chat, they wanted a very private chat. This just got better and better. "So what's this all about?"

"The Spiders have a problem," Hermod said gravely. "One which may well determine the future of the entire galaxy. They thought you might be able to help them with it."

"What makes you think that?" I asked, feeling sweat popping out all over my body.

"You're a well-trained observer, investigator, and analyst," he said. "Trained by one of the best, in fact: Western Alliance Intelligence."

"Who sacked me over a year ago," I reminded him, passing over for the moment the question of whether Westali really *was* one of the best.

"But not for lack of ability," Hermod reminded me right back. "Merely for—what did they call it? Professional indiscretion?"

"Something like that," I agreed evenly. That was what the dismissal papers had called it, anyway. *Professional indiscretion,* like I'd been caught stealing hotel towels or something. I'd sparked a major furor in the press, been responsible for a handful of political scapegoats having their heads handed to them in the hallowed halls of the United Nations, and earned myself the permanent loathing of both the secretary-general and the Directorate in the process.

And all they'd had the guts to call it was professional indiscretion.

But I let that one pass, too. "There are plenty of other ex-

Westali people around who are as good as I am and a lot more respectable," I said instead. "So again: Why me?"

Hermod's forehead wrinkled. "Your reticence puzzles me, Mr. Compton," he said. "I would think that, considering your present circumstances, you'd jump at the chance for employment."

My *present circumstances*. On the surface, an innocent enough expression. Nearly as innocent, in fact, as *professional indiscretion*.

Did he and the Spiders know about my new job? It was hard to imagine how they could, not after all the paranoid-level convolutions we'd gone through to keep it secret.

On the other hand, it was equally hard to imagine how they could *not* know. Their messenger had been right there, after all, right outside the New Pallas Towers the evening the whole thing had been finalized.

But there was no hint of any such secret knowledge in Hermod's face or body language. There was no anticipation I could detect, no sense of the hunter waiting eagerly beside his trap as the prey wanders toward the tripwire. There was nothing there, in fact, except an almost puppy-dog earnestness set against a background of distant fear and unease. If he *did* know about me, he was being damn coy about it. "So my present circumstances aren't as good as I might like," I said. "How about some information instead of flattery?"

His lips puckered. "There are many mysterious places in this galaxy," he said. "One of them, which the Spiders have dubbed the Oracle, sits a short distance from a siding similar to this one. Occasionally, Spiders passing through the area see visions of future events." He gestured at the Spider standing over him. "Five weeks ago, this Spider saw the future destruction of a Filiaelian transfer station."

I sat up a little straighter in my chair. Filly transfer stations were among the biggest and best-protected in the galaxy. "How sure are you that it was a Filly station?"

"Very sure," Hermod said, his voice darkening. "Because there were the remains of two gutted *Sorfali*-class warships drifting alongside it."

I threw a look at the Spider. "Your friend's been hallucinating," I said flatly. "Filly soldiers are genetically programmed against rebellion or civil war."

"I never said it was a civil war," Hermod countered, his voice going even darker. "The attack came from somewhere *outside* the system."

I looked over at The Girl's expressionless face. If this was a joke, no one was laughing. "Now *you're* the one hallucinating," I told Hermod. "You can't smuggle weaponry through the Tube. Certainly nothing that could take out a *Sorfali*. You know that better than I do."

"It seems impossible to the Spiders, as well," Hermod agreed. "Nevertheless, that *is* what he saw. And since the Oracle's past visions have subsequently proven valid, the Spiders have no choice but to assume this one may, too." His eyes locked onto mine. "I trust you don't need me to spell out the implications."

"No," I said, and I meant it. There were twelve empires spanning the galaxy, or at least twelve species-groups the Spiders officially recognized as empires. A few of them, like the five worlds of our pathetic little Terran Confederation, weren't worthy of the name; others, like the Filiaelian Assembly and Shorshic Domain, were the genuine article, consisting of thousands of star systems spread across vast reaches of space. Historically, at least on Earth, powerful empires seldom bumped into each other without eventually going to war, and from what we knew of alien psychology there was no reason to assume anyone out there would react any differently if they had a choice.

Only in this case, they didn't. The only way to cross interstellar distances was via Quadrail, and there was simply no way to stuff a war machine into a group of Quadrail cars. The only exception was interstellar governments, who under very special and very strict transport conditions were allowed to ship the components of planetary defenses through to their own colonies.

Which meant that anyone who wanted to make war against his neighbor would find himself facing as much military nastiness as the intended victim had felt inclined to set up. In a Quadrail-run galaxy, defense was king.

But if someone had figured out how to take out not only a transfer station but a couple of warships along with it, cozy peacefulness and stability were about to come to a violent end. "Was there anything else in this vision?" I asked. "Any idea which of the Fillies' stations it was, or who might have been involved?"

"Neither," Hermod said. "But he did see that the Filiaelian warships carried both the insignia of the current dynasty and the one scheduled to come to power in four months. We can therefore assume the attack will take place sometime during the transitional period."

Four months. This just got better and better. "That's not much time."

"No, it's not," Hermod agreed. "The Spiders will, of course, give you all the assistance they can, including unlimited use of the Quadrail system."

I felt my eyes narrow slightly. "Including access to places like this?" I asked casually, gesturing around me.

"Yes, if you need them," he said, frowning a bit. "Though I can't think why you would need that."

"You never know," I said, my heartbeat starting to pick up a little. Suddenly this was becoming more than just interesting. "How exactly do I get all this unlimited access? Pass key? Secret handshake?"

"You begin with this," he said, nodding to The Girl. Right on cue, she dug a small folder out of her belt pouch and handed it to me. It was the same sort of folder I'd taken off the dead kid in Manhattan, except that instead of being made of cheap plastic this one was a high-end variety of brushed leather.

And instead of the copper-edged ticket of a third-class Quadrail seat, this one held the diamond-dust-edged tag of a first-class, unlimited-use pass, something I'd never seen before except in brochures. "Nice," I said. "How long is it good for?"

"As long as you need it," Hermod said. "Assuming, of course, that you take the job. Will you?"

I angled the ticket toward the light for a better view, my brain spinning with the possibilities. If they were on to me and this whole thing was a trick, then whatever answer I gave him wouldn't matter in the slightest. Whatever I did or said, I was already sunk.

But if they *weren't* on to me and this offer was legit, then I was being offered a gift on a platinum platter.

Of course, if I took the job I'd also be morally obligated to put some actual effort into it. Four months wasn't a lot of time to figure out who was planning to start an impossible interstellar war and find a way to stop it.

Still, this was way too intriguing to pass up. And despite the old saying to the contrary, it was surely possible for a man to serve two masters. "Sure, why not?" I said, tucking the folder into my inner jacket pocket. "I'm in."

"Excellent." Again, Hermod gestured to The Girl. "This is Bayta. She'll be accompanying you."

I looked at her, found her looking back at me with her usual lack of expression. "Thanks, but I work alone," I told him.

"You may need information or assistance from the Spiders along the way," Hermod said. "Only a few of them can communicate with humans in anything more than a handful of rote phrases."

"And, what, Bayta speaks their language?"

"Let's just say she knows their secret handshake," Hermod said with a faint smile.

I suppressed a grimace. I didn't want company on this trip, particularly company who might have come off a mannequin assembly line. Still, I should have expected that the Spiders would insist on assigning me a watchdog. "Fine," I said. "Whatever."

"One other thing," Hermod said. "The messenger who delivered your ticket was supposed to accompany you here. Did he happen to mention why he had chosen not to do so?"

I hesitated, but there didn't seem to be any point in lying.

"I'm afraid choice had very little to do with it," I said. "He died at my feet."

Bayta inhaled sharply, and the whole room suddenly went very still. "What happened?" Hermod asked.

"He was shot," I said. "Multiple times, actually. Someone was very serious about getting rid of him."

"Did you see what happened?"

"All I know is that he was already bleeding when I found him," I said, choosing my words carefully. If they already knew about me, mentioning the New Pallas Towers wouldn't be telling them anything new. But if they *didn't* know, I certainly wasn't going to be the one to point them that direction. "Considering the shape he was in, I'm surprised he made it as far as he did."

"He knew the importance of his mission," Hermod said soberly. "Do you know what kind of weapon he was shot with?"

"Snoozer and thudwumper rounds," I told him. "Fortunately, they didn't need to escalate to shredders."

"Human ordnance, then?"

"Yes, but that doesn't necessarily mean anything," I said. "Terra Station's *very* particular about keeping alien weaponry out of the system."

"Except at the various nonhuman embassies on Earth and Mars," Bayta said. Her face, which had gone rigid at my announcement of the kid's death, was back to an expressionless mask. "I understand embassy guards are permitted to carry and use equipment that would otherwise be interdicted."

"True," I said. "Which means using one to commit a murder would be about as clever as leaving a sheet of the ambassador's personal stationery pinned to the body. As I say, the choice of weapon doesn't tell us anything. Forensics might have had better luck if they got around to putting him through the sifter."

"Why wouldn't they have?" Hermod asked, frowning. "He *was* a murder victim."

"He was also a man with no ID, credit tags, or apartment key," I said. "Dit rec mysteries notwithstanding, in the real world we'll be lucky if they even stored away his ashes after the cremation."

Hermod sighed. "I see. Well . . . thank you, Mr. Compton. And good luck."

Neither Bayta nor I spoke again until we were settled into the Quadrail car, me in my original seat, her in the one behind me. "I presume you aren't planning to gas me for this leg of the trip?" I asked, swiveling around to look at her as we started moving.

A flicker of surprise touched her eyes. "You knew about that?"

"It was pretty obvious," I said. "I don't suppose it ever occurred to you or Hermod that all you had to do was ask me in for a chat?"

"We needed to keep the conversation a secret," she said. "A conductor came in shortly after we left Terra and told the rest of the passengers that there was extra space in the main third-class area two cars up and that as a result they'd all been upgraded. We needed you asleep so he'd have an excuse to leave you behind until later."

"Again, you could have just asked me."

"It was thought it would look more realistic if you didn't know what was going to happen," she said. "That was why the ticket was made out to Yandro, too."

"That part certainly caught my attention," I said sourly. "I take it we're not actually going there, then?"

"Not unless you want to. At any rate, the bags the Spider took from you at Terra Station are waiting in the front car in a first-class compartment that's been reserved for us. We can move up there as soon as we're back with the train."

Not just a first-class ticket, but a compartment, as well. They were definitely rolling out the red runner here. "Nice," I commented. "Any chance of similar accommodations if and when we change trains?"

"Of course," she said, as if it were obvious. "There'll be an empty compartment kept available for our use on all Quadrail trains in our vicinity for the next four months."

"Even better," I said. "Okay, first things first. Do you have a map of the Quadrail system? A *complete* map, I mean, one that shows these sidings and any other hidden goodies?"

"I don't know what you mean by *goodies*," she said as she selected a data chip from her belt pouch. "And you'll need to use my reader," she added, pulling it out and plugging in the chip. "The data is masked on normal readers."

"Good idea," I said, taking the reader from her. "What's your last name, by the way?"

"I don't have one," she said, adjusting herself in her seat. "We'll be rejoining the train in about an hour. If you have any questions, please wake me."

She closed her eyes, and for a moment I studied that nondescript face of hers. She'd be watching every move I made from now on, I knew, ready to whistle up the nearest Spider at the first wrong step.

I turned back around to face forward. I still didn't know if the Spiders were on to me or not. But if they were, they were certainly giving me plenty of rope with which to hang myself. It would be a shame to let that much good rope go to waste.

Settling back into my seat, I got to work.

FOUR :

Exactly one hour and nine minutes later I felt a slight jolt run through the car. Two minutes after that, the connecting door at the front of the car irised open and a conductor appeared from the vestibule, its slender legs picking their way carefully down the narrow aisle toward us. I watched it come, listening to Bayta's slow breathing behind me; and as the Spider came within five meters of us I heard a sudden catch in the rhythm as she came awake. "Yes?" she called.

"I think we're here," I said, half turning to look at her.

"Yes, we are," she said, her fingertips rubbing the skin on either side of her eyes. "He's come to show us to our new compartment."

"Do you know which one is ours?" I asked.

"Yes."

"Then tell it thanks, but we'll get there on our own," I said. "An escort will just draw unnecessary attention."

She hesitated, then nodded. "All right," she said, locking her eyes onto the conductor. Its globe dipped slightly in response, and it reversed direction and left the car. "So?" she prompted. "Are we going?"

"Patience," I said, studying my watch. So apparently all she had to do was to look at a Spider to communicate with it.

Interesting. "In another twenty minutes we'll reach New Tigris. There won't be a lot of traffic coming and going, but at least we won't be the only ones on the move."

We sat in silence until, twenty minutes later, we decelerated to a stop. Then, as the expected trickle of passengers began, we headed forward.

The walk proved more interesting than I'd expected. On the Quadrail trips I'd taken while working for Westali I'd normally traveled third class, making it up to second only on the rare occasion when some nervous medium-level bureaucrat insisted on having an escort assigned to him. In each of those latter instances I'd ended up in cars dominated by other humans, either business or government types or minor celebrities who couldn't swing the price of a first-class seat.

Now, as we passed through the last of the second-class cars into the first-class section, I got to see how the galaxy's elite and powerful traveled.

The seats themselves were, not surprisingly, larger and better furnished than those in second and third class. They were also far more mobile. Third-class seats were fixed in place, with only limited adjustability. Second-class seats were a step up from that, attached to small floor circles that permitted them to both rotate and also move laterally to a limited extent, allowing passengers to create little conversation circles for themselves. The first-class cars had gone this one better, with seats that could be moved anywhere in the car, allowing a lounge atmosphere in which neat rows and aisles were pretty much nonexistent.

What was surprising to me was how the occupants had used this flexibility to sort themselves out. Unlike the lower classes, where travelers tended to congregate with their own species, the first-class cars were much more heterogeneous. Shorshians and Bellidos sat together, engaged in serious discussions, while here and there humans conversed as equals with Halkas or Juriani, despite the fact that both those races had been busily colonizing their home solar systems when Charlemagne was still planning his conquests of Central Europe.

Even political differences didn't seem to matter. The Juriani and Cimmaheem were currently embroiled in a major controversy regarding the development of a half dozen worlds bordering their empires, yet I saw a mixed group of them sitting around a table playing a card game and chatting quite amicably.

The bar end of the first-class dining car was much the same, with the social lubricant of alcohol and other intoxicants adding an extra layer of goodwill and camaraderie. Only in the restaurant section did the travelers largely segregate themselves, and I suspected that had more to do with the challenges of species-specific food aromas than any xenophobia.

The car in front of the dining car contained more first-class seating, with more of the social mixing I'd already seen. Finally, in the compartment car ahead of that one, we reached our new home.

It was as nice as I'd expected, and then some. It was small, of course, but the space had been utilized so efficiently that it didn't feel at all cramped. Attached to the front wall was a narrow but comfortable-looking bed that could be folded up for extra floor space. Above the bed was a luggage rack with my two carrybags sitting neatly side by side. Against the outer wall was a lounge chair with a swivel computer beside it on one side and an expansive display window—currently blank—on the other. On the opposite side of the display window was a fold-down clothes rack, with memory-plastic hook/hangers that could stretch or shrink as needed, plus a built-in sonic cleaning system with a quick-turn cycle for half-hour freshening. A tiny human-configured half bath was tucked into the corner beside the door, the whole cubicle converting into a shower stall for use after long overnight trips. Finally, the back wall contained a curve couch with a set of reading and ambiance lights strategically placed above it. The room was done up in a tasteful color scheme, with decorative moldings and small cameo-style carvings where the walls and ceiling met. "I could get used to this," I commented as I circled the room, touching the various controls and running my fingers over the moldings and the sections of polished wood and metal. The lounge chair had a leathery feel to it, while the curve couch was done up in something midway between velvet and very soft feathers.

"I trust you'll find it adequate," Bayta said. She stepped past me as I finished my tour and touched a control beneath the display window. In response, the curve couch and lights collapsed neatly into the back wall, which then retracted into the side of the half-bath cubicle to reveal a mirror image of the compartment we were standing in. "This one's mine," she said, a subtle note of warning in her tone.

"Of course," I said. Not that I was likely to have made a swing for her even if I hadn't had more important business on my mind. Walking back to my bed, I reached up to the luggage rack and hauled down the smaller of my two carrybags.

And as I did so, a quiet alarm went off in the back of my skull. Earlier, when I'd carried the bags out of the transfer station restaurant, the leatherlite grip that rode the handle straps had been flexible, even a little squishy. Now there was virtually no give to the grip at all. "Bayta, can you pull up a dining car menu for me?" I asked casually as I popped the bag open.

"Certainly," she said, sitting down in the lounge chair and swiveling the computer around to face her.

And with her attention now safely occupied, I gave the handle a close look.

The reason for the change in its feel was instantly obvious. The space between the grip and the strap, the looseness of which had given the handle its squishiness, had been completely filled in, like an éclair with a double helping of cream. The material matched the leatherlite's color and texture perfectly, but somehow I doubted that was what it was.

"Here it is," Bayta announced, swiveling the display around. "But I thought you ate at Terra Station."

"A good traveler learns to eat whenever he gets the chance," I said, stepping to her side and paging quickly through the menu. "I don't suppose first-class has delivery privileges."

"Not usually," she said. "Do you want me to ask one of the servers or conductors if he'll bring you something?"

"No, thanks," I said. "That's what I've got *you* for. Be a

good girl and go get me an order of onion rings, will you?"

In the past, I'd found the be-a-good-girl line to be a remarkably effective way of getting a quick reading on a woman's temperament. Unlike most of those I'd tried it on, Bayta didn't even bat an eye. "As you wish," she said, sliding out of the chair. Crossing the compartment, she touched the door control to open it and disappeared into the corridor.

I went over to the door and made sure it was locked. Then, returning to the bed, I hauled down the other carrybag. In a galaxy where self-propelled luggage was the norm, I doubted that one in a hundred travelers had more than a vague idea what their handles really felt like. The only reason I'd caught the alteration so quickly was because of my carrybags' chronic motor problems, the very problems I'd been cursing five hours ago.

There was a lesson there, or at least a bit of irony, but at the moment I couldn't be bothered with either. Like the smaller carrybag, the larger one's handle had also been padded out. Pulling out my pocket multitool, I extended the fingertip-sized blade—the biggest knife permitted aboard a Quadrail—and began digging carefully beneath the grip.

My first guess was that the Spiders had decided to backstop their watchdog by planting a tracer or transmitter on me. But as I scraped millimeter after millimeter away without finding anything except whisker-thin embedded wires, that idea began to fade. I kept at it; and finally, two centimeters in, I struck something familiar.

Only it wasn't a transmitter. It was, instead, a short-range receiver connected to a small pulse capacitor, which was in turn connected to the whisker wires buried in the material.

The sort of setup you might find in a remotely triggered antipersonnel bomb.

Pulling out my reader, I selected a data chip from my collection marked *Encyclopaedia Britannica*. So Bayta had a specially-gimmicked reader, did she? Fine. So did I. Plugging in the chip, I touched the reader's activation control and held one corner close to the material I'd scraped out of the handle.

It was not, in fact, a bomb, antipersonnel or otherwise. This sensor was the most advanced bit of technology in the Terran Confederation, a gadget any Westali field director would probably give his best friend's right arm for, and it wasn't picking up even a hint of the fast-burning chemicals all explosives had in common. I retuned the sensor twice, just to be sure, then switched to scanning for poisons. Again, nothing.

But *nothing* in the case of poisons could merely mean that the stuff was too well disguised for a normal scan. Fortunately, there were ways of teasing such things into the open. Pulling out my lighter, I flipped the thumb guard around, swinging it over the flame jet where it would serve as a specimen holder. I put a single grain of the mystery material on top, set the sensor at the proper reading distance, and ignited the lighter. The flame hissed out, clean and blue-white, and there was a brief burst of pale smoke as the grain burned as well. Shutting off the lighter, I set it aside and keyed for analysis.

And this time, the sensor finally found the active ingredient carefully buried beneath the inert containment matrix.

Saarix-5 nerve gas.

The image of the Spiders' dead messenger rose unpleasantly in front of my eyes as I unplugged the data chip and returned it and the reader to my pocket. In the absence of any move against me during the voyage from Earth, I'd begun to wonder if his death might have been a bizarre coincidence, the result of some random crime that had nothing to do with me.

Now it was looking like whoever was behind his murder had simply been biding his time.

Only here it wouldn't be just me who went down. Depending on what percentage of the packing material was Saarix-5, there could be enough there to kill every oxygen-breather within ten meters. If my assailant set it off in the enclosed space of a Quadrail car, the effects would go even farther.

Which led to another interesting question. Namely, how had this little conjuring trick been performed in the first place? The only time the bags had been out of my sight after leaving the transfer station was right after we'd docked, as the passengers climbed up the ladder and the shuttle's conveyer system pulled the luggage from the racks and shoved them up into the Tube after us. The sheer mechanics required for someone to insert a pair of booby traps in such a brief time was bad enough. What was worse was why the Spiders' sensors hadn't picked up on it.

Or maybe they *had* picked up on it. Maybe that was why that drudge had swooped down on me and walked off with the bags. But then why hadn't they detained me, or kicked me off the Quadrail, or at least removed the Saarix?

Unless it was the drudge itself that had gimmicked them.

I stared at the bags, a hard knot forming in my stomach. The Spiders had been running the Quadrail with quiet efficiency for at least the past seven hundred years. In all that time there had never been a report of conflict among them, which had naturally led to the conclusion that they were a monolithic culture with no factions, disagreements, or rivalries.

But what if that wasn't true? What if there *were* factions, only one of which wanted me to investigate this impending interstellar war? In that case, there might be another group seriously opposed to the idea of airing their secrets to a lowly human, especially a lowly human whose own government wanted nothing to do with him.

They might even be opposed enough to look for a permanent way to make sure that didn't happen.

Gathering up the material I'd scraped out, I began stuffing it back beneath the grip. Bayta could return at any moment, and if she didn't already know about the Saarix this wasn't the time to break the news to her. If she *did* know, it was even more vital that she didn't find out I was on to the scheme. It would have been nice if I could have disabled the receiver or capacitor, but a properly designed detonator came with built-in diagnostics, and I didn't have the equipment to trick the gadget into giving itself false readings. If my would-be poisoner found out I'd neutralized this particular threat, he would just come up with a different one, and it was always better to face a trap you knew about than one you didn't.

I was sitting in the lounge chair, skimming through a colorful computer brochure on Quadrail history, when Bayta returned with the onion rings.

"Thanks," I said, taking the basket from her. The aroma reminded me of a batch I'd had once in San Antonio. "Have one?"

"No, thank you," she said, stepping back to the middle of the floor. "Have you come up with a plan yet?"

"I'm still in the information-gathering phase," I said, crunching into one of the rings. They tasted like the San Antonio ones, too. "For starters, I want you to ask the Spiders for a list of situations under which weapons are allowed aboard Quadrails."

"I can answer that one," she said. "Personal weapons like Belldic status guns can be put in lockboxes at the transfer station, which are then stowed in inaccessible storage bins beneath the cars. Larger weapons and weapons systems can be sent by cargo Quadrail only with special governmental permits."

"Yes, I know the official exceptions," I said. "I want to know the *un*official ones."

She shook her head. "There aren't any."

"That you know about."

"There *aren't* any," she repeated, more firmly this time.

I took a careful breath, willing myself to be calm. Dogmatic statements always drove me crazy. "Ask the Spiders anyway," I said. "I also want to know everything about the Tube's sensors. How they work, what they look for, and what exactly they do and don't detect."

She seemed a bit taken aback. "I'm not sure the Spiders will be willing to give you that kind of information," she warned.

"They're not being offered a choice," I said. "*They're* the ones who asked *me* in on this, remember? Either I get what I need or I'm walking."

Her mouth twitched. "All right, I'll ask," she said. "But none of the conductors will have that kind of information."

Another dogmatic statement. This one, though, I believed. "Fine. Who will?"

"It'll have to go through a stationmaster," she said, her forehead wrinkled in thought.

"Is that a problem?" I asked. "I assumed you could talk to *all* the Spiders."

"Yes, I can," she said. "But there aren't very many of them at Yandro Station. Probably not enough for a clear relay to the stationmaster's building."

"A clear what?"

"My . . . communication . . . method has a limited range," she said reluctantly. "For longer distances a message can be relayed between Spiders, but only if the Spiders are physically close enough to each other."

"I see," I said, nodding. So apparently she didn't even have to look at a Spider to communicate, as I'd first thought. Some form of telepathy, then?

Problem was, as far as I knew no human being had ever demonstrated genuine, reproducible telepathic abilities. Also as far as I knew, neither had any of the galaxy's other known species.

Which made Bayta . . . what?

"On the other hand, we're only in the station for fifteen minutes," I reminded her. "That's not much time."

"No, but I'll only need to deliver that one short request," she pointed out. "The information itself will have to be gathered and sent to us farther down the line."

"I suppose that'll work," I said, thinking it through. Cargo and passengers traveled at the Quadrails' standard light-year-per-minute, but the news and mail in those message cylinders somehow managed the trick of crossing the galaxy over a thousand times faster. The most popular theory was that once the Quadrail got up to speed, the Spiders used the dish antenna in front of the message cylinder slot to transmit everything to a train farther up the line, using the Tube itself as a gigantic wave-guide.

The messaging apparatus was supposedly sealed and self-contained, impossible for even the Spiders to reach while the

Quadrail was in transit. But of course that didn't stop the conspiracy theorists. The more paranoid among them were convinced that the Spiders read everything, encrypted or otherwise, before they transmitted it.

If we were dealing with two different factions, the question of Spider eavesdropping might be a highly important one. Unfortunately, I couldn't think of anything I could do about it one way or the other. "I presume you can arrange for them to deliver the data to us aboard whatever train we're on at the time?" I asked.

Bayta nodded. "I'll tell the stationmaster when I put in the request."

"Good," I said. "Tell him to deliver it to us at Kerfsis."

She drew back a little. "Kerfsis? The Jurian colony world?"

"Regional capital, actually," I corrected her. "Why? You have a problem with Juriani?"

"No but—" She seemed to flounder a moment. "I assumed we'd be transferring to a cross-galactic express at Homshil and heading straight to Filiaelian space. That's where the attack is supposed to take place."

With a sigh, I popped the last onion ring into my mouth and stood up. "Come on," I said, brushing off my hands.

"Where are we going?" she asked cautiously.

"To the bar," I told her. "I need something to drink."

She followed me silently down the corridor to the rear of our car, through all the genial camaraderie in the forward first-class coach, and back into the dining car. The bar was reasonably busy, but most of the patrons were drinking in groups and there were a few unoccupied tables for two. Choosing one in a back corner, I steered Bayta over to it. The chairs were lumpy and uncomfortable-looking, which probably meant some Shorshians had been using them last. "What'll you have?" I asked, gesturing her to one of the chairs as I sat down in the other. The chair sensed my weight and body temperature, correctly deduced my species, and reconfigured itself into something a lot more comfortable.

"Something nonalcoholic," she said a bit stiffly.

"Teetotaler, huh?" I hazarded, touching the button in the middle of the table to pull up the holodisplay menu. I gave it a quick scan, then tapped for a lemonade for her and an iced tea for me. "Too bad. Alcohol can be a nice little social equalizer."

"Or it can be a way to cloud your mind and put you at a disadvantage with your enemies," she countered.

I thought about the dead man in Manhattan and the Saarix-laden carrybags back in my compartment. "Lucky for me, I don't have any enemies," I murmured.

Her eyebrow may have twitched, but I could have imagined that. "Why exactly did you bring me here?" she asked.

"I wanted to go someplace where we could talk in private," I said. "I thought the Spiders might have the compartments bugged."

"They wouldn't do that," she insisted.

"You never know," I said. Actually, I *did* know; and no, they hadn't. My watch came from the same stratospherically priced tech people as my disguised sensor system, and it would have tingled a warning if it had picked up any sign of eavesdropping equipment. Another trinket my old Westali colleagues would probably give spare body parts to possess.

"Think whatever you want," Bayta said. Her voice was still stiff, but now it was a tired sort of stiff. "What do you want to talk about?"

I took a deep breath, let it out in a soft sigh. My attempts to get a reaction with the good-little-girl gambit had failed, and my take-it-or-leave-it arrogance about the weapons data hadn't done any better. Maybe a sincere, humble, heart-on-the-sleeve approach would hit a resonance and give me a handle on this woman. "Look," I said. "According to every bit of conventional wisdom, what Hermod says the Spider saw is impossible. The Spiders screen everything coming into the Tube; and the Fillies' own transfer station screens everything coming *out*. There should be zero chance of getting any serious weaponry close enough to a Filly station to take it out."

"Which is why you were asked to investigate it."

"What I'm trying to say is that the whole thing has me completely flummoxed," I said. "Frankly, I'm not even sure where to start."

She started to reach out toward my hand, resting on the table. Midway through the gesture she seemed to think better of it and let her arm fall instead into her lap. "The Spiders wouldn't have hired you if they didn't think you could do it," she said.

Encouraging words, and with some genuine concern behind them. The compassionate type, then, only she was afraid to show it?

Perhaps. Still, I couldn't quite shake the impression that she was more like an observer watching a dit rec drama unfold than one of the people actually in the middle of the action. "Thank you," I said humbly. "I just hope you're right."

"I am," she said firmly. She glanced around the room, as if making sure no one was close enough to hear us, and leaned a little closer across the table. "But why go to Kerfsis? Do you suspect the Juriani?"

"Not really," I said as a Spider arrived with our drinks. I handed Bayta her lemonade and took a sip of my iced tea. It was strong and sweet, just the way I liked it. "It's more likely that one of the Fillies' neighbors will be the ones making the trouble," I continued. "Serious grievances typically ferment close to home. Mostly, I want to see if the Jurian entry procedures have changed any in the couple of years since I've ridden the Quadrail."

She took a sip of her lemonade, her eyes fluttering with clear surprise at the tang. Her first experience with the drink? "May I ask why?" she asked.

I nodded upward toward the bar's slightly domed ceiling. Spread across it was a glowing map of the galaxy and the Quadrail system. "Here's the problem," I said. "The Fillies are all the way across the galaxy, about as far from Earth as you can get. Even if we take express trains the whole way, that's still nearly two and a half months of travel. We simply don't have the time to go there and start working our way back."

"We have four months."

"No, the *Fillies* have four months," I corrected her "*We*, on the other hand, do not . . . because the Fillies aren't going to be the first ones attacked."

Her eyes narrowed. "What do you mean?"

"I mean that whoever these warmongers are, they'd have to be insane to take on the Fillies first crack out of the box," I said. "Filly soldiers are genetically programmed for loyalty, their overall defense network is second to none, and depending on who's doing the counting, their empire is either the biggest or second biggest in the galaxy. Would *you* try out a brand-new attack plan on someone like that?"

Her lips compressed briefly. "I suppose not."

"Following that same logic, the test subject is likely to be one of the newer, younger, and therefore less dangerous races," I continued. "If we limit ourselves to those who've joined the galactic club in the last two hundred years, that means the Juriani, the Cimmaheem, the Tra'ho'sej, and the Bellidos." I took a sip of my tea. "And, of course, us."

For a minute the only sound was the muffled background hum of a half dozen different conversations and the click-clack of the Quadrail's wheels beneath us. Quadrail dining cars, I remembered from previous trips, were acoustically designed in such a way that the volume and intelligibility of a conversation dropped off sharply half a meter away from the center of the table. It made for considerably more privacy than one would expect just from looking at the layout, which was why I'd been willing to talk about this here at all. "And whoever they decide on," Bayta said at last, "they'll need to make their test at least a couple of months before the Filiaelian attack."

"Right," I said. "Which basically means any time from now on."

She took another sip of her lemonade. "All right," she said. "But if it's entry procedures you're interested in, wouldn't we do better to go straight to Jurskala?"

"I don't think so," I said. "A homeworld station—*any* homeworld station—will be too crowded for us to get a really good look at their setup. A regional capital like Kerfsis should have all the same stuff, but without all the busyness. We'll take the shuttle out to the transfer station, look around a bit, then come back, pick up the next train, and move on."

"To where?"

"I'm not sure," I said. "I'm guessing our warmongers will want a test subject a little more advanced than us or the Tra'ho'sej. That leaves the Juriani, Cimmaheem, or Bellidos."

She pondered a moment. "The Bellidos might be a good choice," she offered. "They're farther out on the arm than the Terran Confederation, which makes them even more isolated."

"Right, but at the moment we're heading the wrong direction," I reminded her. "Rather than spend time backtracking, we might as well continue on and check out the Juriani and Cimmaheem."

"There are a lot of worlds out there," she murmured, looking down at her glass.

I nodded agreement, taking another swallow of my tea as I let my gaze drift around the bar. There were Jurian foursomes occupying two of the tables, with a scattering of Shorshians and Bellidos taking up most of the rest of the space. In the far corner two Cimmaheem sat across from a lone human, their features obscured by the swirling blue smoke of a traditional *skinski* flambé as a hardworking vent fan kept the fumes from bothering anyone else in the room. "We can look through the system listings along the way and see if we can figure out what sort of test area our attacker might like," I said. "But no matter how you slice it, we're talking a lot of search area." I raised my eyebrows. "I just hope you and I aren't the only team on the job."

"What do we do if we find them?" she asked, ignoring the gentle probe. "The attackers, I mean?"

"*That'll* be the easy part," I said. "All your Spider friends have to do is shut down Quadrail service to those worlds."

There was something about the way she took her next breath. Nothing obvious, but still noticeable. "Maybe," she said.

"What do you mean, *maybe*?" I asked, frowning. "It's their train system, isn't it? Why can't they classify someone as persona non grata and refuse to stop at their stations?"

"I don't know," she said. "Maybe they can. I just don't know."

I studied her face, trying to read past that neutral expression. On everything else, she seemed so certain about what the Spiders could or couldn't or would or wouldn't do. Now, suddenly, she wasn't sure if they could shut down a few Quadrail stations?

Because if the Spiders couldn't do that, maybe they weren't the ones in charge of the system after all. And that was *not* something I wanted to hear right now. "Well, however they want to deal with it is their problem," I said. Even to my own ears it sounded pretty lame. "*Our* job is just to figure out the who and where." I yawned. "And it's probably time we got a little rest."

"Yes," she said, taking another sip of her lemonade and getting to her feet. "And don't worry. I won't tell the Spiders about . . . you know."

"Thank you," I said, standing up as well. Actually, I didn't much care whether or not the Spiders heard about my crisis of confidence. My main reason for having this conversation somewhere other than in my compartment was to see if there would be any obvious fuss on the Spiders' part when I moved out of range of their little Saarix booby trap.

But there hadn't been any such reaction, or at least none I'd been able to see, which left me basically where I'd started. Maybe all the fuss would happen later.

Still, the conversation had given me at least a partial handle on Bayta. That was worth something.

And at the very least, the iced tea had been good.

FIVE :

Eight hours later, right on schedule, we pulled into Yandro Station.

I had set the compartment's display window to show a dit rec of travel through the Swiss Alps, mostly because west-central EuroUnion trains and this kind of intrigue just seemed to go together. Now, as we angled downward from the main Tube into the station, I shut down the dit rec and turned the window transparent.

All the Quadrail stations I'd ever been to had looked pretty much alike, all of them variations on the same basic theme. Yandro's was no exception, the variation in this case being the number and distribution of the support buildings. Only two of the thirty tracks spaced around the cylinder carried trains that actually stopped here, all others merely passing through on their way to more important places. Ergo, only two of the tracks had passenger stations and cargo loading cranes built alongside them.

Considering the minuscule level of traffic involved, even that was overkill. I found the old frustrations rising again like stomach acid as we pulled to a halt and I saw there were only six passengers waiting to board. At a trillion dollars to put in the station, Yandro's colonists were going to have to sell a hell of a lot of fancy lumber to ever earn back that investment.

At the far edge of my view, I saw Bayta striding across the platform toward one of the two maintenance buildings, trying not to look too much like she was hurrying. She disappeared inside and I checked my watch, hoping she was doing the same. A fifteen-minute stop wasn't very long, and for all their professed willingness to cooperate I doubted the Spiders would go so far as to make the train late for us.

Bayta apparently didn't have any illusions in that regard, either. She emerged from the building with ninety seconds to go and crossed the platform in a sprint that would have done an Olympic runner proud. Even then, I wasn't sure she'd actually made it aboard until she arrived at my compartment two minutes later, still breathing a little heavily. "All set," she said as she dropped onto the curve couch. "The stationmaster will pass on the request. The data should be ready by the time we reach Kerfsis. It'll be delivered to our compartment on the next train we take."

"Good," I said, checking my watch, now set to our particular Quadrail's internal time. It was just after ten in the evening of the Spiders' standard twenty-nine-hour day, with nine more hours to Kerfsis Station. Enough time for a good night's sleep plus breakfast before we arrived.

I was just wondering if I should go to the bar first for a quick nightcap when the door chime sounded.

I looked at Bayta. "You expecting someone?" I asked in a low voice.

She shook her head, the corners of her mouth suddenly tight. "It's not a Spider," she said.

The chime came again. I thought about sending Bayta back to her own compartment, decided there wasn't enough time to unfold the wall without the delay looking suspicious. "Washroom," I ordered her, standing up and crossing to the door. I waited until she had disappeared into the cubicle, then touched the release.

It was a pair of Halkas: flat-faced, vaguely bulldoglike beings who could talk a man's leg off at twenty paces and had a passion for Earth-grown cinnamon. "Whoa," the shorter of them announced, his breath thick with the distinctive burnt-acetate smell of their species' favored intoxicant. "This isn't Skvi. It's a Human."

"I believe you're right," the taller one agreed, leaning forward and squinting as if having trouble focusing on me. "Interesting snouts on this species."

"Can I help you?" I asked, stepping into the doorway just in case they had it in mind to come in without waiting to be asked.

The shorter one waved a hand, his hollow double-reed claw sheaths whistling like a distant oboe with the gesture. "We seek a friend," he said. "A fellow Halka. Our apologies for the disturbance."

"No problem," I said, smiling genially as I gave his eyes a quick but careful look. "I hope you find him."

"If he is here, then we shall," he intoned solemnly, pulling his lips back in a smile which made his face look even flatter. Taking his companion's arm, he turned and continued unsteadily down the corridor, tapping his claws rhythmically against the side wall as if trying to make sure it didn't get away from him.

I stepped back into the compartment and touched the control. The door started to close; and as it did so, I quickly leaned my head back out again.

The two Halkas were still walking away from me. But there was no longer any sign of staggering or wall-tapping. Just as there hadn't been the pupil dilation of a real Halkan high.

Fake drunks. And by inference, a fake errand.

I pulled my head back again before the door could close far enough for the automatic safeties to kick in, letting it slide shut in front of me. "Who was it?" Bayta asked, coming out of the washroom.

"A couple of Halkas looking for a friend," I told her as I snagged my jacket from the clothes rack. "You didn't happen to notice anyone following you when you got back onto the Quadrail just now, did you?"

Her forehead creased. "I don't know—I wasn't really watching. I'm sorry."

"It's okay," I said as I punched the door release. "Don't wait up."

The two Halkas were already out of sight, having either passed through the car's rear door or else gone into one of the other first-class compartments along the way. Not especially feeling like ringing door chimes at this hour, I continued to the end of the car and pushed the release. The door slid open, and I crossed the swaying vestibule into the first-class coach car beyond.

Late evening it might be by the Spiders' clocks, but you wouldn't have known it from the activity level. The card games were still going strong, several of the chairs having been repositioned as old conversation circles had broken up and new ones formed. The overhead lighting had been dimmed to a soft nighttime glow, but with each seat sporting its own reading light the only difference was that the brightness started at chest height instead of up at the ceiling. A few of the passengers were dozing in their seats, sonic neutralizers built into their headrests suppressing the commotion around them.

There were several Halkas in evidence, some of them playing cards, others conversing or snugged down for sleep. I zigzagged my way slowly through the car, looking at each of them in turn. Halkan faces were difficult for human eyes to distinguish between, but I'd had some training in the technique, and I was eighty percent sure that none of these were the ones I was looking for. Certainly there wasn't anyone dressed the way my visitors had been.

I'd made it halfway through the car, and was starting to pick up my pace toward the rear door, when a human voice cut through the general murmur. "And Yandro makes five."

I froze in my tracks, my eyes darting that direction. An older man in a casual suit was sitting a couple of seats to my right, his face half in shadow from his reading light, his lips curled in a sort of half smile as he gazed up at me. "Come, now," he said reprovingly. "Don't tell me you've forgotten your own catchphrase."

For another second I stared at him, my mental wheels spinning on their tracks. Then my mind edited in the missing mustache and beard, and it abruptly clicked: Colonel Terrance Applegate, Western Alliance Intelligence. Once upon a time, one of my superiors. "It wasn't *my* catchphrase," I said stiffly, and started to move on.

"My apologies," he said, holding up a hand. "A poor attempt at humor. Please, sit down."

I hesitated. As far as I was concerned, tracking my two Halkas was way higher on my priority list than reminiscing about the bad old days. Especially with one of the people who had made the last of those days so bad in the first place.

But on the other hand, we were on a Quadrail, and aside from the restrooms and first-class compartments there weren't a lot of places aboard where anyone could hide. And I had to admit a certain curiosity as to what a midlevel Westali officer's rear end was doing in a first-class Quadrail seat. "An extremely poor attempt, Colonel," I told him, stepping through the maze of chairs to an empty one at his side. Swiveling it around to face him, I sat down. "So how are things at Westali?"

"About the same, or so I hear," he said. "And it's *Mr.* Applegate now. I resigned my commission eight months ago."

I looked significantly around the car. "Looks like you traded up."

He shrugged, retrieving a half-full glass from his seat's cup holder. "Debatable. I'm working for the UN."

"How nice for you," I said, keeping my voice neutral. I'd never been able to prove it, but I'd long suspected there had been UN pressure behind Westali's decision to sack me. "And you're already up to whatever rarefied level gets you expense chits for first-class Quadrail travel?"

"Hardly," he said dryly. "I'm just here to hold the hands of those who are."

"Don't tell me you're back on bodyguard duty."

"Don't laugh," he warned, his lips smiling but his voice

only half joking. "I could still take on five of you young whelps and beat you to a pulp."

"I'm sure you could," I said, deciding for once in my life to be diplomatic.

"But, no, I'm actually more of a consultant," he went on. "Deputy Director Losutu is on his way to talk with the Cimmaheem about buying some starfighters, and he wanted a military expert along to check them out."

So Biret Losutu was here, too. This just got better and better. "Isn't that a little risky, politically speaking?" I suggested. "I thought the UN's official stance was that Terran-built starfighters are as good as anything else on the market."

Applegate snorted. "And you and I both know what a piece of Pulitzer-Prize-winning fiction *that* is. But then, the UN hardly invented the art of hypocrisy."

I thought of all the crocodile tears shed on my behalf as I was summarily kicked out of my job, some of those tears coming from Applegate himself. "I don't suppose they invented the art of political spindrift, either."

"Fortunately, that won't be necessary in this case," he said with a wry smile. "The Cimman fighters are slated for duty at Yandro and New Tigris. We both know how many people will see them *there*."

"There's still the hole that much money will leave in the UN's budget," I pointed out. "*Somebody's* bound to notice."

"Maybe," he conceded. "But you know what they say: A billion here, a billion there, and pretty soon you're talking about real money. Anyway, we're only talking about half a trillion for the eight fighters we're looking at, unless we decide to go with something bigger. That's what I'm here to help decide." He took a sip of his drink, eyeing me over the rim of his glass. "But enough about me. What are *you* doing here?"

"Nothing much," I said. "A little sightseeing."

"Really." His eyes flicked to the door I'd come through a minute earlier. "Who died and left you the fortune?"

"It's business sightseeing," I said. Fortunately, I'd already worked out a cover story, though I hadn't expected to need it this early in the trip. "I've been hired by a big travel consortium to scope out new vacation packages to pitch to jaded tourists."

"Ah," he said with a knowing look. "And, of course, a proper scoping requires proper accommodations?"

"Just part of the job," I agreed. "Unfortunately, we also cater to the less than obscenely wealthy, so I'll be switching to second- and third-class seats not too far down the line."

Applegate grunted. "A pity," he said. "I gather you're skipping New Tigris and Yandro and starting your survey with the Jurian Collective?"

"What makes you think I haven't already checked them out?" I countered.

"Two things." He lifted up a finger. "One, because we both know there's nothing at either place that would entertain a tourist for fifteen minutes." He smiled wryly as he raised a second finger. "And two, because I saw you get on at Terra Station."

I blinked. "You were *there*?"

He nodded. "Came in along the diplomatic route via Rome and Elfive," he said. "Damned torchliner ran late, too—we nearly didn't make it. Why, shouldn't I have been there?"

"No, of course you should," I said, feeling some professional annoyance with myself for not having noticed him. Global awareness was something field agents were supposed to cultivate. "I didn't mean it that way. Was Losutu there with you?"

"No, he and the Cimman sales reps came on at New Tigris," Applegate said. "They'd been out there looking over the system."

"And where were you exactly?" I persisted, still not believing I could have missed spotting him.

"I was already at the platform when your shuttle came in," he said with a knowing smile. "Relax—even Westali field training fades away over time. Besides, you were busy glaring at the Spider who walked off with your luggage. Did you get it back, by the way?"

"Yes," I assured him, glancing around the car. This was not a line of conversation I wanted to pursue just now. "And I really should get going."

"Why?" Applegate asked, waving me back down as I started to get up. "Oh, sit—sit. You're not worried about Losutu, are you?"

"What, worry about a man who once said he wished I would just go away or die or something?" I reminded him darkly.

Applegate snorted. "Oh, please. Losutu talks a blustery day, but he has way too big a turnover in enemies to worry about some minor two-year-old political embarrassment. In fact, once he finds out you're aboard, chances are he'll invite you for a drink."

"Why? Does the bar serve hemlock?"

"Hardly," Applegate said, his smile fading as he turned serious. "Off the record, Frank, Director Klein's been having trouble with the Western Alliance Parliament over a couple of his proposals. It could be that a former Westali agent like yourself might be able to suggest ways of soothing their fears and getting them on board."

"Isn't that why *you're* here?"

He shrugged. "It never hurts to get a second opinion."

"Ah," I said, feeling the cynic in me rising to the surface. "Besides which, there's a chance that the handful of Alliance reps who jumped on my bandwagon back then might be favorably influenced if I came out with a ringing endorsement of the Directorate's proposals?"

Applegate's lips puckered. "I see you've lost none of your trademark tact."

"You go with your strengths. I take it this Cimman starfighter deal is the bone of contention?"

"One of them, yes," Applegate said. "But I really ought to let Losutu brief you on that himself."

I nodded as a memory suddenly clicked. The two Cimma-heem in the corner table when Bayta and I had dropped in a few hours ago for our tea and lemonade. The human who'd been sitting with them . . . "That was *you* having the quiet chat over a bowl of *skinski* flambé, wasn't it?"

He smiled. "You see? You haven't lost it completely. Yes, I invited our colleagues for an informal strategy session while Losutu was working on his report. I would have come over and said hello, but you seemed to be having a rather serious conversation of your own."

My stomach tightened, then relaxed. With the bar's acoustic design, there was no way he could have eavesdropped on us. All he would have seen was me having an intimate tête-à-tête with a young woman. Knowing him, he was bound to have instantly jumped to the wrong conclusion. "It was interesting," I said, keeping my voice neutral.

He lifted an eyebrow roguishly. "I'll bet it was." His eyes flicked over my shoulder. "And productive, too, I see," he added, lifting a finger. "Miss?" he said, raising his voice a little. "He's right here."

I half turned and looked around the seat back. Bayta was coming toward us, a frown clearing from her face as she spotted me. "There you are," she said, sounding relieved as she came up. Her eyes flicked to Applegate, back to me. "I was starting to get worried."

"No need," I assured her, gesturing to Applegate. "I ran into an old associate, that's all."

I was facing Applegate as I said that, with Bayta only in my peripheral vision. But even so, I caught the sudden stiffening of her body. "You're one of Mr. Compton's friends?" she asked, her voice suddenly guarded.

"*Mr.* Compton?" Applegate repeated, a touch of amusement in his voice. "Hmm. I may have jumped to the wrong conclusion on this one."

"This is Bayta," I told him. "She's my assistant and recordist."

The minute I said it I wished I could call the words back. Bayta's formal demeanor had unfortunately ruined our best choice of cover story, namely that of a romantic relationship, leaving a business relationship as the only other option.

The problem was, Applegate had seen us on the Terra Station platform going our completely separate ways. The last thing I wanted was for him to remember that and start wondering.

But it was too late now to come up with a better story. All I could do was ignore the inconsistency and hope he would simply assume we'd been doing independent studies for our mythical travel consortium. "Bayta, this is Mr. Terrance Applegate," I continued the introductions. "Formerly a colonel in Western Alliance Intelligence; currently an advisor with the UN Directorate."

Bayta nodded. "Pleased to meet you," she said, her voice still wary.

"Likewise," Applegate said. "Well, it's been pleasant, Frank, but it's been a long day and my eyes are starting to fall asleep."

"Of course," I said, standing up. "By the way, you didn't happen to see a couple of Halkas pass through here a minute or two ahead of me, did you?"

"No, but I wasn't really paying attention," he said. "Is it important?"

"Probably not," I said, privately giving up the hunt. By now the Halkas had had plenty of time to change clothes and go to ground, and I didn't feel like searching the entire Quadrail for them. I would just have to keep my eyes open and wait for them to surface again. "They seemed a little drunk when they came pounding on my door, and I wondered if someone should alert the conductors."

"I wouldn't worry about it," Applegate advised. "I've never yet seen a drunk Halka get violent. And they're not going to crush anyone to death if they pass out on top of him, like Cimma might."

"True," I said. "Good night."

Bayta didn't speak again until we were back in the privacy of our compartment. "Is this Mr. Applegate a friend of yours?" she asked as I locked the door behind us.

"Hardly," I said. "He was one of my superiors at Westali."

"An acquaintance?"

I shook my head. "Given that he was one of the people who voted to kick me out, I wouldn't even put him that high on my list."

"More of an enemy, then?"

"Not really that, either," I said, wondering why Bayta was beating this particular horse to death. "Let's just call him one of life's little disappointments."

She seemed to mull that one over for a minute. "All right," she said. "Are you planning to go out again tonight?"

"Just in the unconscious sense of the word," I said, hanging up my jacket and checking my watch. A little over eight hours to Kerfsis. Still enough time for a decent stretch of sleep, but no chance now for the leisurely breakfast I'd envisioned. "I'm going to bed."

"All right." For a moment her eyes searched my face. "Those two Halkas weren't really drunk, were they?"

I hesitated, the heavily ingrained Westali secrecy reflex briefly kicking in. There was so little I really knew about Bayta. "No," I told her. "I don't think they were looking for any friend, either."

"Were they looking for us?"

"They weren't still chiming doors when I got out into the corridor thirty seconds later," I said. "Draw your own conclusions."

She looked over at the door I'd just locked. "Would you mind terribly if I left the wall open while we slept?"

"As long as you don't snore," I said, going to the luggage rack and pulling down the larger of my carrybags. In point of fact, I'd been trying to find a way to suggest that myself.

After all, if she knew about the Saarix-5 booby trap, it was a good bet that I'd be safe as long as she wasn't demanding an airtight wall between us.

And if she *didn't* know about it, at least whoever wanted to kill me would get a two-for-one deal. For whatever comfort that was worth.

SIX :

The traffic at Kerfsis Station, though light by Jurian standards, was still far more impressive than that of any of the
human stations we'd passed through, including Terra. A
good sixty of us filed off the various cars of our Quadrail,
with an equal number on the platform waiting to board.
Most were Juriani, but there were a handful of other species
as well. Bayta and I were the only two humans in sight.

We were heading across the platform toward the first-class
shuttle when I spotted a pair of Halkas emerging from one
of the third-class cars at the far end of the train. They were
too far away for me to see the subtleties of their faces, but
their rolling gait definitely reminded me of my late-night
visitors. Taking Bayta's arm, I angled us through the crowd
in their direction.

"Where are we going?" Bayta asked. "We're supposed to
take the first-class shuttle."

"I know," I said, picking up my pace a little.

But either the Halkas spotted me on their tail or else they
were in a hurry of their own. Before we'd covered even half
the distance, they reached the third-class shuttle and disappeared down the hatchway.

"We need to take the first-class shuttle," Bayta repeated, more emphatically this time.

For a moment I toyed with the idea of ignoring protocol and staying with the Halkas instead. But the Juriani were sticklers for their particular rules of etiquette and protocol, and they looked very disconcertingly down those hawk beaks of theirs at anyone who dared to break those rules. Bayta and I were first-class passengers, and we belonged on the first-class shuttle, and there would be genteel hell to pay if we tried to hitch a ride elsewhere. It didn't seem worth that kind of grief, especially since all the passengers would be regrouping a few minutes from now anyway in the transfer station's customs area. "Right," I said, and turned us back toward our shuttle.

Like everyone else in the galaxy who could afford them, the Juriani used Shorshic vectored force thrusters for their artificial gravity. That meant an actual stairway inside the shuttle, which meant I could hang on to my carrybags instead of handing them over to an automated system that would leave my hands free to maneuver down a ladder. Considering what had happened to my luggage the last time they'd been out of my sight, I was just as glad to be able to keep track of them this time.

I'd been looking for signs of the Spiders' sensor array as I climbed into the Tube back at Terra Station. I looked just as closely now as I went down the stairs into our shuttle, with no better success. Wherever the Spiders were hiding it, they were hiding it well.

The Jurian sensor system, in contrast, was at the complete other end of the subtlety scale. As our three shuttles glided toward the transfer station, we passed beneath a pair of compact battle platforms, each with a massive sensor array and a matched set of docked starfighters standing ready in case of trouble.

Fortunately, there wasn't any. Our shuttle docked with the station, and a few minutes later we filed into the entry-point lounge. "Are we going through?" Bayta asked, craning her neck to look over the crowd at the customs tables at the far end.

I studied the wide exit doorways in the wall behind the tables. There were almost certainly layered sets of fine-scan sensors up there, and I wondered briefly whether they would be good enough to pick up the Saarix hidden in my bags.

Fortunately, we weren't going to have to find out just yet. "No need," I told her. "We're not staying, remember?"

"I thought you wanted to see the security procedures."

"I've seen enough," I said, scowling as I looked around. There was no sign of the two Halkas I'd been trying to chase down earlier. Had their shuttle been diverted someplace else on the station?

But no. Just after the Halkas had reached their shuttle, I'd seen a little goose-feathered Pirk disappear down the hatchway behind them, and he was visible halfway across the room, standing in the little bubble of open space that tended to form around the aromatic creatures. The Halkas must have slipped out somewhere between the shuttle and the lounge.

Problem was, the only such duck-out places in the corridor *we'd* passed through had been a handful of official-use-only doors. Unless security for the third-class passengers was considerably looser, that meant they must have somehow disappeared into the bowels of Jurian officialdom.

"So where *are* we going?" Bayta persisted.

I looked over at the archway that would allow us to bypass customs and go directly across the station to the departure lounge. The simplest thing to do would be to take that corridor, fly back to the Quadrail, and chalk this whole thing up to coincidence and an overheated imagination.

But it wasn't coincidence, my imagination was strictly room temperature, and what had started as a minor mystery was starting to take on some ominous aspects. Given the Jurian temperament, if my Halkas were sitting around someone's office down there, there had to be a meticulously defined reason for it. "We're going to find those Halkas," I told Bayta. "Come on."

I led her to the information kiosk nestled against the side wall. "Good day, Human," the Juri behind the counter said, nodding her head with the slight sideways tilt that was the proper mark of respect toward an alien of unknown social rank. "May I assist?"

"Yes," I told her. "I'm looking for two acquaintances—Halkas—who were supposed to be aboard the third-class shuttle. They haven't shown up, and I wondered if there was some problem."

"I will inquire," she said, dropping her eyes to her display and tapping briefly at the keyboard. "No, there is no word of any problems or broken protocol."

"May I see a floor plan of that section?"

The scales at the bridge of her beak crinkled slightly, but she worked her keyboard again without comment. "Here," she said, and a display set beneath the countertop came to life.

I leaned over, studying it. There were several offices along the corridor, some maintenance and electrical access areas, and a small machine shop.

And one of the entryways into the secure baggage area.

"How is this door sealed?" I asked the Juri, pointing at it.

"Is this information that you need to know?" she countered, still very politely.

"This is the luggage that isn't accessible to passengers during the trip," I reminded her. "Valuables, oversized bags . . . and weapons."

The beak scales crinkled again. "There is no entry into that area for outsiders," she said firmly.

"I'm relieved to hear that," I said. "Would you mind checking with security anyway?"

Her expression clearly indicated she thought I was crazy. But part of her job was to deal with crazy offworlders, and she merely turned back to her keyboard. "If you would care to wait?" she suggested as a padded bench extruded itself from the wall to the left of the kiosk.

"Thank you." Taking Bayta's arm, I led her over to the bench.

"I don't understand," she murmured as we sat down. "You think the Halkas are up to something?"

"All I know is that they've disappeared," I said, looking back at the crowd. Still no sign of the Halkas. "Things like that bother me."

We'd been sitting there for about fifteen minutes when the Juri called us back. "May I ask your precise relationship to these Halkas?" she asked when we arrived at her counter.

"Casual acquaintance," I said. "I met them on the Quadrail and hoped to talk to them again before we went our separate ways, that's all."

"I see." She seemed to study my face a moment. "If you'll step through that yellow door at the rear of the lounge, the Resolver will see you."

I felt my stomach tighten. A *Resolver* had been called in? "Thank you," I said.

We threaded our way through our fellow travelers toward the indicated door. "Did you mean for them to call in a Resolver?" Bayta asked in a low voice.

"No, of course not," I said. "I was hoping to keep this very unofficial. Too late now."

"We don't have to go see him."

"If we don't, *we'll* be the ones they start looking for," I pointed out. "We'll just have to play it through."

The door opened to admit us, and we stepped into a short corridor with a single door on either side and one at the far end. The door on the right stood open; deciding that was our cue, I walked over and stepped through.

A tall, distinguished-looking Juri seated behind a dark purple desk rose as we entered the room. "Good day, Humans," he said, nodding his head the same way the female in the kiosk had. His scales had the polish of someone of the professional classes, and his beak carried the subtle markings that identified a Resolver. "How may I assist?"

The voice seemed oddly familiar. I took a closer look at the scale pattern of his face; and then, it clicked. "*Tas* Rastra?" I asked.

The scales of his cheeks puckered as he frowned at me in turn. Then, suddenly, they smoothed out. "Mr. Frank Compton," he said, his voice vibrating with the deep subharmonics of Jurian surprise. "An unexpected meeting, indeed."

"For me, as well," I agreed. "It's been a long time since the governor's reception on Vanido."

"Indeed," he confirmed. "You were in command of security for the representatives of Earth's Western Alliance."

"And you were the governor's chief Resolver who made it possible for me to do that job," I said.

"Both our lives seem to have changed since then," Rastra said, gesturing to Bayta. "Please, identify your companion to me."

"This is Bayta, my assistant on my journey," I said.

"Your presence honors the Jurian Collective," he told her gravely. "You have no title of standing?"

"None," she said, her voice oddly tight.

"No, Bayta's not a dignitary," I told Rastra, frowning as I looked at Bayta. Her face, I saw, was as tense as her voice. Had she spotted something I'd missed? "I'm finished with that sort of escort duty," I went on, looking back at Rastra. "How about you? Are you working Kerfsis Station now?"

"Actually, no," he said. "My current position is to travel with a high official of the Halkan government, resolving any problems he might encounter."

"And I'll bet you've had a few," I commented. Halkas often had trouble with Jurian protocol, especially Halkas high on the rank scale.

"Nothing too serious," he said diplomatically. "But as a problem involving other Halkas has now arisen, and as High Commissioner JhanKla and I were awaiting the next Quadrail anyway, I thought I would lend my assistance to your problem."

"Ah," I said. "Actually, it's such a small thing that I hesitate to even mention it. I ran into two Halkas aboard the Quadrail and hoped to see them again before we parted company, that's all."

"And why specifically did you wish this?"

Fortunately, I'd had time during our earlier idleness to come up with what I hoped would be a plausible story. "My current position is with a Terran travel consortium, and the Halkas told me about an interesting recreational area somewhere in the Halkavisti Empire," I explained. "It sounded like the sort of place I should check out; but somehow I never got around to learning its name and location."

"I see," Rastra said, leaning back in his chair. "What sort of recreational area was it?"

"Oh, basically the kind we humans really like," I said, waving my hand. A nice, vague description was what was called for here. "Plenty of outdoor sports, fantastic views, gourmet food. That sort of thing."

"And unique, too, no doubt," Rastra said, his beak flattening with a smile. "You Humans do seem to prize such qualities. Tell me, how did you meet these Halkas?"

"We just bumped into each other, like people do on a Quadrail," I said. "They'd been drinking a little, and we started chatting."

"Did you learn their names, homes, or where and why they were traveling?"

I felt my skin starting to tingle. This was rapidly drifting out of the realm of casual conversation and on to the all-too-familiar territory of an official interrogation. "The conversation never went that direction," I told him. "And before you ask, I'd never met either of them before."

For a long moment Rastra just gazed at me. Then he stirred and stood up. "Come," he said, gesturing toward a door behind him. He started to turn that direction, then paused. "By the way, it's *Falc* Rastra now," he said. "The rank was conferred on me by the governor six lunes ago."

I had the sudden vertiginous sense of the cultural rug being yanked out from under me. With that almost offhanded comment Rastra had suddenly jumped two notches above me on the Jurian social scale, and with a sinking feeling I realized that every tone of voice and nuance of word I'd just used with him had been a violation of proper social protocol. "Congratulations," I managed through suddenly stiff lips.

Fortunately, like the good Resolver that he was, Rastra had already anticipated the problem. "Thank you," he said, giving his beak a pair of distinctive clicks. "It was an unanticipated honor indeed." Shifting his gaze to Bayta, he double-clicked her, as well.

And as quickly as it had been pulled out from under me, the rug was back beneath my feet. With those double clicks officially designating Bayta and me as his social equals—which we most certainly were not—he had graciously relieved us of the onerous task of juggling the complicated forms of address and gesture that would otherwise have been expected of us. "Unanticipated it might have been," I said. "But well deserved."

"Thank you," he said. "But now come and tell me what you make of this."

The door opened as he stepped to it. I started to follow, but Bayta cut halfway in front of me. "This Juri," she hissed in my ear. "He's a friend?"

It was the same question she'd asked about Colonel Applegate aboard the Quadrail. "Not anymore," I murmured back. "When a Juri changes rank, he pretty much has to change all his friends, too. The class lines here are very strictly drawn."

"But he was once your friend?"

I felt my throat tighten. "I don't have any friends, Bayta," I told her. "I have acquaintances, former colleagues, and people who wish they'd never met me. Why? You auditioning for the part?"

A muscle in her cheek twitched. Without another word, she turned and hurried to catch up with Rastra.

We followed him along two more corridors and down a flight of steps to a small and dimly lit office, where we found a grim-faced Juri wearing the uniform and insignia of a midlevel army officer. On the wall behind him was a wide one-way window into a second, better lit room, where two Halkas sat under the watchful eye of a pair of armed Jurian soldiers. "This is Major *Tas* Busksha," Rastra said, indicating the officer. "Mr. Frank Compton of Earth, and his assistant Bayta."

"Mr. Compton," Busksha growled. "Are these the Halkas you seek?"

I went over to the window and studied the aliens, paying particular attention to the shapes of their ears and the pattern of wrinkles angling upward from the centers of their chins. "I think so, yes."

"How well do you know them?" Busksha asked.

"As I told *Falc* Rastra, we met for the first time on the Quadrail," I said. "I trust you didn't detain them just for me."

Busksha rumbled in his throat. "Hardly," he growled. "They were apprehended in the secure baggage area."

So my suspicions had been right. "Who are they?"

"We don't know," Rastra said. "Neither was carrying identification when they were taken. We're searching for it now."

"Any idea what they were looking for?"

"An interesting question," Busksha said, eyeing me closely. "What makes you think they were seeking anything in particular and not merely searching for valuables?"

I shrugged, thinking fast. To me, it was obvious that they were still interested in Bayta and me, and that they'd probably been looking for any secure luggage we might have brought aboard. But saying so would bring more official attention our way than I really wanted. "They don't seem like your average professional thieves to me, that's all," I said.

"They don't *seem*?" Busksha echoed with an edge of sarcasm. "To *you*?"

"Mr. Compton is a former member of Earth's Western Alliance Intelligence service," Rastra said mildly. "His hunches should not be dismissed without consideration."

The major's beak snapped. "And what exactly do these hunches tell you?"

I looked back at the Halkas. "They're well dressed, and their fur shows signs of having been recently scissor-trimmed," I said. "That puts them at least midlevel on the social scale, possibly a little higher. Do we know how they were traveling?"

"First-class," Rastra said. "Yet they arrived at the transfer station aboard a third-class shuttle."

Busksha rumbled in his chest. "Such fraud is the hallmark of thieves and other social outsiders. Why did you inquire of them in the entrypoint area?"

"As I told *Falc* Rastra, I had a brief conversation with them concerning a recreation area in the Halkavisti Empire," I said. "I wanted to find out where exactly it is."

"His current position is to search out such places," Rastra added.

"I see," Busksha said. For a moment he studied me, then twitched a shrug. "Then let us go and ask them."

It was typical interrogation technique, I knew: Put supposedly unconnected people together and watch for a reaction. Unfortunately, showing myself to the Halkas and thereby proving I was on to them wouldn't have been my first choice of action here.

But having come this far, I could hardly back out now. "Thank you," I said. "Bayta, you stay here with *Falc* Rastra."

Busksha led the way out the room's side door and five paces down a short corridor to a similar door in the interrogation room. I watched the Halkas' flat faces carefully as we went inside, but there were no signs of surprise or recognition that I could detect. "You have a new questioner," the major said briefly, and gestured me forward.

"Good day," I said, stepping past him. "You may not remember me, but we met on the Quadrail."

"We met with no Humans," one of them said, looking contemptuously up at me. "We do not associate with Humans."

"You were rather inebriated at the time," I told him. "You may not remember."

"I am never so inebriated," he insisted.

"Nor am I," the second Halka put in.

But even as he said it, his brow fur creased uncertainly. So this one wasn't so sure.

"You can account for every minute of your journey aboard the Quadrail?" Busksha asked. Clearly, he'd caught the twitch, too. "There are no gaps?"

"Only while we slept," the first Halka said truculently.

"Or when you sleepwalked?" I suggested. "Because you *did* speak to me outside my compartment door right after we left Yandro."

The two Halkas exchanged looks. "No," the first insisted again. "We would never associate with a Human that way."

"Fine," I said. "So what were you doing in the secure baggage compartment?"

"You have rights of Jurian prosecution?" the first Halka demanded contemptuously.

"You will answer his question," Busksha said gruffly. Jurian protocol, I knew, made allowances for this kind of guest questioner, whether the Halkas liked it or not. And the major knew as well as I did that the more irritated the prisoner, the less likely he was to think straight.

The Halka shot a glare at Busksha, then made a visible effort to pull himself together. "We were looking for our luggage," he said. "I needed to retrieve an item."

"You couldn't wait for it to clear customs?" I asked.

"It is *my* luggage," he insisted.

"It was inside *our* baggage area," Busksha countered.

"Is our luggage not ours?" the Halka insisted. "Have you a right to keep it from us?"

"While still outside customs?" I asked, frowning. This was about as weak and pathetic a defense as I'd ever heard.

The Halka seemed to realize it, too. "We have rights," he muttered, his righteous indignation fading away.

"I'm sure you'll have all you're entitled to," I said. "How did you get into the baggage area?"

"It was unlocked," the second Halka spoke up. Something seemed to flicker across his eyes—"But tell me, Human. How is it *you* come to question us?"

There didn't seem much choice but to trot out my cover story again. "I wanted some information from you," I said. "While we were aboard the Quadrail you mentioned a vacation spot in the Halkavisti Empire, a place with outdoor sports, a magnificent view—"

And right in the middle of my sentence, the second Halka

reached casually up into his sleeve, pulled out an elaborately decorated knife, and lunged at me.

If I hadn't so utterly been taken by surprise I might have died right there and then. But the sheer unexpectedness of the attack froze my brain completely, freeing the way for Westali combat reflexes to take over. I twisted sideways, taking a step back with my right foot and scooping my left arm down and forward. My wrist caught the Halka's forearm, deflecting the blade past my ribs and throwing him off balance. Grabbing his wrist with my right hand, I slashed the heel of my left hand into the crook of his elbow while simultaneously bending his arm back toward his face.

It was a maneuver that should have sent the knife arcing harmlessly over his shoulder as his entire arm went numb. But either I missed the pressure point I'd been aiming for or else someone had redesigned Halkan physiology while I wasn't looking. The knife stayed gripped in his hand; and with a flash of horror I watched the point zip a shallow cut through the fur of his right cheek.

And suddenly I was in very, very deep trouble. The fact that the Halka had been the aggressor was no longer relevant. I'd been the one to draw blood, and the full weight of Jurian justice protocol was about to come down on top of me.

I let go of the Halka's arm and stepped away from him. But it was too late. Both guards had drawn their lasers, one of them covering the Halkas, the other bringing his weapon to bear on me.

"Don't shoot it!"

It took me a second to identify the voice as Rastra's, coming from a speaker in a corner of the interrogation room. The guard hesitated; then, to my relief, he joined his partner in pointing his weapon at the Halkas.

The door burst open and Rastra charged in, Bayta a step behind him. "Are you all right, Mr. Compton?" he asked anxiously. His expression seemed oddly puzzled, as if he couldn't believe I would do such a thing aboard his station. Shifting his attention to the Halkas, he gestured to the guards. "Take them to the cells," he ordered. "They are to be charged immediately with theft and assault."

"What about the Human?" Busksha demanded.

Rastra's cheek scales crinkled. He knew the protocol on this far better than I did. "He is blameless," he told the major anyway. "The Halka's own hand held the knife that drew his blood."

All things considered, it was a pretty weak loophole. But it was apparently strong enough. Busksha still didn't look happy, but he touched his fingertips together in a gesture of acceptance. "Very well," he said. Shifting his glare to the Halkas, he gestured sharply toward the door. "Come."

For a moment neither of the aliens moved. Then, almost delicately, both of them collapsed onto the deck.

Rastra unfroze first. "Summon the medics," he snapped as he moved forward and knelt down beside them.

"No need," I said, staring down at the crumpled aliens as a sickly sweet odor wafted through the room. They were dead, without a mark on them, and with no one having touched either one.

No one, that is, except me.

SEVEN :

"The protocol is clear," Busksha insisted, pacing around the interrogation room like a caged tiger. "He was involved in the death of two sentient beings."

"The protocol is *not* clear," Rastra countered. He didn't look any happier than Busksha, but his voice was firm enough. "We are witnesses to both his actions and the subsequent deaths. There is no evidence that one had anything to do with the other."

Busksha snorted. "You wish only to save an old friend," he accused.

"I wish to prevent an unnecessary interstellar incident," Rastra corrected stiffly.

"Yet we saw him touch one of them."

"But not the other," Rastra countered. "Yet both deaths came from the same source."

"Perhaps," Busksha growled. "That is for the autopsy to say."

There was a soft twitter from somewhere, and Rastra pulled a small comm from his vest pocket. "*Falc* Rastra," he identified himself, stepping off to one of the corners.

"While he's occupied, perhaps we can focus on the knife

for a moment," I suggested to Busksha. "Do you know yet where they got it?"

"One of the weapons lockboxes in the baggage area," the major said, frowning at Rastra's back.

"One of theirs?"

"Neither of them had a claim marker," he said. "We have not yet determined which lockbox they opened."

"Or how they opened it, I presume," I said. "Interesting, isn't it? First they get past a supposedly secure door, and then into a supposedly secure lockbox."

"As I said, professional thieves," Busksha reminded me.

"Or someone fed them the relevant combination numbers."

He bristled. "Do you challenge the integrity of Jurian workers?"

"Not necessarily," I said. "Some of your workers certainly know the keypad sequence for the room, but they wouldn't know a private lockbox combination. A more interesting question is why the Halkas would go shopping at all before they'd even passed through customs."

The edges of the scales around Busksha's eyes took on a slight purple hue, a color that in a human would probably point to imminent apoplexy. On a Juri, it merely indicated concentration. "The obvious conclusion would be that they intended violence on the station itself," he said. "But against whom?"

Out of the corner of my eye I saw Bayta stir uneasily. "You'd know better than I whether there's anyone aboard at the moment worth killing," I told Busksha.

Busksha's beak clicked once, very softly. "You mean other than you?"

For all his attitude, Busksha was clearly smarter than he looked. "What makes you think I'm worth killing?" I asked.

"I don't know," he said, the bridge of his beak wrinkling. "Why don't you tell me?"

"I know of nothing I've done to these two Halkas to have provoked such an attack," I told him, choosing my words carefully. "Or to anyone else of the Halkavisti Empire, for that matter."

"Well and cleverly phrased," Busksha said. "But not an answer."

I lifted my hands, palms upward. "I'm sorry, but it's the best I can do."

Rastra stepped back to Busksha's side. "The knife has been identified and claimed," he said, his voice suddenly strange.

"By whom?" Busksha asked.

"By the same Halkan official who has forbidden an autopsy," Rastra said. "High Commissioner JhanKla of the Fifth Sector Assembly." His throat scales reddened. "The Halka whom I am currently escorting."

"Wait a second," I said, my mind still two sentences back. "What do you mean, he's forbidden an autopsy?"

"The knife was stolen from his lockbox and used to attempt a killing," Rastra said. "This brings shame onto the High Commissioner, which cannot be eradicated until the perpetrators' bodies have been destroyed by fire."

"He can't claim jurisdiction on a Jurian station," I insisted. "We need to know how those Halkas died."

"It is true that he has no jurisdictional claim," Rastra agreed heavily. "But as a Resolver my job is to smooth over conflicts between the Jurian Collective and the Halkavisti Empire. I have already given the order to permit cremation without autopsy."

"But what about Mr. Compton?" Bayta spoke up. "How can he prove he had nothing to do with their deaths if the bodies aren't examined?"

"High Commissioner JhanKla informs me that he can explain their deaths, though he will do so only in private," Rastra told her. "He confirms that Mr. Compton is in no way involved."

"Yet he drew first blood," Busksha murmured.

"Yes," Rastra said reluctantly. "Mr. Compton, did you intend to remain long in the Jurian Collective?"

I knew a cue when I heard it. "We could be moving along at any time," I assured him.

"Then you shall," he said. "We travel on the next Quadrail

with High Commissioner JhanKla, aboard a private car of the Halkavisti Peerage."

I pricked up my ears at that one. I'd never seen any of the legendary Peerage Quadrail cars, but they were reputed to be rolling versions of the equally legendary Peerage palaces.

They were also definitely not the transport of choice for someone trying to keep a low profile. "The High Commissioner honors me greatly," I said. "But I must humbly decline."

"You have no choice," Rastra said firmly. "I have vouched for your innocence in this matter, and protocol demands that I escort you personally out of Jurian space. Since I travel with the High Commissioner, you and your companion must travel with me. Otherwise, you could be taken into custody at any stop along the way."

"That seems wrong," Bayta said, frowning. "Doesn't that only—"

"Of course it's wrong," I interrupted, throwing her a warning look. "I haven't *done* anything."

"I understand that," Rastra said. "But the protocol must be followed."

"I understand in turn." I lifted my hands again. "In that case, we accept with gratitude."

"Good," Rastra said. "Then let us be off. The High Commissioner awaits us at the Tube. Have you any luggage besides your carrybags?"

"No, we're ready to go when you are." I looked at Busksha, who was still glowering at me. "And the sooner," I added, "the better."

We caught the next shuttle, and a few minutes later were back in the Tube.

"The car's over here," Rastra said, pointing to a warehouselike structure in the maintenance area two tracks around the cylinder from the last of the passenger waiting rooms. "The Spiders will be rolling it out in half an hour, just before our train arrives, and connect it behind the baggage cars. That will give us time to settle in."

"Good," I said, glancing around. If the Spiders had been able to pull together the sensor data I'd asked for, it should be waiting here somewhere.

Problem was, I'd asked for it to be delivered to us aboard whatever train we took out of Kerfsis system. Without a normal reservation, they had no way of knowing we were here and about to leave.

Or did they?

Behind Rastra's back, I looked at Bayta and raised my eyebrows in silent question. She nodded slightly in return, then nodded again over her shoulder. Shifting my eyes that direction, I saw a drone ten meters away suddenly pause and change direction toward the stationmaster's building.

Apparently, the Spiders had been informed of our change in plans.

The inside of the maintenance building was pretty much the same as the one I'd seen once at Terra Station: big and open, with enough room for a Quadrail engine or a couple of cars. Crane tracks crisscrossed the high ceiling, the cranes themselves looking hefty enough to pick up one end of a car without exerting themselves. The Quadrail tracks on the floor mirrored the crane tracks above them, with one set coming straight through the doors at either end while others angled off to miniature sidings along the walls. The walls themselves were lined with toolboxes and parts cabinets, everything clearly designed to be operated by a drone's leg tips.

The Peerage car was sitting on the tracks by the door at the far end. At first glance it looked like every other Quadrail passenger car I'd ever seen, but as we moved closer I spotted the small touches that marked it as something special. An intricate design was etched subtly in the silver metal of the side, with an equally subtle reproduction of the royal Halkan crest beside the door. There was something about the wheels that seemed a little different, possibly an upgraded set of shock absorbers, and at the roof edge there were some embedded greenstone highlights. "Not quite what I expected," I commented.

"It's designed not to be ostentatious," Rastra explained. "Even the most powerful among the Halkas prefer not to flaunt their position."

"I would think the flaunting would be the best part of being in the Peerage in the first place," I suggested.

"The Halkas have always had ambivalent feelings about such things," Rastra said. "The car's interior should prove more to your expectations."

"How many does it sleep?"

"There are ten sleeping compartments, plus dining and lounge areas and a small kitchen," Rastra said. "The staff consists of a chef, two servitors, and High Commissioner JhanKla's guard-assistant. All Halkas, of course."

With the three of us, that made for a total party of eight. "Do you have any other stops planned for Jurian space?" I asked.

"No," he said. "I would not have burdened you with a long schedule if the High Commissioner hadn't already planned to return home."

I tried to figure out how Rastra would have juggled his stated obligations to both JhanKla and me if the Halkas *hadn't* been heading home. But I gave up the effort. Resolvers had a knack for bringing mutually exclusive options together and making them work. "So we're looking at, what, about a five-day trip?"

"Slightly less," Rastra said. "We'll be attaching to an express Quadrail which will stop only once, at Jurskala, before continuing directly on to Imperial Hub Twenty just inside Halkan space. From there you'll be free to travel wherever you wish."

We reached the door, which irised open at our approach, and went inside. Passing the elaborately carved doors of the first set of sleeping rooms, we entered the lounge.

Whatever ambivalence the car's designer had been feeling while working on the exterior, he'd apparently gotten it out of his system well before he switched to the interior. The lounge sported a pattern of living filigree vines on the ceiling, whose delicate scent formed a nice counterpoint to the soft twittering and brilliant colors of the caged rainbirds in the four corners. The display windows were bordered by expensive velvette curtains, though there was no need for curtains of any sort on windows that could be opaqued on command. The chairs were made of hand-carved wood wrapped around memory cushions which, like the bar chairs Bayta and I had used on our last Quadrail, would configure to fit whoever happened to be sitting there. Unlike the bar chairs, though, these looked like they would be comfortable no matter how they were set.

In the center of the room was a low table that seemed to have been carved out of a single piece of geodium crystal. Like the seats in the regular first-class cars, both the table and chairs were set on sliders that would allow them to be moved freely around the room, yet locked securely in place wherever they were placed. Built into the front wall was a top-of-the-line entertainment center, ready to provide music and dit recs to help a traveler pass the time, while late-night thirst or munchies could be taken care of via the rack of beverages and finger foods on the opposite wall. The final touch was the floor design, done in a furstone mosaic that seemed to be commemorating some grand and glorious event in Halkan history.

"Ah," a deep voice said from behind me. "My guests."

I turned, setting down my carrybags beside the geodium table. A medium-sized Juri stood by one of the rainbird cages, poking slender green shoots through the bars for the birds to nibble on. "May I present High Commissioner JhanKla of the Fifth Sector Assembly of the Halkavisti Empire," Rastra said formally. "This is Mr. Frank Compton and his assistant Bayta of the Terran Confederation."

"Yes," JhanKla said, his bulldog eyes gazing steadily at us from his flat face. He wore the distinctive tri-color layered robes of the Halkan Peerage, this particular red/orange/purple color scheme identifying him as a member of the Polobia branch. "The Humans who helped rescue my honor."

The words were polite enough, but I could hear the underlying edge of blame for precipitating the trouble in the first place. "We were glad to assist, Your Eminence," I replied, deciding that the polite thing to do would be to accept the statement at face value. "I'm sure you'd have done the same for us had the situation been reversed."

"The situation would not have *been* reversed," he countered. "Humans do not treasure honor as Halkas do."

"No, some of us don't," I said, looking straight back into those eyes. "But others of us do."

For a long moment he returned my gaze without speaking. I was working on a Plan B, something that would put us at the other end of the Quadrail, when he gave a short bark. "Correction accepted," he said. Flicking his last shoot the rest of the way into the birdcage, he stepped over to join us. "You are not what I expected, Mr. Compton. Welcome aboard this small and unimpressive corner of the Halkavisti Empire."

"We are honored, Your Eminence," I said, making the sort of hunchbacked stoop that was the closest a Human could get to a proper Halkan chest-bow. "And I apologize for whatever discomfort or embarrassment we may have caused you in this matter."

JhanKla made a multifrequency rumble. "The fault lies with the criminals who perpetrated the act," he said. "Their shame is even now being returned to the universe by fire." He paused, then gave me a genuine chest-bow. "I apologize in turn for implying any dishonor rests with you for bringing their crime to light. If such were the case, no officer of the law could ever face his family and people."

"Indeed he could not," I agreed, starting to relax a little. In my admittedly limited experience with Halkas, I'd found they had a tendency to take offense way too quickly, but that most of them calmed down and saw reason if you gave them enough time. JhanKla seemed to be falling nicely into that pattern. "My only regret is that we may never know what it was that killed them."

"Not at all," JhanKla said. "It was their own act of greed that brought their destruction. The knife stolen from my lockbox was an antique belonging to my family. Its blade was protected from corrosion by a chemical which also happens to be a deadly toxin."

"Ah," I said. "That would explain the one who was cut during the struggle."

"Yes," JhanKla said, his sideburn fur bristling in a Halkan shrug. "As to the other, he must have sustained a superficial cut earlier when they first broke into the lockbox."

"Which would explain why the toxin took longer to work on him," Rastra said.

"Yes," I murmured. A nice, neat answer. Far too neat for my taste, especially since it completely sidestepped the question of how the thieves had managed to get into JhanKla's lockbox in the first place.

But I wasn't here to interrogate a member of the Halkan Peerage. Besides, I was pretty sure I already knew the answer. "Lucky for me he didn't connect with that attack," I said instead.

"Indeed," JhanKla agreed, eyeing me curiously. "What exactly did you do to provoke him?"

"I wish I knew," I said ruefully. "I was simply asking about a Halkan resort they'd mentioned to me aboard the Quadrail."

"Which one?"

"I don't know," I said. "That was what I had hoped to learn from them."

"You told me it was a place with outdoor sports and unique views," Rastra said. "Does that sound familiar, High Commissioner?"

"There are only a few million such places in the Halka-visti Empire," JhanKla said dryly. "But I will consider the question." He looked at Bayta and me. "In the meantime, one of my servitors will take your belongings to your rooms."

"Thank you, but we can handle them," I assured him, picking up my carrybags again. "Besides, I'm looking forward to seeing my compartment."

"As you wish," JhanKla said. "They are the last two on the left at the rear of the car."

"Thank you," I said again. "Come on, Bayta."

Beyond the lounge the corridor curved around a compact food prep area and then led into a dining room as lovingly and meticulously decorated as the lounge. Passing the carved-wood table and matching chairs, we reached the sleeping compartments at the other end of the car. "You take this one," I told Bayta over my shoulder, nodding to the first of the two as I passed it. Reaching the second door, I touched the release and went inside.

The Spiders had made a career of moving people around the galaxy in compartments this size, and they'd obviously put a lot of thought into the design and furnishings. Form following function and all that, there had been little the Halkan designers had been able to do to improve on the basic layout, so they'd contented themselves with simply upgrading the pretension level. That meant more carved wood on the walls, more furstone mosaic on the floor, more gold and crystal and marbling everywhere else. But at least they'd passed on the caged rainbirds.

I had just heaved my carrybags up onto the luggage rack—hand-carved, naturally, with some kind of ivory inlays—when a delicate tone issued from the door. "Come in," I called.

To my complete lack of surprise, it was Bayta. "That was quick," I commented as she walked in. There was an odd hesitation to her step, I noted, as if she were afraid of damaging the furstone floor.

"We can't stay here," she said without prologue. "We shouldn't even have visited."

"Oh, come, now," I chided. "How could we be so ill-mannered as to refuse the High Commissioner's hospitality? Especially since the Jurian Collective insists on it?"

"The Collective is wrong," she said flatly. "Here in the Tube, we aren't *in* Jurian territory, and their protocol system has no legal authority." Her lips compressed briefly. "I tried to tell you that, back on the transfer station. You didn't let me finish."

"Of course not," I said. "I couldn't let you ruin such a nicely executed setup."

The skin of her face seemed to shrink back a little. "What do you mean?" she asked carefully.

"You don't think all this happened by accident, do you?" I asked, taking a quick pass by the computer and then circling to the curve couch and sitting down. No warnings from my watch; apparently, the Halkan Peerage didn't stoop to bugging the compartments of their guests. "Come on, sit down," I said, patting the couch beside me. "We might as well be comfortable."

Slowly, reluctantly, she sat down at the far end of the couch. "Do you know what's going on?"

"I know some of it," I said, flipping a mental coin. Bayta was still a big question mark, and my natural impulse was to play my cards as close to my chest as possible. But it might be instructive to give her the whole story, or at least all the story I had, and see if I could get anything from her reactions.

And after all, it *was* possible that she was genuinely on my side. "Bottom line," I began, "is that we've been pinged."

"Pinged?"

"Pinged, as in someone's figured out that we're not your average tourists or businesspeople," I explained. "My guess is that it was when we made that big jump from steerage to first class at New Tigris. This someone has also decided he doesn't like the idea of us poking around, or at least he doesn't like us poking around Kerfsis system. He therefore sent those two Halkan goons into the baggage section to break into a lockbox and get themselves a weapon."

Bayta's face had gone very still, with none of the hints of guilty knowledge I'd been watching for. "They're trying to *kill* us?"

"And this surprises you?" I countered. "People who are planning to start a war?"

"But—" She broke off. "Of course," she said. "Please, go on."

"Unfortunately for them, we picked up on their vanishing act and sicced the cops on them," I said. "They got caught, but by immense good luck I then got hauled in there to talk to them."

"Or maybe it wasn't luck," she said slowly. "Maybe this someone had more agents than just those two Halkas."

"Very good," I said. She had either a very quick mind or else a collection of prior knowledge. Unfortunately, at the moment I couldn't tell which. "JhanKla, at the very least. Possibly Major *Tas* Busksha, too."

"Or possibly your friend *Falc* Rastra?"

"No," I said firmly, feeling a flash of annoyance. "I know Rastra. He wouldn't be mixed up in something like this. And I already told you he's not my friend."

"Yet you say you know him?"

"Would you get *off* that?" I snapped. "I know all sorts of things about all sorts of people. That was my *job*."

"Yes, of course," she murmured. "I'm sorry."

I took a calming breath. I was supposed to be watching for her reactions, and instead *I* was the one doing all the reacting. "Regardless, when the assassination attempt failed, they had to come up with a new plan."

She frowned. "Are you suggesting those two Halkas *aren't* dead?"

"Oh, they're dead, all right," I assured her grimly. "Nothing grabs official attention like someone who tries to kill you and then dies a mysterious death. Plan B was apparently for JhanKla to come charging in on a white horse and rescue us from Kerfsis and the united forces of Jurian legal displeasure."

"But why wouldn't they want us in Kerfsis system? What could be here they don't want us to see?"

"Maybe this is the test system we talked about earlier," I said. "Or maybe some of the preliminary work is being done here. All I know is that someone has gone to an enormous amount of effort to get us out of this specific system onto this specific Quadrail in this specific Quadrail car. I think it would be instructive to follow along for a bit and see where it all takes us."

A sudden shiver ran through her. "Or maybe they just want to get rid of us. Maybe they brought us aboard so they could do it in private."

"That possibility hadn't escaped me," I admitted. "But there are more anonymous ways of killing someone than luring the victims aboard a Halkan Peerage car. No, if it's not Kerfsis itself, I'm guessing JhanKla thinks plying us with hospitality will help him find out how much we know or who exactly we're working for. Speaking of whom, did your friends get that sensor data I wanted?"

"Yes," Bayta said, her brain clearly still working on the possibility of our sudden and violent demise. "The stationmaster will deliver it to the train."

"But not to us directly," I warned. "I don't want JhanKla to see us getting a data chip from a Spider."

"No, of course not," she said. "He'll deliver it to one of the conductors. We can pick it up from him later."

Given our current traveling situation, arranging such a handoff might be a bit awkward. But I had a few days to find an excuse to go wandering around the rest of the train. "Good enough," I said.

"So what do we do once we reach Halkan space?" she asked.

"That depends on what happens between now and then," I said. "If we can act cheerful and stupid enough, maybe we can convince them that it's all a big mistake. That would take some of the heat off."

"And if we can't?"

"Then we'll just have to be careful," I said. "Either way, your next assignment is to get the Spiders busy finding out everything they can about our two freshly dead and cremated Halkas. I want their names, their families, their political affiliations, their business and social associates, their criminal records, their travel records over the past five years, and anything else that seems remotely interesting or unusual. Get the next Spider who wanders into range busy on it."

"That'll take time," she warned. "And it may require sources they don't have access to."

I thought about my original Quadrail ticket with its forged photo and thumbprint. "I get the feeling there isn't very much that's beyond their reach," I told her. "While they're at it, let's have them pull the same information on JhanKla."

"And Rastra?"

My first impulse was to once again leap to Rastra's defense. But she was right. "And Rastra," I confirmed.

"All right." She gazed out the window, her eyes unfocusing for a minute, then nodded. "It's done."

"Good." I looked out the window myself at the drab walls and floor of the maintenance building, all nice and quiet and private. Distantly, I wondered if I might have overstated my assurances that this would be a poor locale for a couple of murders. "Let's get back to the party."

EIGHT :

Four of the chairs had been pulled up to the geodium table in our absence. Rastra and JhanKla were seated in two of them, chatting about the Quadrail and their various travel experiences. Behind JhanKla, a short Halka dressed in the muted plaid of a servitor was busying himself with the refreshments on the far wall. "Ah," JhanKla said, giving a sort of regal nod our direction. "I was starting to wonder if there was a problem with your accommodations."

"Not at all," I assured him, sitting down in the third chair as Bayta took the fourth. "We were simply taking a few minutes to discuss what this change of plans was going to do to our travel schedule."

"We shall do our best to minimize any disagreeable effects," JhanKla promised. "The Spiders have placed a shifter engine into position and will be moving us from the service building as soon as our Quadrail arrives. In the meantime, may I offer you a beverage?"

"Thank you," I said. "Sweet iced tea, if you have it."

"I do." He shifted his attention to Bayta. "And you?"

"Lemonade, please," she said, her voice a little stiff.

JhanKla nodded and half turned in his chair toward the servitor, giving a short fingertip gesture that sounded a brief oboe note from his double-reed claw sheaths. "I have been thinking about the unnamed resort you spoke of earlier," he said, turning back to us. "As I stated earlier, there are many possibilities. But it occurs to me that there is one in particular that might have caught the special attention of thieves."

"Really," I said. In point of fact, my description of the place had been deliberately designed to be as vague as possible. This should be interesting. "Please, continue."

"It is called Modhra," he said. "It is a world located in the Sistarrko system, a minor colony near the end of the Grakla Spur, three stops past the edge of Cimman space."

"Sistarrko," I repeated, trying to visualize that part of the Quadrail map. The Grakla Spur started at the Jurian home system of Jurskala, cut across the edge of the Cimmal Republic at Grakla and connected with two more of their systems, then pushed past their border again into Halkan space. Unlike the Bellis Loop, which linked the Terran Confederation with the Juriani on one side and the Bellidosh Estates-General on the other, the Grakla Spur didn't connect to anything at the far end, requiring travelers to backtrack if they wanted to go anywhere else. That wasn't a terrifically big deal when you could travel a light-year per minute, but it was enough of an inconvenience that worlds served only by spurs tended to be neglected by the main flow of interstellar travel and commerce.

"You have not heard of it, of course," JhanKla said, not sounding offended. "Most of the system is industrial and agricultural, of little interest except to its inhabitants. But Modhra is unique. It is a moon—a pair of moons, actually—circling the gas giant planet Cassp. Both moons are composed of small rocky cores completely covered by water."

"Frozen water, undoubtedly, that far out from the sun," I commented.

JhanKla's flat face creased in a smile. "Indeed. The outer surfaces of the moons are quite solid, the thickness of ice ranging from a few meters to nearly three kilometers. But *beneath* those surfaces, tidal forces and internal heat from the moons' cores have created enclosed seas up to five kilometers deep."

"Interesting," I said, nodding my thanks as the servitor set my tea and Bayta's lemonade on the table in front of us. "Sounds a little like Europa, one of the moons in our own home system."

"So I have heard," JhanKla said. "But unlike Europa, Modhra I has been extensively developed as a vacation resort. There is surface hiking and cliff-climbing, ranging from the simplest to the most challenging of slopes. There are several ski runs, of an equally diverse range of difficulty. There are also three tubular tunnels that have been bored through the thickest parts of the ice for toboggans and luge-boards, with two more under construction. Atop the ice is a lodge of quiet luxury; beneath it lies a hotel that offers access to the galaxy's largest indoor pool."

"With the ice dome above, and the coral formations beneath," I said, nodding as the name suddenly clicked. Modhran coral had been one of the big decorating fads across the galaxy when humanity first stumbled on the Tube thirty years ago. The stuff had been fantastically expensive, accessible only to the fabulously rich and spoiled.

Unfortunately for Earth's own pampered few, by the time we learned about it pressure from the environmental lobby had caused the UN Directorate to slap a complete embargo on the importation of all coral and corallike formations. One of the more arrogant of the rich and famous had tried it anyway. Unfortunately for him, he'd had the misfortune of tangling with an honest customs agent, and his subsequent bribe attempt had raised the incident into Class-B felony territory. When the dust finally settled, the would-be smuggler was doing three to six, a quarter of his fortune had been confiscated, and the rest of the upper crust had suddenly decided Belldic marble was just as decorative as Modhran coral and a lot safer to deal with.

"Yes, there are many beautiful coral formations within submarine range, as well as excellent and intriguing rock formations," JhanKla said. "For those who don't wish to climb or ski or explore the depths, the surface holds spectacular views of the glory of Cassp itself, with its roiling and ever-changing ring pattern, plus the sight of the companion moon Modhra II as it speeds across the sky."

"Sounds intriguing," I said. "And you say you've just opened it to tourism?"

"Within the past year," JhanKla said. "At the moment it is quite expensive, of course, catering to only the richest Halkas and outworlders."

"That would certainly put it near the top of any thief's list of happy hunting grounds," I said thoughtfully.

"It is certainly one possibility," JhanKla said, peering out the window. "Ah—we are moving." We were, too, though so gently that there was no particular sense of motion. Heavy-duty shock absorbers, indeed. "We shall soon be connected to the Quadrail and on our way," he went on. "Are the tea and lemonade to your liking?"

I took a sip from my glass. "Very much so," I assured him. I had suggested to Bayta that the purpose of this exercise had merely been to hustle us out of Kerfsis system. Now I was starting to wonder if the actual purpose had been to point us to Modhra and the Sistarrko system.

Maybe there was a way to find out. "Modhra sounds exactly like the sort of place I'm looking for," I commented. "Too bad we can't swing by and check it out."

"What prevents you?" JhanKla asked.

"I'm sort of in protective custody," I said, gesturing at Rastra. "As a result of the trouble at the transfer station, *Falc* Rastra has to personally escort me out of Jurian space."

JhanKla made a sound that was half snort, half bark. "Ridiculous," he said firmly. "Here in the Tube, you *are* legally outside Jurian space. Provided you don't leave the Quadrail until you arrive at Sistarrko, Jurian law has no authority over you."

"Your pardon, High Commissioner, but that's not the way the protocol is written," Rastra said, a hint of stiffness in his tone. "Mr. Compton was involved in an incident that drew blood, and has been ordered to leave Jurian space."

"An order he will fulfill if he travels to Modhra," JhanKla countered.

"But the intent of the order—"

"The intent is irrelevant, as you have so frequently pointed out on this journey," JhanKla cut him off. "It is the letter of the law that matters. In this case, that letter has been fulfilled." He shrugged, a full rippling of his skin. "At any rate, how did you expect him to return to his home again after his journey? All Quadrails to the Human worlds travel through Jurian space."

"He has a point," I agreed. "You can certainly escort me out of Jurian space now, but I'll still need to get back in at some point."

"True," Rastra said. "Yet . . . perhaps."

"No perhaps about it," I said, looking back at JhanKla. So with a single one-two punch the High Commissioner had pointed me toward Modhra and then cut me loose from the fiction that had brought me into his presence in the first place. Was that all he wanted?

Again, there was one way to find out. "Of course, in that event, there's no need for Bayta and me to impose on your hospitality any further," I said. "We can find accommodations elsewhere in the Quadrail."

"I can't let you do that," Rastra insisted. "Not until I have clarified the protocol."

"And I would not permit it in any case," JhanKla said, just as firmly. "Those who attacked you were shamed Halkas. It is my duty and my pleasure to offer my hospitality in recompense." He looked at Rastra. "So let us compromise," he went on. "You will remain my guests until *Falc* Rastra has had time to study the protocol and come to a decision. Is that acceptable?"

"It is to me," I said. "*Falc* Rastra?"

"Yes," Rastra said, clearly unhappy with the situation. "If the High Commissioner is correct, when we reach Jurskala in three days you'll be free to travel wherever you wish, provided you don't leave the Tube while in Jurian space." He inclined his head to JhanKla. "You may even travel to Modhra, if you so choose."

"That would be wonderful," I said, smiling with thanks and professional admiration. Very nicely, very neatly done.

"Then all is settled." JhanKla said in satisfaction as he gestured again to the servitor. "Let us bring out an Imperium card deck and find a way to pass the time until the meal is ready."

So that was that. Good-bye, interest and intrigue at Kerfsis; hello, interest and intrigue at Modhra. I just hoped all of this was related to the Spider's vision of interstellar warfare. I hoped, too, that it wouldn't interfere too much with the other job I was supposed to be doing.

Most of all, I hoped that it wasn't simply for the purpose of finding a more suitable place to dispose of our bodies.

The first two days of the trip were uneventful. The four of us spent most of our time sitting around the lounge, chatting about issues ranging from interstellar trade and politics to the pluses and minuses of various house pets and the best ways of preparing spiced vegetables. At various points throughout the day JhanKla would declare that it was time for a cultural experience, and we would pause to listen to music or watch a dit rec, taking turns choosing something from the lounge's large and eclectic collection.

Bayta mostly stayed quiet during the conversations, her impassive mask firmly in place, listening closely but only rarely joining in. Her few comments were for the most part factual and neutral, providing no fresh insights into what was going on behind those dark eyes. The dit recs, on the other hand, seemed to fascinate her, particularly one of my choices, a classic Hitchcock called *The Lady Vanishes*, itself set aboard a twentieth-century EuroUnion train.

At prescribed intervals, the aroma of cooking would begin to drift through the car, and in due course a servitor would appear to announce that the next meal was ready. Each day's menu was different, every one of them first-class, and at the end of each I could practically feel another half kilo of weight falling into formation around my waist. Eventually, late in Quadrail-time evening, we would part company with an appropriate round of good-nights and return to our individual compartments.

Theoretically, at any time after that first night I could have excused myself from the group and taken a stroll forward to find the Spider with the promised data chip. Rastra had emerged from his compartment at breakfast the first morning to concede that JhanKla had indeed been correct about my position vis-à-vis Jurian criminal protocol, and that I no longer needed to remain in his custody. Still, as far as I was concerned, cheerful and stupid was still the order of the day, and for those first two days I wasn't able to come up with a plausible excuse to even temporarily abandon the Peerage car's luxury.

Finally, with eleven hours remaining until our arrival at Jurskala, I managed to create my opening.

"No," I said, shaking my head firmly. "I'm sorry, but a proper Chattanooga nightcap can't be prepared with anything but Jack Daniel's."

"None of these will do?" JhanKla asked, gesturing to his array of beverages as, behind him, one of the servitors hovered in tense silence. "I'm told there are three other Human whiskeys available."

"And fine ones they are," I agreed, though two were brands I'd never even heard of. "But this is a *Chattanooga* nightcap, also known as an Uncle T Special. It's a cultural thing," I added, knowing that with JhanKla that would trump all other arguments.

"Very well," he said, throwing an unreadable look at the servitor. Unreadable to me, anyway; the servitor's flat face seemed to shrivel just fine beneath it. "I will send a servitor for a bottle."

"Actually, I'd rather go choose it myself," I said, getting to my feet. "There are several factors to consider—age and blend, for starters—and I'll have to see what they have in stock before I know which one to get."

"Very well," JhanKla said again. "I will summon Yir-TukOo to accompany you."

"No, that's all right," I said quickly. The last thing I wanted was to try to get a data chip from the Spiders with JhanKla's big guard-assistant hovering over me. "I'll be fine."

"I'll go with you," Rastra volunteered. "Without a ticket you'll need someone with diplomatic authority to allow you into the first-class section."

I suppressed a grimace. With the Spiders' diamond-edged pass in my pocket I didn't need his or anyone else's help to go wherever I wanted. But I could hardly tell him that. Still, he should be easier to get rid of than YirTukOo. "Sure," I said casually. "Let me get my jacket and we'll go."

Sixty seconds later I was back in the lounge, with my jacket on and a hastily scribbled note for Bayta lying on my bed: *Contact Spiders—tell them to bring data chip to first-class bar.* Rastra was also ready, and together we headed forward.

The two cars immediately ahead of us were baggage cars, filled with stacks of crates held together by safety webbing. Unlike the hybrid baggage/passenger car I'd started this trip in, the crates here weren't merely lined up along the walls. They were instead arranged in individual clumps, rather like tall islands surrounded by a maze of narrow access corridors that zigzagged around and between them. One cargo island per stop, I guessed, with the access corridors there in case the Spiders needed to get at the ones in back.

Ahead of the baggage cars were four third-class coaches, then the second/third-class dining car, four second-class coaches, one of the first-class coaches, and finally the first-class dining car. "Is it my imagination," Rastra commented as we threaded our way between the restaurant tables, "or are these Quadrails getting longer?"

"It's your imagination," I assured him, glancing around. There were no conductors here in the dining section, but I could see one beyond the smoked-glass divider in the bar.

"If there's anything your taste-tendrils have been missing during the past two days, here's your chance to get it."

"Actually, I rather enjoy Halkan cuisine," Rastra said, diplomatic as always. "Is there something I can get for you?"

"To be honest, I've really been missing my onion rings," I said. "You remember, back on Vanido, the little crunchy round things some of the people in our party were always special-ordering?"

"Yes, I remember," he said. "Shall I see if they have them?"

"Yes, thank you," I said. "While you do that, I'll go get the Jack Daniel's."

Rastra headed toward the carry-away counter, and I continued on through the divider into the bar. The Spider I'd noted, I saw now, was part of a pair, with the second standing near the end of the bar pretending to be a decorative planter.

Mentally, I shook my head. The Spiders might be terrific at running interstellar transport, but they had no sense of subtlety whatsoever. Still, Spider behavior was murky enough that I doubted anyone in here would worry about it one way or the other.

I headed toward a barstool a couple of meters in from the end where the Spider was standing, glancing around the room as I went. Three Cimmaheem were sitting off to one side with a *skinski* flambé going full-blast in the center of their table and a wide berth of empty space around them. A pair of Halkas paused in their conversation long enough to look me over, then returned to their drinks and conversation. A couple of tables over from them, a pair of humans wearing gold-trimmed bankers' scarves didn't even bother to look up as they discussed something in low, intense tones. In one of the other back corners sat a lone Bellido, the grips of his shoulder-holstered status guns poking out from beneath his armpits with the same kind of silent ostentation as the bankers' scarves.

And there was something about him that seemed vaguely familiar.

I reached the stool and sat down. The petite server Spider

tending bar took my order and disappeared into a storage area behind the bar. Out of the corner of my eye I saw the loitering conductor Spider stir and start to move my direction—

"Greetings to you, Human."

I turned my head the other direction. The Bellido had left his table and was settling himself unsteadily onto a stool an arm's length away from me. "Greetings to you and your kin," I replied, hoping fervently that the Spider would have the sense to back off.

For a wonder, it did. As I turned back to the bar, I saw it take a multilegged step backward and go back to waiting. The bartender reappeared, one leg curled around a flexible plastic bottle of Jack Daniel's, which he set on the bar in front of me. "Ah," the Bellido said knowingly. "Stomach trouble?"

"No," I said, frowning. "Why do you ask?"

"Jack Daniel's," he said, gesturing at the bottle. "An excellent stomach tonic. Very good at clearing out intestinal mites."

"Interesting usage," I said, studying the brown and tan facial stripe pattern on his chipmunk face. Unlike some species, Bellidos were fairly easy for human eyes to differentiate between; and up close, I was even more convinced I'd seen this one before. "We use it more like you would use aged Droskim."

"Really," he said, sounding surprised. "Interesting. Tell me, what brings you out into the galaxy?"

I resisted the impulse to roll my eyes. In terms of flat-out, words-per-minute chattiness, Bellidos were even worse than Halkas when they drank. "I work for a travel agency," I told him, getting a grip on my bottle and trying to figure out how to make a graceful exit without him watching me the whole way out. Maybe if I signaled the Spider to follow me to the restaurant area and we made the handoff there—

And then, right in the middle of my planning, it suddenly hit me. This was the same Bellido I'd passed on the way to my seat in the hybrid Quadrail car I'd taken out of Terra Station. The Bellido whose casual look had sent an unidentified but unpleasant tingle up my back.

My eyes flicked to the soft plastic grips of the status guns beneath his arms. Bellidos didn't just roll out of bed in the morning and decide which set of weapons would best suit the day's wardrobe. Those guns were as much a declaration of his societal position as a human banker's scarf or a Cimma's lacquered coiffure. These in particular were copies of Elli twelve-millimeters, a caliber that placed their owner somewhere in the upper middle class, and Bellidos of that class *never* took off their guns in public, not even if they wound up traveling beneath their class.

Back on the hybrid car he hadn't been carrying these guns. In fact, he hadn't been carrying any guns at all. Which meant he'd either been lying to the universe then, or he was doing so now.

And Bellidos never lied like that. Not without a damn good reason.

A renewed tingle ran up my back. Could he be a con artist? Possibly. But in my experience professional criminals were usually smart enough not to get this tipsy in public. A social pretender, then, intent on knocking back the good times and rubbing shoulders with the elite before he got caught? There were severe penalties for such things on Belldic worlds, but of course Belldic law didn't apply on the Quadrail.

"A travel agency, you say?" he prompted.

"Yes," I said, getting back to my explanation and my exit-strategy planning. Now, more than ever, I didn't want him to see me getting a data chip from a Spider. "I'm looking for unusual vacation experiences to offer my fellow humans."

"An enjoyable profession, no doubt," he said. "What is your next destination?"

"A Halkan system named Sistarrko," I said. "There's a resort on a moon there that's been recommended to me." I glanced at my watch. "And I need to get back and prepare for my change of trains."

"Oh, there are hours yet to go," he chided. "Tell me, have you ever tasted *properly* aged Droskim?"

"It would probably eat a hole in my stomach," I told him. "And I really must go."

His expression fell a little. "Then a pleasant journey to you, sir." Lifting his glass in salute, he stood up and made his unsteady way back toward his table.

I stood up, too, picking up my bottle and turning toward the restaurant section. As I did so, the Spider loitering at the end of the bar unglued itself from the floor and started toward me.

I swallowed a curse and picked up my pace. With my Bellido would-be best friend on one side and Rastra's imminent reappearance on the other, I might as well try to make this secret handoff onstage at the Follies.

But Rastra wasn't here yet, and the Bellido was still on his way to his table with his back toward me. If I could do this quickly enough . . .

I cut across the Spider's path, and as I did so one of its legs curled up from the floor and stretched out toward me. I caught the glint of a data chip, and without breaking stride I let my arm swing slightly out of line to pluck it from the pad. Pressing it into temporary concealment in my palm, I continued on, glancing back just as the Bellido dropped heavily into his chair.

I nearly bumped into Rastra as I crossed into the restaurant. "Ah—there you are," he said. "My apologies, but it appears they are out of onion rings. Apparently, they're a delicacy among Pirks as well as humans."

"Too bad," I said, lifting my bottle with one hand as I surreptitiously slipped the data chip into my jacket pocket with the other. "The important thing is that they had the Jack Daniel's. Let's get back to the others."

"I'm afraid you'll have to begin without me," Rastra said regretfully. "I've been informed that one of the first-class passengers has a problem that needs to be dealt with. As senior Resolver aboard, I must see if I can help." The scales around his eyes and beak crinkled slightly. "Try to remember to save me some."

"No problem," I said, a creepy feeling rippling across the skin between my shoulder blades. "Don't be long."

"I won't."

I watched until he'd passed through the door into the vestibule leading forward. Then, for no particular reason, I looked back over at the corner table.

The Bellido's drink was still there. The Bellido himself was gone.

I looked around the room, the creepy feeling turning into a full-fledged unpleasant tingle. The way he'd been moving earlier, he should have had trouble even finding the door, let alone moving stealthily enough to slip out without me noticing. Like the two Halkas before him, he'd apparently decided that the best way to fool a Human was to pretend to be drunk. Unlike the Halkas, he'd had all the nuances of the role down cold.

Which strongly implied he wasn't simply a social pretender, either. So what the hell *was* he?

I didn't know; but suddenly I wasn't feeling very good about hanging around here anymore. Trying to watch every direction at once, I headed back toward the Peerage car.

No one accosted me as I passed through the first- and second-class cars. I paid special attention to the Bellidos scattered among the passengers, but none of them seemed the least bit interested in me.

Which actually wasn't all that surprising. There was no way the fake drunk could have gotten past me while I was talking to Rastra, which meant he was still behind me somewhere in the forward part of the train. Comms didn't work aboard Quadrails, or anywhere else inside the Tube for that matter, which meant there also wasn't any way for him to have communicated with any confederates he might have farther back.

Unless, of course, he didn't need to communicate with them because they already had their orders. Trying not to look too much like I was hurrying, I left the last second-class car and crossed the vestibule into the third-class section.

I hadn't focused on the passengers on my way forward, but to the best of my memory nothing much seemed to have changed since then. Again, I paid special attention to the Bellidos; again, they didn't seem to be paying any attention back.

I was midway through the last of the passenger cars when my eyes fell on a set of three empty seats in the last row.

There had been occasional empty seats on my way forward, their occupants presumably either out having dinner or else communing with nature in one of the pair of restrooms at the front of each car. But there hadn't been any threesomes in the second/third-class dining car just now, and the chances of three passengers in the same row deciding to hit the head at the same time had to be pretty small.

Much smaller, I suspected, than the chances that those same three passengers had drifted off to the privacy of one of the baggage cars to arrange some kind of unpleasant surprise. Still, unless I wanted to wait for the fake drunk to catch up and turn three-to-one odds into four-to-one odds, there was nothing to do but keep going.

But like I'd told Bayta earlier, alcohol was a good equalizer. As my playmates were about to learn, that equalizing capability also extended to nonsocial events.

Anywhere in the galaxy except aboard a Quadrail, there would have been no question about how I would do that. A typical glass whiskey bottle made a natural club, which was probably why the Spiders were careful to package all their beverages in this flimsy plastic instead. One good thump, and the bottle would split along its tear lines and dump its contents all over the floor.

But the warped minds at Westali had been mulling over this for a few years, and they'd come up with a couple of tricks. With luck, maybe I could give any waiting footpads a surprise of their own.

I reached the end of the car and stepped through the door into the vestibule. There, momentarily shielded from view from either direction, I pulled the stopper from the bottle and replaced it just tightly enough to keep it closed. Now, with a good squeeze, I could send the stopper flying straight into an assailant's face, with a slosh of whisky right behind it. I couldn't remember how Bellido eyes reacted to alcohol, but even if it didn't temporarily blind him it should at least slow him down long enough for me to be faced with only two-to-one odds. Still not good, but better than nothing. Holding the bottle at its base, I opened the door and stepped into the first baggage car.

My natural instinct was to pause there, peering down the stacks of safety-webbed crates and listening for some clue as to where they might be hiding. But I overrode the reflex. Showing I was aware of their presence would only make them treat me with professional respect, and I would rather they assume I was stupid and oblivious and hopefully let their guard down a little. Without breaking stride, I headed in, trusting in my peripheral vision to give me enough warning for whatever was about to happen.

It didn't. I was halfway down the car when something exploded against the side of my head and the universe went black.

NINE :

I woke with an ache behind my right ear, an unpleasant half pain across the whole right side of my face, and the odd sensation that I'd been sleeping standing up.

For another minute I stayed as I was, listening for any signs of activity around me. But all I could hear was the rhythmic clicking of the Quadrail's wheels. Apparently, my assailant or assailants were already gone. Carefully, I opened my eyes.

My inner ear hadn't been lying to me. I was indeed standing up, my back pressed solidly up against something hard, my head turned to my left. From the faint light seeping in from below me, I could see I was inside one of the taller crates, which had had a narrow space cleared out for me. The mystery of how I had managed to stay upright while still unconscious was quickly solved: My playmates had simply worked the crate's access panel free—probably sliding it upward—manhandled me in face-first against the safety webbing already stretched around this group of crates, then slid the panel back in place behind me.

It was, I had to admit, a quick and creative way of putting an opponent temporarily out of action. The first person who really focused on the arrangement would instantly spot the webbing anomaly, but people doing a quick search for a wayward Human could easily miss such details.

Still, clever or not, they'd missed an obvious bet: They'd forgotten to gag me. Once the search reached my vicinity, a good shout would bring my rescuers straight to the spot. Experimentally, I started to take a deep breath.

They hadn't missed a bet after all. The webbing was tight enough that I *couldn't* expand my chest that far. Short, shallow breaths were unfortunately going to be the order of the day.

The little knife in my multitool could cut through this stuff with ease, of course. But the multitool was in my right pocket, and my captors had thoughtfully positioned me close enough to the right wall that I couldn't bend my elbow far enough to get my hand into that pocket.

I studied the cargo pressed up against me, or at least the small percentage of it I could see with my head turned to the side. It was too dark to read any of the labels, or even to tell what language they were in, but from the delicate aromas I guessed they were mostly exotic spices. No chance of identifying my assailants by unexplained quantities of merchandise in their possession, then—spices were one of those items that could easily be flushed down the nearest toilet, with their packaging shredded and dumped out the same way. There was no way of knowing my crate's destination, but if my attackers had done their job right it would be someplace far down the line, past Jurian territory and possibly out of Halkan space as well. If they'd been feeling generous, they might have arranged things so that I'd be found before I died of thirst. I wasn't ready to bet on that, though.

And then, as I studied the shadows of my feet against the spice packages, I noticed I'd apparently grown a third leg. For a moment I puzzled at the extra shadow; and then, suddenly, I realized what it was. Rather than burden themselves with the Jack Daniel's, they'd simply set the bottle on the floor between my feet before walling me in.

And I'd already loosened the stopper.

The webbing reached down only to my lower shins. Carefully, wincing as the movement put more pressure on the mesh against my face, I eased my feet together against the bottle, trying to squeeze it open. But my leverage was lousy, and nothing happened.

Besides, what I really needed was to send a spray of the whiskey under the door where it could be seen and smelled, not up across my slacks. Moving my left leg away, I swiveled my right foot around and gave the bottle a tap. It moved over a couple of centimeters, but stayed upright. I tried again, and this time it fell neatly over on its side. With a little careful maneuvering with the tips of my shoes, I got it pointed along the crack beneath the door.

Now came the tricky part. Exhaling as deeply as I could to give myself as much slack as possible, I angled my left foot up at the ankle and set it on top of the bottle. Mentally crossing my fingers, I pushed down.

With a gratifying clatter, the stopper popped out and skittered along the edge of the crate, and the delicate aroma of mixed spices vanished beneath the powerful smell of sourmash whiskey. I took a breath, remembering in time to make it a shallow one, and settled down to wait.

I was just starting to wonder if you could get drunk on alcohol fumes alone when they found me.

"So you never actually saw them," Rastra said.

"Not a glimpse," I told him, gingerly daubing at the lump below my ear with one of the Peerage car's first-aid cloths. "I don't even know what they hit me with."

Standing stiffly to the side, JhanKla made an angry bulldog rumble deep in his throat. "I should have insisted that YirTukOo accompany you."

"Hey, stuff happens," I said philosophically. "No permanent harm done, except that we lost the Jack Daniel's. By the way, did anyone happen to notice where I was heading when you got that crate open? I forgot to check."

"It was addressed to a spice wholesaler on Alra-kae at the inner edge of the Halkavisti Empire," Rastra said. "Only a two-day journey, fortunately, but it still would have been uncomfortable."

"Definitely," I agreed. "You get that problem solved in first class?"

"Yes," he said, the scales around his beak wrinkling. "One took offense at another, with the second unaware that he had even given cause for anger. A brief face-to-face conversation, and it was resolved."

So the whole thing had indeed been a ruse, a heavy-handed but effective ploy to split us up so that they could beat me up in private.

Which had taken some advance planning, which meant that I wasn't just a random victim. Not that I'd really thought that I was.

"I still think you should have that injury examined," Rastra continued. "I'm informed that there are three Human physicians aboard this Quadrail."

"I'll be fine," I assured him. "I got worse lumps than this when I played Sunday afternoon football at college. I just need to take a couple more QuixHeals and lie down for a while."

"As you choose," Rastra said, clearly not convinced. "But if you're still feeling unwell when we reach Jurskala, I'm going to insist. There are specialists in Human medicine on duty at the transfer station."

"Deal," I said, getting a bit unsteadily to my feet. "Bayta, can you give me a hand?"

Silently, she stood up and crossed to my side. She hadn't said a word since she and Rastra and the Spider they'd recruited for the search had pulled me out of that spice crate. Now, still without speaking, she gingerly took my arm. It was the first time she'd ever actually touched me, and even through my shirt I could feel the coldness of her fingers. Letting her take a little of my weight just for show, we headed down the corridor to my compartment.

The door had barely closed behind us when she let go of my arm like she'd been scalded. "How *could* you?" she demanded, her voice shaking, her rigid control suddenly gone. "How could you let them *take* it?"

"Relax," I said, dropping onto the edge of the bed and digging the data chip out of my pocket. "They didn't."

She stared at the chip like it was a gold watch being offered back to her by a dinner theater magician. "But then . . . ?" She trailed off.

"Why did they attack me in the first place?" I finished her question for her. "Good question. Before we discuss it, let's just make sure they weren't cute enough to switch chips on me."

She grimaced, but nodded. "All right," she said, moving toward the door. "I'll get my reader."

She was gone just long enough for me to confirm that the chip registered on my own reader as nothing but an innocuous set of travel guides. "Any chance they could have made a copy?" I asked as she took the chip and plugged it into hers.

"No." She did something with the scroll buttons, peered at the display, and nodded. "There," she said, handing it to me.

Where before there'd been nothing but tourist fluff, the display now showed over fifty files relating to Quadrail security and sensors. "Perfect," I said. "Something to read on the way to Modhra."

"You still want to go there?" Bayta asked, her voice suddenly cautious. "I mean . . . shouldn't you see a doctor first?"

"I'm fine," I assured her. I started to shake my head, quickly changed my mind. "Besides, this is starting to get very interesting."

"Interesting?" she echoed. "You call being attacked *interesting*?"

I shrugged. The gesture turned out to be only marginally less painful than shaking my head. "People don't usually attack you unless they feel threatened," I said. "That must mean we're getting close."

"Close to what?" she persisted. "All we've got is a name—Modhra—and JhanKla telling us we should go there."

"Plus all the maneuvering it took them to get him to drop us that name," I reminded her.

"Which could have just been to get us out of Kerfsis," she reminded me back. "Or to keep us away from somewhere else, for that matter."

I hesitated, once again trying to decide just how much I should tell her. I still didn't know what was really going on, or whose side she was on.

Still, she was clearly in league with the Spiders, or at least some group of them. If I froze her out of my investigation, I'd be completely on my own. Considering what had just happened, even questionable allies were better than nothing. "No, it's Modhra, all right," I said. "I didn't want to say anything with Rastra and JhanKla listening, but there was a chatty Bellido in the bar when I was getting the Jack Daniel's. He asked where I was going—"

"And you *told* him?"

I stared up at her, my head throbbing in time to my pulse, my eyes and ears taking in her expression and her tone and her body language, my Westali-trained brain taking the pieces and putting them together.

And in that single stretched-out moment in time, all my vague suspicions suddenly coalesced into a hard, cold certainty. Whatever was going on with JhanKla and Modhra and the Bellidos, Bayta knew all about it. "It didn't seem like a big deal at the time," I said, keeping my voice even. "The point is, the next thing I knew he'd disappeared somewhere into the first-class cars. And the *next* thing I knew, I'd been clobbered and locked in a spice crate."

"And you think the incidents are related?"

"Absolutely," I said, wondering how much of this she already knew. Still, I couldn't afford to let her know that I knew she knew. "They weren't after the data chip, because I still have that. They weren't after my cash stick, because I still have *that*. What else is there but someone not wanting us to go to Modhra?"

"But how could he have communicated with anyone at the rear of the train?" she asked. "You said he'd gone the other direction."

"That part I haven't figured out yet," I admitted, watching

her closely. But she had herself fully under control again, and her face wasn't giving anything away. "My guess is that he used the Quadrail computer system somehow, or else found a way to piggyback a signal onto the control lines."

She shook her head slowly. "I don't think either is possible."

"Well, whatever he did, he *did* send a message," I growled. "I'm sure of that."

"But I still don't see the point," she said. "What did they hope to accomplish?"

"They hoped to put me on ice long enough for us to go past Jurskala and the Grakla Spur," I said. "That's the only thing that makes sense. Someone, for whatever reason, doesn't want us going to Modhra."

The corner of her lip twitched. "So, of course, that's where you intend to go?"

I shrugged. "I'm following a trail. That's where it leads."

She seemed to brace herself. "I don't want to go to Modhra."

"No problem," I said calmly. "You can wait for me at Jurskala."

"What if I have the Spiders revoke your pass?"

I lifted my eyebrows. "Are you threatening me?"

"There could be danger there," she said evasively. "Terrible danger."

I thought about the Saarix-5 in my carrybag handles. "There's danger everywhere," I said. "Life is like that."

"You could die there."

So there it was, right out in the open. Modhra was indeed the key . . . and our enemies were prepared to be very serious indeed about protecting that key. "I could die anywhere," I countered. "I could fall over a Cimma in the dining car and break my neck. You know something about Modhra you're not telling me?"

A muscle in her jaw tightened briefly. "It's just a feeling."

"Fine, then," I said, pretending to believe her. "I'm going. You've got five hours to decide whether you're coming with me."

"Mr. Compton—"

"In the meantime," I cut her off, "do these feelings of yours include any hints as to which direction the danger might be coming from?"

She looked away. "It could be from anywhere," she said quietly. "You have no friends out here."

"Not even you?" I asked, pitching it like it was a joke. "At least you care whether I live or die, don't you?"

She straightened up. "I'm not your friend, Mr. Compton," she said, her voice and face stiff. "And no, I *don't* care." Brushing past me, she escaped into the corridor.

For a long moment I stared at the closed door, a hard, bitter knot settling into my stomach. I'd hoped for something—anything—that would indicate we were at least on the same side, even if we weren't exactly staunch allies.

But no. *I'm not your friend. And no, I don't care.*

Fine. Then I wouldn't care, either, when I did what I was going to do to her precious Spider friends.

And I would laugh in her face when I did it.

Swiveling my feet up onto the bed, I positioned my throbbing head carefully against the pillow. It would be another half hour before the painkiller I'd taken kicked in and let me get some sleep.

Pulling up the first of the Spiders' security files, I began to read.

TEN :

The Quadrail pulled into Jurskala Station, and with a round of farewells to Rastra and JhanKla I left the Peerage car and headed across the platform toward the track where the Grakla Spur train would be arriving in two hours. Bayta, silent and wooden-faced, was at my side.

I had thought about trying to find a clever way to sneak off the train, but had decided it wouldn't be worth the effort. Even if the Bellidos hadn't yet figured out that I'd escaped their impromptu holding cell, there would be plenty of time for them to spot us as we hung around the station waiting for our next Quadrail. The alternative, to spend that time hiding in one of the Spiders' buildings, would probably just make things worse. Clearly, there were multiple players in this game, and I saw no point in advertising my cozy relationship with the Spiders for anyone who hadn't already figured it out.

Especially when we could use that relationship to other advantages.

"Three more Bellidos have joined with the two from first class," Bayta murmured as we approached the first of the Quadrail tracks we needed to cross to get to our platform. "These three came from third class."

"Are they talking?" I murmured back, resisting the urge to look over my shoulder. The whole point of having the Spiders relay this information to me via Bayta was so that I *wouldn't* look like I had any suspicions about what was going on behind me.

"Yes," she said. "But none of the Spiders are close enough to hear."

"Let me know when they start moving," I instructed her. "Anyone else taking any interest in us?"

We reached the next track, the low protective barrier folding up and over into a little footbridge for us and our trailing carrybags. "I don't think so," she said. "Wait. The five Bellidos have split into two groups again and are moving this way."

"How fast?"

"Not very," she said as we reached the far side of the track and the bridge folded back into its barrier form. "And they aren't following us, exactly, just coming this general direction."

Either being coy about their target or else simply heading for the Grakla Spur train, too. "What about Rastra and JhanKla?"

"They've left the Peerage car and are walking toward the stationmaster's building," she reported. "The guard-assistant, YirTukOo, is with them."

"Probably making arrangements to switch the car to a different train," I said. JhanKla had done his bit by nudging me toward Modhra, and he and his entourage were apparently now out of the game.

We reached the Grakla Spur platform, which was lined by the usual mix of restaurants, lounges, shops, and maintenance buildings. "You ever had a Jurian soda crème?" I asked Bayta.

"A—? No."

"Then you're way overdue," I said, taking her arm and steering her toward the larger of the two restaurants.

"I'm not hungry," she protested, trying to pull away.

"This is more like a dessert than a meal," I assured her,

not letting go. "More to the point, with all those Spider waiters wandering around in there, we'll have a better chance of keeping an eye on everyone than we would in any of the regular waiting rooms."

The resistance in her arm muscles evaporated. "Oh," she said.

About half the restaurant's tables were occupied, a nice comfortable percentage. Suppressing my usual impulse to sit where I could see the door, I led Bayta to one of the tables in the center. "You want me to order for you?" I asked.

She shrugged in silent indifference. I pulled up the menu, found the proper listing, and ordered two of the crèmes. "I gather you haven't spent much time in the Jurian Collective," I suggested, leaning back in my seat.

"Not really." She hesitated. "Actually, not at all."

"Ah," I said, looking around. Unlike the Quadrail bar, this place hadn't been designed with conversational privacy in mind. "How long have you been with your friends?"

"As long as I can remember," she said, lowering her voice. "Is this really the right place for this?"

"Why not?" I countered. "I don't especially like working with someone I know next to nothing about."

She pursed her lips. "If it comes to that, I don't know much about *you,* either."

"Your friends seem to have the full inside track on me."

"That doesn't mean I do." Her forehead creased slightly. "The Bellidos have all gone to one of the waiting rooms by the Grakla Spur platform."

Passing up a possible chance to eavesdrop in favor of not taking the risk of being spotted and spooking the quarry. They certainly seemed to know what they were doing. "So what do you want to know?"

"About . . . ?"

"About me."

She studied my face, her forehead creased, clearly wondering if I was just baiting her. "All right. What did you do to get fired from Westali?"

I felt my throat tighten. I should have guessed she'd pick

that particular knife to twist. "What, you've been asleep the past two years?" I growled.

The corner of her lip twitched. "I'd really like to know."

I looked away from her, letting my eyes sweep slowly around the restaurant. Most of the patrons were Juriani, but there were a few Halkas and Cimmaheem as well.

And, of course, there was us. A pair of Humans, strutting around the galaxy as if we owned it. "Do you know how humanity got to be number twelve on the Spiders' Twelve Empires list?"

"I presume the same way everyone else did," she said. "When a race colonizes enough systems, the Spiders confer that designation."

"You colonize four of them, to be exact," I told her, Colonel Applegate's words from a few days ago echoing through my brain. *And Yandro makes five.* "Which gives you a total of five, including your home system. Yandro was the colony that put Earth over the bar and got us invited into the club."

"And there was a problem with that?"

I sighed. "The problem, Bayta, is that there's nothing of value there. Nothing. A few varieties of spice, some decorative hardwoods, a few animals we may or may not be able to domesticate someday, and that's it."

"And?"

"What do you mean, 'and'?" I bit out. "The UN Directorate dumped a trillion dollars down the drain for that Quadrail station, for no better reason than so they could pretend they were important when they traveled around the galaxy."

Her eyes widened with sudden understanding. "You're the one who blew the whistle, aren't you?"

"Damn straight I did," I growled. "Between the faked resource reports and the carefully prepped enthusiasm of the colonists, you'd have thought Yandro was the next Alaska. I couldn't let them get away with that."

"Alaska?"

"The northernmost state of the Western Alliance," I told her. "Formerly called 'Seward's Folly' after the man who purchased it a couple of centuries ago for a lot of cash that most people thought was being thrown down a frozen mud hole. The ridicule lasted right up until they discovered all the gold and oil reserves."

"You don't think that could happen with Yandro?"

I shook my head. "The reports they released to the public were masterfully done. But I got hold of the *real* ones, and you could literally hear the increasing desperation of the evaluators as they came closer and closer to the end of their survey and still couldn't find anything valuable enough to make it worth exporting in any serious quantities."

"I can see why the UN would be upset with you," she murmured.

"Oh, they were upset, all right," I agreed bitterly. "And the public was pretty upset with them right back. For a while. Problem was, they weren't upset long enough for anything to actually get done about it. The Directorate made a big show of firing a few scapegoats, denied personal responsibility six ways from Sunday, and waited for the ruckus to die down for lack of interest. Then they quietly went ahead and signed up for the station anyway. With their friends and supporters getting most of the contracts for the materials and construction modules, I might add."

"And then they made sure you paid for your opposition," she said quietly. "I'm sorry."

I shrugged, forcing my throat to relax. "It's okay," I assured her. "I'm over it."

Which was a lie, of course. Even after all this time, just talking about it was enough to twist my blood vessels into macramé.

A Spider stepped up to our table, holding a tray with the frothy soda crèmes I'd ordered. "We've got raspberry and Jurian *shisshun*," I told Bayta as I lifted the tall glasses onto the table. "Which one do you want?"

She chose the raspberry, and we settled down to eat in silence. I wasn't in the mood for more conversation, and she was either feeling likewise or was too busy communing with her Spider friends to spare me any attention.

It wasn't until we were heading back toward the platform that I belatedly noticed that her question about my career had completely sidetracked my plan to find out something about *her*.

The train bound for the Grakla Spur was, not surprisingly, considerably shorter than the one we'd taken to Jurskala, reflecting the smaller volume of traffic and cargo involved. The Spiders had another double first-class compartment set aside for us, and we were settling in when the door chimed and a conductor paused in the doorway long enough to hand Bayta a data chip. "That the information on Rastra and JhanKla?" I asked as she pulled out her reader.

"The conductor didn't know, but I assume so," she said, plugging in the chip and peering at the display. "Yes, it is," she said, handing it to me.

I glanced down the directory. "I don't see anything here on the two Halkas who jumped me in the interrogation room."

"They probably haven't had time to pull that together yet."

I grimaced. Still, half a loaf, and all that. "What's happening with the Bellidos?"

"Two of them have the compartment just behind ours," she said slowly. "The other three have gone to the last of the third-class coaches."

"We'll want their profiles and history, too," I said. "Better add that to the Spiders' things-to-do list."

"All right," she said, swaying momentarily for balance as the Quadrail started up. I looked past her at the display window, but there were only a few wandering drones on that side of our track. "I can talk to the stationmaster at the next stop," she went on. "But it's only four days to Sistarrko. They may not be able to get the data collected before then."

"That's all right," I said, sitting down in the lounge chair. "I've got plenty to read already. You want to join me?"

"No, thank you," she said, turning toward the door. "I'll be in my compartment if you need me."

"Hold it," I said, reaching over and touching the switch that opened the wall between our rooms. "Let's not use the corridor any more than necessary, okay? There are nosy neighbors down the hall."

"Oh," she said. "Right." Stepping past me, she went into her compartment, pointedly tapping the control on her own wall as she passed it. I waited until the wall had closed; then, changing my mind, I got up from the chair and crossed over to the bed instead. Throwing my carrybags up onto the rack, I dimmed the lights, propped myself comfortably on the pillow, and started to read.

Given the haste with which the Spiders had thrown together the information package, I hadn't expected anything too extensive or startling. I wasn't disappointed. Rastra had been born to a good if not really highly placed family and had risen through the ranks of Guardians until he showed talent in mediating conflicts, at which point he'd been promoted to Resolver. He'd risen through the ranks there, too, being assigned to increasingly important posts until he'd been promoted to *Falc* and been given his current Resolver-at-large position, going wherever his government needed him. The Spiders had included his last five years' worth of Quadrail travel, which confirmed he'd spent the past three months on the road with JhanKla, no doubt smoothing the High Commissioner's path through the murky labyrinth of Jurian protocol.

JhanKla, in contrast, had been born pretty much at the top of the food chain, to one of the Halkan Peerage families. He'd been schooled and trained in the art of being an aristocrat, and upon completion of those studies had been handed a commissioner's job on Vlizfa. He'd served there for three years, apparently with at least a modicum of competence, then moved on to a succession of more important posts on various Halkan worlds. The details of his promotion to High Commissioner weren't given, but with Halkas that could be a result of merit, a fluctuation in family prestige, or even the serendipity of the right person dying at an opportune moment. Most of his Quadrail travel over the past five years had consisted of trips within the Halkavisti Empire.

As near as I could tell, comparing the two sets of records,

there was no indication that he and Rastra had ever even been in the same solar system together prior to this extended visit to the Jurian Collective.

Something seemed to flicker at the edge of my vision. I looked up, but whatever it was had apparently passed. I looked around the room for a moment, then turned my attention back to the reader and swapped out the chip for the one holding the Tube security data.

I'd had just a few minutes to study the chip earlier, but even through a throbbing head I'd hit enough of the high points to be impressed. Now, as I dug into the details, I found myself even more so.

The Tube sensors spotted explosives, of course, including the explosive loadings of projectile handguns. Everyone knew that much. What I hadn't spotted on my first pass was that the detectors also picked up a wide range of the more innocuous components that could be assembled into things that could go bang in the night. Even homemade explosives were apparently out.

There was also a wide variety of chemical and biological poisons and disease organisms on the list, both fast- and slow-acting varieties, many of which I'd never even heard of. Some were reasonably general threats to the galaxy at large, items like Saarix-5 or anthrax that attacked pretty much every carbon-based metabolism to one degree or another. Things that were more species-specific, like HIV or Shorshic shellbeast toxin, were also screened for.

All the standard tools of mayhem were on the list, from plasma and laser weapons with their huge energy signatures, to the thudwumper and shredder rounds I was most familiar with, to more subtle devices like dart throwers and even such passive devices as nunchaku fighting sticks and police billy clubs. If there was a weapon the Spiders hadn't included, I couldn't think what it might be.

There was obviously way too much for a single set of hatchway sensors to look for, but the chip had the answer to that long-standing puzzle as well. There were definitely hatchway sensors that checked passengers as they arrived from the shuttles, but the deeper and more subtle scanning was done as they made their way to the platforms, via sensors built into the Tube's flooring and support buildings. In effect, each Quadrail station was a massive sensor cavity, discreetly protecting the passengers from each other.

And *that* was certainly not included in the building supplies that made up the major part of a station's trillion-dollar price tag. All of it had to be added afterward, put in by the Spiders themselves. Perhaps, I decided grudgingly, the cost of a new station wasn't quite the extortion I'd always thought.

Above the top of the reader, something again seemed to flicker at the edge of my vision. Again I looked up, and again there was nothing.

But this time I spotted something I hadn't noticed before. Preoccupied with the data chips and my own musings, I'd neglected to opaque the window.

Frowning, I set the reader aside and turned off the room lights completely, and as my eyes adjusted to the darkness I could see a faint luminescence begin to fill the window. For a moment I wondered where it was coming from, then realized that I was seeing a reflection of the Coreline glow from high overhead on the curved Tube wall surrounding us.

Getting to my feet, I walked over to the window, and for a minute I leaned against it and gazed out into the perpetual night of the Tube. How many thousand light-years of Quadrail track was there out there? I wondered distantly. Enough to link all the known inhabited worlds, certainly, with other lines probably already in place waiting for up-and-coming species like us to stumble across. Soon, perhaps, there would be Thirteen Empires, and then Fourteen, and Fifteen—

And without warning, a spot of brilliant red light flashed across my sight someplace far to the rear of the train.

I jerked in surprise as the light winked out again. It hadn't been all that bright, I realized now, except relative to the soft Coreline glow and my own dilated pupils. I stared at the spot where it had been, wondering if that had been what had caught my attention earlier and what in the world it could be. Some kind of erratic running light? But Quadrails didn't carry running lights, at least as far as anyone knew. Some kind of warning beacon, then? Out here in the middle of nowhere, I hoped to God not.

The light flashed on again. Experimentally, I turned my eyes slightly away, and this time I thought I could detect a slight flicker in it.

And as it winked off again, I suddenly understood.

My jacket was hanging beside me on the cleaning rack. I dug madly into the pockets, pulling out my reader and data chip pack and swearing under my breath as I tried to read the chips' labels by the dim reflected Coreline light. Finally, I located the right one. Jamming it into the slot, I turned the reader on and pressed it against the window.

It was obvious now, with the crystal clarity only hindsight could bring to a situation. My playacting Bellido back on the Jurskala train hadn't needed anything so esoteric as a tap into Spider computer or control systems to keep in touch with his buddies back in third class. He'd had a compartment window, a simple low-power laser pointer, a fluctuation modulator, and the whole Tube wall to bounce messages off of. No wonder his friends had been ready for me—they'd probably had their orders before I'd even made it out of the last first-class coach.

The red light came on again, and I pressed the reader hard against the window, keeping it as steady as possible. The modulation sequence was far too fast for human eyes to register, but the sensor built into the reader ought to be able to capture it and slow it down enough for me to make some sense of it later.

The light came and went three more times in the next few minutes. Apparently, the Bellidos were feeling chatty today. Three minutes later it flashed one final time, then went silent.

I waited by the window another half hour before finally calling it quits. Making my way back to the bed, I turned the lights up to a dim glow and got to work.

With the basic mode of their communication so unlikely to be spotted, I'd hoped the Bellidos might have gone with something simple like digitized text or voices. But no such luck. The modulation turned out to be some sort of Morse-style code, and it wasn't following any of the usual Belldic encryption systems.

Still, at least I knew now how it had been done. That was worth a lot right there, especially since it offered a little more insight into the people I was up against. Cleverness and simplicity seemed to be their style. I'd do well to remember that.

But for now, my head was starting to hurt again and fatigue was dragging at my eyelids. Going to the tiny washroom, I got some water and took another painkiller and QuixHeal, then turned off the light and got undressed for bed.

My last act before crawling under the blankets was to set my reader on "record" and prop it up in the window. Just in case.

I slept long and deep and awoke ravenously hungry. I checked the other compartment, found Bayta already up. I had a quick shower and shave, and together we went back to the dining car.

None of the Bellidos were there at the moment. Bayta's Spider friends reported to her that the two in first class had already eaten and returned to their compartment, while the ones back in third had eaten in shifts. I kept an eye on the handful of Halkas in the room, wondering if JhanKla had put someone on our tail straight from the last station, or whether he'd just sent a message on ahead.

But no one seemed to be taking any particular interest in us. Which didn't prove anything one way or the other, of course.

We finished eating and returned to my compartment, where we spent a few minutes sifting through the tourist brochures on the Modhra resort and discussing what exactly we would do when we got there.

Surprisingly, the choice of lodging turned out to be our

biggest sticking point. Bayta wanted to take the lodge on the surface, where we would have a view of Modhra II and the gas giant Cassp, while I pushed equally hard for the underwater hotel JhanKla had mentioned. Eventually, Bayta gave in, though clearly not happily, and stalked back to her own compartment.

When the wall between us was closed again, I checked my reader to see if the Bellidos had transmitted any more secret messages during the night. They hadn't.

The rest of the trip passed uneventfully. Bayta stayed alone in her compartment most of the time, joining me only for meals, and I did what I could to catch up on my sleep and healing.

It was only as I was repacking my carrybags in preparation for our arrival at Sistarrko that it belatedly occurred to me that information wasn't the only thing I should have asked the Spiders for when this whole thing had started.

I should also have asked for a gun.

ELEVEN :

JhanKla had described Sistarrko as a minor colony system, but from the size and design of its transfer station I would have guessed it to be more along the lines of a regional capital like Kerfsis. From the size of the two warships that had silently escorted us in from the Tube, I would have put it even higher than that.

Of course, the system *was* the home of the famous Modhran coral, and an up-and-coming tourist center to boot. Maybe that explained it.

Maybe.

We made it through customs without incident, the Saarix in my carrybag grips whispering right past their sensors. I didn't spot any of the Bellidos, but that wasn't surprising. The Halkas had separate customs areas for the different traveling classes, and I'd already seen how this bunch shifted class and status without batting a whisker. They were probably two levels below us, working their humble way through the third-class stations.

And of course, after they did that, they'd be getting their genuine status guns out of their lockboxes. The next time I faced them, they would be fully armed.

What a lovely thought.

Like Quadrail Tubes everywhere in the galaxy, the Grakla Spur cut through Sistarrko's outer system, in this case just outside Cassp's orbit. That would put the Modhra resort at a considerable distance from the station for much of any given decade, which I suspected would cause trouble for the tourist logistics a few years down the line. Fortunately, at the moment the planet was nearly at its closest approach, which meant the travel time would be measured in hours rather than days. The transport rep directed us to the proper departure lounge, where we found a fifty-passenger short-haul torchferry waiting, and we climbed aboard with thirty fellow travelers. I'd expected at least one of the Bellidos to join the party, if only to keep an eye on us, but none of them did.

We took off in a blaze of superheated heavy-ion plasma, and five hours later reached the delicately ringed gas giant. Shutting down the drive well clear of Modhra I's icy surface, we switched to Shorshic vectored force thrusters, and a few minutes later settled gently onto the light-rimmed landing pad.

The view was everything JhanKla had promised. Bulging up over the resort area's horizon, Cassp had the same turbulent cloud bands and thousand-kilometer-wide storms as Jupiter and Saturn back in Sol system, but with a wider range of coloration than either of those two worlds. Its ring system was at least as impressive as Saturn's, as well, with much of it extending well past us. Overhead, Modhra II moved across the sky, a glistening ball of stone and ice arcing its way along the Modhra Binary's common orbit.

As an extra bonus, some quirk of celestial mechanics had put the Modhras' combined orbit at right angles to Cassp's ring system. That meant that as the two moons moved around their combined center of gravity, our view of the rings shifted from slightly above to a straight edge-on view to slightly below, then rose back through them again. It made for an ever-shifting, ever-changing panorama that all by itself would probably have justified the development of the place as a tourist getaway.

The lodge-style building we set down beside was a sprawling copy of an ancient Halkan High Mountain fortress, complete with distinctive star-shaped turrets. The modern airlock entrances spoiled the illusion a bit, but neither of the two moons was large enough to hold much atmosphere. Bayta and I joined the rest of the passengers in climbing into the torchferry's vac suits, and a few minutes later we all headed out across the frozen surface.

The lodge's interior décor was High Mountain style, too, with several centuries' worth of Halkan armor replicas standing in front of equally ancient wall hangings. The motif was carried even to the check-in procedure, which was handled by desk clerks in half-scale mail instead of by self-serve computer terminals. When our turn came I asked about the underwater hotel and was directed to a bank of ornate elevators waiting across the entry foyer. We joined five of the other guests, and fifteen minutes later emerged into the hotel lobby and what could only be described as an undersea wonderland.

The whole place was decorated with a graceful mixture of wispy sea plants and multicolored rock, all overlaid with a filigree of ice and frozen sea foam. Large convex windows showcased the view here beneath Modhra's ice cap, illuminated by an array of floodlights. JhanKla had said these oceans ran up to five kilometers deep, but the resort had been built in one of the shallower areas, and some of the famous Modhran coral ridges could be seen snaking their way across the ocean floor below.

The desk clerks here were dressed in outfits that looked vaguely mermaid and merman, though I couldn't remember any such legends in any Halkan mythos. The single-room rates were outrageous enough, but the two-room suite we needed was astronomical, far beyond what I had in any of my cash sticks. The Spiders hadn't thought to include any actual money with their Quadrail pass, which left me no option but to put the room on my credit tag. I did so without actually wincing, though I suspected there would be all sorts of unpleasant future ramifications for this kind of unauthorized usage.

But then, according to Bayta, odds were I'd be dying here anyway. No future; no future ramifications; no worries. I signed the authorization, and we were directed to the elevator for one final descent.

Our suite wasn't quite as luxurious as JhanKla's Peerage car. But it was lavish enough, and the view beat the car hands down. We were on the hotel's lowest level, with a transparent floor and two transparent corner walls giving us a spectacular wraparound view of the rippling water and coral ridges below. In the center of the room a pair of couches faced each other over a glowing fire pit—artificial, of course, but very realistic. There were two comfortable lounge chairs and six carved wooden uprights, the latter group arranged around a similarly carved wooden dining/conference table. Set against the two nontransparent walls were a computer desk and a huge entertainment center.

The bedroom was just as nice, though smaller, with its floor and its single outside wall again transparent. Here the center was dominated by a gargantuan bed big enough for a Cimmaheem couple or at least four standard-issue humans, with a duplicate of the living room's entertainment center on one wall and a large walk-in closet on the other. The closet, I noted, came prefurnished with clothing in a wide range of styles and sizes.

There were also no bugs anywhere in the suite. For me, that was the biggest surprise of all. "Nice enough for you?" I asked Bayta as I emerged from my bedroom sweep into the living area.

Bayta was standing beside one of the outer walls, gazing out at the coral and the lights from a group of divers and a couple of midget submarines that were moving around among the ridges. "I mean, there *was* a Grand Suite listed if you think we should upgrade," I added.

"What exactly are you planning to do here?" she asked, not turning around. She'd hardly said two words since our arrival at Sistarrko Station, and the muscles of her neck seemed to have settled into a permanently taut state.

"We start by trying to relax," I told her, stepping to her side and taking her hand. Trying to take it, anyway, before she deftly pulled it out of my grip. Her skin was icy cold. "No one's going to try to kill us here. It's too public and way too high-profile."

"So they'll wait until we're off in some quiet and lonely place?" she asked with only a trace of sarcasm.

I shrugged. "Something like that."

"And, of course, we *will* be going to some quiet and lonely places?"

"Well, *I* will," I told her. "Like I said before, you're welcome to stay here, or even go back to the Tube." I crossed toward the desk and computer terminal. "Let's see what they've got in the way of entertainment."

There were, as it turned out, quite a few options to choose from. JhanKla had already listed the outdoor activities for us, but the resort had a large number of indoor ones as well. There were half a dozen restaurants, ranging from casual to formal-wear-fancy, two theaters with rotating stage shows designed to appeal to a wide range of Halkan and offworlder tastes, and a fully equipped casino for anyone who still had money left after paying for their room and meals. Our entertainment centers had access to a wide range of music and dit recs, as well, more extensive even than JhanKla's private collection. "Let's try the casino first," I suggested. "Unless you'd rather start with a swim."

"Shouldn't we be focusing on our investigation?" she countered.

"We've got time," I assured her, getting up from the desk and crossing to her side. "I'm expecting our Bellidos to show up before anything interesting happens, and they definitely weren't on our torchferry. Either they decided to take a later one, which according to the schedule won't be in for another eight hours, or else they've gone into the inner system to Sistarrko itself, which means they can't be here for a minimum of thirty."

"Why would they go to Sistarrko?"

"No idea," I said. "Maybe there's some prep work they still need to do."

"Or maybe that's where this theoretical test of yours will take place?"

"I suppose that's possible," I conceded. "Still, JhanKla pointed us here, not Sistarrko, and Modhra's the name that apparently also caught my fake drunk's attention. No, *something's* going to happen here, and most likely within the next hundred hours."

She frowned. "How do you know that?"

"Because the crate they stuck me in was bound for Alra-kae, nearly two days past Jurskala," I reminded her. "If I hadn't been found until then and had had to backtrack, it would have cost us just about a hundred hours. If the idea was to get me out of the way while something happened here, we can assume it'll all be all over by then."

I gestured to the view. "But until they arrive, the point is moot. So let's spend some time getting the lay of the land."

"How will you know when the Bellidos arrive?"

"There are ways," I assured her. "So again: casino or swimming?"

"Casino," she said reluctantly. She turned toward the bedroom, paused. "This whole place will probably be decorated with Modhran coral," she said, her voice suddenly very strange. "Whatever you do, don't touch it. All right?"

"The stuff's not fragile," I soothed her. "I've seen pictures of it being used—"

"Just *don't touch it*!" she cut me off sharply. "Promise me you won't touch it." Her shoulders rose slightly as she took a deep breath. "Please," she added more quietly.

"Okay," I managed, trying to unfreeze my brain. An outburst like that from my calm, unemotional Bayta? "Since you say *please* . . . sure."

"Thank you." Her shoulders rose and fell again. "All right. Let's go."

* * *

Halkan casinos were invariably formal, and I hadn't brought anything nearly classy enough to wear. Fortunately, the hotel had that covered with several formal outfits, both male and female, tucked away in the bedroom closet. They were all Remods, no less, which meant that once we'd donned the ones closest to our sizes, we were able to plug them into the room's computer and have them fine-tuned to a perfect fit. One of the more useful toys of the rich and famous.

It was the middle of the afternoon, local time, and the casino was doing a brisk business. I spotted a couple of other hotel-issue Remods, but most of the patrons had brought far more elaborate outfits of their own to show off to each other. Two of the room's corners sported drink and snack areas set off from the rest of the casino by what looked like waist-high walls with chunks of Modhran coral submerged in swiftly moving canals. In the center of the casino was a five-meter-tall waterfall/fountain with more of the coral in the rippling pool area around it.

"I see a Bellido," Bayta murmured as we paused at the top of the entrance ramp leading from the elevator bank to the main floor. "Over by that long green table."

"The daubs table," I identified it for her. The Bellido in question was in full army uniform, watching intently as the Halka currently handling the dice ran through the traditional prethrow good-luck routine. I couldn't make out his rank insignia from this distance, but there were a pair of gun grips sticking out from beneath each of his arms, which probably pegged him as at least a lieutenant general. "It's the Halkan equivalent of craps."

"That's a military uniform, isn't it?"

"It is indeed," I agreed, putting my hand against the small of her back and starting down the ramp. "Come on, let's mingle. You go left; I'll go right."

"You want us to split up?" she asked, a fresh note of trepidation in her voice.

"Public and high-profile, remember?" I soothed her. "Just smile a lot, listen to what people are saying, and don't leave the casino without me. We'll meet in an hour in that blue-colored snack area in the back corner."

We reached the bottom of the ramp. Giving her arm a reassuring squeeze, I let go and headed into the genteel chaos.

In real life, I knew, gambling usually wasn't nearly as dramatic as it was portrayed in dit rec dramas and mysteries. Rarely if ever were pivotal decisions made at the poker tables, nor did the chief villain meet the hero over baccarat to trade witticisms and veiled threats.

Still, gambling turned people's minds toward money and recreation, and as a result tended to make tongues wag more freely and with less caution than they otherwise might. Keeping my ears open, I wandered through the crowd, pausing at each table to study the game in progress and do a little professional eavesdropping.

Like the first-class coach cars on the Quadrail, this seemed to be a place where the galaxy's various species mixed freely. Unfortunately, as I made my rounds I discovered that business interests seemed to have been left back in the guest rooms. All the conversations I dipped into seemed related either to the current game in progress, the profit and loss levels of previous games, or the other activities available on Modhra I. Even a trio of Cimmaheem, who generally avoided exercise like the plague once they'd reached this age and status level, were talking enthusiastically about taking a submarine tour to one of the cavern complexes nearby and suiting up to go explore it.

Eventually, my wanderings brought me to the central waterfall/fountain.

It was one of the standards of Halkan décor, consisting of several small fountains at different levels squirting water upward where it then tumbled down layers of molded rock. Each fountain had its jets set at different heights and intervals, the whole group working together in a nicely artistic pattern. Additional injectors at various levels of the waterfall added more variation to the flow, stirring up the water, sending it into small whirlpools, or whipping it into brief whitewater frenzies. The reservoir pool stretched out a meter from the base of the rock pile, though the water itself was only about half a meter deep, and the waist-high wall around the whole thing was embossed with colored light ridges running a counterpoint pattern of their own.

And as I'd observed from the entrance ramp, the pool itself was full of coral.

Considerably more coral than I'd realized, too. The bits I'd spotted sticking up out of the water were only the tips of much larger formations snaking along the floor of the pool, covering it completely in places, with hidden colored lights creating contrast and dramatic shading.

Anywhere else in the galaxy, a display with this much Modhran coral would have cost millions. Here, fifty meters above the spot where the stuff grew, it was rather like decorating a Yukon winter scene with ice sculptures.

"What do you think?" a voice rose above the general murmur of the crowd.

I turned. The military-clad Bellido Bayta had pointed out earlier was standing behind me, idly swirling the dark red liquid in his glass as he gazed up at the waterfall. I could see now that his insignia identified him as an *Apos,* the equivalent of a brigadier general. "It's beautiful," I said.

"Isn't it, though," he agreed, lowering his eyes back to me. "*Apos* Taurine Mahf of the Bellidosh Estates-General Army Command."

"Frank Compton," I said in reply. "No position in particular at the moment."

He made a rumbling noise. "And they were fools to allow your departure."

I frowned. "Excuse me?"

His chipmunk face creased with a smile. "Forgive me," he said. "You are the Frank Compton once with Earth's Western Alliance Intelligence service, are you not?"

"Yes, that's right," I said, studying his face. As far as I could recall, I'd never run into this particular Bellido before. "Have we met?"

"Once, several years ago," he said. "It was at the ceremony marking the opening of the New Tigris Station. I was one of the guard the Supreme Councillor sent to honor your people."

"Ah," I said. In fact, I remembered that ceremony well . . . and unless *Apos* Mahf had had extensive facial restriping I was quite sure he hadn't been there. "Yes, that was an adventure, wasn't it?"

"Indeed," he said, taking a sip from his drink. "What exactly do you do now?"

"At the moment, I work for a travel agency," I told him. "A much simpler and safer job."

"Even so, you cannot seem to avoid adventure," he said. "I understand you nearly vanished from your last Quadrail."

An unpleasant tingling ran across my skin. "Excuse me?" I asked carefully.

"Your adventure with the baggage car and your unknown assailant," Mahf elaborated. "He *was* unknown, was he not?"

"Yes, unfortunately," I said.

"No idea at all?" Mahf persisted. "Even knowledge of his species would be of help to the authorities."

"I didn't see or hear a thing," I said. "Is keeping track of Quadrail incidents part of your job?"

He waved his hand in the Belldic equivalent of a shrug. "Not at all," he said. "But this topmost level of galactic society is a small and tightly bound machine. Gossip and rumor are the fuels that drive it."

"Ah," I said, deciding to try a little experiment. "Yes, it was an unexpected adventure, all right. Rather like that of the old woman in the classic dit rec drama, in fact."

Mahf's whiskers twitched with uncertainty, then smoothed out again. "Yes, indeed," he said knowingly. "*The Lady Vanishes.* Very much like that, in fact. Still, I'm pleased you won out in the end."

"As am I," I said between stiff lips. There should have been no way for him to have caught on to which specific dit rec drama I'd been referring to. No way in hell.

Unless he had a direct pipeline to someone who'd been in that Peerage car with us.

The Spiders had told Bayta that everyone from that group

had stayed behind at Jurskala. I'd checked the schedule for Sistarrko-bound Quadrails, and there wasn't any way for someone to have caught a later one and arrived here by now. JhanKla or Rastra would have had to send a message on ahead, a message apparently detailed enough to include even the dit recs we'd watched. Either that or the Spiders had lied to Bayta.

Or else Bayta had lied to me.

"I see you admiring the coral," Mahf said into my thoughts.

I had been doing no such thing, but I nodded anyway. "Beautiful, isn't it?" I said. "Unfortunately, our laws don't permit it to be imported to our worlds."

"A pity," he said, gesturing toward the fountain. "I presume that means you've never had the chance to actually touch it."

Bayta's strange warning flitted through my mind. Was everybody in the whole galaxy obsessed with this damn stuff? "No, but I've touched Earth coral a couple of times," I told him. "Very rough, very pointy, very scratchy."

"But this is *Modhran* coral," he said reprovingly. "It has a texture far different from that of any other coral in the galaxy. Different from anything else, for that matter."

I stepped to the wall and looked down. I'd never seen Modhran coral up close, and as I gazed into the pool I was struck by how vibrant and colorful and glittery it was. Human coral just sort of lay there, silently warning the unwary diver with its sharp brittleness, but this had an odd look of suppleness, even cuddliness, that I couldn't quite explain, even to myself.

"Go on," Mahf murmured. He was right beside me now, practically breathing onto my neck. "Touch it. It's quite safe, and very pleasant."

"No, that's all right," I said, straightening up and taking a long step back from the pool. "Mother taught me never to pick up strange things. You never know where they've been."

For a long moment he stared at me, his earlier cheerfulness suddenly hidden beneath an almost wooden mask.

Then, to my relief, the smiles came out again from behind the clouds. "I would never seek to overturn such counsel," he said, lifting his glass to me. "Farewell, Compton. May your stay be pleasant."

There were half a dozen cashiers seated in booths along the walls, walled off behind traditional flame-patterned iron gratings. "Your desire, sir?" one of them asked as I stepped to his window.

"Do you have link-games?" I asked.

"Yes, indeed," he assured me, selecting a link chip from a bowl. "Do you need a reader?"

"Got one, thanks," I said, taking the chip and heading for the bar. Choosing a table that gave me a view of the rest of the casino, I pulled out my reader, palming my sensor chip as I did so. Switching on the reader, I made as if to plug in the link chip, then did a flip-switch and put in the sensor instead. Settling back into my chair, pretending I was playing the link-game, I keyed for a scan of the comm-frequency transmissions.

Considering the size of the resort, there was an amazingly low level of comm traffic going on, though in retrospect I should have realized that these people had come here to get away from it all, not bring it all with them. All the transmissions that were zipping around were encrypted, of course, and I had nothing with me nearly powerful enough to dig through all that protection.

But then, actually eavesdropping on the conversations wasn't the point of this exercise.

The bulk of the traffic, not surprisingly, was running civilian Halkan encryptions, and I tackled those first. They varied in complexity and layering, depending on how leakproof their owners wanted them to be, but they all followed a very distinctive, very Halkan pattern. The next most common encryption pattern was Cimman, again not surprising given the proximity of the Cimmal Republic. I eliminated those, plus the dozen civilian Jurian systems, and finally the two Pirkarli ones.

And that was all. There was nothing with the Peerage-type patterns that a Halkan high official like JhanKla would use. There was also nothing that followed any standard Belldic patterns, military *or* civilian.

There was a movement at the corner of my eye, and I looked up as Bayta slid into the chair across from me. "Is anything wrong?" she asked. "You said an hour."

"Nothing's wrong," I told her, keying off the reader and pulling out the chip. "I just got tired early. How sure are you that JhanKla or one of his people didn't get on our Quadrail at Jurskala?"

"The Spiders said they'd all stayed behind."

"So we're as sure as the Spiders are," I concluded, wishing I felt reassured by that. "Fine. Hear anything interesting out there?"

"Not really," she said, frowning slightly. "They mostly seemed to be talking about whatever game they were playing."

"Yeah, I got a lot of that, too," I said. "You happen to listen in on any Cimman conversations?"

"There was one," she said. "They were talking about taking a submarine cruise to an underwater cave a few kilometers from here."

"So were mine," I said. "Interesting."

"Doesn't sound very interesting to me," Bayta said. "None of it did."

"My point exactly," I said, looking out past the low wall at the milling gamblers. "When did you ever wander around this many people and not find *someone* talking business?"

She pursed her lips. "Maybe they save all their business talk for somewhere else."

"Maybe," I said. "But I didn't hear anything about family or politics, either. They save all that for somewhere else, too?"

She gave a hooded look to the side, toward a pair of Halkas sitting two tables away. "What are you implying?" she asked in a low voice.

"I'm not sure," I said. "Normally, you never make the assumption that everyone's in on a gag except you. But in this case, I'm starting to wonder."

"You mean like a conspiracy?"

"I admit it's an overused presumption," I said. "But you said yourself that I had no friends out here. And *Apos* Mahf did say the ultra-rich were a close-knit community."

"*Apos* Mahf?"

"The Bellido you pointed out earlier," I told her. "He claims to know me."

"A friend?" she asked, her tone suddenly cautious.

"So he claims," I said. "He named a ceremony I was at several years ago, but he apparently doesn't know how good my memory is for faces. Even Belldic faces."

"But how could he have known you were at the ceremony unless he was there, too?"

"Because some of the news footage of the VIPs happened to catch a couple of us security grunts in the background," I told her. "I got chewed out royally about it afterward, in fact. As if it had been my fault." I stroked my lip as a sudden thought struck me. "Come to think of it, it was our old friend Colonel Applegate who did most of the chewing. Our old *acquaintance,* that is," I corrected myself.

It was a small joke, and I hadn't expected much of a response. Bayta didn't give me any response at all. "What did you and Mahf talk about?" she asked instead.

"He tried to renew our nonexistent acquaintanceship and then asked me about the incident aboard the Jurskala Quadrail. Interestingly enough, he mentioned details about that trip that he has no business knowing. That's why I asked if the Spiders could have missed someone following us from Jurskala."

"No." Bayta was positive.

"Then someone must have sent one hell of a detailed message here ahead of us," I grunted, slipping my reader back into my pocket. "Come on, let's get back to the room and check the submarine tour schedule."

She seemed taken aback. "The what?"

"Submarine tours seem to be the hot item today," I pointed out. "Why, is there a problem?"

"No, of course not," she said, suddenly sounding flustered. "It's just . . ."

"It's just that you don't like being led around by the nose?" I suggested.

Her lips compressed. "Something like that."

"I don't much like it myself," I said pointedly. "But someone has again gone to a lot of effort to lay out a trail of bread crumbs. I want to see where it leads."

"What if it leads into a trap?"

I shrugged. "Hopefully, we'll figure that out before we get there."

The hotel offered three different submarine cruises, two of them traveling to distant coral formations and one hitting the caverns Bayta and I had heard so much about in the casino. All of the day's cruises were full, but there was a cavern trip scheduled for early the next morning that still had a half dozen vacancies. I booked us two seats on that one, and while I was at it made reservations for an early evening dinner.

With a couple of hours to kill, Bayta went into the bedroom for a nap. Drawing myself a drink from the room's dispenser, I settled down at the computer desk to learn all there was to know about Cassp, the Modhra Binary, and the Modhran resort.

Dinner that evening was very much in the five-star range I would have expected from a place like this. Afterward, we browsed through one of the rows of shops for a while, and I bought Bayta a set of hair fasteners and a compact travel makeup kit.

I could tell she wasn't particularly impressed with the gifts. For that matter, it was clear that the whole idea of a leisurely shopping trip bored her to tears. I could sympathize, but it was something a good travel scout would be expected to do.

Not that I thought anyone out there really believed that story anymore. But by sticking with the cover, it might be possible to fool them into thinking *I* still thought I was covered, which might lead them to underestimate my competence. Sometimes this got too complicated even for me.

Finally, our token shopping out of the way, we returned to our suite and locked ourselves in for the night. It was still too early to go to bed, so we opaqued the walls and floors and I pulled up another classic Hitchcock dit rec drama to show her. This one was called *North by Northwest,* a story of a man on the run pursued by shadowy forces he didn't understand. If the theme tugged at Bayta's conscience, it didn't show.

With an early wake-up required for the tour, we made a point of turning in early. As I had already noted, the bed was huge and very comfortable-looking. Fortunately for me, the living room couch was comfortable, too.

TWELVE :

"And now it is the time for the adventurous among us to leave the safety of our vehicle and explore the caverns," the guide intoned, switching from Halkan to English for our benefit. "I must warn you, though, that the caverns are extensive, and only a small percentage has been explored and mapped. Please stay in the areas with marker lights."

I nodded to Bayta, and we put on our helmets. Only a half dozen of the twenty passengers seemed interested in joining us, I noticed, the rest content to stay aboard the sub for another pass around the outer sections of the caverns. I also noted that, despite their verbal enthusiasm of the previous day, there were in fact no Cimmaheem on our sub.

We finished our preparations and lined up at the exit. Each of us was given a quick equipment check by the guide, then sent two by two into the airlock. Bayta and I received our check, listened to one final warning about staying on the marked paths, and went outside.

The water was icy cold, I knew, but the pressure suits were well designed and only a hint of that chill made it through to my skin. With Bayta beside me, I touched my jet control, and as the pressurized water streams brushed past my heels we headed into the wide opening of the caverns, following the lights of those who had gone before us. Right at the opening we hit a current that tried to push us aside, but a little maneuvering and re-angling of the jets and we got through it.

I'd toured a few other caverns back when I was young, two of them underwater, and compared to those these weren't all that impressive. Still, the lighting had been arranged for maximum effect, and I could see a few interesting formations in the various side tunnels. "Did you want to see any of the tunnels in particular?" Bayta's voice came through the small speaker in my helmet.

"Not really," I said casually, knowing that our comms also linked back to the submarine. Nothing we said out here would be private. "Let's try over here."

I pointed my light toward a passage no one else seemed interested in. We jetted our way across to the tunnel and peered inside. "Pretty twisty," Bayta pointed out. "The marker lights don't go back very far, either."

"Oh, it's not *that* twisty," I admonished her, studying the rocky walls. It *wasn't* that twisty, at least not for us. But even from here I could see a couple of spots that would be problematic for Halkas to get through.

Was that why we'd been maneuvered into coming out here? To do some cave exploration for them?

And then, as I moved my light around, something in the rock a few meters ahead caught my eye: a flattish spot that stood out glaringly amid the rest of the textured bumpiness. "Anyway, we're not here to stay on the beaten path," I added, kicking my feet and moving into the passage. "Let's see where it goes."

My eyes hadn't been playing tricks on me. The spot I'd noticed was indeed flat, and it definitely hadn't gotten that way by itself. Something hard and probably metallic had brushed up against the rock, hitting it with enough force to grind off the bumps. Someone, probably fairly recently, had moved something large and heavy through here.

I shone my light farther down the passage. Now that I knew what to look for, I could see a couple more smooth spots ahead, one of them just in front of the last marker light.

I caught Bayta's eye and pointed to the spot, then at the others down the tunnel. She frowned, then lifted her eyebrows questioningly and tapped her backpack with its air generator and jet system. I shook my head, pressing my fingertip into the plasticized coating to show that it had too much give to have scraped the rock that way. "Looks like we're running out of markers," I said aloud for the benefit of our other listeners.

I gestured emphatically, and Bayta nodded understanding. "We could at least go to the end," she suggested. "We've got plenty of time."

"Sounds good to me." Giving her a thumbs-up, I started forward.

The other flat spots looked pretty much the same as the one I'd already examined. Interestingly, none of them were at particularly narrow spots in the tunnel. It was as if whoever had been maneuvering the object had been careful enough at the tricky places but had gotten careless when the going was easier.

We reached the last marker, and I shone my light into the tunnel beyond it. Just past the marker was another flat spot, bigger than the others, as if the movers had been seriously rushed at the end and desperate to get behind the light where they wouldn't be so visible.

So rushed, in fact, that they hadn't just bumped the side of their burden against the wall. Just ahead of the flat spot was a large protrusion with an abrupt indentation where they'd apparently run the object's nose straight into the rock. A nose, I could see from the impression, that was about fifteen centimeters across, pointed, and had a hint of an angled, spiral shape behind the point.

Exactly like the shape of an industrial-sized drill bit.

I pointed it out to Bayta. She frowned, clearly puzzled, but nodded when I gestured ahead. Throwing a glance over my shoulder to confirm that no one was coming in after us, I eased past the marker and swam into the tunnel.

The first part was the trickiest. A meter past the drill-bit indentation was the narrowest spot yet, complicated further by a sharp left turn just past the narrows. I had to bend at the waist to get through it, then roll over midway to keep my legs from becoming lodged against the side. The lads with the drill had clearly had similar problems, leaving two more marks where they'd bumped their burden getting around the turn. Fortunately, the water was calm; with a current like the one we'd run into outside, it would have been well nigh impossible.

Past the turn the tunnel straightened and widened again. I waited until Bayta had worked her way through, then together we moved on.

A few meters beyond the turn the tunnel became a confused honeycomb as it joined up with other passages and sent branches of its own in several directions. Fortunately, I'd taken the precaution of bringing along the tube of bright red lip gloss from Bayta's new makeup kit, and at each intersection and potential confusion point I marked the stone to show us the way back out.

But whoever our clumsy driller had been, he'd apparently cleaned up his act. I found two more wall marks within the first couple of meters; and then, just as the labyrinth started to get particularly tangled, the marks disappeared completely. I went a short distance down several of the side passages, but saw nothing to indicate whether he'd been that way or not.

I'd just given up on the eighth side passage when Bayta tapped me on the arm and pointed significantly to her wrist. Reluctantly, I nodded agreement: If we didn't start back soon the Halkas were likely to send out a search party. Turning around, I led us back to the bottleneck and then out again into the reassuring glow of the marker lights.

We were just in time. Even as the passage widened enough for us to use our jets, I could see that the rest of the divers had gathered around the submarine and were awaiting their turns in the airlock. We jetted out and joined them, and a few minutes later were back aboard.

"Welcome," the guide greeted us as we unfastened our helmets and shook off the excess water. "I trust you had an enjoyable and enlightening visit?"

"Oh, yes," I assured him, smiling. "We did indeed."

We made our way back to the hotel, passing a couple of the smaller maintenance subs we'd seen the previous day through the walls of our suite. Stripping off our suits, we returned them to the preparation room and headed out of the docking area. It was close to lunchtime, and even though it was clear Bayta was anxious to get back to the suite where we could talk, I insisted we stop at one of the restaurants first. We had a quick meal, then returned to the suite.

And as I ushered Bayta inside and closed the door behind us, I finally felt something I'd been expecting ever since leaving New York: the gentle tingling of my watch against my skin.

While we'd been exploring the ocean depths, someone had bugged our rooms.

"Were those marks what I think they were?" Bayta asked as I locked the door behind us.

"Probably," I told her, gesturing her toward one of the couches as I scrambled furiously to revise the conversation I'd been planning to have with her. There were some things I didn't mind unknown listeners knowing—in fact, there were a couple of half-truths it might be very useful to feed them. But there were other topics I needed to avoid at all costs. "Assuming, that is, you think they were made by someone bouncing an industrial-sized drill around off the walls," I continued.

"Okay," she said slowly as she sat down. "But what would the Halkas want in there with a drill?"

"Well, for one thing, it wasn't the Halkas," I said. "That dogleg would have been impossible for anyone with their joint arrangement. To me, that strongly suggests whoever did it chose that tunnel precisely because the Halkas *couldn't* go in after him."

"But why?" she persisted. "What's in there anyone would want?"

"Empty space, of course," I said. "You remember the guide mentioning that the caverns were huge and hadn't been completely explored? What better place to stash something big that you didn't want anyone else stumbling over?"

"But how big could it *be*?" she asked. "We barely made it through ourselves."

"Hence the drill," I said, nodding. "I'm thinking someone went off into a far corner of the caverns and found himself a nice open space like the entrance area we went through. He then drilled himself a private entrance, doing all the work from the inside so as not to leave telltale chips lying around, brought in his prize, and camouflaged the entrance. Bingo: instant storage unit."

"For what?" Bayta asked, her voice gone cautious. "What are they hiding?"

"My guess?" I said, thinking again of our silent audience. "One of the hotel's submarines."

Her eyes widened. "A *submarine*?"

"Oh, not one of the tour ships," I hastened to add. "One of those midget maintenance jobs we saw poking around on our way in this morning. You'd need something like that if you wanted to move anything sizable around out there."

"So you're saying they stole a submarine so they could move something bigger," Bayta said slowly, clearly having trouble working through this. "What is it they're trying to move?"

"No idea," I said. Unfortunately, that one was a hundred percent truth. "All I know is that a rock cavern on Modhra, under all this water and ice, is about as private as you can get and still have regular Quadrail and torchferry service." I looked at my watch. "But there's nothing to be gained sitting here wondering about it. The next torchferry from the Quadrail is due in a couple of hours. Let's go to the surface and watch it land, maybe do some hiking or lugeboarding."

Her mouth dropped open a couple of millimeters. "You want to go *lugeboarding*?"

"Absolutely," I said. "We don't want anyone wondering what we're doing up there watching Modhra II go around and around, do we?"

Her mouth closed tightly. "Of course not."

"Good," I said, standing up. "Let's see what kind of outdoor wear we've got in the closet."

Along with its various formal outfits, the closet also included several sets of the thin but warm clothing designed to complement the insulation of a standard vac suit. While Bayta changed into one of them I called up to the lodge to check on the procedures for going outside and reserved us a couple of suits. The very nature of a place like this would make it impossible for us to slip out unnoticed, but hopefully the hidden listeners had bought into the excuse I'd given Bayta and wouldn't pay much attention to our sortie into the great outdoors.

The pale disk of Modhra II was high overhead as we emerged from one of the airlocks onto the surface, with Cassp's glowing, multicolored bands filling most of the sky to the north. We were currently below the ring plane, and the distant sunlight playing off the floating bits of ice and rock created a striking pattern of light and shadow above our heads. "Have you ever lugeboarded before?" I asked Bayta as we bounced our way along a line of tall red pylons marking the way to the toboggan tunnels.

"No, and it sounds rather dangerous," she said, her voice coming from a speaker in the back of my helmet. "Rather pointless, too." She gestured up at one of the pylons as we passed it. "Aren't these awfully tall for trail markers?"

"Actually, they're the pylons for a future ski lift system," I told her. "Eventually, the red lift will go to the toboggan tunnels, with the blue and green ones taking you to the ski runs."

"How do you know that?"

"It was in the brochures."

"Oh."

We reached the base of the hill that the map indicated was the starting point for the toboggan tunnels and started up. I'd worried a little about climbing upslope on ice, even with the special grips on our vac suits' boots, but it turned out not to be a problem. The ice's texture was reasonably rough, and the gravity and ambient temperature too low for our weight to form the thin layer of water that normally made ice so treacherous. Briefly, I wondered how that would affect the performance of our lugeboards, then put it out of my mind. People had been dealing with this kind of extreme physics for a long time, and the resort's designers had presumably known what they were doing.

The entrances to the three tunnels were grouped around a common staging area, from which they headed underground in different directions. A circle of lights had been embedded in the ice around each entrance, and from the glow coming up from the tunnels I guessed there were lights all the way down. Three vac-suited figures—Halkas, probably, though I never got a look through their faceplates to confirm that—were just getting their toboggan ready to go at Number Three, and as we unfastened our lugeboards from our backpacks they headed in. I watched them drop out of sight beyond the first slope, then turned my attention to the east, where the red pylons we'd been following marched up the next group of hills and disappeared over the other side.

"You said you'd show me how this worked," Bayta reminded me.

"Sure," I said. Hoping I remembered how to do it, I popped my lugeboard's straps. "First, you get it open. . . ."

We got the boards set up and headed down Number One. It was just as well I'd chosen the most undemanding of the tunnels, as it turned out, because even that was well beyond my modest abilities. Not only had the designers smoothed the ice to a high polish, but they must have installed heaters under the surface to bring it to precisely the optimal temperature to form that thin water layer I'd noticed the lack of while climbing the hill.

Worse yet, Bayta, with no experience whatsoever with

these things, turned out to be better at it than I was. She fell probably once to every two tumbles I took, and near the end of the run was even daring enough to take a shot at one of the three-sixty spirals I wouldn't have tried on a bet. The lower gravity made such stunts easier, of course, but that wasn't much help to my bruised pride.

We reached the bottom, our momentum running us smoothly across the long flat area to a gentle stop near the elevators. Unfastening our boards, we headed inside, and I punched for the surface. "This goes *down*, too?" Bayta asked, pointing at the lower button.

"Yes, back to the hotel," I told her. "This particular run ends just above the lobby. Probably planned that way so that bruised amateurs could go staggering straight home and collapse into bed or a whirl bath."

"I guess," she said. "That was fun."

I looked through her faceplate. Bayta, the girl with no last name, who had once calmly told me she didn't care if I lived or died, was actually smiling, her cheeks red with exertion, her face more alive than I'd ever seen it. "It was, wasn't it?" I agreed. "We'll have to do it again after my knees stop hurting."

She looked back at me, her smile fading as she suddenly seemed to remember why we'd come to the surface in the first place. "Yes," she said. "Well . . . maybe we could just climb one of the hills near the lodge and watch the ring pattern for a while. Until you feel better."

"Sounds good to me," I said.

The elevator let us out inside the lodge, just off the equipment rental area and near one of the airlocks. We headed back outside and walked along the red pylons to the top of the first big hill. There we found a comfortable place to sit together, and as I snuggled close and put my arm around her shoulders, I motioned for her to turn off her comm.

I leaned my helmet against hers, hoping that to any observers we looked like two lovers getting as romantically physical as it was possible to get in vac suits. "Can you hear me?" I called.

"Yes," she called back, her voice sounding tinny as the sound transmitted across the contact between our helmets. "Why did you want to watch the torchferry arrive?"

"I don't, actually," I told her. "But someone bugged our suite while we were on our submarine tour, and I needed to find a reason to get you out here where I could be sure no one could eavesdrop."

"We were *bugged*?" she demanded. "Why didn't you *tell* me?"

"You mean while we were there in the suite?" I asked.

"Oh," she said, her annoyance fading into embarrassment. "Right."

"Which is also why I had to tell you a few half-truths," I went on. "Starting with those drill marks on the tunnel wall. Someone made them, all right, but whoever it was didn't stash anything in there. At least, nothing important."

She drew away to frown at me, and I saw her lips moving. I tapped her faceplate in reminder; grimacing with a little more embarrassment, she turned again and leaned her helmet against mine. "Sorry," she said. "I said, how do you know?"

"First of all, because it was a little *too* obvious," I said, watching her face out of the corner of my eye, hoping her reactions would give me some clue as to how much of this she already knew. So far, it all seemed completely new to her. "The marks were right there in the lighted areas, there hadn't been any effort to disguise or obliterate them, and they quit showing up past that bottleneck, past the point where there was no chance of the Halkas getting in and finding any more of them."

"Maybe they just got more careful."

"No," I said. "Remember that current we ran into outside the cavern? That showed Modhra's underground ocean keeps itself moving, probably driven by tidal forces from Cassp. But there *weren't* any currents inside the tunnel we explored. If someone had made the kind of opening in the far end that we talked about, even if they camouflaged it afterward, the water would have been sloshing back and forth and we'd have been tossed around like guppies."

"Then what was the point of the marks?"

"The same point as the drunk act that Bellido put on for me on the Quadrail," I said. "Something big and bold and obvious to get people looking and thinking the wrong direction."

"So they *didn't* actually steal a submarine?" she asked, sounding thoroughly lost now.

"Actually, I'm guessing they did," I said. "The fake drunk had all the right cues and telltales, which tells me these people pay attention to the details. If you want someone to waste their time searching the caverns, you need to give them a good reason to do so."

"Yes, I see," Bayta said. "And you don't want the Halkas to know about this?"

"No," I said, watching her closely. "Because I think the Bellidos are on our side."

There was a moment of silence. This was the perfect moment, I knew, for her to confess that she already knew that. The perfect moment to finally fill me in on everything else she knew about Modhra and what was going on here.

Only she didn't. "You mean the people who hit you on the head and locked you in a spice crate?" she asked instead.

"I mean the people who *didn't* injure me," I growled, a sudden stirring of anger sending heat into my face. "I mean the people who could have simply broken my leg if all they'd wanted was to put me out of action for a while." I slid my helmet around the side of hers so that I could glare straight into her eyes. "I mean the people who *haven't* been lying through their teeth to me since this whole thing started."

Her face had gone suddenly rigid. "What do you mean?" she asked.

"You know what I mean," I bit out, suddenly sick of it all. "You know what's going on here. You know all about JhanKla and the Bellidos. You've known right from the beginning."

She tried to pull away from me. I grabbed the back of her helmet and yanked it back, pressing it firmly against mine. "Go ahead—tell me I'm wrong," I invited harshly. "Tell me that I'm imagining things."

"Frank—I'm sorry," she said, the words coming out in little puffs of rapid air. Her face had come alive with fear, her throat muscles working rapidly. "I couldn't—"

"Of course you can't," I cut her off. "So now tell me why I shouldn't just go ahead and bail on this whole damn thing."

"No!" she all but gasped. Her face shot through the whole range of fear and landed squarely on sheer terror. "Please. You can't leave."

"Why not?" I demanded. "The Bellidos didn't hurt me because the fake drunk saw me take the chip from the Spider and figured I was on their side. Only I'm *not* really on their side, am I? I'm not on *anyone's* side. All I am is a dupe."

I let go of her helmet, suddenly too disgusted with her to touch even that. "I won't be a dupe, Bayta," I said. "Not for you; not for your damn Spiders."

Her breath was coming in hyperventilating huffs, her face still rigid with fear. "Please, Frank," she managed. "Please. You can't leave me here alone—"

I didn't want to hear it. Standing up, I turned my back on her and strode off down the ice hill. I kept walking, up the next small hill and down into its valley, until she was out of sight. Then, folding my arms across my chest, I stopped and glared up at the shifting ring pattern blazing softly across the Modhran sky.

I should do it, I told myself firmly. I should turn around, go to the hotel and pack my stuff, and then head straight back to the Tube on the next torchferry. Maybe I'd drop her fancy unlimited-travel pass in the fire pit before I left, a nice dramatic gesture that would make it clear to her and the Spiders what I thought of them. I had places to go and things to do, and the last thing I needed was to hang around here in the cold and dark with a bull's-eye painted on my chest. The sooner I shook the dust of this off my feet, the better.

I had just about made up my mind to do it when the face of the dead messenger outside the New Pallas Towers floated up from my memory.

The Spiders had gone to a lot of trouble to entice me into

this game. Someone else had gone to even more trouble to keep me out of it.

And I was damned if I was going to quit before I knew what the game was.

Bayta was sitting where I'd left her, her knees hunched up against her chest, her arms wrapped tightly around them. Her whole body seemed to be quivering as I approached, perhaps shaking in fear or anger. I sat back down beside her . . . and it was only then that I realized what the shaking actually was.

She was crying. My stoic, wooden-faced Bayta was actually crying.

I leaned my helmet against hers. "One question," I said, forcing calmness into my voice. "*Are* the Bellidos on our side?"

Her eyelids fluttered as she tried to blink away the tears. "I think so," she said, sniffing. "I mean, I think we ultimately want the same thing. Only they're . . . sort of independent."

I grimaced. Independent operations were always wasteful, usually counterproductive, and way too often dangerous. But in the world of intelligence and covert ops, they were unfortunately a fact of life. "Do you know what their plan is?"

She closed her eyes, squeezing out another couple of tears in the process. "No."

I took a couple more calming breaths. I didn't need this. I really didn't. "Fine," I said. "Let's see if we can find out."

She opened her eyes, gazing nervously at me as if expecting another outburst. "Does that mean you're staying?"

"For now," I told her, unwilling to commit myself to anything long-term at this point. "Go ahead and switch your comm back on, and let's head back to the toboggan tunnels."

I started to reach for my own comm switch, but she snaked a hand up and caught my arm before I could reach it. "I told you once I wasn't your friend," she said, her voice shaking with emotion. "But I'm not your enemy, either."

I stared into her eyes, eyes from which all the defenses had crumbled. There was indeed a real, live person back there. "Glad to hear it," I said. "Be ready to switch off again when I give you the signal."

I turned on my own comm, and we headed back upslope. She was clearly still too shaken to counterfeit a casual conversation, so instead I kept up a more or less running monologue about how her first lugeboard run had been beginner's luck. About halfway there, she was finally able to ease back into the conversation.

We reached the lugeboard tunnels; but instead of stopping, I motioned her to keep going, and we followed the pylons as they headed up the next hill. JhanKla had said there were two other toboggan tunnels in production, and it seemed logical that the Halkas would have laid out their future ski lift to serve all five.

We reached the top of the hill, and there they were: two large openings facing each other from the sides of another pair of hills. Like the first set of tunnels, a flattened staging and preparation area had been created between them, this one crowded with heavy equipment and crates of supplies. Some of the equipment was attached to conduits and cables of various colors and diameters that snaked their way down into the tunnel mouth. No one else was visible, and the tunnels themselves seemed dark.

I motioned to Bayta, and we switched off our comms. "There you go," I said, pressing my helmet against hers again.

"There I go where?" she said, frowning.

"It's classic diversionary technique," I said. "You get your opponents looking one direction while you set up your operation in the other. The Bellidos get the Halkas looking down at the underwater caverns, then settle themselves into a nice little staging area up here. An unused tunnel, complete with stacks of stuff where you could probably hide pretty much anything you wanted."

"But there are Halkan workers here," she pointed out.

"Only during the day," I said, checking my watch. "Then they go inside, which is where they all are now, leaving the place nice and deserted."

I started forward, but Bayta grabbed my arm and pressed her helmet against mine again. "What if the Bellidos are in there?"

"They aren't," I assured her. "They can't be back from Sistarrko yet."

"Unless they took a later torchferry from the Tube and never went to Sistarrko at all."

I shook my head. "I poked around the resort computer system for a while last night after you went to bed. Room registration listings are always protected, but the restaurant and room-service records are usually more accessible. There were only two sets of Belldic meals served yesterday, and one of those has to have been to *Apos* Mahf."

"Do you think he's working with them?"

"Definitely not," I said. "For one thing, he tried too hard for information as to who had left me in that spice crate. For another, he tried to get me to touch the coral."

I heard her inhale sharply. "You didn't, did you?" she asked anxiously, her grip tightening on my arm.

"No, no, I didn't even get close," I assured her hastily. The sudden dark tension in her face was unnerving. "Maybe you should tell me why that's such a big deal to you."

Through her faceplate, I saw her throat work. "I can't," she said, letting go of my arm. "You just have to trust me."

For a moment I was tempted to again threaten to walk. But I'd already made my decision on that, and I knew better than to bluff when there was nothing to back it up. "Sure," I growled. "Come on." I stalked off across the ice toward the leftmost of the two tunnels, the one on the north side of the staging area. With only a slight hesitation, Bayta followed.

The tunnel was clearly being planned as a more challenging run than the one Bayta and I had gone down earlier, with a much steeper initial plunge. Fortunately, the Halkan workers weren't relying on the nonsmoothed ice to get back and forth, but had rigged a corrugated walkway along the tunnel's left-hand side. Pulling out my light, I got a grip on the handrail and started down.

The first fifty meters of the tunnel floor were smooth and clean. Past that point we hit an area of work in progress, and got a hint of just how complicated these things actually were. My earlier speculation about an embedded heater system was confirmed: Wide sheets of fine mesh encircled the entire tunnel, buried a few centimeters beneath where the toboggan surface would ultimately be. Every few meters we came upon large holes that had been dug in the tunnel walls, with various bits of machinery tucked away inside. Some of the devices were easily identifiable: area minigenerators for the lights and heaters, and impact registers like those used in sports arenas for alerting the staff to possible medical emergencies. Others I didn't have a clue about.

We followed the twists and turns for another hundred meters to where the tunnel ended at a concave wall. Several heavy-duty melting units were on the floor in front of the ice face, along with a pair of high-pressure pumping units connected to two of the thicker conduits.

Bayta touched her helmet to mine. "Nothing here," she said. "Maybe the other one."

"Maybe," I said, eyeing the wall on the far side of the tunnel. On the other hand, if *I* were hiding something, I would put it on the side farthest away from the traffic zone. "Go ahead and start back," I told her. "I'm going to take a stroll."

I crossed to the far side and started up, alternating my light and attention between the ice wall and the cables and hoses running alongside it. Even in the low gravity there were a couple of spots where I had to use one of the cables to pull myself up.

Midway through one of the tighter curves, where the slope made a particularly sharp drop, I found it. Catching Bayta's eye, I waved her over.

It took her a minute to backtrack to a spot where she could cross the tunnel and join me. "Take a look," I told her, pointing to the drain hose, our helmets again touching for private communication. "See here, where the color is just slightly off the rest of the hose?"

She peered at it. "Looks like a patch."

"Very good," I said. Working my fingertips under one edge, I peeled the patch back a couple of centimeters to reveal a handful of small punctures below it. "Behold: a homemade mister. Something to make liquid water mist, which will then freeze on contact with a wall." I touched the tunnel wall beside me. "This wall, for instance."

She shook her head. "I don't understand."

"Let's say you want to burrow into a tunnel wall," I said. "The digging itself is trivial; all you need is a tight-beam plasma cutter or nuke torch. Hiding the hole afterward is the tricky part. You need liquid water and a way to deliver it to the hole."

I gestured at the hose. "Luckily for you, there's a fresh supply available at the tunnel face for you to tap into. A few small holes, a good aim, maybe a small grinder to smooth out any big lumps afterward, and you're done."

"But the hose only carries water when the workers are here."

"Sure, but the equipment stays here all day," I reminded her. "It wouldn't be hard to sneak out at night and fire up the pump just enough to bring through the water you needed to close up the opening." I cocked an eyebrow as a new thought struck me. "Or they might even have slipped into the work team and done it right in front of the Halkas' flat little faces. A lot of Bellidos are able to speak alien languages without an accent—I've heard some of them do it— and once they're wrapped up in vac suits no one's going to pick them out of a crowd without a good look through their faceplates. With a chaotic enough workplace, they could conceivably pull it off."

Tentatively, she touched the ice wall with her fingertips. "So how do *we* get in to take a look?"

I studied the wall, wishing I'd brought my sensor with me. "Well, we can't do it now," I said slowly. "We may be under surveillance, and I don't want to blow the Bellidos' cover before we know what they're up to. Our best bet would be to wait until they get here and let them open it for us."

I looked over my shoulder down the tunnel. "*Or* we could help ourselves to a couple of workers' suits and drop in on tomorrow's work party."

Bayta's eyes went wide. "Are you *crazy*?"

"Probably," I conceded. "But it's still worth thinking

about. Let's check out the other tunnel, and then we'll have that lugeboard rematch."

We climbed the rest of the way up and headed across the staging area. The work in the south tunnel was about as far along as that of the north, and I searched it with the same degree of care. But if anyone had been doing unauthorized work, I couldn't find any sign of it. Finally, and to Bayta's obvious relief, we left and headed back to the finished tunnels.

I did considerably better on this run, falling down less than half as often as I had on the first run. Unfortunately for my pride, Bayta's learning curve was steeper, and she still came out looking better than I did. We took the elevator down this time, turning in our vac suits and other equipment at the hotel's service desk.

"Now what?" Bayta asked as we headed across the lobby.

"Dinner, then an early bedtime," I said as we passed one of the observation lounges on our way to the guest room elevators. "Tomorrow could be a very busy—"

"Compton!" a voice from the lounge cut across the low buzz of conversation. "Frank! Over here!"

Clamping my teeth down onto my tongue, I turned to look.

It was Colonel Applegate, seated at one of the lounge tables, a friendly smile on his face as he waved a hand invitingly.

And seated across from him, his own expression studiously neutral, was Deputy UN Director Biret Losutu.

A man who once said he wished I was dead.

THIRTEEN :

"What do we do?" Bayta murmured.

For a long moment I considered turning my back on them and continuing on my way. But that might look like I was afraid to face Losutu again, and there was no way in hell I was going to give anyone *that* impression. "We see what they want, of course," I told Bayta. Taking her arm, I led us over to their table. "Good day, gentlemen," I said. "This is a surprise."

"For us, as well," Applegate said. "Though now that I think about it I suppose it shouldn't have been. Sooner or later, a travel agent searching for exotic locales would have to find his way to Modhra."

"It *is* spectacular, isn't it?" I agreed, shifting my attention to Losutu. "Good day, Director Losutu."

"Good day, Mr. Compton," he replied, his dark eyes steady on mine, his face settled into the half-contemptuous, half-amused expression I'd found so irritating at the UN hearings a year and a half ago. "So you're a travel agent now, are you? Interesting career move."

"I mingle with a better class of people this way," I replied. "I see you're being as careful as ever with Confederation money."

The amused half of Losutu's expression vanished. "Meaning?" he asked, a note of warning in his voice.

"Meaning I must have missed the brochure that talked about Modhra I's prominence as a weapons purchasing center."

Losutu's eyes shifted to Applegate. "Colonel?"

Applegate's lip twitched. "I may have mentioned something of our mission to Mr. Compton," he admitted. "As a former Westali agent, I thought—"

"*Former* being the operative word," Losutu cut him off, shifting his glare back to me. "What exactly do you know, Compton?"

"You're looking to buy some expensive starfighters to guard the transfer stations at New Tigris and Yandro," I said, forcing myself to meet his glare. I was a private citizen, and we were a long way from his little fiefdom. "Strikes me as a good-money-after-bad sort of thing."

"There are three million Confederation citizens in those two star systems," he said, a little stiffly. "Yandro itself is up to nearly half a million, I might add, despite your predictions to the contrary."

"I never said no one could live there," I countered. "All I said was that the place wasn't worth the cost of putting in a Quadrail station."

"Those half million colonists would disagree," he said, calmer now as he settled into the rote rationalization he'd probably used a thousand times in the last couple of years. "Frontiers are important for the human spirit, whether they immediately earn their keep or not. Give the people there another twenty years, and I think you'll be surprised at what they create. In the meantime, they deserve the same degree of security and protection as you do." He pursed his lips. "And whatever you may think of me personally, that *is* part of my job."

"A job you may be able to help us with," Applegate jumped in. "The Western Alliance is having some problems over Director Losutu's proposals. You might be able to help smooth the way."

I thought about reminding him that he'd already made this pitch to me back on the Quadrail. But it was obviously supposed to be a secret, and getting him deeper in trouble with Losutu than he already was wouldn't gain me anything but a little petty vengeance. "I think you overestimate my influence," I said instead.

"You might be surprised," Applegate said doggedly. "The least you could do is check out the fighters we're looking at and give us your opinion."

I shook my head. "Sorry, but we don't have room in our schedule for any side trips into Cimman space."

"No need," he said. "Two of the fighters are stationed right here at Modhra."

Pressed close beside me, I felt Bayta stiffen. "What for?" I asked.

"Protection of the resort and coral harvesting areas, of course," Losutu said. He was looking at me more thoughtfully now, like a tool he might be able to find some practical use for. "They're actually stationed over at the other moon, Modhra II, where they're more unobtrusive."

"No, we wouldn't want to upset the paying customers," I agreed cynically. "But I thought you were looking at Cimman fighters."

"We are," Applegate said. "Chafta 669s, which are a joint project between the Cimmaheem and Halkas. We were scheduled to have our talks at Grakla, but there was a scheduling foul-up and the people we needed to talk to were all the way across the Republic and wouldn't be back for a few more days. The nearest Chaftas were here at Modhra, so one of the negotiators suggested we come here and have the Halkas run them through their paces for us."

"So when is this supposed to happen?" I asked.

"Tomorrow morning," Applegate said. He looked questioningly at Losutu, got a microscopic shrug in reply. "Would you be interested in joining us?"

"Actually, afternoon would be better for my schedule," I said.

Losutu rumbled something under his breath. "We're already set up for morning," Applegate said, warning me with his eyes not to be difficult.

But I was nowhere near his little fiefdom, either. "In that case, enjoy yourselves," I said, taking Bayta's arm. "And have a pleasant evening."

We retraced our steps back through the lounge and were nearly to the elevators when I heard a set of rapid footsteps coming up behind us. Turning, I saw Applegate, the dark look of an approaching storm on his face. "Damn it all, Compton," he snarled. "Anyone ever tell you what a flaming uncooperative son of a mongrel you are?"

"Once or twice," I said. "Is this one private citizen to another, or UN flunky to private citizen?"

He glared at me, but his heart clearly wasn't in it. "Look. I know you don't like Losutu, but he really *is* looking out for the Confederation's best interests. Isn't there some way you can rearrange your schedule to come with us tomorrow?"

I shook my head. "I want to take one of the tours out to the Balercomb Formations, and the bus leaves in the early morning. Did you read about the formations?"

He snorted. "We're not here on vacation."

"They were formed a hundred years ago when a fragmented comet slammed into the surface about forty kilometers from here," I told him. "Between the multiple impacts and the resulting shock waves, they shattered and boiled off a lot of the ice, which naturally started refreezing almost at once. The result was a dozen square kilometers of pitted landscape with lots of hills, caves, and weird formations."

"Fascinating," he growled, clearly not interested in the slightest. "What if we can arrange to drop you there after we look at the fighters? You could do your exploring and take the bus back with the rest of the group."

"I don't know," I said, thinking hard. With the new toboggan tunnels at the top of tomorrow's itinerary, the last place I had actually planned to be was on a tour bus. But unless I came up with something quick, my bluff was going to be called right out from under me. "They're supposed to give you a lot of the historical background on the ride there. I really ought to go along to see what that's like."

He exhaled loudly in exasperation. "Will you at least give me a chance to talk you into it?"

"I'm listening."

"I meant over dinner," he said. "I'd like you and Bayta to join us." He managed a faint smile. "On the UN's credit tag, of course."

"Better check with Losutu first," I warned. "Anyway, Bayta wouldn't be able to join us. I have a research project for her to do in our room."

"Well, just you, then," Applegate persisted. "And don't worry about Losutu. I can handle him."

I shrugged. "If you can persuade him, why not? Where do you want to meet?"

"Let's make it the Redbird Restaurant on the fourth level," he said. "Say, in two-thirds hour?"

"Fine," I said. "By the way, you said one of your contacts suggested you come here to Modhra. Which contact was it, exactly?"

"I don't know his name," Applegate said, frowning slightly. "One of the Halkas. Why?"

"Just curious," I said. "Two-thirds hour in the Redbird, then."

He turned and headed back to the lounge, and I touched the button to call the elevator. "What is this research you suddenly want me to do?" Bayta asked suspiciously.

"Something I should have thought of days ago," I told her. The elevator arrived, and we got aboard. I focused my attention briefly on my watch; no tingling. "If the Bellidos were taking a later torchliner from the Quadrail, they should have been here by now. The fact that they're not implies they went to Sistarrko after all. Right?"

"*If* you're right about them not being here," she agreed cautiously. "So?"

"So why go to the inner system?" I asked. "Answer: Either they needed to do some prep work away from Modhra, or they needed to take something there or pick something up."

"Okay," she said, still sounding puzzled. "Again: So?"

"Remember what the Spiders said about the Bellidos who followed us onto the Sistarrko train? The third-class group were in the last coach, the one right in front of the baggage car. I never got around to telling you, but the ones who jumped me in the Jurskala Quadrail also seemed to have been in the very back, too, the seats just in front of the baggage car. You seeing a pattern?"

"But all the cargo back there is unsecured," she said. "If they had something valuable to transport, shouldn't they have put it in the secured cargo areas instead?"

"Normally, yes," I agreed. "But secured cargo automatically gets more attention, official *and* unofficial. Maybe they preferred to go low profile, trusting in their own ability to protect it if necessary."

"All right," she said slowly. "What do you think they were transporting?"

"No idea," I said. "That's where you come in. I want you to send a message to the Spiders and get a list of all the cargo and baggage that came off our Quadrail. I presume you have an encryption you can use?"

"Well . . . yes," she said. "But I'm only supposed to use it for emergencies."

"Close enough," I said. "And get everything, not just stuff coming in under Belldic registration—they might have used a dummy name. And don't forget about the bugs in the suite."

We arrived at the suite, and Bayta got started on her message while I took a quick shower and chose some nice semi-formal clothing from the closet. One other chore and I was gone, feeling a little guilty at leaving Bayta alone with the room service menu.

I needn't have rushed. Losutu and Applegate, as befitted their high-level bureaucrat and high-level bureaucrat flunky status, were nearly fifteen minutes late. "Compton," Losutu greeted me curtly as they sat down at the table I'd procured for us. "Got us something not too close to the damn coral, I see. Good."

"You don't like Modhran coral?" I asked, focusing for a moment on the decorative waterfall/coral arrangement in the center of the room. It wasn't as impressive as the display in the casino, but of course the Redbird wasn't as large and impressive a place to begin with.

"Hate the stuff," he declared as he punched up the menu. "I will never understand the obsession the rest of the galaxy seems to have with it. It's not particularly attractive in the first place, and after a few bumps it's going to look like a badly trimmed hedge."

"It's also apparently the Halkan equivalent of cuddlestuff animals," Applegate added. "You talk with anyone here long enough, and sooner or later he'll try to get you to go over and touch it."

"Yes, I've had one or two such invitations myself," I said. "I can't say I see the attraction."

"Coral's such rough, pointy, scratchy stuff," Applegate agreed with a grunt as he studied the menu. "Someone really needs to introduce these people to satin and velvet."

"Nice that we can all agree on something," Losutu said, eyeing me. "Now convince me we can agree on something important. Applegate seems to think you can be helpful to the Directorate on this starfighter deal."

"I've been thinking about that," I said. "My primary obligations are still to my employer, but I should be able to take a quick trip to Modhra II with you and look at the Chaftas. Provided you can drop me off at the Balercomb Formations afterward."

"The what?" Losutu asked, frowning.

"That's where he was planning to go tomorrow morning on the tour bus," Applegate explained.

"The bus is a ground transport, I presume?" Losutu asked.

"Yes," I said. "They don't want even Shorshic thrusters coming too close to the formations."

Losutu grunted. "Fine. We'll see if Applegate can work his diplomatic magic and can get us permission to land you nearby."

"Good," I said. "The next question is how much use I'll actually be to you. Starfighters are hardly my area of expertise."

"Cards on the table, Mr. Compton," Losutu said. "Your technical expertise or lack of it is irrelevant. All I need from you is an endorsement that would help sell this plan to the Western Alliance."

"I understand," I said evenly. I'd been fairly repulsed by the whole cynical scheme when Applegate had first suggested it, and it didn't sound any better coming from Losutu. But at least he was being honest about it. "Let me look at the fighters and I'll let you know."

For a moment Losutu studied my face. Then his lip quirked microscopically, and he nodded. "Fair enough," he said. "We'll expect you at the lodge's main entrance tomorrow morning at ten."

The toboggan tunnel work schedule I'd pulled from the hotel computer just before coming to dinner had indicated the crew was due on site at seven. That should give me plenty of time. "I'll be there," I promised.

"Good," Losutu said, leaning back in his seat and gesturing to the menu. "Then while we eat you can tell us all about this new travel job of yours."

"Certainly," I said, shifting my brain into liar mode. It was becoming an increasingly easy transition for me to make. "I was approached about three months ago. . . ."

The evening turned out to be considerably more pleasant than I'd expected, despite the fact that I didn't particularly like or trust either of my dinner companions. Losutu could be rather charming when he chose, in a cold-fish sort of way, and Applegate had apparently decided to abandon the comrades-in-arms approach he'd tried on the Quadrail and let Losutu do most of the talking.

We had a long and leisurely dinner, the full traditional

Halkan five courses plus the knotting of wish sticks at the end. Once I'd finished my travel-agent story the conversation turned to Losutu's dealings with the rest of the galaxy on the Confederation's behalf, a monologue heavy on amusing stories and light on useful information.

As promised, Applegate picked up the tab on the UN's behalf, and I was making my farewells when Losutu suggested we go see a show. For no particular reason I said yes, and we headed up to the theater section nestled just beneath the ice. The show he chose was a Cimman production, but it had been written broadly enough to be at least marginally accessible to other species. I'd always thought of Cimman drama as a cross between Japanese Kabuki theater and English Reformation comedy, and this one in particular seemed to hit just the right notes. I enjoyed it thoroughly, and by the time it was over I was feeling more relaxed than I'd been since I'd walked down the steps at the New Pallas Towers that dark evening seventeen days ago. Leaving Losutu and Applegate at the elevator bank—they were going to the theater lounge to hammer out final details for the morning's inspection tour—I got into one of the elevators and punched for my floor.

At least, I thought I'd punched for it. But when the doors slid open, I found myself gazing instead down into the casino.

My first impulse was to stay in the car and simply make sure I hit the right button this time. But between the background hum of conversation, the clicking of the dice and chips and chinko tiles, and the effervescent sparkle of the waterfall, I found myself instead stepping out of the elevator and walking down the ramp to the main floor. No matter how quickly Bayta had gotten her message off she couldn't possibly have gotten an answer yet, so there really wasn't any need for me to hurry back to the suite. Besides, a little judicious eavesdropping might sift out a useful nugget or two.

I spent some time wandering the casino, watching the games and keeping my ears open. Again, though, all the conversations seemed to center on fluff and trivialities. I made a complete circle of the floor, shifted to a sort of lopsided figure eight, then finally went with a straight inward vector.

And so within a few minutes of my arrival, I found myself standing by the central fountain.

I gazed down into the pool, watching how the lapping water gently surging around the coral caught the casino's lights, adding an extra sparkle to the subtle color display. It really *was* an intriguing substance, I had to admit, and in this light it didn't look nearly as scratchy as Earth coral. Earlier, I'd agreed with Applegate's curt dismissal of its unfriendly texture; but as I stood here now, I wondered if perhaps I'd been overly hasty. Everyone else seemed to think it was no big deal to pet this stuff. What if they were right?

Besides, even if they weren't, what was the big deal? At worst, I'd get a scratch or two. At best, I'd be able to go to Bayta and tell her what a rewarding experience it had been—

I frowned, my train of rationalization braking to a sudden halt. Bayta, who had gazed into my eyes with a face more filled with concern than any of my superiors at Westali had ever shown, and had begged me to promise I would never touch Modhran coral.

And I'd looked back into that face, and made a little joke, and said yes.

It was ridiculous, of course. Bayta was a casual companion, thrown at me without invitation on a job I'd essentially been press-ganged into doing. She was also a liar, at least by omission, with a private agenda that may or may not have my own best interests at heart. And it wasn't as if I'd sworn a solemn oath on a multitranslation Bible or anything.

Which was, a small corner of my mind noted, more rationalization.

I didn't need to rationalize. I was a big boy, and I could do what I wanted. And I didn't need to care about anyone's opinion, especially Bayta's.

So why was I spending all this effort to talk myself into this?

I focused my eyes on the coral in front of me . . . and it was only then that I discovered that my hand was already stretched out over the pool and starting down toward the sloshing water.

I snatched the hand back, feeling sweat suddenly breaking out on my face. What the *hell* was going on here? I took a long step away from the pool, looking over my shoulder to make sure I wasn't going to back into anyone.

I froze. All around me, everywhere I could see, the casino patrons had paused in their games and their conversations.

And they were all watching me.

The tableau lasted only a fraction of a second before they turned away again, casually resuming their activities as if it had all been a giant coincidence, that they'd all merely happened to be looking in the same direction at the same moment. But I knew better.

Earlier, I'd wondered whether Bayta and I might have stumbled into the middle of some strange conspiracy. Now I knew that we had.

I headed straight for the exit ramp, senses alert, face set into a combat mask that dared anyone to try to stop me. Fortunately for them, no one did. I reached the elevators and punched the call button, and a few seconds later was on my way down to our suite.

I arrived to find Bayta slouched low into one of the couches, gazing dully at some unfamiliar dit rec. She looked up as I came in, a flicker of relief crossing her face. "There you are," she said, her tone a subtle mixture of petulance, concern, and relief. "I was starting to worry."

"Sorry," I said, keeping my voice casual as my watch tingled the news that the hidden microphones were still on duty. "Losutu insisted on dragging me to one of the shows afterwards." I gestured toward the bedroom. "Going to be a busy day tomorrow. We'd better get to bed."

She twitched, her eyes widening a little. Up to now, we'd never even slept in the same room, let alone together in the same bed. "To—?"

"To bed," I repeated, leaning a little on the last word as I touched my ear in warning.

She swallowed visibly. "All right," she said. Turning off the dit rec, she disappeared into the bedroom.

I shut off the lights and opaqued the walls and floor in the main room, then double-checked that the door was triple-locked. By the time I joined her she had similarly opaqued the bedroom wall and floor and was lying rigidly in the middle of the bed with the blanket and overblanket pulled up to her chin. I turned off the light, took off my shoes, and crawled in from the near side. "Mm—you smell good tonight," I commented aloud for the benefit of listening ears as I maneuvered close to her.

She didn't say anything, but just lay silently, her body as rigid as a board. Like me, she was still fully clothed. "Sorry about this," I whispered in her ear. "But the bugs are still active. The ones in this room are over by the bathroom and closet, so we should be able to talk here without them listening in."

"What do you want to talk about?" she whispered back.

"Let me start by telling you about my evening."

I recounted everything that had happened, from the dinner to the play to my unplanned detour into the casino. When I had finished, she was silent so long that I wondered if she'd fallen asleep. Then she turned her head to put her lips by my ear. "Are you sure you didn't touch the coral?"

"I'm positive," I assured her.

"How can you be?" she demanded. "You said you blacked out for a second. Could you have touched it, then dried your hand on your jacket?"

I shook my head. "The coral where I was standing was deep enough for my cuff to have gone into the water, too. There's no way I could have dried that off." I turned my head a little and gazed down at the top of her head. "I think it's about time you told me just what the hell is going on here, Bayta. Especially what the hell is going on with the coral."

I felt her body stiffen. "I can't tell you," she said, the words coming out almost too quiet to hear. "Not yet. I'm sorry."

"You may be sorrier than you think," I warned. "I can't protect you against danger I don't understand."

She hesitated, and I held my breath. But no. "The coral's not dangerous if you don't touch it," she said. "That's all I can say right now."

Earlier, up on the surface, I'd thought about simply walking out on this mess. Now, after the eeriness of the casino, I was even more inclined to do so. *And* to take Bayta with me, whether she wanted to go or not.

But down deep, I knew it wouldn't work. Whoever our mysterious enemies were, we were already in their sights. One way or another, we had to see this through. "Have it your way," I said. "Just remember that your neck's on the line here, too."

She shivered. "I know," she murmured. "What are we going to do?"

"We're going to stick with Plan A, and try to get a look at what the Bellidos have been up to," I said.

"Before or after you go to Modhra II with your friends to see the starfighters?"

It was usually hard to distinguish emotions in a whisper, but I had no trouble hearing the harshness in hers. "They're not my friends, and I don't give a damn about the starfighters," I growled back. "What have you got against friends, anyway? Or do you just like to rub in the fact that I don't have any?"

For a moment she didn't speak. "How are you going to do it?" she asked at last.

I grimaced. For a moment there . . . But that was all right. I didn't particularly want her friendship, either. "There's an employees-only door up in the lodge near the airlocks that's probably a ready room. I'll sneak in after the main work force has left and get a suit."

"Won't that be dangerous?"

"Depends on whether the whole resort staff is in on the conspiracy or if it's just the upper-crust elite who come here to play," I said. "Anyway, assuming I get that far, and further assuming I have enough time in that bend of the tunnel with no one watching, I should be able to poke a small hole through the ice, take a quick look, seal it up, and be back in time for my ten o'clock appointment with Losutu."

"And then you *are* going with him to Modhra II?"

"At the moment, I can't see any plausible way to get out

of it," I said regretfully. "But I'll say all the things he wants to hear and get back here as quickly as I can. With luck, we'll be able to grab the afternoon torchferry to the Tube."

She hissed out a sigh. Clearly, she wasn't happy with any of this. "What do you want me to do?"

"That's up to you," I said. "You can stay here, or you can join the tour group and go ahead of me to the Balercomb Formations. That's where Losutu's going to drop me off, so if you do that we can ride back together on the bus."

"I'll go on the tour, I guess," she said. "When does it leave?"

"Seven-half from the lodge," I said. "I'll already be gone, so you'll have to get there on your own. You think you can handle it?"

"I made it to Earth and back on my own," she said a little tartly.

"I know," I said. "But everyone on Earth wasn't out to get you."

She shivered again. "I'll be all right."

"Good girl," I said. "Did you get that message off to the Spiders?"

She nodded, her hair brushing against my cheek. "But we won't get an answer before tomorrow."

"Understood," I said. "Where is it? I'd like to take a look."

"On my reader, in the outgoing message folder."

"Okay," I said, gathering myself to slide back to the edge of the bed. "Try to get some sleep."

"Are you coming back?" she asked.

"Of course," I said, trying for a confidence I didn't feel. "I was trained by one of the best, remember?"

"No," she said hesitantly. "I meant . . . are you coming back now?"

I frowned in the darkness. "What?"

Her sigh was a breath of warm air against my skin. "I'm afraid," she said simply. "I don't want to be alone."

I looked down again at the top of her head, wondering how much it had cost her pride to admit something like that.

Still, now that she mentioned it, I realized I didn't especially want to be alone right now, either. "It's okay," I assured her, groping beneath the sheets to find and squeeze her hand. For once, she didn't pull it away. "I'll look at the message and check on a couple of other things, and then I'll be right back."

Her reader was on the desk by the computer. I turned it on, went through the convoluted access procedure she'd taught me, and found the message. I glanced over it, noting with approval that it was exactly what I'd asked her to send, then scrolled down to the encrypted version. Pulling out my own reader, I scanned her message in and keyed for an analysis. I watched the procedure long enough to confirm that it wasn't a Halkan military encryption, then turned on the room's computer and again skulked my way into the hotel's food service records.

As with the previous day, only two Belldic breakfasts and midday meals had been ordered. The evening meals, however, were a different story. A total of twelve had been ordered and consumed, nine of them via room service.

Either *Anos* Mahf had suddenly developed an enormous appetite, or else our wayward Bellidos had finally arrived.

By the time I returned to my reader it had finished its analysis. Bayta's code wasn't related to anything Halkan, military *or* civilian, or to any of the known Cimman or Jurian or Human systems.

It was, however, the same pattern as the laser-code system I'd spotted and recorded aboard the Quadrail. The system the Bellidos had been using.

The suite's refreshment center was well stocked with beverages of all sorts, all of them in nice sturdy glass bottles. Selecting two with a good size and heft, I turned off the computer and readers and returned to the bedroom.

Bayta had rolled away from the middle of the bed in my absence, hunching up onto her side facing away from me. She didn't move or speak as I climbed in under the blankets, but from her restless movements I could tell she was still awake. I laid my hand reassuringly on her shoulder for a moment, then slid back to my edge of the bed to give her as much privacy as I could.

One of the two bottles went under my pillow where it would be close at hand. The other went on the floor just under the edge of the bed where I could get to it if I had to roll out in a hurry. Settling myself comfortably on my side where I would be facing the door, I got a loose grip on the bottle under my pillow and closed my eyes.

Tomorrow promised to be a busy day. If whoever was behind all this wanted to start that day a little early, I was willing to oblige him.

FOURTEEN :

The morning work crews dribbled into the ready room as I sat on the far side of a nearby lounge pretending to read the latest Quadrail-delivered *Intragala News*. Promptly at six-two-thirds, they came out again in a group, forty-five of them, all properly vac-suited, and made their way out the airlock in groups of four. I waited another third of an hour to make sure there weren't any stragglers, then tucked my reader into my side pocket and casually wandered over and slipped through the door.

Ten minutes later, attired in a vac suit only slightly too large for me, my faceplate darkened enough to hide my features, I followed them onto the ice.

I headed up the hills along the line of red pylons, listening to the Halkan chatter coming through the helmet speaker. All the discussion seemed to be about the two new toboggan tunnels, but as I flipped through the various frequencies I discovered three more clusters of conversation. Apparently, there were a *lot* of Halkas out on the surface today.

But wherever they were, they were keeping out of sight. Aside from a group of lodge guests heading toward the ski slopes, I saw no one until I came within view of the new tunnels. There, in the staging area between the openings, were a pair of workers, one handling a spurting drain hose, the other squatting by an open pump and fiddling with the equipment inside.

I started down the slope, making my stride and gait as much like a Halka's as I could. From the number of voices and names I could pick out of the chatter, I estimated there were fifteen to twenty other workers at the site. That should be enough of a crowd for me to lose myself in. I could burn a peephole through the ice with the plasma torch on my tool belt, have a quick look, and be out again before anyone even started wondering. A quick wink-and-wag, easy as pie.

Maybe a little *too* easy.

I studied the two workers in the staging area as I continued down the slope, quiet alarm bells starting to chime in the back of my head. There was no reason to tie up a worker on water-dump duty—a couple of anchor staffs, and the hose could take care of itself. As for the lad at the pump, he seemed to be doing more staring and poking than actual repair work. He did, however, have an open toolbox sitting conveniently beside him, which could conceal any number of unpleasant surprises. And to top it off, they were facing opposite directions, giving themselves a panoramic view of all possible approaches.

They weren't workers at all. They were sentries. Apparently, my attempts at sneakiness had been a waste of time.

My first impulse was to turn around and head straight back to the lodge. But doing a sudden about-face would clue them in that I was on to the charade.

Still, there was no point making it easy for them.

I reached the staging area; but instead of heading into the north tunnel, I turned to the south. If someone was expecting me to instantly damn myself by making a beeline for the Bellidos' work area, he'd now have to wonder if I was genuinely involved or just an inquisitive but stupid tourist.

The south tunnel looked much the way it had the previous day except that now the lights were on. I worked my way down the walkway, mentally running through the Halkora phrases I would use to explain myself if and when someone demanded to know what I was doing.

And with my mind and attention preoccupied, I made it perhaps thirty meters into the tunnel before it dawned on me that something was wrong.

I stopped. Twenty or more Halkas, I'd estimated earlier from the comm chatter, all of them packed into two fairly compact work sites. And yet, I hadn't seen a single person since leaving the staging area.

Yet the comm continued to crackle with orders and comments and casual conversation. Had the whole troop gathered over in the north tunnel? I took a few more steps, trying to sift through the rapid-fire Halkora blaring from my helmet speaker, and rounded a sharp turn in the tunnel.

I'd been wrong about the tunnel being empty. There were two vac-suited figures waiting silently for me around the curve, legs spread in low-gravity marksman's stances, their guns held in double-handed grips.

Pointed at me.

I froze in midstep, keeping my hands open and visible. They'd darkened their faceplates even more than I had, and despite the bright light I couldn't see even an outline of the faces inside. But guns had been my business, and these were definitely Belldic design.

I'd hoped to get in and out before the Bellidos made their move. Apparently, I was too late.

One of the Bellidos shifted to a one-handed grip on his gun, lifting the other hand vertically to his faceplate in the Belldic version of a finger to the lips. I nodded understanding, and he shifted the hand to point behind me. I half turned, saw nothing, and turned back. He pointed again, stepping toward me in emphasis, and this time I got it: We were going back outside. Turning, I headed up the slope.

We reached the surface, and my escort pointed past the two workers toward the other tunnel. I nodded and started across the staging area, noting peripherally that my escort was making no move to follow. The workers ignored me as I circled around them, and as I reached the north tunnel I looked back and saw the other Bellido turn and disappear back down his tunnel.

For a moment I wondered what would happen if I changed direction and instead headed back toward the lodge. But only for a moment. Taking a deep breath, I started down the tunnel.

Two more Bellidos were waiting just around the first curve, their transparent faceplates and quadruple shoulder holsters leaving no doubt of their identity this time. The one in the lead stepped up to me, flicking off my suit comm with one hand and pressing the small black disk of a short-range remora transceiver to the bottom of my faceplate with the other. "Can you hear me?" a voice called faintly from that direction.

"Yes," I replied, feeling my lip twitch as I recognized the stripe pattern across his chipmunk face. It was my fake drunk from the Quadrail, the one whose buddies had stuffed me into the spice crate. "One of us seems to be the bad penny that keeps coming back."

"Whose side are you on?" he asked.

"Mine, mostly," I said. "Other than that, I'm not even sure what the sides are."

"Not good enough," he said, his voice firm. "You stand with us and the galaxy, or you stand with the Modhri." His shoulder dipped; and suddenly the muzzle of one of his guns was pressed against my faceplate. "Choose now."

My first impulse was to do a slipstep and take the gun away from him, or at least try to get it pointed in a different direction. But he had three more guns, he had a partner standing nearby with another four, and their low-gravity combat training was probably a lot more up-to-date than mine was. "You know whose side I'm on," I said as soothingly as I could. "I'm working with the Spiders. They're trying to stop the war before it gets started."

He snorted, a high-pitched barking sound. "It is far too late for that."

I thought about Hermod, and the secrets hidden behind Bayta's troubled eyes. "Apparently I was misinformed," I said.

For a long moment he just stared at me, his expression impossible to read. Then his whiskers stiffened once and relaxed, and he returned his gun to its holster. "Spiders," he said, his voice edged with contempt. "Come."

He turned and headed down the walkway. I followed, the second Bellido bringing up the rear. "Where are all the Halkas?" I asked as we headed down.

"Under guard at the tunnel face," the first Bellido said. "We took them silently as they arrived for work."

"And you left their comms on?"

"Of course not," he said. "One of us monitored and recorded several days' worth of their conversation and created a compilation."

"Which you're now broadcasting on the appropriate channel," I said, nodding. "With one of your people no doubt standing by with a voice synthesizer to handle any direct questions from base. Very neat."

"Though perhaps pointless," he said grimly. "These workers are supposed to all be newcomers. If that's untrue, then the alarm is already out." He half turned to look at me. "Though with you here even that may now be irrelevant."

"I haven't said anything about you," I assured him, wondering what that comment about newcomers had been all about.

"That, too, may not matter," he warned. "He almost certainly has been on to you from the beginning."

"Possibly," I said, wondering who *he* was. "Of course, so have you."

"Yes," he said. There was no boast or malicious amusement in his voice; he was simply stating a fact. "Still, perhaps it's too late for him to stop us."

"We can hope," I agreed. "I don't suppose you'd like to tell me who we're talking about?"

"The Modhri, of course," he said, his voice suddenly as cold as the tunnel around us. "He and his walkers."

"You mean the big conspiracy going on at the resort?"

He stopped so abruptly I nearly ran into him. "You see this as merely a *conspiracy*?"

"Well, it's definitely a *good* conspiracy," I floundered, startled at the intensity of his reaction. "They've got excellent lines of communication, for starters."

He snorted a sort of barking laugh. "Human humor in the midst of danger," he said. "A strange but interesting gift."

We continued on in silence, the Bellido apparently no longer interested in conversation, me trying to figure out what the hell he'd meant by that last comment. If this wasn't a conspiracy, what was it? And if this so-called Modhri wasn't one of the Halkas, then who was he?

It had been obvious from the instant that first gun had been pointed at me that the Bellidos had already had a busy morning. It wasn't until we reached the area I'd found yesterday that I saw just how busy they'd been. A two-by-three-meter section of the tunnel wall had been melted away, revealing a good-sized cavern carved out of the ice behind it. Two more Bellidos were standing inside, training plasma cutters on the floor around a pair of massive telescoping elevator beams poking vertically through the cavern.

And as the water runoff flowed out into the tunnel to be siphoned away by the drain hoses, I saw a wide metal plate working its way upward. I studied it through the swirling mist of condensing ice crystals, trying to figure out why it looked familiar.

Then, suddenly, I got it. It was the upper surface of a maintenance submarine. Most likely the very submarine the Bellidos had tried to convince everyone was hidden in the underwater caverns Bayta and I had visited.

Only here it was, magically transported hundreds of meters up from where it had last been spotted. And through solid ice, yet.

I turned to my guide, to find that he in turn was watching me. "You seem surprised," he said.

I looked back into the cavern, scowling. My professional pride was at stake here. I studied the sub's emerging upper surface, particularly where it connected to the elevator beams, noting the interesting texture of the beams themselves. "Not really," I said. "Those elevator beams are rigged with microwave surface/point heaters. You got them in place here, walled them up where they wouldn't be seen, then sent them telescoping downward, melting the ice as they went.

Once they broke through to open water, you stole a sub, attached it to them, and started it melting its leisurely way back up again. Nice and quiet, no massive energy spikes for detectors to latch on to, and the water even froze again beneath the sub as it went up so that it wouldn't leave a telltale hole in the icepack."

"Excellent," he said, and I thought I could detect a note of respect in his voice. "And now?"

"You got me," I admitted. "A submarine a hundred meters from actual water seems kind of useless. Unless you're building a clubhouse."

"Your sense of humor is—" He broke off, his head tilting slightly to one side as if listening . . . and when it straightened again, I could see his whiskers had gone rigid. "They're calling for you," he said.

There was something in his tone that sent a sudden chill up my back. "Who?"

"Your friends." Reaching to my helmet, he flipped on my comm.

"—ton," a familiar voice called tautly. "Repeating: Terrance Applegate calling Frank Compton. Damn it, Frank, I know you're out there somewhere."

I flipped off the comm. "What do you want me to do?" I asked.

"What do *you* want to do?" the Bellido countered.

I grimaced, but I didn't have much choice. "I have to go," I said. "I know Applegate, and he won't quit looking until he finds me."

"Then go," the Bellido said.

I'd always thought of Bellidos as being somewhat abrupt, but even by their standards it was a pretty curt dismissal. "Fine," I answered him in kind. Turning around, I brushed past his friend still standing behind me and started up the slope.

I was thirty meters away before I noticed I still had his remora transceiver attached to my helmet. Pulling it off, I tucked it away in my top pocket.

I waited until I was within sight of the entrance before I

turned the suit's regular comm back on. Applegate was still burning up the frequency, his tone sounding more worried now than angry. "I'm here, Applegate," I called the first time he paused for air. "Stupid comms in these things aren't worth—"

"Forget the comm," he cut me off. "There's been an accident with the Balercomb tour."

I felt my heart seize up. "Bayta?" I demanded, breaking into a gliding, bobbing run.

"I don't know," he said. "Where are you?"

"Over by the new toboggan tunnels, at the far end of the red pylon line," I told him as I emerged onto the surface. "I'm heading back."

"Just stay put," Applegate ordered. "I'll be right there."

I frowned; and then, belatedly, I noticed the faint sound of Shorshic thrusters in the background. I turned toward the lodge and saw a sleek Chafta 669 starfighter settle onto the ice twenty meters away. "Come on!" Applegate's voice barked in my helmet.

He had the canopy popped by the time I reached him. "Take the ops seat," he ordered, gesturing over his shoulder at the padded chair above and behind him.

"What's this doing here?" I asked as I pulled myself up the handholds along the side and dropped into the seat. "I thought we were going to Modhra II to see them."

"Losutu's idea," he grunted as the canopy swung closed and we lifted from the surface. "He thought it would save time if we brought one of the starfighters here for you to look at. Never dreamed we might actually need it for anything. Hang on."

He kicked in the drive, the acceleration shoving me back into my seat. "What happened?" I called over the roar coming from behind me.

"Sounds like the driver lost control somehow and rammed the bus into one of the ice pillars," he said. "I heard that Bayta was calling for you, and that no one could find you, so I fired up the Chafta and headed out to look."

I felt a sudden crawling on my skin. Bayta had called for

me? Knowing where I was and what I was doing, she'd still called for me? Not likely.

"Your turn," he said. "What were you doing in a restricted area in a resort worker vac suit?"

"I wanted to check out the work on the new toboggan tunnels," I said, sliding into liar mode with half my brain while the other half sifted through the potential traps. "If I'm going to recommend this place, I have to know everything about it, including how it's being expanded."

"Why didn't you just ask for a tour?"

"Tours only show what the management wants you to see," I said, peering out the side of the canopy. We were passing over the lodge, and I saw that the morning torchferry from the Tube had landed and was cooling down in preparation for the return trip.

But there was a second ship on the ice, as well, a ship with the boxy lines and soft-focus anti-sensor hull of a military troop carrier. Pressing my helmet against the canopy, I caught a glimpse of figures in dark green Halkan military vac suits moving toward the lodge.

And then, even as I craned my neck to try to see more, Applegate rolled the starfighter a few degrees to port, cutting off my view. "Hey!" I protested.

"Hey, what?" he called back.

I clenched my teeth. "Nothing," I said. "How much farther?"

"About thirty kilometers," he said. "Don't worry, I'm sure she's all right."

The crash site was bustling with activity when we arrived. Three ambulances were already on the scene, clustered around the bus, with half a dozen Halkas helping passengers out of the damaged vehicle. The bus itself was tipped nearly up onto its left side, its nose crunched into a huge ice stalagmite. Applegate set us down fifty meters away and popped the canopy. "What frequency are we on here?" I asked as we hurried toward the scene. "I'm still on the workers' channel."

"General Two," Applegate told me.

I switched over, and the silent scene erupted with the terse orders of command, the moans and whimpering of injured or scared tourists, and the soothing voices of the medics themselves. "Bayta?" I called.

"She's over here," a Halkan voice replied, and a medic squatting by one of the ambulances raised a hand. The figure sitting limply at his feet looked up, and I saw that it was indeed Bayta, her face tense and pinched. But at least she was alive. I started toward her—

And came to an abrupt halt as a tall Halka suddenly loomed in my path. "You are Compton?" he demanded. He was wearing one of the military vac suits, with major's insignia around the collar.

"Out of my way," I growled, trying to get around him.

But he wasn't about to be gotten around. "You are Compton?" he repeated.

"Yes, this is him," Applegate spoke up, taking my arm. "Sorry, Frank, but we've got a situation here."

"No kidding," I said, trying to pull away.

"Bayta's all right," Applegate soothed, steering me toward the wrecked bus. "This will just take a minute."

He led me around the back of the bus to where we could see the underside, the major staying close behind us. Up close, the damage to the vehicle's nose looked worse than it had from the air, and I found myself wondering what speed the lunatic had been doing when he rammed the ice. "There, beneath the overhang," Applegate said, pointing to the chassis between the two right-hand wheels. "You see it?"

"Of course I see it," I said with as much patience as I could manage. From this angle, with the bus tilted up on its side, the long plastic-wrapped package would have been hard to miss. Given the three Halkas standing there poking and prodding at it, the thing was as obvious as a Times Square holodisplay. "So?"

"You know what it is?"

"I left my X-ray glasses in my other suit," I growled. "You consider just unwrapping it?"

"No need," the major put in, his tone dark. "It is a phased

sonic disruptor, designed for underwater dredging and shock-mining."

"Okay," I said. "And this concerns me how?"

In answer, the Halka gestured to two of the three figures who'd been inspecting the disruptor. They walked over to us; and before I could react, there was a glint of metal and a sudden flurry of hands, and my arms had been neatly pinioned in front of me in a set of wristcuffs.

My heart, which had already been doing overtime over Bayta, kicked into full jackhammer mode. "What the *hell* are you doing?" I snarled.

"You are wanted at the lodge," the major said, getting a grip on my upper arm and leading me toward the ambulance. The medic had Bayta on her feet now, I saw, and was helping her inside. "You and your female both."

"Yeah, whatever," I muttered. In the distance I could see the bumblebee shape of a heavy lifter approaching, its underside grapples looking like giant insect legs. "This had better be good," I warned.

"It's not good, Frank," Applegate said quietly. "It's not good at all."

FIFTEEN :

Applegate and the major seated me between them in the forward section of the ambulance, while Bayta was taken aft to the pressurized treatment area. Ostensibly so the medics could check her over; in actual fact, I had no doubt they just didn't want us within helmet-touching range of each other where we could compare notes without anyone else listening in.

We were met by four other militarily vac-suited Halkas when we touched down outside the lodge. One of them took a moment to put wristcuffs on Bayta, then they formed a standard escort box around us as the major led us through a cargo airlock big enough to accommodate the whole group. Once inside, our escort handed us off to two more armed Halkas in regular army uniforms, the vac-suited batch then returning outside. Applegate and the major popped their helmets and slung them onto their shoulder clips, then did the same for Bayta and me. With our new escort flanking us, we went through a series of service corridors to a door marked WATERCOURSE CONFERENCE ROOM.

As the ready room had been of typical layout, so, too, was the conference room. In the center was a long rectangular table ringed by nicely padded rolling chairs, while the far end was dominated by a media setup with all the equipment necessary for a business or social dit rec presentation. A few sculptures and paintings were scattered around, and along one wall was a narrow water channel with a babbling brook running over more of the ubiquitous Modhran coral.

There were three people seated on the side of the table nearest the coral, obviously waiting for us. One of them was a Halkan Peer, wearing a tricolor scheme I didn't recognize, with a Halka in an upper-class layered suit seated beside him. The third was my Belldic acquaintance *Apos* Mahf. "Mr. Compton," the latter said, nodding as our two Halkan escorts took up positions just inside the door. "Again we meet."

"So we do," I agreed as Applegate led me to a chair across from Mahf and sat me down, taking the seat to my left. "Perhaps *you* would like to explain what exactly is going on."

"I think you know," Mahf said darkly, his eyes shifting to Bayta as the Halkan major put her at the end of the table by the door and sat down beside her. "Perhaps your companion will begin by telling us what happened aboard the tour bus."

"I really don't know," Bayta said, her voice trembling. I'd watched her as they'd marched us from the ambulance into the lodge, and as far as I could tell through a vac suit she didn't seem particularly injured. But she was obviously still pretty shaken. "One minute we were traveling along the ice and the driver was describing some of the formations. The next minute we were all suddenly thrown against the seats and walls as the bus crashed and fell over on its side."

"You saw none of your fellow passengers approach the driver just before this happened?" Mahf asked.

Bayta shook her head. "I was looking out the window."

"You saw no one struggle with the driver, or try to take the control wheel from him?" Mahf persisted. "Nor did you see anyone try afterward to escape onto the ice?"

"No, nothing like that," Bayta insisted. "I was looking out—"

"Out the window," Mahf finished for her. "Of course you were." Abruptly, he shifted his glare to me. "What about you?"

The quick-change attack was a time-honored way of throwing interrogation subjects off step. Unfortunately for Mahf, I'd read the same manuals he had. "What about me?" I countered calmly. "I was thirty kilometers away when it happened."

"In an area where you had no business being," the non-Peer Halka put in.

I focused on him. "And you are . . . ?"

"This is Superintendent PrifKlas," Applegate said. He had the look and sound of a man in the middle of trouble not of his own making who would rather be almost anywhere else. "The administrator of the resort."

"Ah," I said, looking him up and down. "My apologies. I was under the impression that *Apos* Mahf was the one in charge here."

PrifKlas bristled—"I'm here solely as an advisor," Mahf said hastily. "Full Colonel AvsBlar of the Halkan army is the commander on the scene."

"And where is he?"

"Deploying his troops," Mahf said.

"Not that this is any of your business," the Peer said.

"And you are . . . ?" I asked.

"My name is unimportant," he said. "Superintendent PrifKlas asked me to sit in on the proceedings."

"Ah," I said, turning back to PrifKlas. "So where exactly did you scare up a full colonel on such short notice?"

"From the garrison on Modhra II, of course," PrifKlas said, a note of malicious satisfaction in his voice. "You didn't know we had a garrison here, did you?"

Beside me, I sensed Applegate squirm in his seat. Perhaps he and Losutu had overstepped their bounds when they'd told me about the Modhran military presence. Still, they'd never actually mentioned a garrison. "No, I didn't," I said truthfully.

"Good," PrifKlas said. "Now tell me why you were at the work site."

"I wanted to see how the resort expansion was progressing," I said.

"Even though that area is strictly off-limits to guests?"

"I saw no such signs to that effect," I said. "Besides, what could you be doing out there you'd want to hide?"

Beside Bayta, the major snorted, a wet, whispery sound. "You are here to answer questions, Human, not to ask them."

I shrugged. "Fine. So ask."

"I told you he was a cool one, Superintendent," Mahf murmured. "Very cool, very professional. More than ever I see the hand of *Korak* Fayr in this."

I pricked up my ears. *Kora* was the Belldic equivalent of major; adding the final *k* made it a major of commandos. That sounded rather like the sort of person I'd been shadow-boxing with for most of this trip.

"Yet you have no proof Fayr is even on Modhra," PrifKlas countered.

"He's here," Mahf assured him grimly. "And he will hardly let a mishap like this discourage him. You've moved all submarines away from the hotel?"

"Yes, and have deployed them around the caverns," PrifKlas confirmed.

"And the troops?" Mahf asked, looking across at the major beside Bayta.

"Deployed around the formations." The major launched into a list of numbers and map coordinates.

And as he did so, I eased my bound wrists beneath the edge of the table. The Halkas had put the cuffs on while my vac suit was fully pressurized, and no one had bothered to refasten them since I'd had my helmet removed. If the suit depressurization had left enough slack, there was a chance I could pop them and get free.

There was indeed a little slack. Not much, but maybe enough.

Beside me, Applegate cleared his throat softly. I turned to find him gazing at me, a knowing expression on his face as he glanced down at my wrists. He gave me a microscopic nod, then turned casually away.

The major finished his recitation. "Which again brings us

to you," PrifKlas said, turning back to face me. "You'll find things much easier if you cooperate."

"I'd love to," I said. "But I have no idea what this is all about."

"Actually, Superintendent, he may be telling the truth," Mahf spoke up reluctantly. "I've read his file, and cannot envision him involving himself in something like this. Do you agree, Colonel Applegate?"

"I never knew him all that well," Applegate hedged. "He was just one of many investigators under my overall command."

"Yet if he is innocent, how do you explain his presence?" PrifKlas demanded.

"We were invited," I told him. "High Commissioner JhanKla of the Fifth Sector Assembly recommended the place."

"And all the rest is pure coincidence?" PrifKlas asked sarcastically.

"All the rest what?" I asked.

PrifKlas snorted. "So now you play a waiting game."

"Or he is in fact an innocent dupe," Mahf persisted. "If so, he would have no reason to protect information that might lead us to Fayr."

For a moment the two of them locked eyes, and I had to suppress a cynical smile. Did they really think I would be so easily taken in by the old good-cop/bad-cop routine? Especially with Applegate, the obvious good-cop candidate, clearly not interested in playing along? "You may try," PrifKlas said grudgingly. "Be brief."

Mahf turned to face me. "We believe there to be a rogue Belldic commando team in the area," he said, his voice low and earnest. "They are most likely already on Modhra I, though some may still be offworld. They have come"—he grimaced—"to destroy the coral beds."

I felt my eyebrows crawling up my forehead. Of all the possible scenarios running through my mind, ecoterrorism was probably the last one that would have occurred to me. "What in the world for?"

"We don't know," Mahf said. "An imagined Halkan offense, or perhaps he has simply lost his mental soundness. It began two months ago with the theft of one of the resort's maintenance submarines. From small bits of evidence, we believe it is hidden somewhere in the cavern complex you visited two days ago."

"Yes, I wondered about that myself," I agreed, deciding to pretend I didn't know they'd already heard me come to that conclusion via the bugs in our suite.

"That was where matters rested until today," Mahf continued. "The Halkas have attempted scans of the caverns, but none was successful—too much rock, and Modhran water is heavy with dissolved minerals. Still, a single submarine wasn't thought to be a serious threat, particularly since we were now keeping a close watch on all approaches to the caverns."

"Ah," I said, noting with interest his continued use of the word *we*. Apparently, he'd been working with the Halkas on this longer than simply since this morning. "Why didn't you just watch for Fayr to show up at the resort? You *do* know what he looks like, don't you?"

"Of course," Mahf said. He pulled out a reader, tapped a couple of keys, and slid it across the table to me. "Do you recognize him?"

It was my fake drunk, all right, the one I'd left chopping ice in the new toboggan tunnel an hour ago. "I saw him on the Jurskala Quadrail," I said, sliding the reader back. "So why haven't you arrested him?"

"Because until this morning we didn't even know which species was involved in this plot," PrifKlas growled. "Let alone which individuals."

"And you're sure Fayr's the one?"

"Very sure," Mahf said grimly. "It was one of his commandos whose attempt to wrest control from the bus driver caused the crash."

I frowned. "You've lost me."

"Really," PrifKlas said, his voice cold. "You hadn't noticed that those ice formations are situated directly over the caverns where the stolen submarine is hidden? Or that the ice there is barely thirty meters thick, easily shattered by a series of properly shaped thermistack charges?"

"No, I hadn't noticed any of those things," I said evenly. Seen from their point of view, there was definitely a certain logic to it.

Except for the possibly inconvenient fact that the sub was nowhere near where they thought it was. What was Fayr up to, anyway?

"Really," PrifKlas bit out again. "Is it also pure coincidence that you just *happened* to be out on the surface, in a place where you had no business being, at the precise time all this was happening?"

And with that, it finally clicked. "Wait a minute," I said. "Are you suggesting I was Fayr's *diversion*?"

"Why not?" PrifKlas demanded. "Particularly since you performed the same task yesterday, and in the same place, when the commandos concealed the disruptor aboard the bus. Why not use a successful feint twice?"

"Except for why anyone should have been distracted by my movements in the first place," I countered stiffly. "What did I do to justify you putting me under surveillance?"

"It's nothing specific, Frank," Applegate spoke up. "But you have to admit there's been a whole pattern of strange things that have happened around you since you came aboard the Quadrail at Terra." He gestured toward Mahf's reader. "And now we hear that you actually rubbed shoulders with this Fayr character. What *should* we think?"

"One: There wasn't any rubbing of shoulders," I said, lifting up my bound hands and ticking off fingers. "I saw him in the bar, period. Two: Bayta and I wouldn't even *be* on Modhra if JhanKla hadn't suggested we come here. You want to blame somebody, blame him. Three: If you've got one of Fayr's people in custody, why aren't you interrogating *him* instead of me?"

Mahf looked over at the Halkan major scowling at me from beside Bayta. "Do you care to respond?" he invited.

The major scowled a little harder. "He is no longer in custody," he said, his tone a swirling mix of anger and embarrassment. "He was brought to the lodge, but escaped his guards. We're searching for him."

"Really," I said, swallowing a three-course meal's worth of sarcastic remarks that very much wanted to come out. "At least you can't blame me for *that* one."

"Don't be so certain," PrifKlas warned. "Halkan conspiracy laws are both clear and unforgiving."

"Which means this is the time to cut a deal," Applegate urged. "If you have any idea where Fayr is, or how he's planning to get to that sub, you need to tell them. Now."

I looked over at Bayta. She was gazing back at me, her throat tight, her eyes pleading.

But pleading for what? That I should give in and tell Mahf and PrifKlas about the gimmicked toboggan tunnel? Or that I should keep quiet and give Fayr and his people time to complete their mission, whatever the hell that mission was?

For that matter, why should I even care what Bayta wanted? She'd lied to me from the start, claiming not to be in league with Fayr and yet using the same encryption system he did. I didn't owe her any loyalty. Turning back to Mahf, I opened my mouth—

And paused. He was gazing hard at me, his whiskers stiff, an almost breathless anticipation on his face.

And it occurred to me that, once again, I was rationalizing.

Mahf was still waiting. "I was just thinking," I said, speaking slowly as if my hesitation had been due to a long train of thought. "Even if Fayr gets to the sub, doesn't he still have to smuggle in some explosives or something if he's going to damage the coral beds?"

Some of the stiffness went out of Mahf's whiskers. "Not if he has a second sonic disruptor," he said, a hint of disappointment in his voice. Clearly, he'd been primed and ready for me to spill my guts. "With that he could shatter the coral matrix, scattering and killing the polyps inside."

"This is a waste of time," PrifKlas cut in harshly. "Tell me, Compton: How much longer were you planning to stay here?"

"I reserved our suite for another two days," I told him. "As I presume you already know."

"Then how do you explain *this*?" Reaching down to the floor by his feet, he hauled up my carrybags and slammed them triumphantly onto the table beside him. "Or do you claim this is not your luggage?"

I suppressed a grimace as he retrieved Bayta's carrybag from the floor and added it to the lineup. Of course Bayta would have packed our bags before heading out on the tour; I'd told her we'd be leaving on the afternoon torchferry. "No, it's our luggage, all right," I conceded.

"And how do you explain that you have packed if you intend to stay two more days?"

"Bayta's the one who handles our transportation schedule," I said. "She must have learned that our original plans wouldn't mesh with the Quadrail schedule and decided we had to leave this afternoon."

A flicker of annoyance crossed his flat bulldog face. Naturally, they would already have pulled the resort's long-range comm schedule from last night and learned she'd sent a message to the Tube. Nothing there they could use to trip me up.

But that didn't mean they wouldn't try. "And what precisely was this scheduling conflict?" PrifKlas demanded.

Beside him, the Peer stirred in his seat. "With all due respect, Superintendent, we are getting nowhere," he said.

"Yes, Honored One," PrifKlas said, going instantly servile. "Your suggestion?"

The Peer gave a microscopic nod behind him. "There is a bed of coral right here," he pointed out. "It is time we used it."

And with that, the atmosphere in the room abruptly changed.

It wasn't anything specific I could put my finger on; no pregnant silences or sharp inhalations, no stunned changes in expression or restless shifting of chairs. But in that moment, somehow, something changed. Something vitally important.

"Yes," PrifKlas murmured, looking back at me with the same subtle fire I'd just seen in Mahf's eyes. "Very well."

"Wait a minute," Applegate put in cautiously, his eyes flicking back and forth between them. "I don't think this is something you really want to do."

"You presume to speak to us thusly on our own world?" the Peer asked. His voice was calm, but his eyes were focused on Applegate like a pair of plasma torches.

"He's a citizen of the Terran Confederation," Applegate said, refusing to shrivel. "As such, he has certain rights."

"You may lodge a protest when this is over," the Peer said, motioning to the two soldiers flanking the door. "Guards: Remove his vac suit." He cocked his head thoughtfully. "And the female's suit, as well."

"I can find him for you," Bayta spoke up as the two soldiers started forward.

All eyes turned to her. "You mean Fayr?" PrifKlas asked.

"Yes," she said. Her voice was tight, her expression that of someone facing a firing squad. "I just need the reader from my carrybag."

I frowned, trying to read past the taut skin and haunted eyes. There couldn't possibly be anything on her reader that would tell her where Fayr was. What was she up to?

"Very well," PrifKlas said slowly, standing up. Turning her carrybag on its side, he popped it open.

And then, with a sudden rush of heat across my face, I understood. Rather than let them make me touch the coral, she was going to trigger the Saarix-5.

I looked back at PrifKlas as he rummaged through Bayta's carrybag, freshly aware of the gentle weight of the vac helmet hanging from my shoulder clip. Depending on the poison's dispersion radius, Bayta and I might be able to get our helmets on and sealed before the Saarix reached us. Applegate might possibly manage it, too, if he figured it out and reacted quickly enough.

But that left all the others.

What was my obligation to them? Certainly none of them had threatened us or made any other move that justified deadly force. How could I just sit by and let Bayta murder them?

PrifKlas had the reader out now, fingering it as he eyed Bayta suspiciously across the table. He wasn't fooled; he knew something here was off-key. "Very well," he said at last. "But first, you and Compton will remove your vac suits."

The skin of Bayta's face went even tighter. She shot a look at me—

"Well, come on," I seconded, putting a little impatience into my voice. "Get it off and tell them what they want to know so we can get out of here."

For a split second she just stared at me, a whole series of emotions flicking across her face. Then, with a final twitch of her lip, her expression went back to its usual wooden flatness.

A flatness I was doing my best to emulate . . . because in order to remove our vac suits, the Halkas were first going to have to take off our wristcuffs.

Of course, that would still leave a ratio of two Halkan soldiers plus a major to one of me. But it was still our best chance. Probably our only chance.

The two soldiers stepped to either side of Bayta and hauled her to her feet. I watched their procedure, planning when and how I would make my move when it was my turn.

And then, as one of the soldiers reached for the fasteners at her collar, the conference door slid open behind them.

Both soldiers spun around, hands dropping automatically to their weapons. But it was only a Cimma in a bright orange vac suit, his faceplate darkened as if he'd just come in from outside but his pear shape unmistakable as he waddled into the room. He saw us and came to an abrupt halt. "Does this be the ski instruction group?" he asked tentatively, his gravelly voice through his helmet sounding like it was coming from a deep pit.

"You have the wrong room," PrifKlas said tartly.

Keeping my upper body motionless, I gathered my feet beneath me. One did not turn down a gift from heaven, and with the Cimma's appearance my odds had suddenly improved. The two soldiers now had their backs to me, and the others had at least part of their attention distracted toward the end of the room.

It was time to make my move.

The two soldiers were the obvious targets. But with Applegate and most of the table between us, I knew I'd never reach them in time.

But Mahf was another story. He was sitting directly across from me, his status guns gleaming in their shoulder holsters. If I could get across the table fast enough, I might be able to grab one of those guns before he could react. Getting a grip on the edge of the table, I eased my weight off the chair, preparing to kick it backward out of my way.

"My apologies," the Cimma said, bowing low and stretching his arms out as if preparing to bless us. I caught a glimpse of a pair of slender orange tubes fastened to the undersides of each of his forearms—

And with a double snap like the breaking of small branches, a pair of projectiles shot out to catch the two Halkan soldiers squarely in their torsos.

They staggered back into the table, clutching at their chests and fumbling for their guns. A quarter second later their legs folded beneath them, dropping them onto the floor, even as the major seated beside Bayta caught a round of his own and collapsed onto the table. Across from me, Mahf snarled a curse, shoving his chair violently backward and throwing himself after it as he grabbed for his guns. But the Cimma was already tracking his movement, and again the wrist guns snapped, turning the dive into a crumple and sending his guns skittering uselessly away across the floor.

PrifKlas and the Peer, older and more cultured and far less accustomed to sudden and violent action, didn't even make it out of their chairs.

Which left just Bayta, Applegate, and me. "Easy," I cautioned, holding my cuffed hands up for the Cimma's inspection. "We may be on the same side here."

"Perhaps," the other said. "One moment, if you please."

Keeping one of his wrist guns pointed at Applegate, he systematically fired three more rounds with the other into each of the figures already sprawled in chairs or on the floor. "It requires more than one snoozer to put a walker completely to sleep," he commented. With his one hand still trained on Applegate, he reached up now with the other and touched his faceplate control. The darkening cleared away . . .

And to my complete lack of surprise, I found *Korak* Fayr gazing back at me. "Thanks for the assist," I said. "And in the traditional nick of time, too."

"You were in need of assistance," he said, eyeing Bayta and Applegate. "These are trusted colleagues?"

"Bayta is," I said, bending the truth only a little. "I'm afraid I can't vouch for Mr. Applegate."

Applegate sent me a surprised look. "Well, thank you," he growled. "Thank you very much."

"Nothing personal," I assured him as I lowered my wrists to my lap and started working my fingers along the edges. "Right now I don't trust much of anyone on this rock."

"Unless they're renegade Bellidos, of course," Applegate countered tartly, brushing my fingers aside and starting to work on the cuffs himself.

"Who said I trust them, either?" I said, looking back at Fayr. He was busily stripping the sleeping Halkan soldiers of guns and comms, the orange of his chameleon vac suit fading rapidly to dark green and the pear-shaped lower bulge collapsing in on itself as it reconfigured from its Cimman profile. "And I think it's about time someone told me what exactly is going on."

Fayr's eyes flicked to Applegate. "Later."

"Or I could just tell you now," Applegate offered, still fiddling with my cuffs. "It turns out that Modhran coral has some properties the Halkas have been careful not to mention to the rest of us. To be specific, chemicals in the shell material that create a mild narcotic effect in most species. For a small percentage of the populace, it can be as addicting as heroin-3 or Redpeace." He looked over at Fayr. "We're not *that* far out of the loop, *Korak* Fayr."

"Never mind the loop," I growled. As bad as heroin-3? "And they've been shipping this stuff across the galaxy for *how* long?"

"The officials claim they didn't know," Applegate said. "Maybe they didn't. But someone's been using the coral to manipulate people. Important people, corporations—maybe even entire governments."

"Including some in the Estates-General?" I suggested, lifting my eyebrows at Fayr.

Fayr didn't reply, but Applegate nodded. "There's a fair chance of it. Those who've been caught, needless to say, haven't been very forthcoming."

"So who's behind it?" I asked.

Applegate shrugged. "Some secret group calling themselves the Modhri," he said. "Whoever they are, the source of their power is sitting right here, a kilometer below our feet. Destroy that, and they're finished."

I looked at Fayr again. Both he and Bayta, I noted with interest, had been remarkably quiet during this whole conversation. "Comments?" I invited.

"Mr. Applegate has caught the essence," Fayr said, his voice neutral as he circled the table and gathered up Mahf's guns.

"Just the essence?" I asked.

"There are a few other details." Fayr gestured toward the sleeping Peer. "For one, that this Halka is one of them. He controls the company that mines, packages, and ships the coral."

"Ah." I looked back at Applegate. "What's the Confederation's position on this?"

He made a face. "Officially, we haven't got one. We don't have any of the coral on our worlds, and we mean to keep it that way. Unofficially"—he gave my cuffs a final tweak and popped them free—"the UN supports any action that keeps dangerously addictive drugs off the streets. As far as I'm concerned, Modhra I is fair game. If you want to assist them, I won't stop you."

I looked at Bayta. "You want to go?"

"Yes," she said, her voice trembling slightly.

"*Korak* Fayr?"

The Bellido gave a slight bow. "Your assistance would be valuable."

"Then we're on," I said, getting to my feet.

"Go get 'em, tiger," Applegate said, a slight smile touching his lips.

I got out of my chair and circled around behind him, then paused and turned back. "There's just one other thing," I said, gesturing to Fayr. "We wouldn't want PrifKlas and Mahf to wonder if you betrayed them, now, would we?"

Applegate's eyes went wide. "What? Wait a—"

His protest was cut off by the snap of Fayr's wrist gun. He had just enough time to send me a baleful glare, and then his eyes rolled up and he slumped unconscious in his chair. "Good shot," I said, pulling my helmet off its shoulder clip and putting it back on. I turned off the suit's comm and retrieved the remora transceiver from my pocket, sticking it back onto my faceplate. "What's our first move?" I asked, choosing one of the Halkan guns from the neat row Fayr had laid out on the table and sliding it into a side pocket where it would be handy.

"You shall see," Fayr said, his voice coming distantly from the remora as he fixed another of the little transceivers to the bottom of Bayta's faceplate. His chameleon suit had settled into a nice copy of a Halkan military outfit. "Bring your carrybags," he added, picking up the other Halkan gun. "We will not return to this place."

SIXTEEN :

The corridor outside the conference room was deserted. We saw a few people as we made our way to the airlocks, including a couple of Halkan soldiers. But it was always at a distance, and as far as I could tell none of them gave us a second look.

Everything outside looked pretty much the way we'd left it a few minutes earlier. The torchferry was still sitting on the ice, with the Halkan troop carrier squatting nearby. We headed toward the landing area, Bayta and me in front with our luggage, Fayr walking behind us with his gun out like a good Halkan prisoner escort should. "I hope you're not relying on this charade to get us aboard that troop carrier," I warned. "Halkan commandos have chameleon suits, too."

"No fears," Fayr assured me. Faintly through my remora I heard the sound of someone reporting to him on his own suit comm. "Other transportation has been arranged."

Right on cue, a large bulky vehicle hove into view over the horizon, heading our direction. It took me a couple of puzzled seconds to identify it as the heavy lifter I'd seen earlier, now with the damaged tour bus clutched beneath it on its grapples. The lifter continued toward us, flying low and much faster than I would have expected something lugging that much mass could manage.

I was still watching when the grapples released in midair, sending the bus arcing sedately toward the surface. I heard Bayta's sharp intake of air; and a second later the bus slammed squarely into the aft section of the troop carrier.

Even in Modhra's thin atmosphere the impact was loud enough to hear, like a meat grinder that had had a bone tossed into it. "To the torchferry," Fayr ordered over the noise.

We picked up our pace, fighting to maintain the delicate balance between maximal speed without hitting the ground hard enough to go bounding kangaroo-style into the air. Behind us, people were starting to pour from the lodge's airlocks in response to the crash, and I saw a dozen figures in military vac suits hurrying in from over two of the nearby hills. The lifter itself, now relieved of its burden, shot past the lodge and disappeared over the horizon in the direction of the toboggan tunnels.

We reached the torchferry's open outer door without incident and slipped inside. I drew my gun, just in case, as Fayr closed the door and cycled the airlock. The inner door slid open, and we went inside.

I needn't have bothered with the gun. There were two figures already at the torchferry's command and copilot stations, and though their vac suits were pure Halkan military it was obvious from their nonchalant glances our direction that they were in fact two of Fayr's commandos. "I guess this explains where the Halkas' prisoner went," I commented as Fayr gestured us forward.

"Actually, he is piloting the lifter," Fayr said. "I assumed that the last direction the Modhri would expect him to flee would be to the scene of his previous activity. Can you fly this vehicle?"

"Probably." I stepped between the two Bellidos and gave the controls a quick look. All the labels were in Halkora, but the layout was standard enough. "Make that yes," I said. "Provided you don't want anything too complicated."

"Nothing complicated at all," Fayr assured me, gesturing

the Bellidos out of their seats. "We need only return to where you found me earlier this morning."

"Got it," I said, slipping into the pilot's seat and strapping in. I checked the thrusters and ion-plasma drive, confirmed they'd been run properly through their warm-up. "Say when."

"Lift now," Fayr said.

My limited Westali flight training had centered around starfighters and other military craft, and the first thing I noticed was how sluggishly the torchliner responded. But as I got us pointed the right direction and fed power to the ion-plasma drive it became considerably more lively, and we were pressed gently back into our seats as we shot over the frozen landscape below. A minute later, we'd reached the end of the red pylons and the unfinished toboggan tunnels. "Now what?" I called.

"We must melt the ice over the north tunnel," Fayr called from the rear of the compartment. "You know where."

I glanced back over my shoulder, paused for a longer look. While I'd been concentrating on my flying, Fayr and his buddies had been putting together a pair of very nasty-looking 15 mm hip-mounted packet guns. "Nice," I said. "You get all this stuff from Sistarrko?"

"Yes," Fayr said. "Military-class weapons cannot be transported via Quadrail, so we brought in trade goods and purchased the equipment we needed from local manufacturers."

"By way of the black market, I'd guess," I said. "Incidentally, you *do* realize those are outside toys, right?"

"No fears," he assured me. "Concentrate on melting the ice, and leave us to deal with the starfighters."

"The—?" I checked my board, then lifted my eyes to look out the canopy.

There they were, all right: a matched pair of Chafta 669s hovering watchfully over the ice, their bows pointed our direction.

And as I watched, one of them dipped its bow and then raised it upward again, tracking its weapons-lock systems across our hull in the universal command to surrender. "They're not looking very happy," I warned Fayr.

"Ignore them," he said as he helped one of his armed compatriots into the starboard airlock. The other gunner was already in the portside lock, the inner door closing behind him. "This is a civilian craft," he added, coming forward and taking the copilot's seat. "They won't fire on us until they realize we have not been fooled."

"Fooled how?"

"Later," Fayr said. "Now—carefully."

I eased the torchferry to a hovering halt a dozen meters off the surface and perhaps thirty past the spot in the north tunnel where the buried sub waited. Tilting the bow upward—no simple task the way our force thrusters were vectored—I slowly fed power to the drive. "How exactly haven't we been fooled?" I asked again as the ice began to boil away in a tornado of swirling white.

"I told you earlier that several of Applegate's details were incorrect," Fayr said, alternating his attention between the aft display's boiling ice and the starfighters hovering in front of us. So far, he was right about them not seeming all that worried about what we were doing. "One of the more critical is the nature of the threat we face," Fayr continued. "The Modhri is not simply a group of drug distributors. He is instead the coral itself."

I frowned. "He—I mean they—*what*?"

"Modhran coral consists of many small polyps within a shell-like matrix," he explained. "Unlike other corals, these polyps in large numbers form the cells of a group mind. A little more to the left."

I eased the drive stream a few degrees that direction. "What do you mean, a group mind?"

"The polyps function like the cells of a normal brain, except that instead of connecting neurons they are linked telepathically," he said. "A few thousand together can create a rudimentary self-awareness, and a large enough group can link with others up to hundreds of kilometers away to create a larger and more capable intelligence." He eyed me. "You don't believe me, of course."

"I wouldn't say that," I said cautiously. Certainly not to

someone with a pair of packet guns at his beck and call. "How do you know all this?"

"There," he said, pointing at the display. "You see it?"

I looked at the display, fully expecting to see some amorphous mass of coral rising from the steam and freezing rain, like Count Dracula in a classic dit rec horrorific. But there was nothing; and it was only as I took a second look that I realized he was pointing to a pair of gray-metal pillars, the elevator beams attached to the stolen sub. We were almost there. "So what exactly is the threat?" I asked. "The chunks that have been exported spy for the main branch or something?"

"The exported masses of coral—we name them *outposts*— are too far from the homeland for direct linkage," Fayr said. "The danger lies in the mobile colonies, or walkers, which they have created in most of the galaxy's social and governmental leaders."

A creepy sensation was starting to twist its way through me. "What do you mean, created? Created how?"

"By touch," he said. "A polyp hook can enter a person's skin and bloodstream via a small scratch when the coral is touched. Once there, it grows into a complete organism, then divides and grows and creates its own colony."

"And then?"

"The colony creates a hidden secondary personality," Fayr said. "It normally remains in the back of its host's mind, offering subtle suggestions for behavior and decisions. Usually very reasonable suggestions, which the host can easily rationalize away."

Go on, Mahf had urged that afternoon in the casino. *Touch the coral.*

And a day later, strangely and inexplicably asleep on my feet, I'd nearly rationalized my way into doing just that. "Do you need one inside you to get these suggestions?" I asked, not at all sure I wanted to hear the answer. If they'd gotten one of these things into me without my knowledge . . .

To my relief, he shook his head. "No, a large enough colony has the ability to offer suggestions at a distance," he said. "We call them thought viruses. They can linger in a person's mind for minutes or sometimes hours."

"Giving the victim plenty of time to talk himself into going along with them," I said grimly.

"Indeed." Fayr pointed. "There."

The top of the sub was visible now through the steam, its sides emerging as the ice melted away. "So if you're trying to destroy the coral, what's the sub doing way up here?" I asked.

"Shut down now so that the lifter may attach," he said. "Once that's done, we can melt away the rest of the ice."

There was fresh movement on the aft display: The heavy lifter that had dropped the bus on the troop carrier had appeared from inside the south tunnel and was maneuvering carefully through the ice storm toward the sub. "Beware," Fayr warned. "The starfighters will soon make their response."

I looked back at the Chaftas. Neither had moved; but suddenly I had the sense that they were bracing for action. "Against us or the sub?"

"The sub," Fayr said. "But—"

His protest was cut off as I threw power to the maneuvering baffles, turning us ponderously around and vectoring the thrusters to slide us directly between the Chaftas and the sub. "You *did* say they wouldn't fire on us, right?" I shouted over the roar.

The words were barely out of my mouth when the starfighters attacked.

They split their formation, one going high, the other going low, both trying to do an end run around the bulk of the torchferry I'd now moved to block their direct line of fire at the sub and lifter. I cut back on the thrusters, dropping closer toward the ice to further block the low-run attacker. He dropped lower in response, apparently figuring that in a game of chicken his maneuverability would beat out mine. His partner, with me obligingly clearing the high road for him, swooped in for the kill.

To be met by a withering hail of anti-armor packet fire from the Bellido in my portside airlock. The Chafta twisted hard around, trying to get out of way as a portion of his starboard engine nacelle shredded under the multiple impacts.

The first starfighter was still trying to slip beneath me. Setting my teeth, I started to drop us lower—

And twitched in surprise as Fayr reached over to his copilot's board and threw full power to the thrusters instead. "What are you doing?" I snapped as the torchferry lurched upward like a slightly drunk cork.

"Clearing the path," he called back. "Brace yourself."

I was taking in a fresh lungful of air when a slender black cylinder riding a streak of yellow fire shot horizontally beneath us. It caught the low-road starfighter squarely in its forward weapons cluster.

With a brilliant flash of smoke and fire, the Chafta disintegrated.

I shifted my attention to the other direction. Standing side by side in the opening to the south tunnel were a pair of Bellidos with shoulder-mounted missile launchers. Even as I watched, the second launcher flared with yellow fire, sending its missile shooting over the top of the torchferry into the remaining starfighter. Another explosion, and the fight was over.

With an effort I found my voice. "Well," I said as conversationally as I could manage. "That went well."

"For the moment," Fayr agreed tightly. "The question will be what surprises he may yet have waiting."

"This was surprising enough for me," I assured him. The two Belldic gunners had discarded their launchers and were heading down into the crater I'd melted in the ice, while the rest of the Bellidos I'd seen that morning appeared from the tunnel behind them and followed. The group reached the half-exposed sub and the lifter hovering above it and began connecting them together via the elevator beams. "As long as we have a minute, you want to finish your story?" I suggested. "Starting with what the sub is doing up *here* if you're gunning for the coral down *there*."

"Because we're *not* gunning for the coral down there," Fayr said. "That was the other critical error in Applegate's story." He pointed downward. "This, you see, is not the world where Modhran coral originates."

"That's ridiculous," I said, forgetting for a moment the packet guns behind me. "Every report I've ever seen says it does."

"True, the reports state that it comes from Modhra I," he said, his whiskers stiffening in a tight smile. "But *this* is not Modhra I. The Modhri, in an effort to confuse potential attackers, has switched the names of the two moons."

I stared at him. "You're joking. How do you rename two entire worlds without somebody noticing?"

"Who would notice?" Fayr pointed out reasonably. "Those who do the harvesting, packing, and shipping are all walkers, firmly controlled by the Modhri whispering in their minds. All others simply accept official designations as to which moon of the Modhra Binary is which."

I chewed the inside of my cheek. There *was* a certain weird logic about it, I had to admit. "And you're sure *you've* got it right?"

He pointed to the smoking rubble that had once been a Chafta starfighter. "Their own actions prove it," he said. "Do you think the Modhri would have attacked that way unless he'd suddenly realized we knew the truth, and that the genuine coral fields were under threat?"

"I meant do you have any *other* proof of this name switch?"

His eyes bored into my face. "You are a curious species, Human," he said. "You base many of your actions on strange leaps of illogic and hunch, beyond even those of the Shorshians. Yet in the same moment you demand proofs and evidences far beyond that which others would declare sufficient."

"We're a mass of contradictions, all right," I agreed. "Do you have independent confirmation, or don't you?"

"We have," he said, his voice starting to sound a little strained. Maybe he was regretting saving us from the coral, after all. "The Modhri was clever enough to alter official records and even historical documents. But he neglected to change the early oceanographic data. A careful study of the depth charts clearly shows that the other moon is the one formerly called Modhra I, and the source of the coral."

I nodded as the pieces started to finally fall together. So that was why Fayr had absconded with one of the lodge's submarines and gone to all the trouble of bringing it up through the ice instead of simply purchasing one of his own and flying it here along with his guns and other equipment. He'd been deliberately playing the Modhri's game, pretending he'd bought into the moons' name switch. "So does the whole Modhri know they're—it's—in trouble yet?" I asked. "Or is it only the local group?"

"No, the homeland branch knows," Fayr said, his eyes on the operation going on below us. "There are several walkers here who carry large colonies within them, plus there are many coral outposts in various parts of the resort. This mind segment can easily unite with the homeland branch."

He gave me a sideways look. "Which is probably why you were invited to come here," he added ominously. "An agent of the Spiders is a rarity the Modhri would certainly wish to study. Before he enslaved you."

My stomach tightened. "Instant spy, huh?"

"It's worse than that," he said. "A Modhran colony normally stays in the background, but in need it can push the walker's own personality aside and take complete control of the body."

I thought about the two Halkas back at Kerfsis. "Complete enough to make the walker attempt theft or murder?"

"The wishes or scruples of the walker are completely irrelevant at such a point," he said. "The walker's own personality is suppressed and experiences a total blackout. If the Modhran colony is clever enough, the walker may never even realize anything has happened."

"And that lodge is filled with Modhran walkers?"

He snorted. "The lodge is filled with the rich and powerful of the galaxy," he said. "That makes your question redundant."

I looked toward the lodge, half expecting to see the traditional dit rec horrorific mob coming at us with pitchforks and torches.

But the ice was empty. Anyway, torches wouldn't work in the thin atmosphere. "What kind of reception can we expect at the main base?" I asked.

"The harvesting complex has ten small submarines and fifty divers at its disposal," Fayr said. "They also have perhaps fifty other vehicles, including ten or twelve lifters and other small flyers."

"Not to mention whatever's still at the garrison."

"They have no more than five vehicles left, now that the troop carrier and Chaftas have been disabled," Fayr said. "And with many of the soldiers already here, they may not have the trained personnel to operate them."

"Unless they commandeer the rest of the resort's lifters and take the troops back home," I pointed out, glancing up at the sky. Nothing was coming at us from that direction, either.

"The resort has no more spaceworthy flyers," Fayr assured me. "Their long-range communications have been dealt with, as well."

"That helps," I said. "How about ground-based defenses?"

"The harvesting complex has antiair weapons in place," he said. "Fortunately, we won't land within range of them. We'll open a hole in the ice at a safe distance from the complex, and from there our submarine will travel along the coral beds, using sonic disruptors and small explosives to destroy them."

"How do we retrieve them afterward?"

"We don't," Fayr said. "For those two, this has always been a suicide mission."

I felt my stomach tie itself into an extra-tight knot. I had always hated suicide missions.

Fayr apparently had no trouble reading my face on that one. "I don't like it any better than you do," he said grimly. "But I see no other alternatives."

"Let me work on it," I said.

"Do so." He gestured. "They are ready."

I looked down. The lifter and sub were connected together now, and the Bellidos were hurrying in our direction. "We'll take the others aboard," Fayr said, notching back on the thrusters and lowering us to the surface. "We will then melt the submarine free and be on our way."

I gave one last look at the sky. Still clear. "Sounds a little too easy," I warned.

"Perhaps we have taken the Modhri by surprise," he said.

"Yeah," I said. "Maybe."

Three minutes later, with the commandos aboard and the sub freed, we were on our way.

The torchferry flew in front, with the lifter/sub combo riding our aft starboard flank like a baby whale staying close to mama. No one challenged us as we made our way across the short distance separating the two moons. The harvesting operation was on the far side, Fayr informed me, out of sight of any curious eyes from the resort, and he kept us low to the surface as we headed in that direction. As promised, he stopped us well short of the complex, picking a spot where a past meteor impact had made the ice relatively thin.

Relatively being the operative term, of course. With a limit to how hot we could run the drive without sending the torchferry skittering out into space, it was going to take a while to burn our way through.

We had made it about halfway when our opponents finally made their move.

We spotted them in the distance, sixty flyers and ground vehicles lumbering across the ice en masse like the proverbial lemmings heading for the cliff. At first glance they seemed to all be civilian craft, but our lifter, detached now from the sub and flying high cover, reported a handful of armed military roamers scattered throughout the convoy. Maybe they were hoping we wouldn't notice the ringers in the crowd, or maybe they thought we would hesitate to shoot through civilians to get to them.

If that was their strategy, it didn't work. The civilian craft pressing in close around them limited their own combat capabilities, and the Bellido packet gunners riding the lifter had the necessary marksmanship to single out the military craft and destroy or disable them well before they got within their own firing range.

I hoped at that point the civilians would take the hint and back off. But the Modhri was apparently more interested in stopping us than in conserving troops. The vehicles kept coming, maneuvering around the piles of debris but otherwise seemingly oblivious to the destruction going on around them. The Bellidos responded by first taking out the rest of the flyers, then dropping shatter charges in front of the ground vehicles to try to block their path.

But they kept coming. With a complete slaughter of the civilians as the only other option, Fayr reluctantly broke off our digging project and took the torchferry to a spot well ahead of the lead vehicles. There he used the drive to carve a trench in the ice in hopes of blocking any further advance.

It was a noble move, and it nearly cost us our lives. The Bellido gunners had indeed taken out all the military vehicles, but the Modhri had been crafty enough to hide a pair of Halkan soldiers in one of the civilian transports. I looked up from our work just in time to see them lean out from opposite sides with a pair of missile launchers.

I was also just in time to see their transport blown into shrapnel before they could bring the launchers to bear. Fortunately for our side, the Bellidos in the lifter knew all the tricks, too.

We finished the trench without further incident and headed back. "I wonder what they expected that to accomplish," I commented as we resumed our attack on the ice.

"Obviously not to stop us," Fayr muttered. "It can only have been to delay us while he prepares his submarines for defense of the coral."

"It's going to be ten-to-one odds down there, isn't it?" I agreed soberly. "Not to mention whatever mischief the divers can cause. You *have* planned for that, I hope?"

"No fears," Fayr assured me. I'd never heard that peculiar phrase from a Bellido before, but Fayr had apparently adopted it for his own. "The submarine has been equipped with sensor decoys and other countermeasures. I also expect the ongoing destruction of the coral to have a certain confusing effect on the defending walkers, as well."

"But you don't know for sure."

"No," he conceded. "To the best of my knowledge, an attack on the Modhri has never before been attempted, much less successfully."

"Mm," I murmured, gazing out in the direction of the now-stalled ground vehicles. "So after we drop the sub into the water, you're planning to just leave?"

"Do not misunderstand," Fayr said, his voice tight. "I do not wish to leave anyone behind. But we cannot assume that no messages were sent before we dealt with the resort's transmitter. The Halkan warships at the Tube transfer station could be here in four hours, and it will take the submarine at least two and two-thirds to destroy the coral between here and the harvesting complex. If we wait the extra two-thirds hour for them to make the return trip, we could find ourselves trapped with little margin for error."

"Okay, but what if we go to the harvesting complex and meet the sub there?" I suggested. "That would at least save us that last two-thirds hour."

"And could end matters even more quickly," Fayr countered. "Or had you forgotten the ground-based weapons at the complex?"

"Not at all," I said. "It just seems to me there are a couple of points that may make it worth considering." I gestured out at the horizon. "For one thing, I'm wondering how well those weapons will be manned, given how many of the residents are sitting out there in that convoy."

"Possibly not as fully as usual," Fayr conceded. "Certainly with his flyers destroyed he will have less capability against ground troops." He eyed me curiously. "I find it interesting that you would care so much about two Belldic lives."

"I don't like wasting lives, human or otherwise," I told him. "But I'm also thinking it might also be a good idea to take a good, hard look at the records they have in there."

"What sorts of records?"

"All sorts," I said. "I'm still wondering why the Modhri threw all the workers at us just now like cannon fodder, but didn't do the same with the guests at the resort."

"Those at the resort are the rich and powerful," Fayr reminded me. "Perhaps the Modhri feared the repercussions that would follow such a high number of important deaths."

"Yes, but why?" I persisted. "Isn't this place right here his must-win stand?"

"It is his homeland and the center of his intellect and power," Fayr agreed thoughtfully. "But as I said earlier, he has many outposts across the galaxy, and many, many walkers. Perhaps he still feels he can stop us here without risking his secret."

"How secret can it be?" I pointed out. "*Your* government at least seems to know all about this. Don't they?"

"Do they?" he said bitterly. "Like many others, my government has been enslaved. What is actually known of the Modhri, and what has been carefully suppressed, I cannot say."

"But I thought—" I floundered.

"That we represent an official Belldic mission?" Fayr shook his head. "No. On this point, at least, *Apos* Mahf spoke the truth: My squad and I *are* renegades. We recognized that something was amiss and from various records were able to piece together the truth. But we have no official orders or sanction for what we do."

His whiskers twitched. "In fact, any of us who survive will undoubtedly be brought before a military court upon our return."

I grimaced. But it was not, I reflected, all that different from the reception I was likely to get when I got back to Earth. "I still want some answers," I said. "And the harvesting complex is still the place to get them."

"Perhaps," he said. "You said there were two reasons you thought it would be worth the risk?"

I nodded. "You seemed concerned earlier about the idea of flying into a place guarded by antiair defenses. Right?"

"Correct."

"But assuming you're right about this whole setup being designed by the Modhri for his own benefit, where are those defenses likely to be centered? On the administration center, which holds the records we're looking for? Or on the access to the harvesting areas, where the coral is?"

"Mmm," he murmured. "Interesting."

"Of course, once we're down you'll still have to get to the admin areas on foot," I went on. "You'll also have to neutralize enough of the weaponry around the access areas to get your people out once they've brought in the sub. But as you've already pointed out, the Halkas have lost most or all of their air power, which is usually the trickiest part."

For a long minute Fayr gazed at me, his striped face expressionless. "You humans are without a doubt the most hunch-driven species in the galaxy."

"Probably," I agreed. "But for us, it works."

"It does indeed," he said, his whiskers stiffening in a tight smile. "Very well. Let us do it."

SEVENTEEN :

We finished blasting our hole and lowered the sub in. It took off with a will, diving deep toward the coral beds and the Halkan subs no doubt already arrayed in its path.

But those defenders would be mostly civilians, whether they had some bizarre group mind helping them or not. The attackers were warriors, and I had no doubt that the Bellidos would make it through.

Especially with us throwing in a double helping of chaos at the other end of the rabbit hole. With the lifter again hugging our flank we took off, flew past the mass of ground vehicles still uselessly trying to get to us, and made for the harvesting complex.

My first thought as we approached was that someone must have seriously overestimated the importance of the place as well as the amount of profit coming out of it. All that was visible was a modest trio of single-story buildings set around a docking and under-ice access area.

It wasn't until we were nearly on top of it that I realized the truth. The three buildings were merely the front of the operation, a deliberately deceptive façade designed to throw off inquisitive eyes and minds. The rest of the complex had been built almost invisibly into the ice, probably constructed on the surface with ice then layered over it.

The true access to the coral beds was camouflaged even better. The only way we knew where it was, in fact, was by backtracking the antiair fire that erupted in our direction as we approached.

But my hunch paid off. The defenses were geared toward protecting the coral beds, with the workers' safety running a distant second. As a probably unintended consequence, several of the larger ice-sheathed buildings lay squarely in one line of fire or another, creating a whole set of kill-zone shadows in the outer parts of the complex. Fayr landed us in the most convenient of them, and with weapons at the ready he and the rest of his team headed off into battle.

Bayta and I stayed behind in the torchferry. Our vac suits didn't have the protective armor and heavy-duty puncture-sealant systems their chameleon suits did, and I doubted either of us had the training and stamina to keep up with a commando squad, anyway.

Besides which, it was time she and I had a little talk.

"So," I commented, swiveling around in my seat to face her. We had taken off our helmets so that Fayr and his squad couldn't listen in, keeping them handy in case of trouble. "Interesting theory, isn't it?"

"What is?" she asked cautiously.

"Fayr's fever dream about malevolent coral that wants to rule the universe," I said, watching her closely. "Malevolent telepathic coral, yet. Crazy, huh?"

Her eyes slipped away from my gaze. "Very interesting," she agreed, her voice studiously neutral.

"Never heard anything like it, myself," I continued conversationally. "How about you?"

She didn't answer. "There never was any vision of an attack on the Fillies, was there?" I asked, letting my voice harden. "In fact, this whole thing has been a scam from square one, hasn't it?"

"No," she protested, her eyes coming up to meet mine.

Her lips compressed, and she again dropped her gaze to the floor. "No, there *is* a threat to the galaxy. A terrible threat."

"From power-crazed coral?"

She glared at me. "You shouldn't make jokes about things you don't understand."

"So enlighten me," I countered. "Starting with what exactly my role was in all this."

"What do you mean?" she asked, her voice gone cautious again. "You were hired to help us in the war against the Modhri."

"No, I was hired to be your diversion," I said bluntly. "Your Spider friends knew all about Fayr and his private little battle plan. You wanted to give him the best shot you could; and since you knew the enemy was watching, you brought me in to give them someone handy to watch."

Her lip twitched. "It wasn't like that."

"Wasn't it?" I bit out. "You have a drudge accost me and walk off with my carrybags in front of God and everyone at Terra Station. Then you throw everyone else off my car midway to New Tigris with the flimsiest excuse possible and hustle me off to a meeting on a secret Quadrail siding. And *then* you march both of us up from third-class steerage to a first-class compartment. You might as well have pinned a sign on my back that said *Spider Agent—Kill Me* in three languages."

Her face looked like she was getting ready to cry. "We didn't expect him to try to kill you," she said earnestly. "You have to believe me. We thought he would think you were our latest attempt to find him and just watch you. That's all. Just watch."

"That's very comforting," I growled. "Unfortunately, good intentions don't feed the bulldog. They knew about Fayr, too, or at least suspected something was in the works." I paused, studying the shame and self-reproach in her face and feeling a small twinge of conscience. "And for whatever it's worth, I don't think those two Halkas back at Kerfsis were really trying to kill me," I added reluctantly. "That incident was mainly designed to give Rastra and JhanKla an excuse to get us aboard the Peerage car."

She shivered. "To try and make friends with us, so that they could bring us here."

There it was, that whole friend thing again. "You keep talking about friends," I said. "What do friends have to do with it?"

"There are natural emotional barriers between people that tend to block thought viruses," she said. "Only between friends or trusted associates are there the emotional connections that allow the thought virus to pass."

"Uh-*huh*," I said, a few more pieces falling into place. "Which is why Mahf tried to pretend we'd met before that afternoon in the casino. *And* why you kept asking if Rastra or Applegate were friends of mine."

She nodded. "I didn't know if either of them was a walker. But if they were, I was afraid you'd trust them enough for a thought virus to get through."

"Is that why you picked me for this job in the first place?" I asked. "Because you figured I'd become something of a loner?"

"Partly," she admitted. "Mostly it was because you'd been ostracized by all your former official Terran government contacts. That was the pattern the Modhri followed with all the other species: An officially sanctioned team would go in to investigate, be infected by the Modhri, then go home to infect and conquer the rest of the upper military and government levels. With thought viruses passing freely between close friends and associates, it can happen very quickly."

She gave me a wan smile. "Humans are almost the last ones left unconquered. We didn't want to risk your people by getting someone who was still involved with important government officials."

"And so you picked me," I said, a small part of me appreciating the potentially lethal irony of the situation. If only they knew who I *was* involved with. "Why didn't you tell me all this last night when I asked?"

She looked away from me. "I wasn't sure I could trust you."

"And now?"

She shrugged noncommittally.

Which was pretty damn ungrateful, I thought, especially after all I'd done for her and her Spider friends. A surge of annoyance threatened to wash over me; ruthlessly, I forced it back. A combat situation was no place for stray emotional reactions. "What makes you think humanity hasn't been conquered yet?"

"The Spiders have been watching the top levels of Human government very closely," she said, clearly relieved to be back on less personal ground. "So far, they've seen no sign of Modhran influence."

"Only you said the people themselves don't even know when they're carrying a colony," I pointed out. "You have some kind of Rorschach test?"

"I wish we did," she said ruefully. "But since the colony usually stays in the background of the walker's mind, there usually isn't anything that would show up on psychological tests."

"Or emotional or skin/eye reaction tests, either, I suppose," I said. "That just leaves straight-out physical tests."

"Which also aren't usually very helpful," she said. "The polyps tend to gather in hidden areas, especially around and beneath the brain. It would take a very careful microscopic examination to spot them."

"Is that why JhanKla insisted those two dead Halkas be cremated?"

"Yes, though of course he himself wouldn't have known the true reason," she said. "He would have had his own set of perfectly good excuses. And we've never found a scanning technique that can pick the polyps out from the organism they've attached themselves to."

"So again, what makes you think Earth hasn't been infiltrated?"

"There are patterns of behavior and decision that can be seen, especially on a group level," she explained. "Neither the UN nor any of your nation-state governments have shown signs of such behavior."

"We just too small for the Modhri to bother with?"

"The reasons are probably more practical," she said. "For one thing, you have no coral outposts on your worlds, which by itself would make conquest difficult. There's also your political structure, with its many nation-states and lack of a truly central governing body. That holds challenges they won't have found elsewhere among the Twelve Empires."

I'd never before thought of Earth's political chaos as being a possible military asset. Usually just the opposite, in fact. "What would have happened if I'd touched the coral last night? I'd be a walker now, too?"

"Not yet," she said. "It takes days or weeks for an implanted hook to grow into a polyp and then to reproduce enough to form a complete colony."

"Okay, so back to current events," I said, picking up the logic trail again. "We had Fayr and his commandos on one hand, and us on the other. The Modhri knew about both of us; but he *didn't* know what the connection was. So he maneuvered us here, hoping we would trip over Fayr's scheme and expose it for him." I lifted my eyebrows. "Damn near worked, too, didn't it?"

She grimaced. "I know," she murmured.

"So if this is their homeland, why don't the Spiders just lock them in? They have to travel by Quadrail like everybody else, don't they?"

"Yes, of course," she said. "But all we knew at first was that various leaders were being controlled and governments were being corrupted. It was a long time before we learned the mechanism and, later, where it was coming from."

"But you know now," I said. "So why not just keep the coral off the Quadrails?"

"Because the sensors can't detect it," she said. "I mean, they *can,* but the chemical composition is so close to a hundred other things that it would require hand searches." She shrugged uncomfortably. "Besides, by now the coral's been distributed so widely that locking down Sistarrko system wouldn't gain us anything."

And with that, the final, ugly piece dropped into place.

Modhran outposts all over the galaxy, accessible only via the Spiders' own Quadrail system . . . "You didn't hire me to find out how to stop a war," I said quietly. "You hired me to figure out how to *start* one."

She turned her face away from me. "You have to understand," she said, her voice suddenly very tired. "We'd finally learned where the enemy was located, but we knew the same limitations that keep one empire from attacking another would also keep us from taking any action against them. We suspected Fayr was up to something, but we assumed he was still just investigating. And here especially the Modhri would make sure that the warships guarding the Tube transfer station were exclusively manned by walkers. We needed a way to break the stalemate."

Involuntarily, I glanced back out the canopy. I'd forgotten all about those warships, and the fact that they might be burning space on their way here at this very moment. I hoped Fayr wasn't taking time to smell the flowers. "You could have saved all of us a lot of time if you'd been up front with me in the first place," I told her. "I could have told you that you do exactly what Fayr did: Bring in stuff to sell and then buy or create your weapons there in the target system."

She sighed. "I understand that now," she said. "But the Spiders thought the story of an attack on the Filiaelians would be the only way to get your attention."

"Especially since Fayr's technique wouldn't work on the Fillies," I conceded. "No weapons black market, and too many genetically loyal soldiers wandering around watching everything."

"Yes." Bayta ran a hand through her hair. "But at least now it's almost over."

"Maybe," I said. "Maybe not."

She frowned at me. But before she could ask, there was a ping from my helmet. "Compton?" a voice called faintly.

I picked up the helmet and slipped it over my head. "Here," I said.

"We have the records and are moving to support the half squad at the dock," Fayr reported. "Estimate arrival and retrieval in one and two-thirds hours, return one-third later. Hostiles?"

"No sign," I said, looking out the canopy and giving the displays a quick check. "I think all the unfriendlies must be on your side of the fence."

"Acknowledged," he said. "Be watchful."

"You, too."

He clicked off, and I took my helmet off again. "He says they'll be back in about two hours," I told Bayta. "Then maybe we'll find out whether it's over or not."

They were back exactly two hours and five minutes later. Rather to my surprise, all of them made it, including the two commandos from the sub. They had apparently succeeded in destroying all the coral they could find, while Fayr had located and pulled all the records stored in that part of the complex. He ordered a few quick preparations, and we were ready to go.

Unfortunately, the unwanted company was already coming up the walk.

"There," Fayr said, pointing at the long-range display as we ran up the torchferry's thrusters and eased cautiously away from the now out-of-business harvesting complex. "You see it?"

"It would be hard to miss," I said. In actual fact, of course, most people *would* miss it: A small sensor dot nearly hidden behind the glow of its decelerating ion drive, hardly big enough to identify as an ore tug. But to someone with the right training, the sensor footprint of a stealthed warship was unmistakable. "Coming in fast, too," I added. "I hope you have a plan for getting past him."

"It won't be possible to get past him," Fayr said calmly as we reached a safe distance from the complex's remaining defenses and lifted away from the surface.

"We're sure not going to talk our way out of it," I warned, frowning as he punched in our course. He was turning us toward the edge of Cassp's disk, sitting directly ahead like a huge black hole in space with only its edge lit as the outer atmosphere refracted the light from the distant sun.

The Tube, though, was in exactly the opposite direction. The only thing in that direction was—"*Sistarrko?*"

"Why not?" he replied calmly. "It has a population of over three billion, including at least a hundred thousand resident Bellidos and three thousand Humans. There are also several smaller mining centers, colonies, and homesteads in the inner system. What better place for a small group of fugitives to hide until they can arrange passage back to the Quadrail?"

"Except that all those colonies and homesteads have bright shiny police and military units standing around with nothing to do," I countered. "We'd never even get close before we got cut into bite-sized chunks."

"Unless we have a plan to avoid that," Fayr said, examining the power readings and adding a little more juice to the drive.

"Do we?"

"No." His whiskers twitched. "But the Halkas don't know that, do they?"

I frowned at him . . . and then, finally, I understood. "Cute," I said. "You think they'll fall for it?"

Hunching his shoulders once, he settled himself down into his flying. "We shall find out together."

We pulled away from Modhra I, picking up speed as we drove inward through Cassp's massive gravitational field, still heading for the gas giant's edge. I alternated my attention between our projected course and the aft displays, and less than ten minutes after our departure I saw the warship's drive wink out. "He's turning over," I reported. "Apparently decided we're serious about heading inward and doesn't want to get left behind."

"A reasonable concern," Fayr said. "Even without leaving Cassp there are four ring and far-moon mining operations we could be making for."

I nodded. Torch ships were the fastest civilian spacecraft in the galaxy, but military ships were even faster. But this particular warship had been braking toward an arrival at the

Modhra Binary, while we were now blazing away from the twin moons for all we were worth. If the Halkas back there let us build up too much of a velocity difference, they would have a hard time catching up.

Sure enough, the warship's drive came on again, only now showing behind the sensor dot that represented the hull. "There they go," I informed Fayr. "Flipped"—I checked the sensor reading—"and pulling pretty close to top acceleration."

"Intercept point?"

I checked the computer's projection and made a quick calculation of my own. "About eight hours," I told him. "More importantly, we'll be well within Cassp's outer atmosphere before they're in missile range."

"Excellent." He sent me a sideways look. "I'm told you were fired in disgrace from your empire's service. Apparently it was not for lack of competence."

"The wrong political toes got underfoot," I said. "I'll tell you all about it someday if you're interested."

"I am," Fayr said. "Let us first see if we survive the next few hours."

Thirty minutes later, we entered Cassp's outer atmosphere.

In many ways, it was a good place to be. True, the roiling gases created a certain amount of friction on the hull, which always had the potential to be a problem. It also added drag, which required us to run the drive above its normal operating range in order to maintain our acceleration. But on the plus side it helped diffuse the glow from the drive, which made our position that much harder to pick up on both visual and nonvisual sensors. Fayr continued to move us inward, and the torchferry began to vibrate with turbulence, occasionally picking up more significant bumps and twitches. The glow of our pursuers' drive faded behind us as we put increasingly thick layers of methane and hydrogen between us, until finally it disappeared entirely behind the planet's edge.

And with us temporarily out of each other's sight, Fayr shut down the torchferry's drive and released the lifter that had been riding our hull since leaving Modhra. Activating its preprogrammed course, he sent it blazing off toward Sistar-rko and the inner system.

I watched it fly away with a warm and slightly malicious sense of satisfaction. On paper, of course, it was a ridiculously tissue-thin trick. The lifter's drive was nowhere near as powerful as the torchferry's, and even if our pursuers concluded that we'd deliberately decreased our drive level to confuse them, a single clear view at the sensors would show the craft's true nature.

But they wouldn't be getting that clear look, at least not anytime soon. Unless they could push their acceleration a lot more than they already had, they would be spending the next couple of hours peering at the departing lifter through a haze of Cassp's dit-rec-drama-fog atmosphere. By the time they got clear, they would be pretty well committed to the chase.

And in the meantime, we in the torchferry would do a nice tight slingshot around Cassp and emerge from its atmosphere with a vector two hundred seventy degrees off from the one we'd gone in at, driving outward toward the Quadrail station. And, as an extra added bonus, we would have picked up close to twice Cassp's orbital speed in the process.

All of that assuming, of course, that the Halkas fell for it.

Four hours later, when we finally keyed the drive to full power again and headed off on our new course, we saw that they had.

"They will, of course, try to alert the transfer station as soon as they discover their mistake," Fayr pointed out as we watched the distant blaze of the warship's drive. "We'll have to trust that the Halkas on Modhra won't be able to repair the damage to their long-range transmitters before we reach there."

"There may be a way to avoid the problem entirely," I suggested. "If we head directly to the Tube from here, we can slip around to the far side and run parallel to it until we reach the station. As long as the second warship stays close to the transfer station—and I see no reason why it shouldn't—we ought to be able to sneak in without anyone noticing."

"We will still have to find a way into the station once we arrive," Fayr pointed out doubtfully.

"I don't think that'll be a problem," I said, looking sideways at Bayta. "There are service airlocks all around the station's outer surface that the drudges use to move heavy equipment in and out. I'll bet we can get someone to open one of them for us."

Fayr gave me a strange look. "You *are* joking."

But I'd caught Bayta's microscopic nod and merely smiled back. "Not at all," I assured him.

He eyed me a moment longer, then shrugged. "Very well," he said. "It is insane. But so was the rest of it. We shall try."

We'd never tried Bayta's telepathy trick through a Tube wall, and privately I wondered whether she'd be able to punch a signal through material that blocked sensors and comm systems as efficiently as this stuff did. But in the end, it all went as smoothly as a frictionless airfoil. We eased along the Tube to a halt at the back side of the station, apparently unobserved by anyone at the transfer station a hundred kilometers away on the other side.

There had been some discussion about whether we should try to dock with one of the service hatchways. But the torchferry was just too big for that kind of delicate work, and so we simply parked it a few hundred meters away, and with luggage in hand we space-walked across the gap. Even before Fayr, bringing up the rear, had made it all the way to the Tube, the hatchway began to iris open in response to Bayta's silent request.

Unlike the usual shuttle hatchways, this one was equipped with an actual airlock and was large enough for our whole group. We piled in and waited with varying degrees of patience and trepidation while it ran through its cycle. When the inner door finally opened, we found ourselves in a maintenance area half a kilometer from the more central, public areas of the station.

We also found ourselves surrounded by a solid wall of drudge Spiders.

They collected our luggage, making a special point of relieving the Bellidos of their status guns, then escorted us into a large machine shop nearby. Inside, a half dozen small Spiders of a type I hadn't seen before took over, sifting deftly through our luggage and pulling out small weapons and other forbidden equipment that the station's sensors had spotted. As they loaded the contraband into lockboxes, a pair of conductors appeared and started taking ticket orders.

Bayta and I used our passes to get our usual double first-class compartment. Fayr got a single compartment for himself, while the rest of his team took second- and third-class accommodations. The plastic imitation status guns came out of the carrybags and were sorted out into the commandos' empty shoulder holsters, the sizes and numbers matching their appropriate travel classes. Fayr, as befit a first-class traveler, loaded four of the toy pistols into his holsters.

And with our informal entry procedure complete, we collected our luggage and followed one of the conductors back outside the shop.

There were a couple hundred people waiting on the various platforms, most of them Halkas, all of them gazing in obvious fascination as the Spider guided us across the maze of service tracks to the public areas. I heard Fayr muttering under his breath about stealth and secrecy, but there wasn't much any of us could do about it. The conductor led us to our platform, bade us a pleasant journey, then headed off to whatever routine we had so rudely interrupted. The rest of the passengers, clearly intrigued by all this, nevertheless were either polite enough or wary enough to give us plenty of room.

Not surprisingly, the Spiders had booked us on the very next Quadrail headed down the Grakla Spur toward Jurskala. With a number of well-dressed Halkas in evidence, at least some of whom probably included Modhran walker colonies, I figured that news of our arrival had most likely made it across to the transfer station by now. I kept one eye on the nearest shuttle hatchways, half expecting Halkan official-dom to make one last-ditch effort to grab us.

But no one had appeared by the time our Quadrail arrived. We let the departing passengers off, then climbed aboard and made our ways to our various accommodations. Fifteen minutes later, while I continued to watch the hatchways through my compartment window, the Quadrail pulled smoothly and anticlimactically out of the station.

For the moment, at least, we were safe.

EIGHTEEN :

It was another four days back along the Grakla Spur to Jurskala, and for every minute of each of those days I fully expected the Modhri—or whatever was left of him—to make his move.

But the Quadrail made its stops, picked up and dropped off its passengers and moved on, and nothing happened. It was as if with the destruction of the homeland branch the other outposts and walkers had gone completely dormant.

Fayr didn't believe it for a minute. "He's planning something," he declared two days into the trip as we pulled out of one of the Cimman stations on our way back toward Jurian space. "He surely won't allow such an attack to succeed without at least an attempt at retribution."

In principle, I agreed. Still, whatever desires for vengeance the Modhran remnant might be feeling, the fact was that we'd gotten out of the Sistarrko system about as fast as anyone could, and he was now up against the purely practical problem of coming up with a plan on the fly.

Of course, it wasn't something he had to rush on. Even if Bayta was right about him not yet having infiltrated Earth and the Confederation, that still left damn few places where the walkers couldn't get to us whenever they wanted to.

Still, while we continued to keep an eye over our shoulders, the four days ended up being completely uneventful. What the rest of the Bellidos back in second and third class did to fill the hours I never found out, but the three of us in first spent much of it listening to each other's stories.

For Fayr, it had started several years earlier when the Belldic intelligence service had discovered secret dealings going on between the Spiders and the Tra'ho'sej. The Bellidos had investigated, eventually digging up a trail leading to the Modhra Binary and the discovery of some kind of influence emanating from it. The Tra'ho'sej themselves had been in the middle of setting up some kind of military operation when they suddenly and inexplicably abandoned it.

The Bellidos, now more than merely curious, had tried to pick up the operation. But instead of simply following their own leads, the heads of the investigation had made the fatal mistake of contacting their counterparts in the Tra'ho intelligence community in hopes of getting inside information. Naturally, they'd gone to the Tra'ho'sej with whom they had the closest professional and personal relationships, and Modhran thought-viruses had done the rest. In rapid succession the upper levels of Belldic intelligence had fallen to the silent invasion, followed by the military leaders who controlled them, followed by the political leaders to whom they all reported. For the Modhri, it was just one more conquest, one more potential threat that had been eliminated.

Or so he thought. What he hadn't realized was that the Belldic intelligence service was a strongly compartmentalized organization, consisting of many independent groups that had for centuries maintained their own identities for historical reasons that were only vaguely remembered. Fayr had been in one of those groups, and as he and some of the others had noticed odd behavior and decisions from their superiors they had started a fact-finding mission of their own.

They'd also attempted to contact the Spiders. The Spiders hadn't been very enthusiastic, apparently still smarting over their failure with the Tra'ho'sej. Still, they had given the group some logistical support, including the encryption system I'd seen Fayr use with his pulse laser communications aboard the Quadrail. The Bellidos had moved with careful deliberation, bringing spices and gourmet foods and high-end electronics to Sistarrko over a period of two years as they studied the situation, building up their network of trading partners and black market contacts in the system for the time when they would be ready to make their move. They'd also sent members of the team to the Modhran resort, who mingled with the rich and powerful and scouted out the battle zone.

Fortunately for them, many of the resort's patrons were of the newly rich and powerful whom the Modhri hadn't yet had a chance to infect, which meant the uninfected Bellidos didn't completely stand out of the crowd. By the time Fayr launched Phase Two, the theft of the resort maintenance sub, the infiltrators had become so much a part of the general background that the Modhri apparently couldn't even figure out which species had been responsible.

As for me, I'd caught Fayr's attention on the very first leg of my Quadrail journey. He had taken a seat in the hybrid passenger/baggage car so that he could keep an eye on their final shipment of antique jewelry, and his suspicions had been aroused when the Spiders unceremoniously promoted everyone except me up to the next car. When he'd subsequently seen Bayta slip back there, then discovered the door to the car had been locked, his suspicions had turned to near-certainty. By the time we reached New Tigris and he saw us head straight up to first class, he had concluded that the Modhri had ferreted out his plot. When Bayta and I had disembarked at Kerfsis, he'd taken four of the group and followed, sending the rest of the team on ahead with the jewelry to make the final arrangements on Sistarrko. When we'd returned to the Quadrail in the company of a high Jurian official, he'd made sure to place his three commandos in the rear coach where they could alert him if I made any movement out of the Peerage car.

His theory had then done a screeching bootlegger reverse when he'd spotted the conductor slipping me that data chip in the first-class bar. That had quieted his fears that I was a Modhran walker, but now he was faced with the possibility that the Spiders were launching an operation of their own that could easily blunder into his plan and wreck them both. Rather than take that risk, he had me waylaid on my way back to the Peerage car and stuffed in the spice crate where I would hopefully be out of the way long enough for his team to finish their job.

It hadn't worked, though, and from that point on we'd been rather informal and slightly problematic allies, right up to the moment when he'd eavesdropped on the conference room conversation via the remora transceiver still in my pocket and decided I was worth the risk of rescuing.

We also spent a lot of time going over the data chips his people had taken from the harvesting complex. There were three of them, all of a slightly non-standard size which only Bayta's reader could accept. They were also copy-proofed, which meant we had to either take turns sifting through the numbers or else stare at them over each other's shoulders.

None of the staring did us much good. The Halkas had been shipping out Modhran coral for nearly a hundred fifty years, though these particular records only went back the last ten of those. Even so, that turned out to be a *lot* of coral. Fayr, we now learned, had agreed to the data raid in the first place because he'd hoped there might be a way to identify the Belldic outpost and walker colonies. But there turned out to be so many transfers and middleman operations that we couldn't even be sure where all the coral had gone, let alone who might have come in contact with it.

My reasons for wanting the data I kept to myself. There was no point in worrying the others until I was sure.

And so matters stood when we reached Jurskala. Again, I expected some sort of reception to be waiting. Again, the Modhri was apparently still a couple of steps behind us. If that held until we made it aboard our next Quadrail, maybe I could relax a little.

It was as we went to check the schedule that the secret I'd

been carrying since the New Pallas Towers finally caught up with me.

"No," Fayr said firmly, gesturing at the floating holodisplay. "Agreed, the Bellis Loop will take several extra days to bring you to your people. But it will depart from here in less than an hour, three hours earlier than the direct Quadrail to your own empire. Equally important, it will also permit us to stay together until we are clear of Jurian territory."

"Only to take us straight through the Estates-General," I pointed out, hoping he'd get the inference. There were several other beings crowding around the three of us, also checking the listings, and I didn't want to make any overt references to the Modhri. "I'm not sure what this gains us."

"The Juriani have had the problem for nearly a hundred years," Bayta murmured from beside me. "The Bellidos have had it for less than ten."

"I suppose," I said, studying the schedule. Actually, the most important difference as far as I was concerned was the fact that the Bellis Loop Quadrail stopped at fewer Jurian stations along the way than the next train to the Confederation. The fewer the stops, the fewer the opportunities for any Modhran walkers to put something together against us.

From my other side came a tentative plucking at my sleeve. I turned, tensing, but it was only a slightly hunched-over middle-aged Human with white-flecked brown hair tied back in a short ponytail, muttonchop whiskers, and a rather bewildered expression as he blinked at the schedule. "Excuse me, sir," he said in a quavering voice. "I can't seem to locate my train. Could you possibly help me?"

"I can try," I said. "Where are you going?"

"I can't pronounce it," he confessed, pressing a folded and dog-eared piece of paper into my hand. "Here's the name."

I opened the paper. But there wasn't any station name written there, pronounceable or otherwise.

Tlexiss Café. Now. Mc.

I took a second, longer look at the man . . . and only then

did I see past the whiskers and the slightly disheveled hair and the overall air of harmless helplessness.

It was Bruce McMicking, bodyguard and general trouble-shooter for multitrillionaire industrialist Larry Cecil Hardin.

My boss.

"It's right there," I said between suddenly dry lips as I pointed to a random line on the schedule. McMicking here . . . and Bayta standing right beside me. This was not good. "Track Five in thirty-five minutes."

"Thank you, sir," he said. Plucking the paper out of my hand, he turned and made his uncertain way out through the other bystanders.

Fayr and Bayta were still waiting for my decision. "Fine, we'll do the Loop," I told them. "You two go make the reservations. I need to check on something—I'll meet you at the platform in twenty minutes. Hang on to my carrybags, will you?"

I headed away before either of them could object, passing two of Fayr's commandos on my way out of the crowd. One of them gave me a questioning gesture; I motioned for him to stay with Fayr and Bayta. If McMicking was here, there was a chance Hardin was, too, and I didn't want even the Bellidos to see us together.

McMicking was about fifty meters ahead of me, walking with a sort of shuffling step that fit the rest of the persona he'd adopted for the occasion. I followed, keeping my distance, marveling again at the chameleonlike abilities of the man. I'd seen him in person three times now, and never did he look exactly the same twice. He changed his hair and beard like other people switched socks; whether he saw that as part of his job or whether it was some strange psychological quirk I didn't know.

The Tlexiss Café was one of the half dozen restaurants serving the Jurskala Station. Unlike the others, it boasted an open-air section dressed up with trellises and arbors like something you'd find in a EuroUnion countryside. McMicking led the way between a pair of potted bushes, pausing just inside to wait for me to catch up.

"Compton," he greeted me as I came up to him. The quavering uncertainty was gone from his voice and his manner as if they'd never been there. "Mr. Hardin would like a word with you."

"Of course," I said, trying to sound calm. So Hardin *was* here. Bracing myself, I stepped between the bushes and into the café.

It wasn't a normal mealtime by the station's clock, but eight of the twenty tables were nevertheless occupied by a variety of beings sipping or eating various drinks and foodstuffs. Seated at the far end beneath an arching latticework arbor laced with delicate purple vines and brilliant red and purple flowers was Larry Cecil Hardin.

Even by Earth's perpetually starstruck standards, Hardin stood head and shoulders above the crowd. He'd started life as an inventor of high-end precision optics and optical switches, had taken up a business role in order to market his creations, and had managed to hit a couple of economic waves that had made him a more or less overnight billionaire. Never one for laurel-resting, he'd kept at it, and after another few business cycles and a few more small but timely inventions he hit the one trillion mark. After that, there'd been nowhere to go but up.

No one actually knew how rich he was, except possibly Hardin himself, and he wasn't talking. But that didn't stop the media from speculating on it. And Hardin played the game right back at them, inviting them in to see his planes and cars and antique motorcycles while at the same time playing it all very coy and modest.

The irony of it, at least for me, was that there were at least eight men and women in the Confederation who were richer than he was. But he was the one the media had latched onto, so he was the one everyone knew. A place like Jurskala Station, where humans were barely even noticed, let alone lionized, was probably an interesting change of pace for him.

Hardin was the sort who liked to get in the first word. Perversely, I decided to beat him to it. "Mr. Hardin," I said, nodding as I sat down uninvited across the table from him. "This is a pleasant surprise. How did you find me?"

Behind me, McMicking made a soft noise in the back of his throat. But Hardin didn't even twitch. "There's only one exit from the Grakla Spur," he said calmly. "Once I knew you'd been there, it was a simple matter of having my people check all inbound Quadrails until you showed up."

"Of course," I said. "I hope you didn't come all this way just for me."

"I had other business to attend to," he said, his eyes and voice cooling a few degrees. "Tell me, did you think I wouldn't notice if you slipped off to a high-class resort for a few days?"

So he'd taken time out of his busy schedule to keep up-to-date track of the credit tag he'd given me. I'd been afraid of that. "That was business," I said.

"*My* business?"

"Of course," I said striving for snow-pure innocence. "What other business could I be on?"

"I don't know," he countered. "Maybe something having to do with that dead man at the curb the night you left?"

I looked up at McMicking, a piece clicking into place. "So that was *you* standing over the body as I was leaving," I said.

He inclined his head in an affirmative. "You should have told me about that in advance," he said. "It could have been handled much more quietly."

"I didn't *know* in advance," I said, looking back at Hardin. "What, you think *I* killed him?"

"You tell me," he invited. "All I know is that there seem to be an extraordinary number of dead bodies in your wake. First the kid in New York, then those two Halkas at the Kerfsis transfer station—"

"Those weren't my fault, either," I interrupted.

"Of course not," he said. "And now I'm hearing reports of some sort of disturbance at that resort you were just at?"

I hesitated, wishing I knew exactly what those reports had said. Had they mentioned a pair of Humans, or just Fayr and his Bellidos? "That wasn't really my fault, either," I hedged.

"Of course not," Hardin said. "You know, Compton, when I hired you I thought it was understood that you were to keep a low profile. Is this what you consider a low profile?"

I spread my hands, palms upward. "I know, and I'm sorry," I apologized. "Sometimes things happen that are out of anyone's control."

Hardin exhaled heavily. "I'd like to believe that, Frank," he said. "But the damage has already been done." He held out his hand. "I'll take that credit tag now, and all the equipment I gave you. I trust you can find your own way home?"

I stared at him. "You're joking," I said. "You came all the way out here just to *fire* me?"

"As I said, I have other business out this way," Hardin said, his hand still outstretched. "Finding you was just an extra bonus. My credit tag?"

"I *am* making progress," I insisted. Oddly enough, it was even true.

"I'm sure you are," he said. "But I'm starting to wonder whether it is, in fact, the progress I hired you to make. You see, even while you're running up bills at fancy resorts, I've noticed you're *not* using my credit tag to pay for your Quadrail travel."

I suppressed a grimace. I should have known he'd spot that, too. "I'd have thought you'd be pleased that I'd found a way to save you a little money."

"What pleases me is to have someone who's supposed to be in my pocket actually stay there," he said. "When a person starts climbing out on his own, he gets assisted the rest of the way. My credit tag and equipment?"

I grimaced. But there was nothing for it. "Fine," I said, fishing the credit tag out of my pocket. Ignoring his outstretched hand, I dropped it on the table between us, then added my watch, reader, and gimmicked data chips to the pile.

"Thank you," he said, pulling everything to his side of the table. "Good day, Mr. Compton."

For a long moment I considered pressing my case. I still needed all those items, especially the credit tag. And though

Hardin had no way of knowing it, I could guarantee he would never, *ever* find another investigator with my current qualifications.

But I knew it would be just so much wasted breath. And in the meantime, I had more important things to worry about than my professional pride. Standing up, I turned my back on him and headed back across the café, trying not to think about the long and expensive torchliner trip from Terra Station to Earth that I no longer had the funds to pay for. Maybe I'd wind up going to the Bellidosh Estates-General with Fayr, after all.

I was nearly to the café exit when I discovered McMicking was still at my side. "What do you want?" I growled.

"Just escorting you back to your platform," he said mildly. "Why? Don't you like my company?"

I didn't, but since he already knew that there wasn't much point in saying so. "He's making a mistake, you know," I said instead, trying one last time.

"That's possible," he agreed. "Happens to all of us. Speaking of mistakes, you haven't been kicking dust at the Halkan Peerage lately, have you?"

I looked sideways at him. "Why do you say that?"

"No reason," he said. "I've just been noticing there are a lot of Halkas out here in those three-colored robes the Peerage always wears."

"Really," I said, my throat tightening. I'd been assuming that if the Modhri wanted to make a move, he would use the local Juriani to do it. It had never occurred to me that he might nudge a group of Halkas into coming down to Jurskala for the occasion. "Maybe it's a convention."

"Or not," he said, and I could feel his eyes on me. People like McMicking had a keen sense of atmosphere, and he was clearly picking up my sudden tension. "I count at least five different color combinations, with five to ten Halkas in each group. This have anything to do with that resort incident Mr. Hardin mentioned?"

"Could be," I conceded, craning my neck over the crowd.

I could see Bayta and Fayr ahead at our platform now, both of them looking around for me.

And McMicking was right. There were a *lot* of Halkan Peers here. "Thanks for the heads-up," I told him. "I can make it the rest of the way on my own."

"It's no problem," he assured me.

"It is for me," I countered tartly. "I don't want my friends to see us together."

"Ah," he said with a knowing smile. "Of course not."

"And if you're smart," I added, "you'll get Mr. Hardin out of sight and onto the next train back to Earth."

The smile faded. "Just what kind of trouble *are* you in?" he asked quietly.

"Nothing that concerns you anymore," I said. "Now get out of here. I mean it."

He held my eyes a half second longer. Then, with a curt nod, he turned and melted back into the crowd. Trying to watch all directions at once, I made my way to the platform.

"There you are," Bayta said, her tone halfway between relieved and accusing as I came up beside them. "Where have you *been*?"

"Scouting the territory," I said. "We've got a problem. The entire Halkan Peerage seems to have come by to see us off."

Fayr's eyes flicked over my shoulder, and I saw his whiskers stiffen. "Any ideas?" he murmured.

"I suggest we take the next Quadrail as planned," I said. "They can't all get tickets before it arrives.

"Perhaps," he said slowly. "It will be as safe as we're likely to get."

His eyes met mine, flicked to Bayta and then back to me. "Agreed," I said, giving him a microscopic nod in return. Two warriors, taught from the same handbook, understanding each other. "Let's do it."

NINETEEN :

Three minutes later, the Quadrail pulled into the station and began discharging its passengers. Two minutes after they were off, Bayta and I were in my compartment.

"Don't get comfortable," I warned her as I dropped my carrybags on the bed and crossed to the window. We were on the side the train was loading from, and I felt my stomach tightening as I spotted all the tricolored robes climbing aboard.

And not just in first class, either. A number of them were getting on in second and third class, too, as far back as I could see. Places where a Halkan Peer usually wouldn't be caught dead.

There was a multiple tap on the door, the distinctive rhythm I'd set up earlier with Fayr. Bayta opened the door and he slipped inside, locking it behind him. "It doesn't look good," he warned.

"No kidding," I said. "You told us earlier that Modhran colonies can take over their hosts' bodies if they want to. Any idea how long they can hold them that way?"

"None," he said. "As far as I know, it could be indefinitely."

"But the longer the host is under control, the more likely he is to realize afterward that something strange has happened," Bayta added. "The Modhri might be able to pass off a few seconds' blackout as daydreaming, but he'd have a harder time covering up one that lasts longer than that."

"In that case, there must be a lot of pretzel-twist rationalization going on out there," I said. "They're piling in all the way back to third."

"Planning on having his revenge during the trip," Fayr rumbled. He fingered his plastic status guns, undoubtedly wishing he had the real ones instead. "He therefore arranges his walkers so that there will be no safe haven for us anywhere aboard."

I looked out again at the crowd. A lot of the Peers had gotten on our train; but there were a lot more still hanging around on the nearby platforms. "No," I said. "This is way too elaborate for simple revenge."

"Then what *is* it about?" Fayr asked.

"I have an idea," I said. "But I may be wrong, and we sure as hell don't have time to discuss it now. Grab your bag, Bayta—we're getting off."

"We're *what*?" Bayta demanded, her eyes widening.

"We're splitting up," I explained, thinking hard. Unfortunately, with that many walkers still wandering the station, following my plan of hopping off the train as it pulled out wasn't going to gain us anything.

We were going to have to play it a little trickier.

"My team will remain aboard and deal with the walkers here, while the three of us switch to a different train," Fayr told her. "A classic deception—"

"Which isn't going to work," I cut him off. "Bayta, can you get the door open while we're moving?"

Her eyes widened still further. "The door to the *outside*?"

"We're going to jump?" Fayr demanded, sounding as surprised as she did.

"Yes, and yes, and we haven't got a choice," I told them, touching the control to opaque the window. "If we just go back out onto the platform, the rest of the walkers will be right on top of us. Can you open the door, or can't you?"

"No," Bayta said, still clearly struggling to catch up with me. "But a Spider might be able—"

"Get one to the car door right away," I ordered, scooping up my carrybags. "And it's not the three of us, *Korak* Fayr, just Bayta and me. Considering the number of walkers aboard, your team's going to need you here."

He gazed at me, and I braced myself for his protest. But to my relief, he merely nodded. The fewer people involved in this kind of stunt, the better the chances it would work, and we both knew it.

From beneath us came the multiple thud of brakes releasing, and the Quadrail started to move. "Very well," Fayr said, lifting his arms with the wrists crossed in a Belldic military salute. The flourish ended with his hands on his upper set of guns; and suddenly he drew them, flipping them around so that their grips faced me. "Here," he said. "You may need these."

There wasn't time to ask what on Earth I might want with a set of plastic toy guns. I stuffed them inside my jacket, nodded a quick good-bye, and made for the corridor.

I wondered if I would ever see him again.

There was a conductor waiting when we arrived at the outer door. The Quadrail was already going too fast for comfort, but it was still picking up speed and any delay would only make it worse. "Bayta?" I called.

She didn't reply; but a second later the corridor suddenly filled with a swirling slipstream of air as the door reluctantly irised open. I tossed out my carrybags, grabbed Bayta's, and threw it after them. Then, wondering whether this was the stupidest thing I'd ever done in my life or merely one of the top ten, I grabbed her wrist and jumped.

We hit hard, the next few seconds becoming a swirl of confusion and dizziness and agony as we tumbled and rolled along the station floor. Eventually we came to a halt with me on my back and Bayta lying half on top of me. "You all right?" I asked, doing a quick inventory of my own bones and joints. My knees were aching fiercely, as was my left shin and elbow, and every bit of exposed flesh felt like I'd caught a bad sunburn. But nothing seemed sprained or broken.

"I think so," she murmured back. With a muffled groan, she started to get to her feet.

"No—stay down," I said, grabbing her forearm and pulling her back down. Beside us, the Quadrail was still roaring along, still picking up speed. The last baggage car shot past, and I watched as the train angled up the slope and disappeared into the darkness of the Tube. The usual light show from the Coreline faded away, and only then did I cautiously raise my head a few centimeters to assess our situation.

If I'd planned this whole thing deliberately, I couldn't have done a better job of it. We were in one of the service areas of the station, similar to the one we'd back-doored our way into at the Sistarrko Station after our mad-dash escape from Modhra 1. Two sets of tracks away, a large service hangar sat conveniently just opposite us. Barely three meters past the spot where we'd ended our tumble was a crisscrossing of tracks that would probably have left us with multiple broken bones if we'd landed there instead of where we actually had.

Most important of all, the passenger platforms and all those brooding walkers were a good kilometer and a half away.

"What now?" Bayta asked.

Abruptly, I realized I was still holding her pressed beside me. "We need to get aboard another train and get out of here," I said, letting go of her arm. "Any chance of talking the Spiders into rigging a private train and bringing it out here to pick us up?"

"I don't think so," she said. "There's a certain amount of momentum needed to get up the slope and through the atmosphere barrier. It usually requires the entire distance from the platform for a train to make it."

"Even if the train consists of just an engine and a single car?"

"Even then." She hesitated. "And even if we could, I'm not sure it would do any good. The walkers would surely see the train stop, figure out what had happened, and send warning messages ahead. We'd just have to face the same trouble at the next station. Unless," she added thoughtfully, "we don't *stop* at any other stations."

"No, that wouldn't help," I said, shaking my head. "We still have to go through those stations, even if we don't stop there. The walkers would message ahead and have their buddies either destroy the rails or throw debris onto the tracks. Maybe even throw themselves."

"That can't be," she insisted. "Surely he wouldn't waste all those walkers just for revenge." She gazed down the tracks toward the platform, at all those Halkan Peers still milling around. "Unless this isn't about revenge."

I sighed. "It was staring us in the face as far back as when we were melting the sub free," I told her. "That was where the Modhri should have thrown everything he had to try and keep us from getting off Modhra II and within range of his homeland coral beds on Modhra I. But he didn't."

"Yes, you mentioned that at the time," Bayta said, her voice dark.

"And then afterward, after we got away, we were locked into a Quadrail train for four days," I went on. "If it was vengeance he was after, why didn't the walkers get together to hit us then?"

"Not enough time to organize?"

"That was what I thought, too," I said. "Right up until we got to Jurskala and saw the number of walkers he'd gathered here."

I waved a hand toward the distant platform. "The fact of the matter, Bayta, is that he didn't particularly care whether we destroyed the Modhra coral beds or not. Not until someone got into the harvesting complex and realized we'd taken their records." I took a deep breath. "Their *export* records."

She stared at me, her eyes suddenly gone dead. "Oh, no," she breathed.

I nodded. "He was already gone from Modhra when we hit it, Bayta. Not all of him, certainly, and I'm sure Fayr's people hurt him terribly when they wiped out the coral that was left there. But he's moved enough of it to establish himself a brand-new homeland.

"Only this time we don't know where it is."

* * *

It seemed like a long time that we lay there, each of us wrapped in our own thoughts. "What *about* the records?" Bayta asked at last. "He must think we can locate the new homeland that way or he wouldn't be trying so hard to stop us."

"Possible, but I doubt it," I said. "Fayr couldn't even track the stuff bound for the Estates-General, and the homeland data will be scrambled a lot more. My guess is that he simply doesn't want to take the chance."

"We can still try," she said, a spark of renewed spirit sifting in through the despair in her voice. "And the first thing we have to do is get out of here."

"Absolutely," I agreed, an idea starting to work its way through my still-throbbing skull. "You think you can get the Spiders to bring a few items to that hangar over there?"

"If they can get hold of them, yes," she said. "You have a plan?"

"Maybe," I said. "Think back to *The Lady Vanishes,* that Hitchcock dit rec drama we watched with Rastra and JhanKla. Remember how they smuggled that other woman aboard the train?"

"They had her wrapped up as if she'd been in an accident," Bayta said slowly. "But there isn't supposed to be anyone except Spiders at this end of the station. If the Modhri sees someone coming from here, won't he suspect something?"

"Right, which is why we won't be coming from here." I nodded toward the hangar. "First thing to do is crawl over to that hangar and get out of sight. Once we're inside, whistle up a couple of drudges to retrieve our bags. After that, here's what we're going to need. . . ."

The trick, as always, would be in the timing.

There was every chance that the Modhran mind segment on the Bellis Loop train would quickly figure out that Bayta and I were no longer aboard, and probably be rather miffed about it. But by that time he would be well out of communication range of the Modhran mind segment still here in Jurskala Station. He would have to wait until the next stop, four hours away, before he could send a message back this direction.

At the moment, the rest of the walkers here were probably preparing to head home, believing whatever rationalizations they'd come up with to explain why they'd come here in the first place. Once the other mind segment alerted them, though, the hunt would be on again.

But an hour before that message could get here there would be a Quadrail leaving on a direct shot to Earth. If we could get aboard that train without anyone fingering us, we could be gone while the Modhran segment here was still trying to figure out where on Jurskala Station we might be hiding.

At first blush, that looked like a pretty serious *if*. We had limited time, limited resources, and the limited changes of clothing in our carrybags, plus whatever the Spiders could scrounge for us. And it was probable that any human male/female combination would automatically come under at least casual scrutiny.

But just as Halkas were difficult for humans to distinguish between, the reverse was also true. That would make the job much easier than if we were trying to slip past a group of other Humans.

As to the Modhran parasites inside them, I still remembered *Falc* Rastra's own colony taking control of him long enough to shout *don't shoot it* to the Jurian soldiers in the Kerfsis interrogation room. Referring to me as *it* rather than *him* implied that the Modhri didn't see us as much more than organic autocabs. A minimal bit of deception on our part ought to be adequate, provided we didn't call attention to ourselves by strolling in from the Spider end of the station.

Fortunately, we wouldn't have to.

The maintenance skiff they brought for us was small and cramped, designed mainly for transporting repair materials while drudges hung onto the outside. It normally wasn't pressurized, but the Spiders had plenty of oxygen cylinders lying around to replenish the slow leakage through the atmosphere barriers at the ends of the stations. We had loaded a couple of them into the skiff with us, just in case, and the soft hissing added to the basic eeriness of the situation as the Spiders maneuvered us around the station. I'd specified that we use the hatchway closest to our departure platform; and with exactly fifteen minutes remaining until our Quadrail arrived, the skiff locked itself against the outside of the station.

I looked at Bayta, wrapped in a sterilizer gown and strapped to a self-powered medical stretcher. Her face was completely covered in white bandages, a false beak pressing up against them from the center of her face above the breather mask connected to the stretcher's own medical oxygen tank. More makeshift prosthetics under the swathing disguised the shape of her forehead and chin, while others padded out her shoulders and created three-toed claws at her feet. "Ready?" I asked.

Her answer was a soft grunt around the oxygen mouthpiece, and I felt a pang of sympathetic edginess. To have to pass through a group of enemies was bad enough; to have to do so totally blind and strapped to a rolling table had to be a hundred times worse.

But we had no choice. The Modhri would be looking for a pair of humans, and only with her face and body completely covered could we transform her from a woman into a badly injured Juri.

I ran a hand carefully over my hair, darkened and slicked back with a few drops of motor oil, and smoothed out the slightly scraggly mustache I'd thrown together out of tack sealant and some bits of Bayta's hair. That, plus the protective smock we'd taken from one of the emergency medical kits, would have to do for me. "Okay," I said. "Here we go."

I touched the hatch release. It slid open, the station's hatch did likewise behind it, and I looked up to find a pair of drudges looming over us. "Quickly, now," I said in my best dit rec medical professional's weighty yet compassionate voice, standing upright and gesturing down into the skiff. Behind the Spiders, a small crowd had gathered, clearly curious as to what the two drudges were up to. "But carefully," I added, stepping up out of their way. "Don't jostle him."

They reached in a pair of legs each and carefully retrieved the stretcher. I helped guide it up, some of my tension easing as the hatch closed beneath it. Any of the gawking bystanders who got a good look in there would have instantly spotted that it wasn't a normal medical shuttle. But the drudges' long legs had kept the crowd back far enough and long enough, and now that particular danger was past.

I touched the control at the stretcher's side, unfolding its wheeled legs. "Thank you," I said to the Spiders as they set it down onto the station floor. "I can take it from here." Pulling the leash control from its clip, I started toward our platform, the stretcher rolling beside me.

The crowd, still staring in fascination at the spectacle, parted in front of us like the Red Sea in front of Moses. Out of the corner of my eye I spotted a couple of Peerage robes wandering in our direction, and forced myself not to speed up.

"What happened?" a short Juri on the sidelines asked, stepping close to the stretcher and gazing down his beak at Bayta, as if trying to glean through the bandages whether it was someone he knew.

"Acid accident," I said, waving him back. "Please—keep your distance. He's had terrible burns and his immune system is very weak."

"Shouldn't you take him to the transfer station?" someone in the crowd suggested. "It has the nearest hospital."

"We've just come from the station," I said. "This is a job for specialists."

"Surely there are specialists on Jurskala?" someone else chimed in.

"Please," I said between clenched teeth. Why couldn't these people gawk in silence like every other accident crowd? "Just make room—"

"Thank God you made it," a relieved voice cut me off, and a business-suited man stepped boldly to the other side of the stretcher.

I opened my mouth to tell him to back off— "I got your message, and I've been in contact with the office," he went on before I could speak. "They're collecting the specialists—

should be ready by the time we arrive. And they repeat that absolutely no expense should be spared."

I stared at him, a nondescript man with midlength hair and clean-shaven face . . . and then, abruptly, I got it. This was not some random raving lunatic, or even a bizarre case of mistaken identity.

The man facing me across the stretcher was Mr. Chameleon himself, Bruce McMicking.

My sudden confusion wrapped around my tongue, striking me momentarily speechless. Not that it mattered. McMicking's own spiel was already in full gear. "How bad is it?" he asked as we wheeled our way onto the platform. "They told me it was mostly hydrochloric, but that there were some other chemicals involved."

"Yes, there were," I said, finding my voice at last. Down at the far end of the station, I could see the laser light show of the approaching Quadrail. "That's what did the most serious damage. Once the skin was broken and the parichloric and fluoro-di-monistak got in—well, you understand."

"Yes, of course." McMicking hissed under his breath. "Parichloric. What a terrible, terrible thing."

The Quadrail roared down the track and came to a halt in front of us. McMicking and I kept up the pseudomedical jargon until the flow of departing passengers finally ended. Then, as the crowd continued to keep a respectful distance, we rolled the stretcher through the door and into the first-class compartment car. Two conductors were waiting at our door, and with their help we got the stretcher inside.

I stood over Bayta's swathed form, making soothing noises for the benefit of any passengers passing through the corridor until the Spiders tapped their way out, closing the door behind them. "Don't take this the wrong way," I said, opaquing the window and turning to face McMicking. "But what the hell are you doing here?"

He shrugged. "Protecting Mr. Hardin's investment, of course."

I glanced down, wondering how much Bayta could hear in there. "I thought he fired me," I said, lowering my voice.

"He decided to give you one more chance," McMicking said, eyeing me curiously as he pulled my watch, reader, and credit tag from his pocket and dropped them onto the bed. "So you *are* in trouble with the Halkan Peerage."

"With the Peerage and every other upper-class business and political leader in the station," I told him. Unfastening the straps that held Bayta to the stretcher, I started to undo the bandages around her head. "And I thought I told you to get Mr. Hardin out of here."

"He's on his way," McMicking assured me, watching in fascination as Bayta began to emerge from her cocoon. "He went across to the transfer station with the rest of our people to check on some of his investments in the system. He'll stay another day or two, then head home." He lifted his eyebrows. "I trust whatever trouble you've stirred up will be over by then?"

"Don't worry, the trouble will be following me," I said. "Thanks for the assist, but you'd better get going."

"I appreciate the warning," he said. "Hello, there," he added as I finished pulling the bandages clear of Bayta's face.

Bayta's eyes widened, her breath catching in her throat. "It's all right," I told her quickly. "He helped us get past the walkers out there."

"Name's McMicking," McMicking introduced himself calmly. "A colleague of Mr. Compton's."

Bayta's eyes shifted to me. "A colleague?" she asked, her tone suddenly ominous.

"More like second colleague, twice removed," I said. "He works for Larry Hardin, one of Earth's men of wealth." I gave McMicking a warning look. "I've had some dealings with Hardin in the past."

McMicking, as I'd expected, had no trouble picking up on the cue. "That's right," he confirmed easily. "I happened to notice your quick departure from your last train, and figured you were in trouble."

"How did you know we'd come back in this way?" Bayta asked, her expression still tight.

"I didn't, exactly," McMicking said with a shrug. "But I

spent ten years as a bounty hunter before I started working for Mr. Hardin. I know a little about how fugitives think." He favored me with a thin smile. "Especially clever ones like Mr. Compton. How about telling me what's going on?"

I could feel Bayta tense up as I continued unfastening her bandages. Fortunately, I'd already worked up a story, one that McMicking might actually believe. "It's basically a blackmail and extortion scheme," I said. "One that's sucked in most of the top people across the galaxy."

"Our people haven't heard anything about this," he said, eyeing me closely.

"It's been going on very quietly," I explained. "And so far Humans and the Confederation seem to have been ignored. But that's about to change; and when they *do* come for us, I guarantee Mr. Hardin will be one of the first on their list."

McMicking's eyes narrowed. I had his full attention now. "Let them come," he said, a soft menace in his voice. "We'll be ready."

"You may not even know it's happened," I warned as a small additional spark of inspiration struck. Applegate had been content with half the Modhran story. Maybe McMicking would be, too. "They make their conquests through a highly addictive chemical found in Modhran coral."

He frowned. *"Coral?"*

"Goes in through small scratches in the skin," I said. "One touch, and they've got you."

He snorted. "You need to *touch* it? *Coral?* You've got to be kidding."

"Their agents are very persuasive."

"Not *that* persuasive," he countered with a sniff. "I can't imagine anyone speaking well of grabbing a chunk of coral."

I stared at him, a sudden tingle at the back of my neck. *I can't imagine anyone speaking well of grabbing a chunk of coral . . .*

And with that, the rest of the pieces fell into place.

That was it. God above, that was *it.*

"So what are they after *you* for?" McMicking continued.

"You get on someone's list of the rich and famous when I wasn't looking?"

"Hardly," I said mechanically, dragging my mind back to the conversation at hand. "Some of us made a mess of their main base a couple of days ago. They're not happy about that."

There was a tap at the door. "You expecting anyone?" McMicking asked, his voice suddenly taut as he stepped to the door.

"No," I told him, lowering my voice.

"It's all right," Bayta said. "It's just our luggage."

McMicking threw her an odd look. "Your luggage has its own secret knock?"

"Just open the door," I growled.

He transferred the odd look to me, then turned and opened the door. A conductor stood there, our carrybags dangling from three of its legs. Wordlessly, McMicking took them, dropped them onto the bed, then closed and relocked the door. "So," he said conversationally as he stepped over to the curve couch and sat down. "We have just this one compartment?"

"No, *we* have two compartments," I said "*You,* on the other hand, are getting off this—"

I broke off as the thud of releasing brakes sounded from beneath us. "Afraid not," McMicking said calmly.

"McMicking, you *son* of a—" I choked off the curse and grabbed for his arm. I'd throw him off bodily if I had to.

But he evaded my grab with ease. Besides, it was way too late. Even as I made a second and equally futile grab, the train started moving. "McMicking!" I snarled again, dropping my hands uselessly to my sides.

"Relax," he said. "You didn't think I came just to help you aboard and then let you ride off down the rabbit hole, did you? A man like Mr. Hardin didn't get where he is by not protecting his investments."

"Investments?" Bayta asked.

I sighed. "I'll tell you later."

"In the meantime," McMicking continued, lacing his fingers comfortably behind his head, "where exactly do I sleep?"

TWENTY :

It was a four-day trip from Jurskala to Terra, and like the journey from Sistarrko to Jurskala, this one quickly settled into a fairly dull routine.

Dull, but with a dark edge of tension. We couldn't let Bayta out in public, for starters, and even in disguise I didn't dare poke my own nose out for anything beyond a thrice-daily trip to the dining car to get our meals. The fact that I was supposedly the physician to a badly injured Juri made it worse, since one of those meals each time had to be Jurian sickbed fare. The necessary blandness of the diet got old after about the middle of the second day.

At each stop I stood at the compartment window, watching the arriving passengers and trying to gauge which of them might be Modhran walkers. It was a pretty futile exercise; if the walkers themselves didn't know what they were, I didn't have much hope of figuring it out. Still, Bayta had suggested it was the rich and powerful who were first targeted, and the farther we got from Jurskala the more infrequent the first-class travelers seemed to become.

Unfortunately, there was enough traffic in the corridor outside our door to show that the first-class compartments remained full, and first-class passengers of any species were automatically suspect.

And then, of course, there was McMicking.

I had had serious reservations about sharing my compartment with him right from the start, but once the Quadrail left the station there wasn't much I could do about it. Our dramatic entrance to the train might have been quickly forgotten by the rest of the passengers; but on the other hand, it might not. I couldn't simply cut McMicking loose after he'd publicly attached himself to us the way he had, particularly since he probably didn't have a ticket for any of the other seats on the train. We were stuck with each other until we got to Terra Station, and would just have to make the best of it.

Not that he was a particularly unpleasant guest. On the contrary, once I got over my initial annoyance at being scammed I found him to be a reasonable enough traveling companion. He made a point of taking walks several times a day, going up and down the train to keep tabs on what was happening, at the same time giving Bayta and me a little breathing space. Occasionally, when we were all together and the right mood struck him, he would tell a story about his life as a bounty hunter.

Three days later, we pulled into Kerfsis Station, the last big colony system before Earth. Given the trouble we'd had the last time through, I half expected to find Major _Tas_ Busksha waiting on the platform with a warrant in hand for my arrest. But we pulled out again without incident, and I finally began to feel some of the tension draining away. After Kerfsis came Homshil, a transfer point where several cross-galaxy lines intersected, and beyond that there were only two more stops in Jurian space, both of them small outpost colonies not much further along in their development than New Tigris or Yandro. Twenty-three hours and five stops from now, we would be pulling into Terra Station and as safe a haven as we were likely to find anymore in the galaxy.

We were two hours short of Homshil when it all went straight to hell.

* * *

". . . and a bowl of frisjis-broth soup," I told the Spider at the dining car carry-away counter. I was, in fact, getting royally sick of frisjis, and I'd only had it three times since leaving Jurskala. But the medical section of my encyclopedia said it helped promote tissue regeneration in Jurian burn victims, which meant we were pretty well stuck with it.

The Spider dipped its globular body slightly in acknowledgment and headed back into the service area. I stepped away from the counter and took a seat at an empty table nearby. Now that we were almost to Earth, it was time to start thinking about what we were going to do once we got there. The Modhri may have been content to leave humanity alone up to now, but my guess was that that neglect was about to come to an abrupt end.

The problem was that the very quality that had made me a good candidate for the Spiders in the first place was now going to work against me. I had no close contacts, personal *or* professional, with anyone in the government, certainly no one who would listen to me. Hardin was the only influential person I knew, and I could just hear what he would say if I trotted an insane story like this in front of him.

Out of the corner of my eye, I caught a glimpse of movement as someone stepped to my side. Sighing, I settled my face into kindly physician mode and ran my concerned-physician spiel through a quick update. Most of the Jurskala passengers who had seen me bring Bayta aboard were long gone, but there were still a few aboard, at least one of whom cornered me for updates whenever he spotted me out and about. "Yes?" I asked mildly as I looked up.

But it wasn't an inquisitive passenger. It was, in fact, the last person I would have expected to see.

"Well, well," Losutu growled, his voice dark and sarcastic as he glared down at me like a summer thundercloud. "Look who we have here."

"Director *Losutu*?" I gasped, scrambling quickly to my feet. Beyond his glare I saw Applegate hurrying toward us from the bar section, a look of consternation on his face. "What are *you* doing here?"

"I could ask you the same question," he bit back. "I'd have thought the Halkas would have you strapped to a torture rack by now."

I just shook my head, my brain frozen with the impossibility of it. Fayr had gotten us to Sistarrko Station in time to catch the first Quadrail out of the system, and even with the extra three-hour delay in our departure from Jurskala there was no way Losutu and Applegate could have caught up with us via a later connection from Modhra.

Which meant they must have been aboard the same trains with us the whole way. But how could they have gotten to Sistarrko Station ahead of our borrowed torchferry?

"I don't know what possessed you to participate in such an insane venture," Losutu was saying, in full chew-out mode now. "Applegate told me you—"

"Sir, please," Applegate cut him off urgently as he came up to him. "Not here. I told you—"

"And I'm tired of listening," Losutu snapped, sparing him a brief glare before turning his attention back to me. "I'm waiting, Compton. Give me a reason why I shouldn't turn you over to High Commissioner JhanKla right here and now."

I felt my heart try to seize up. "High Commissioner *JhanKla*?"

"We just left his Peerage car," Losutu said, and even through his anger I could hear the self-satisfaction that he'd been afforded such an honor. "He was kind enough to give us a ride from Sistarrko Station after Superintendent Prif-Klas ordered us off Modhra."

"And who then called the other warship in from the transfer station to take you to the Tube," I said as it finally came together. No wonder we hadn't had any trouble with that second Halkan warship; it had been pressed into transport duty to get Losutu and Applegate to the Quadrail in time to shadow us. And of course, sneaking up around the back of the Tube as we had, we hadn't seen that it was missing from its post.

"And thanks to you, we'll be lucky if the Halkas don't block our purchase of those Chaftas," Applegate put in indignantly. "You've wrecked an entire diplomatic initiative—"

"Forget the Chaftas," Losutu cut him off. "I'm still waiting for Compton's explanation about Modhra."

"Yes, sir," Applegate said. "But again, we shouldn't be discussing this out in the open. Perhaps the High Commissioner would permit us to continue the discussion in the Peerage car."

"I'm sure he would," I said, my brain finally starting to kick into gear. "But there's no reason for us to go all the way back there. I have a very comfortable compartment two cars forward."

"No," Applegate said sharply before Losutu could answer.

A UN deputy director, I suspected, was not used to having his decisions made by underlings. "What did you say?" Losutu asked ominously.

Applegate flicked a look at me, the wrinkles around his eyes deepening briefly as if he were just as startled as Losutu that he'd spoken out of turn. "My apologies, sir," he said. "But the High Commissioner needs to be a part of any conversation that deals with the Modhran attack."

"You disappoint me, Colonel," I said. "This isn't the attitude you showed back on Modhra, when you were trying so hard to be my friend."

"That was before you joined ecoterrorists and participated in an attack on Halkan soil," Applegate countered stiffly.

"Is that what it was?" I asked. "Or is it that you were still trying to get me to trust you, hoping to give the Modhri one last crack at me?"

Applegate's forehead wrinkled. "I have no idea what you're talking about."

"Actually, you probably don't," I conceded. "But you see, I'm on to your quiet little friend. You and he made a slip when we were all having dinner together in the Redbird. Not a big slip, nothing I noticed at the time, but something that came back to me later when I heard someone else comment that he couldn't imagine anyone speaking well of grabbing a chunk of coral."

"I didn't say anything good about touching coral," Applegate said, still frowning. "In fact, I think I said just the opposite."

"Yes, you did," I agreed. "The slip was in the specific words you used. You said that coral was such rough, pointy, scratchy stuff."

"You have a point here?" Losutu put in. His voice hadn't lost any of its anger, but there was a hint of curiosity starting to edge its way through. For all his dislike of me personally, he knew the kind of Westali agent I'd once been.

"Yes, sir, I do," I assured him. "Because just one day earlier I'd used those same words, in that same order, when *Apos* Mahf was singing the praises of Modhran coral. Rough, pointy, scratchy. Tell me, Colonel: How likely is it for you to have come up with all three of those words on your own unless there was someone whispering them in your ear?"

"This is insane," Applegate insisted. "Completely insane."

"I agree," Losutu seconded. "If you've got something to say, Compton, say it."

"I'll be happy to, sir, if you'll just step over to my compartment," I said. "And if JhanKla wants to join us, he's also welcome."

"So now you want a Halkan High Commissioner to leave the comfort of his Peerage car for your convenience?" Applegate demanded contemptuously.

"Is it his comfort you're worried about?" I asked. "Or his safety?"

"His *safety*?" Applegate echoed, frowning.

"Yes," I said, suddenly feeling tired of this whole thing. Applegate had never been a friend; but even so, it was strangely debilitating to fight a man who didn't even know he was an enemy. Maybe that was where the true strength of the Modhri lay. "Tell me, Colonel, what's he afraid of? Me? Bayta?"

"Stop calling him *Colonel*," Losutu growled. "He's a civilian now."

I shook my head. "No, sir, he's just with a different army. The army of the Modhri."

"The *what*?" Losutu demanded.

But I wasn't looking at him. Applegate's eyes had gone oddly flat, the muscles of his face sagging visibly as if he had fallen asleep on his feet. Before I could react, his face tightened up again, and his eyes came back to focus.

Only now the eyes were too bright, his posture too stiff, his face a subtle parody of the man who had once gazed coolly at me across a Westali desk and told me I was fired. It was no longer Colonel Terrance Applegate who stood before us.

The real enemy had finally come out to play.

"Ah," I said, trying to keep my voice conversational. "Do I finally have the honor of speaking directly to the Modhri?"

"You do," Applegate said. It wasn't quite his voice, either.

Losutu apparently heard the difference, too. "Applegate?" he asked uncertainly. The anger was gone now, a growing apprehension in its place. "What's going on?"

"Shut up," Applegate said. He stepped to Losutu's side, and the other inhaled sharply as his right wrist was suddenly pinned in a control lock. "You win, Compton. Let's go to your compartment."

"What for?" Losutu asked, fighting to keep his composure as Applegate marched him across the dining car.

"We're going to talk," Applegate told him calmly. He looked at me, the strange eyes gone suddenly dead. "And then," he added, "I'm going to end it."

The entire contingent of first-class passengers was in motion as we stepped through the connecting door into the coach car, their drinks and readers and cards abandoned as they strode purposefully toward us like soldiers marching into combat. I tensed, hardening my hands into fists; but to my surprise they merely swerved both ways around us and continued on, heading back through the vestibule toward the dining car. "Where are they going?" Losutu asked, craning his head to watch as the last of them filed out of the car. "Applegate?"

"It's no concern of yours," Applegate said. Or rather, the thing possessing Applegate said. When the time came, I would have to remember that it was no longer a human being that I would be facing.

We were halfway across the now-empty car when the door ahead of us opened and a second stream of passengers appeared, heading aft with the same air of purpose as the first. Apparently, the Modhri was clearing out his walkers from all of the first-class compartments, too.

By the time we reached the compartment car itself the corridor was empty. "Which one?" Losutu asked.

"These," Applegate said, gesturing toward the doors of our two compartments. "They're the only ones I didn't control."

"We'll go in here," I said, stepping to Bayta's compartment and touching the door chime. "We might as well bring Bayta in on the conversation."

"And your other companion, too," Applegate said. "The one posing as another doctor."

The door opened, and I saw a flicker of surprise on Bayta's face as she realized I had company. A second flicker followed as she saw who the company was. "Yes?" she asked carefully.

"Sorry," I said, gently easing her aside and stepping in. The connecting wall between the two compartments, I saw, was partially open, just the way I'd left it. "Afraid we've miscalculated."

"What do you mean?" she asked as the others came in behind me, Applegate closing the door behind him.

"He means the game is over," Applegate said, releasing Losutu's wrist and giving him a shove toward the bed. "Sit down, all of you. I'll make this as quick and painless as possible. You—in the other compartment! Come here. Now."

There was no answer. "You—Human!" Applegate called again, putting an edge to his voice. "Come *now*."

"Just a minute," a timid voice came at last. McMicking's

voice, but quavering like a frightened accountant. "Please. I'm not dressed."

Applegate hesitated, probably wondering whether it would be safe to leave us alone while he went to the other compartment and dragged McMicking in by his neck. His eyes touched mine, and he apparently decided against it. "You have one minute," he called.

Losutu cleared his throat. "You promised to tell me what's going on, Compton."

"Basically, Colonel Applegate has been turned into a sort of pod person," I told him, making sure my voice was loud enough to carry to McMicking. "I say *sort of* because up to now he's been completely unaware that he's playing host to a section of a group mind called the Modhri."

"Even now he isn't aware of it," Bayta said, her voice so low I could barely hear her. "The Modhri has taken control by putting his personality to sleep. When he releases him, Applegate will return, with no memory of what happened. He'll think he simply blacked out."

"Only this time that may be a problem," I warned, eyeing Applegate thoughtfully. "He'll remember that I was talking about you just before he suffered an unexplained blackout. He's too good an intelligence agent not to connect the dots."

"I doubt it," Applegate said calmly. "Primitives like you are amazingly good at rationalizing away events you don't understand."

"Why are you doing this?" Losutu asked, and I had to admit a grudging flicker of admiration for the man. All of this dumped on him like a truckload of rocks, and yet he was already thinking like a diplomat. "What exactly do you want?"

"I want to be all, and to rule all," Applegate said, as if it were obvious. "And that day will come. But to business," he went on, shifting those dead eyes back to me. "You took three data chips from Modhra 1. Give them to me."

"If you insist." I gestured toward the lounge chair where Bayta's reader and the chips were lying on a pull-out armrest table. "They're right there."

Applegate backed over to the chair, keeping his eyes on

us, and picked up the chips. A quick confirming glance at them, and he dropped them into his pocket. "Now tell me what you've learned from them."

I thought about playing dumb, but it didn't seem worth the effort. "You've shipped out a hell of a lot of coral recently," I said. "Aside from that, nothing."

His eyes glittered. "Nothing?"

"Absolutely nothing," I assured him truthfully. I *hadn't* figured it out from his precious data chips, after all. "Though it wasn't for lack of trying."

"I see," Applegate murmured. He started to turn away—

And before I could react, he stepped to the bed, grabbed a handful of Bayta's hair, and yanked her upright. "You lie," he said calmly, twisting her around and pulling her close in front of him. "Tell me where it is, and I'll release her."

"I don't *know* where it is," I protested, feeling sweat breaking out on my face as he shifted his grip, wrapping his right arm around her throat. "Leave her alone."

"Where *what* is?" Losutu demanded.

"Fine," Applegate said. "Have it your way." His left hand dipped into his side jacket pocket and came out again.

Holding a lump of Modhran coral.

"Now," he said, holding the coral up for my inspection. "Will you tell me the truth? Or do I simply scratch her so"—he pantomimed running an edge of the coral along her cheek—"and turn her into the thing she fears most in the universe?"

"Leave her *alone,* damn it," I snarled, half rising to my feet. Applegate twitched the coral warningly; clenching my teeth, I sank back down again. "I tell you we don't know."

"Do you agree, servant of the Spiders?" Applegate asked Bayta, his lips almost brushing her ear.

She didn't answer, her eyes blazing with anger and terror. "Well?" he prompted.

"You *will* die," she said, her voice strained but firm. "Do you hear me?"

"I hear you," Applegate said calmly. "A final chance: Tell me where the homeland is, or join us. I assure you—"

"I'm coming out," McMicking called from the other compartment, his voice still trembling. "Please don't hurt me."

Applegate flicked a glance at the open wall, clearly annoyed at the interruption. "Just come," he snapped. There was another moment of hesitation, and then McMicking appeared, sidling nervously through the gap.

He hadn't changed his hair in the past twenty minutes. But even so, for that first couple of seconds I almost didn't recognize him. The air of professional awareness and competence had vanished into a bubbling nervousness. His eyes were bulging in panic, his fingers and lips and throat working with barely contained terror, his face halfway to bursting into tears. "Please don't hurt me," he begged.

"Sit down," Applegate said disgustedly, jerking his head toward the bed. He turned his eyes back to me, as if even the alien within him was embarrassed at the sight of such a pathetic excuse for a Human being. "Well?" he demanded, again lifting the coral toward Bayta's cheek.

And in that moment, McMicking struck.

He threw himself at Applegate in a flat leap that covered the two-meter gap between them, his fist slamming hard into Applegate's exposed right armpit. Applegate bellowed with pain, and Bayta twisted away from him as the arm holding her suddenly went limp. Applegate twisted around as well, his left hand slashing out with the coral toward McMicking's face.

But McMicking was no longer there. Even before Bayta was completely free he had dropped into a low crouch; and as the coral swung through the air above his head he swiveled around, his right leg sweeping Applegate's legs out from under him.

With a curse, Applegate toppled over, slamming hard onto his back on the floor. I jumped up to assist, but there was no need. McMicking finished his sweep and hop-switched legs, jabbing his left foot out like a Russian dancer to catch Applegate solidly behind his right ear. There was a sickening thud, and with a single convulsive spasm, Applegate collapsed and lay still. His left hand opened limply, the coral rolling a few centimeters away across the floor.

"Everyone okay?" McMicking asked, giving Applegate's ribs a test nudge to make sure he was going to stay down.

"We're fine," I said, getting up and kneeling over Applegate. "Did he get you with the coral?"

"Not even close," McMicking assured me.

"Be careful," Bayta warned as I checked Applegate's pulse. "Modhran walkers aren't easy to knock out."

"I don't think we'll have that problem," I said grimly, getting back to my feet. "He's dead."

"*What?*" McMicking demanded, dropping down and checking for himself. "That's crazy—I didn't hit him that hard."

"The colony must have suicided," Bayta said with a shiver. "Like the two Halkas at Kerfsis."

"This Modhri sounds like a sore loser," McMicking said with a grunt, straightening up and prodding the coral with his shoe. "What should I do with this?"

"Don't touch it," I warned. Nudging him away, I kicked it under the bed where it would be out of the way. "I wonder where the hell he got it from."

"From the Peerage car," Losutu murmured mechanically, still staring at Applegate's body. "JhanKla has a long spine of it in a pool in his sleeping compartment."

So the Peerage car wasn't just a walker's convenient and comfortable transport. It was also a full-fledged mobile command center. "Should have guessed," I said. "Bayta, do you know if it can hear us?"

"You mean the *coral*?" Losutu asked, breaking his gaze away from Applegate to stare up at me. "What in the—?"

"Director, please," I said. "Bayta?"

"I don't think so," she said. "The polyps can detect and interpret vibrations, but only under water."

"What about Applegate?"

"But you said he was dead," Losutu protested.

"Director, *please,*" I said, trying hard to hold on to my temper.

"He might," Bayta conceded. "The—I mean—the neural degeneration hasn't yet started—"

"Out in the hall with him," McMicking said briskly, grabbing Applegate under the armpits. "Better kick that coral thing out there, too, just to be on the safe side."

A minute later we had dumped both the body and the coral out in the corridor, making sure to retrieve the data chips first. "What about you?" I asked Bayta when we were back in the compartment. "Did he get you with the coral?"

"No," she said, rubbing gingerly at her cheek.

"You sure? No—hold still," I ordered as I took hold of her chin and tilted her head up toward the light. "Let me see."

"See what?" she retorted, pushing my hand away. "A microscopic scratch? I tell you, he didn't touch me."

"Okay, okay," I growled. "I was just trying to help."

"Help by figuring out what he's going to do next," she growled back. Dropping back down onto the bed, she pulled her knees up to her chest and hugged her arms tightly around them as she stared off into a corner.

"What do you mean, what he's going to do?" Losutu asked, his expression unreadable. "He's *dead,* right?"

"She means he, the Modhri, the group mind," I told him. "Weren't you listening?"

"Yes, but . . ." He trailed off. "You were serious, weren't you? But that's . . ."

"Insane?" I suggested tartly. "Ridiculous? Horrifying? Pick an adjective and move on, because it's also true."

Losutu took a deep breath, let it out slowly. "All right," he said. "Assume for the moment it's true. As she says: What now? What exactly are his options?"

"You saw all the first-class passengers moving like zombies while we were coming here," I reminded him. "All of them are Modhran walkers, just like Applegate was, all of them apparently being directly controlled by the group mind." I patted my pocket. "And their sole purpose in life is to get these data chips back."

"How many of them are there?" McMicking asked.

"At least everyone in first class, plus JhanKla and his entourage, plus probably a few others scattered around for insurance," I told him. "The odds here are not good."

"Yeah, but it's only another hour to Homshil," McMicking pointed out. "Maybe we can barricade ourselves in until we get there."

"And then fight our way through them to get off?" I asked doubtfully. "Worth a try. Let's see if we can get these beds off the walls—"

And from behind me, Bayta screamed.

"What?" I snapped, spinning around to face her.

Her eyes were staring into infinity, her face gone deathly white, her chest heaving with short, rapid breaths. "Bayta?" I asked, dropping down on the bed beside her and taking her hand. It was icy cold. "Bayta, what is it?"

"They killed him," she whispered, her voice shaking. "They killed one of the Spiders."

"Who did?" I asked, a creepy feeling running up my back.

"The crowd," she whispered. "The mob. All of them."

"That can't be," McMicking objected. "You said it was just first class. There can't be enough of them to take out a Spider."

"He was wrong," she murmured, her eyes still blank. "They're all part of the Modhri now. They're attacking the Spiders, and they're going to kill them all."

She closed her eyes. "And then they're going to kill us."

TWENTY-ONE :

For perhaps half a minute no one spoke. I looked at Bayta, then McMicking, then Losutu, seeing my own disbelief reflected in their faces. For centuries the Spiders had been the most stable and unchanging part of the galactic landscape: enigmatic and anonymous, striding silently through the background of interstellar events even as they enabled those events to happen. They had no faces or personalities; no apparent desires other than to serve; no hopes or dreams or joys or sorrows of their own.

And there had never, ever been any indication that they, like all the rest of us, might be mortal.

"What do we do?" Losutu asked at last. "We can't hold off a whole train full of people until we reach Homshil, can we?"

"It doesn't matter if we can or not," Bayta said. The horror had faded from her face, leaving only a bitter resignation behind. "The Spiders are the ones who control the Quadrail."

"You mean they've gotten to the engine?" McMicking asked.

Bayta shook her head. "There isn't anyone in the engine," she said. "They control it from back here. Once they're all dead, we'll just keep going until we run out of fuel. Or until we hit something."

"At a hundred kilometers an hour," Losutu murmured.

"Or a light-year per minute, depending on how you look at it," I said grimly. "But this doesn't make sense. You told me it takes days or weeks for a colony to form inside someone."

"That's if you start with a single polyp hook from a single pinprick," she said with a sigh. "If you put full-grown polyps in to begin with, and a lot of them—" She swallowed. "You could create a new walker within hours. Maybe even minutes."

So that was what Applegate had been threatening her with. A slash across the cheek with the coral would dump dozens of the damn polyps straight into her bloodstream. "Zero to Modhri in fifteen seconds," I said. "I guess that explains where everyone in first class was going. Back to the Peerage car for a lump of coral, then off to the first annual Modhran recruitment drive."

"Stop babbling, Compton," Losutu bit out. "What I want to know is, how does this gain them anything? Now they'll *all* die."

"Unless he doesn't realize he's killing the drivers?" McMicking suggested.

A spasm of pain flashed across Bayta's face. "He's killed another one," she murmured.

"No, he understands, all right," I said. "Remember, the Modhri is a group mind, with each colony forming connections with any others nearby. That's what's happened here: The colonies in Applegate and JhanKla and the first-class passengers were linked up with the coral back in the Peerage car. Now the mind segment's apparently been extended to the rest of the passengers as well."

"So they'll still all die," Losutu protested.

"He doesn't care if this mind segment dies," I told him. "All he cares about is making the segment big enough that he'll be able to link to whatever mind segment is waiting in the Homshil Station when we go roaring through."

"Where he can pass on the information," McMicking said, nodding. "Sure."

"What information?" Losutu asked. "What's so important?"

"The fact that we have their stolen data chips," I said. "Up to now, the Modhri didn't know whether we had them, or Fayr had them, or whether we'd passed them off to someone else."

"But if the train crashes, he'll never get the chips back."

"He doesn't need them back," I said. "He just needs to make sure no one else has them."

"And this is worth sacrificing JhanKla and Applegate and all the rest of them for?" Losutu persisted.

"To the Modhri, the individuals don't matter as long as the whole remains," I said. "Would you worry about sacrificing a few brain cells?"

Losutu hissed between his teeth. "This can't be happening," he muttered.

"Trust me, it is," I said, trying to think. I didn't know how many Spiders there were aboard, but it was surely going to be a while longer before even a whole train full of walkers could take out all of them. We had that much breathing space to work with. "Bayta, is there anything *you* can do with the engine?" I asked. "Speed us up, slow us down—anything?"

"No," she said dully. "Not from here."

"But you talk to the Spiders," I reminded her.

"It's not the same," she snapped suddenly. "If I was in the engine, I could do something. But I'm not." She gave another spastic twitch, and her shoulders sagged. "And there's no way to get there."

"Why not?" McMicking asked.

"Because there just isn't," she said. "There aren't any passageways between the engine and the rest of the train."

"But it's obviously connected to us," I said. "Can we get to it from the outside?"

"There's no air out there," Losutu said. "Not enough to breathe, anyway."

"There are medical kits in every car," McMicking pointed out. "They all have emergency oxygen breathers, right?"

"Yes," Bayta said slowly, a note of cautious hope starting to creep into her voice. "And there are bigger cylinders, too, for emergency repressurization. We could maybe use one of those to pressurize the engine compartment once we're there."

"Then we're in," I said. "How do we get the doors open?"

Bayta sighed. "We can't," she said, the spark of hope going out again. "They're pressure-locked."

"All of them?" Losutu asked.

Bayta nodded. "We'd need someone with the strength of a drudge to force one open." She hesitated. "But there *are* some roof panels in the baggage cars for getting extra-large cargo crates in and out. They're heavy, but they're not air-locked. We might be able to get one open."

"But they're all the way at the back of the Quadrail," Losutu objected. "How are we going to get there with the Modhri in the way?"

"Leave that to us," I said, lifting my eyebrows questioningly at McMicking. "You game?"

"Absolutely," he said grimly. "Let's show this Modhri what a couple of primitives can do."

Our first task was to collect all the oxygen tanks we would need. McMicking and I did that, slipping back to the first-class coach and retrieving the emergency medical kit and its oxygen breather. Fortunately, the passengers were still gone, apparently out beating Spiders to death. The breather's tank wasn't very big, but it ought to be enough to get one of us to the engine.

The actual mechanics of which I hadn't quite worked out yet. As far as I knew, when Bayta and I had jumped off at Jurskala we'd been the first people to even stick our noses outside a moving Quadrail. Climbing on top of one going full tilt down the Tube was at least an order of magnitude crazier. There were so many unknowns, in fact, that it didn't even pay to start listing them, and I would probably have voted to try the barricade approach if it hadn't been for the absolute certainty that that would leave us all dead.

We also found and removed the emergency repressurization tank Bayta had mentioned. It turned out to be not just a simple tank, but a complete self-controlled supply/scrubber/regulator system. It also weighed nearly as much as Bayta, but fortunately it came with a built-in carrying harness that would easily convert to a backpack.

We returned to the compartment and dropped off both tanks, then pulled the medical kit from our own car. That gave us two personal-sized tanks, which added to the stretcher's tank and the spare we'd brought from Jurskala Station gave us the four we would need for the trek across the top of the train.

Meanwhile, Bayta and Losutu hadn't been idle. As per our instructions they'd set the stretcher up on its wheels and loaded it with spare clothing and bedding and everything else flammable they could find or tear loose from the compartments' furnishings. They'd also rigged up shoulder or belt harnesses for the four oxygen tanks.

And with that, we were ready.

"As ready as we're going to be, anyway," I said, adjusting the small personal oxygen tank at my waist and manhandling the big one onto the stretcher's center equipment rack. Now, more than ever, I wished I'd asked the Spiders for a gun when I'd had the chance. "Oh, and grab those two carrybags, too," I told McMicking, pointing at my luggage.

"You want to bother with *luggage*?" he demanded, crossing the room and bringing back the bags.

"Trust me," I told him as I stowed them on the stretcher's lower rack. "Bayta? You ready?"

"I think so," she said. She was still pale, but her voice was firm. Whatever black valley she'd gone through when the Spiders started dying, she'd worked her way through it.

"Director?"

"I don't like any of this, if you want to know the truth," Losutu said, his voice heavy. "Attacking and maybe killing a whole group of people, especially people who aren't accountable for their actions—"

"They're not people," McMicking interrupted. "They're targets, or enemy combatants, or bug-eyed monsters. Not people. You start thinking about them that way and you'll be dead."

"I understand the emotional necessities of warfare, thank you," Losutu said icily. "I just wish we didn't have to do it."

"*I* wish we had Fayr and his commando squad along," I countered. "You don't always get what you wish for."

"If we did, we'd have some real weapons," McMicking added sourly. "Unless those Spiders are putting up one hell of a fight, none of this is going to get us very far."

He was right, of course; our gimmicked stretcher was hardly battlefield shock armor. But it was all we had. "You want some plastic Belldic status guns to wave around?" I offered, nodding toward the bed where they'd ended up when Bayta had pulled the clothing out of my carrybags. "Fayr gave them to me before we left him."

"Really," McMicking said, frowning over at the guns. "Why?"

I opened my mouth . . . closed it again. "Good question," I said, going over and picking them up. *You may need these,* Fayr had said. Not exactly the sort of comment a person usually makes when offering someone else a souvenir.

But right after that, Bayta and I had jumped off the Quadrail, and I'd stuffed the guns into my luggage, and somehow I'd never gotten around to wondering what he might have meant. "See what you can find," I told McMicking, handing him one of the guns.

We examined them in silence as Losutu and Bayta watched over our shoulders. The entire gun was made of soft plastic, except for a decorative braided tassel attached to the bottom of the grip which seemed to be some sort of synthetic silk. The gun was definitely hollow, but a methodical squeezing didn't reveal any telltale lumps that might have indicated something hidden inside. Not that they could have gotten anything dangerous past the Spiders' sensors anyway. The oversized barrel was closed at the business end, and had some ribbing running lengthwise at various points along its surface that gave it a certain rigidity. Not enough to make it a useful weapon, though, given how light it was.

Unless . . . "Check the barrel," I told McMicking, running my fingers around the socket where it fit into the rest of the gun. "See if you can find a way to get it— Never mind," I interrupted myself as the barrel snicked free. The tube was closed at both ends, I saw now, but the inner end had the look of a pressure-threaded cap. There were also a pair of eyelets on the cap that had been concealed by the socket, eyelets that extended upward from the cap without opening into the interior of the tube itself.

"Toy nightsticks?" Losutu hazarded as McMicking also pulled his gun barrel free.

"Better than that," I assured him, unscrewing the cap and handing it and the barrel to Bayta. "Here—fill it with water. All the way up—no bubbles. Yours, too, McMicking."

"Okay, that'll make them heavier," Losutu said, still frowning as the others headed for the washroom. "They're still too short to be much good as clubs."

"Watch and learn," I told him, turning over what was left of my gun and starting to unfasten the tassel. "Westali did a study once on how someone might improvise weapons from things available on a Quadrail. Looks like the Bellidos did us one better."

I had the tassel unbraided into a single smooth silk cord by the time McMicking and Bayta returned with the water-filled barrels. They held them steady while I threaded the cord through the eyelets on the tops of both barrels, leaving a few centimeters of slack as I wove the cord back and forth between them. When I was finished, I tied the cord in a secure knot beside one of the eyelets. "And there we have it," I said, taking the barrels and snapping them apart to take up any slack I'd left in the cord. "One improvised but very serviceable nunchaku combat flail."

"I'll be damned," Losutu said, sounding like he wasn't sure whether to be impressed or appalled. "Do the Spiders know about this?"

"Don't know," I said. "Don't care, either. McMicking? You or me?"

"Me," he said firmly, taking the nunchaku from my hand and giving it an experimental swing. The swing turned into a bewildering and convoluted routine that ended up with one barrel in his hand and the other tucked securely under his arm. "This should work just fine," he said, giving Losutu a tight smile. "You see, Director? Sometimes you *do* get what you wish for."

Losutu didn't reply. "Then I'm driving," I said, pulling out the stretcher's leash control. "Let's go."

The hallway was still deserted as we made our way aft, as was the first-class coach car behind it. As I maneuvered the stretcher along the twisted aisle created by the rearranged chairs, Bayta and Losutu collected the cards and other flammables that had been left behind and added them to the pile on the stretcher, dousing everything with the remnants of the various alcoholic drinks. Passing through the vestibule, we entered the bar end of the dining car.

And found ourselves in a scene straight out of the Reign of Terror. In three different places around the room well-dressed Juriani, Halkas, Bellidos, and Cimmaheem stood in tight knots, silently and methodically attacking the dented spheres and broken legs of the Spiders in the centers of their circles, beating them with fists and chairs and tables and anything else they could find.

Beside me, I heard a strange gurgling sound from Bayta, and sensed her start to totter. Grabbing her arm, I pulled her close to me and kept moving.

We'd gotten perhaps four paces into the room when someone noticed us, and the whole crowd stopped what they were doing and turned in our direction. I braced myself, but the Modhri apparently had more important things on his mind right now. Again in perfect unison the walkers turned back and resumed their attacks on the Spiders.

"What are they doing?" Losutu muttered from beside me. "Don't they realize who we are?"

"Of course they do," I muttered back. "Group mind, remember? What one walker sees, the whole Modhri sees. He just figures that whatever we're doing, we're dead anyway." I nodded toward the bar. "You and McMicking—go."

Losutu hesitated, reluctantly detached himself from Bayta and me, and followed McMicking to the bar, the two of them slipping through the opening and disappearing into the storage room beyond. I kept an eye on the three lynch mobs, watching for any sign of trouble and trying not to think too hard about what they were doing. It was clear that these particular Spiders, at least, were already goners, and that there wasn't anything we could do to help them. But that didn't make it any easier to watch.

Two minutes later McMicking and Losutu reappeared, their arms laden with bottles of *skinski* flambé fluid. "Great," I said as we loaded as many as we could onto the stretcher's lower rack, tucking the rest awkwardly under our arms. With the leash control again in hand, I eased us past the nearest lynch group and into the restaurant end of the car.

The same spectacle was taking place there, except that the mobs in that half of the car seemed to be mostly second-class passengers. The Modhri had apparently promoted them to first-class for the occasion. "Anybody know how many cars there are in this train?" I asked as we reached the far end and opened the door.

"There are eleven total in front of the first baggage car," McMicking said. "Three down; eight to go."

I nodded as we all crowded into the vestibule. "Let's just hope the Modhri keeps thinking we're not worth bothering with. Hold it here a second," I added as the dining room door closed behind McMicking. "Dump the rest of these bottles on top of the stretcher."

"This isn't going to buy us anything, you know," Losutu warned as we began opening the flambé bottles we were carrying and dumping the contents onto the stretcher. "Doing it in here, I mean. They're bound to smell it as we go past."

"Probably," I agreed, hunching down to loosen the stoppers in the bottles we'd racked on the bottom so that they would be ready when we needed them. "But it's better than letting the Modhri watch us while we do it. Every few steps we can buy for ourselves are worth it."

"That should be enough," McMicking said, emptying one final bottle over the stretcher. "Better get going before he misses us. And here," he added, pressing an igniter into my hand. "This'll have a longer reach than your lighter."

The next car back was a second-class coach. There were a few people sitting around, mostly panting or nursing arms and legs where flailing Spider legs had apparently caught them, but there weren't nearly enough to account for the entire passenger list. Some of the missing were probably the ones we'd just seen in the dining car, with the rest presumably gone somewhere aft. Draped across the seats, I also saw the battered remains of four more Spiders.

Fortunately, this bunch didn't look like they could stop us even if the Modhri had wanted them to. None of them made any kind of move as we worked our way through to the rear of the car. Unlike the previous groups, though, they watched us closely as we passed through their midst. Whether or not the Modhri had decided we were a threat, he was definitely starting to get curious. Bracing myself, I led the way into and through the vestibule.

The next car was much like the one preceding it, with only the injured and those too tired to fight still present. There were definitely more of them, though, along with the crumpled remains of six Spiders. I wondered how many were left, decided it was a mostly moot point. Bayta was still twitching occasionally, so apparently they weren't all gone yet.

We were midway through the next car when our luck finally ran out.

I'd noticed the difference the instant we'd stepped through the door. Before, the walkers had either merely given us a cursory glance and returned to their other activities or watched us more closely without showing any interest in taking action. Here, in contrast, we were the center of attention as soon as the stretcher cleared the vestibule.

And unlike the previous two cars, this one wasn't populated only by the injured and the stragglers. The majority looked like they'd been through the wars, but were just as clearly ready for round two.

Bayta noticed it, too. "Frank?" she murmured tautly.

"Just keep walking," I murmured back. "McMicking?"

"I'm on it," he said, brushing past Losutu and me to take point. "You said this group mind thing sees everything everybody else sees. Does he feel what they all feel, too?"

"I think so," Bayta said.

"Good," McMicking said grimly. "Let's see how much he likes pain."

Second-class seats weren't quite as mobile as those in first class, but they were maneuverable enough that the walkers had been able to clear a large area in the center of the car. I expected the Modhri to make his move when we reached that open area, and I wasn't disappointed. The stretcher had just rolled past the last row of seats when a group of ten Juriani and Halkas got up and strolled almost leisurely to form a line blocking our path. Some of them carried bits of table or chair from the dining cars, while others had shiny metal rods that had probably once been parts of Spider legs. Others, mostly the bigger ones, seemed to have only their fists. I glanced over my shoulder, saw a similar group moving up behind Losutu to block our retreat.

"Keep going," McMicking said, picking up his pace as he strode forward to intercept the group ahead of us. They watched him come, their faces carrying bizarrely similar looks of anticipation, and raised their makeshift weapons for the kill.

They never had a chance to use them. McMicking was two paces away when he pulled his new nunchaku out of concealment beneath his jacket and slammed it hard across the biggest Halka's head.

The alien staggered back, and I could see a ripple of shock run through the whole group as the sharp and unexpected pain jabbed through the combined mind. McMicking didn't give the Modhri a chance to recover, but continued whipping the nunchaku across heads and arms and ribs and legs, going first for disabling shots and second for blows that would cause the most pain.

A pair of Cimmaheem who had been sitting on the sidelines heaved themselves to their feet and started toward me. I grabbed one of the flambé bottles from the stretcher's rack and squeezed it hard, sending the stopper and a spray of fluid into their faces. They bellowed, a subsonic roar that rattled my head, and staggered back, clawing at their eyes.

"Come on!" Losutu snapped, giving me an urgent shove forward. I saw that McMicking had cleared us a path, and with the stretcher rolling ahead of me I broke into a jog. We cleared the little circle—

"Behind you!" McMicking snapped.

I twisted my head around. The rear guard was moving forward, their mutual expression no longer one of anticipation. Snatching another bottle and igniter, I squeezed the fluid out onto the floor of the aisle behind us and tapped the edge with the igniter.

Blue-white flames crackled up, bringing the posse to a sudden stop. I squirted another bottle onto the fire; and as the heat washed across my face Losutu grabbed my arm and we made a mad dash for it. We reached the vestibule and squeezed inside, closing the door behind us. "That won't hold them for long," Losutu panted, his voice tight. "All the Modhri has to do is throw a couple of them over the fire to make a bridge."

"Maybe," I said. "On the other hand, he *does* feel all the pain coming in through his walkers, and burns are something you can't suppress just by sitting quietly or keeping pressure on them. He may still hesitate at letting himself in for that sort of grief."

"Are we talking, or are we going?" McMicking growled.

"We're going," I said. "Me first."

He frowned briefly, then nodded. Holding the igniter ready, I pushed through the door and into the second/third-class dining car.

They were waiting for us: a triple semicircle of walkers standing well back from the door, several with towels or napkins hastily wrapped around their heads and low over their eyes to help protect against flambé sprays. All of them gripped weapons of some sort. Behind them, I could see more walkers awaiting their turn. "Hell," I said.

"What did you expect?" McMicking countered. "This is the last really open area on the train, the last place they can effectively gang up on us."

"What do we do?" Losutu asked nervously.

The walkers were still standing motionlessly, apparently waiting for us to make the first move. "No way out but through," I told him. "Cannonball express?"

"Cannonball express," McMicking agreed.

Taking a deep breath, getting a solid grip on Bayta's arm, I flicked on the igniter and tapped the edge of the stretcher.

The whole top burst into flame, the blue-white fire quickly taking on a yellow edge as the cards and clothing and other flammables caught fire. Grabbing one of the flambé bottles in each hand, wincing at the heat singeing my face, I charged forward.

The triple semicircle gave way before the blazing cart. But as I guided the stretcher through the center of the line the walkers folded in from both sides, moving in to flank us. Aiming one of my bottles at the center of each side, I squeezed hard, angling the spray so that it caught the edge of the stretcher fire. The fluid ignited in midair, and a shudder ran through the group as suddenly two of their members were engulfed in brilliant blue-white halos.

But that brief shudder was all the breathing space we got. A second later they surged forward again; and this time I knew there would be no stopping them. Behind me I could hear the rhythmic cracking of bone as McMicking worked his nunchaku, but even he couldn't handle this sheer weight of numbers.

Which left us only one option. "Masks!" I shouted at the others, snatching up another bottle with one hand as I grabbed my oxygen mask with the other. Squeezing the bottle into the face of a lunging Juri, I followed it up with a hard side kick to his midsection and clamped the mask over my face. "Masks?" I called again.

I got three terse acknowledgments. "Bayta—go!" I called, mentally crossing my fingers as a dozen weapons swung into the air around us. From the stretcher rack came a sort of sizzling *pop*—

The front group of walkers came to an abrupt halt, their chests heaving, a look of bewilderment on their faces. The group behind them, trying to push their way through, suddenly froze as well. I cocked my leg for another kick . . . and then, as if their strings had been cut, every single one of the walkers collapsed onto the floor.

"My God," Losutu's muffled voice murmured. "What—?"

"Saarix-5 in my carrybags," I told him, breathing hard through my mask, the cold oxygen tingling my nostrils as I gave the car a quick sweep of my eyes. They were dead, all right. "A little gift from the Spiders."

"Oh, my God," Losutu said again. "We've just—we've just—"

"Would you rather *we* be the dead ones?" McMicking growled.

"No, of course not," Losutu said. "But *this*—"

"They were already dead," I cut him off, peering at the door at the far end of the car as I forced the stretcher over a couple of Halkan bodies. So far, the Modhri didn't seem inclined to send in reinforcements. "Even if he somehow managed to stop the train, the Modhri couldn't have let any of them live. They'd seen too much before he took them over."

Losutu's sigh hissed through his mask. "I suppose," he said reluctantly as he picked his way squeamishly through the bodies.

"Bug-eyed monsters, remember?" McMicking said. "We have any more of that stuff?"

"Yes," Bayta said. Her voice, in sharp contrast with Losutu's, carried an edge of grim satisfaction. She'd hurt the Modhri, and hurt him badly. After having to watch the Spiders die, a little revenge apparently felt pretty good.

"Better save it until we need it," McMicking advised. "This is a good fraction of the passengers, but there are plenty left."

"And keep your masks on once we're out of here," I added, eyeing the black smoke now coming off the stretcher as I pushed it over the last cluster of bodies in front of the door. "This smoke can't be very good for us, and the Saarix on our clothes will linger a few minutes before it oxidizes."

"Will we have enough oxygen to get to the engine if we do that?" Losutu asked.

"We should," Bayta said.

"We might also be able to pick up some spares along the way," I said, pushing open the door and crossing the vestibule. McMicking again moved to take point, and we stepped into the next car.

We had reached the third-class section now, where the chairs were set in permanent rows. As McMicking had pointed out, that meant no more nice open spaces where the Modhri could concentrate his forces.

And it certainly looked like he'd given up the effort. Aside from the remains of two Spiders draped across the seats midway back, the car seemed to be deserted. "Watch it," I warned McMicking as he started down the aisle. "They might be hiding behind the seats."

"Yeah, I hope so," he said with a touch of humor. Small wonder; in the cramped spaces available in here, they couldn't come at him more than a couple at a time, numbers he and his nunchaku should be able to deal with quite handily.

"Watch it anyway," I said, glancing back at the emergency medical kit set against the wall in front of the restrooms. "Director, grab the oxygen cylinder out of that kit, will you?"

"All right," he said, retracing his steps to the kit and retrieving the cylinder.

McMicking had reached the far end of the car by the time

Losutu rejoined us. "All clear," he called back. "Whatever he's planning, looks like he's planning it somewhere else."

The next car was the same: the remains of a few Spiders, no sign of enemies. Again, McMicking headed forward, nunchaku at the ready, while Losutu paused at the medical kit to pick up another oxygen tank.

He had just popped the kit open when the restroom doors at the front of the car swung open and two burly Halkas leaped out.

"Compton!" Losutu gasped, trying to run backward and instead bumping his leg into one of the seats and tumbling off balance into the aisle. "*Compton!*"

Swearing under my breath, I dropped the stretcher's leash control and sprinted toward him. But the Halkas got there first. One of them grabbed him by his jacket and hauled him to his feet, spinning him around to face me as he wrapped an arm around his throat. "Stop, or he dies," he snarled.

There was no time to think, no time to pause and try to figure out what the Modhri was up to. I kept going, my momentum carrying me forward; and as I reached them I shot a hand forward, grabbing Losutu by the temples and slamming the back of his head hard into the face of the Halka behind him.

The Halka staggered back in shock and agony, his grip loosening around Losutu's neck. The other Halka gave the little twitch I was starting to associate with sudden shared pain in the group mind; and then I was on him, slamming my forearm and elbow hard against his neck. He staggered back as well, and I returned my attention to the first alien, gripping the hand still resting against Losutu's throat and twisting it around, pushing against the joint to topple him backward onto the floor between the two restrooms. Another blow to the second Halka's throat, a hard kick to the first's midsection as he tried to scramble to his feet, and it was over.

"You all right?" I asked Losutu as I helped him to his feet. "It's all right," I added to McMicking as he skidded to a halt beside me.

"I think so," Losutu said, his eyes wincing over his mask as he rubbed the back of his head. "I wasn't expecting you to do that."

"Neither was the Modhri," I said, guiding him back down the aisle to where Bayta and the stretcher waited. "There are definitely some drawbacks to fighting with untrained labor."

"Like missing golden opportunities," McMicking grunted, gesturing toward the far door. "They should have charged while we were distracted."

"That wasn't the point of this exercise," I said grimly. "Or didn't you notice that the Halka was very careful not to bump Losutu's oxygen mask?"

"I get it," McMicking said, nodding. "Cute."

"What's cute?" Losutu asked.

"They were hoping we'd use up more of our Saarix to free you," I told him, picking up the leash control and getting the stretcher moving again. "Two cars to go. Any bets on where they'll be waiting?"

"I say they've got both of them stocked," McMicking said as we reached the far door. "Remember, they don't know how much Saarix we've got left."

"Good point," I said. "Maybe we can use that."

"How?" Losutu asked.

"You'll see," I said. Pushing open the door, I rolled the stretcher through into the vestibule. McMicking moved to point position and opened the door into the next car.

Once again, they were waiting for us, a silent line of aliens completely filling the aisle, with others standing in the seating areas ready to take their places if necessary. The four Juriani in front were carrying a large piece of twisted metal, a misshapen sphere and three segmented poles pointed at us like spears. It took me a second to realize it was what was left of a Spider.

"What now?" Losutu muttered.

In answer, I held out my hand. "Hello, Modhri," I called. "Before you do anything rash, you and I need to have a little talk."

TWENTY-TWO :

For a moment there was no response. I watched as a series of expressions flicked across the faces of the assembled crowd, then faded away into a stony mass glare. "What have we to talk about?" the first Juri in line called back.

"I want to offer you a deal," I told him.

"Frank?" Bayta murmured uncertainly.

"Quiet," I told her. "I know what I'm doing."

The Juri clicked his beak. "You think you have anything left to bargain with?"

"Sure," I said. "You see, I can let you win this round. Or, I can make it a complete waste of your time and energy."

The Juri cocked his head slightly. "Explain."

I gestured to the still-smoldering stretcher. "I have enough Saarix-5 to destroy every walker you have between here and the rear of the Quadrail," I said. "You've seen the stuff in action. You know what it can do."

"Even if you kill them all, you will still die," he reminded me.

"I know," I said. "The point is, so will you."

A ripple ran through the assembly. "You see the problem," I went on. "If this mind segment dies now, without passing on the information that we have the data chips, you'll never quite be able to relax." I gestured toward the crowd. "In fact, I suspect that's why you started attacking us so aggressively in the first place. You suddenly woke up to the fact that we were heading straight for the Peerage car and JhanKla's private coral outpost. If we destroy all the walkers *and* the coral, this mind segment is history."

"Very well, I agree," the Juri spokesman spoke up. "You may return to your compartments to await your deaths in peace."

"Such a generous offer," I said dryly. "Fine, but we need to get something from the baggage compartment first."

Another ripple went through the crowd. "No," the Juri said flatly.

I shrugged. "Okay by me." Reaching to the lower rack, I found the carrybag Bayta had already blown and pulled it out. "Here," I said, hiding the damaged handle with my hand as I held it aloft for the Modhri to see. "You want to pass this back to the middle of the room where it'll work the fastest? Or shall I just throw it back there myself?"

"Wait," the Juri growled. "What is it you want from the baggage car?"

"My pinochle deck," I said with exaggerated patience. "What do you care what we want? We're going to die anyway, right?"

Again he paused . . . and suddenly I felt Bayta grip my arm. "Frank—that Spider," she whispered urgently. "He's still alive."

I focused on the tangle of metal the Juriani were holding. "You're kidding."

"No," she insisted. "He's dying, but he's still alive."

And the Spiders were the ones who could control the Quadrail. If we could get it back to our first-class compartment, maybe we wouldn't have to do a Wild West crawl along the top of the train after all.

"Very well," the Juri said. "You may pass."

The crowd began to shuffle out of the aisle into the seat areas. "Hold it," I said. "If you think we're just going to walk your gauntlet, forget it. Everybody back to the second baggage car and stay there. And I mean *everybody*."

"I have given my word," the Juri protested.

"Like I'm going to trust *that*," I said pointedly. "Come on, move it. And leave that thing right where it is," I added, pointing at the crumpled Spider. "It looks way too much like a weapon for my taste."

Silently, the Juriani hoisted the Spider up onto the tops of the seats beside them, then joined the rest of the walkers in backing up toward the rear door. I watched as they filed out, alert for any last-second tricks. The door closed behind the spokesman, and I heard Losutu mutter something under his breath. "I don't like this," he said. "They gave in way too easy."

"Agreed," I said, returning the carrybag to its rack. "McMicking?"

"I'll check it out." Gripping his nunchaku warily, he started slowly down the aisle, checking between the rows of seats for hidden surprises. "All clear," he called when he reached the end. "Let's move before he changes his mind."

I nodded and moved the stretcher forward, stopping as I came alongside the dying Spider. "Director, you want to give me a hand with this?" I asked, getting a grip on the deformed sphere.

"What are we doing with it?" Losutu asked, gathering the legs together and cradling them over his forearms like a bundle of firewood.

"We're taking him with us," I said, starting forward again. "Bayta says he's still alive."

"Can he stop the train?" Losutu asked.

"Not from here," Bayta told him. "But if we can get him to the engine, either he or I will be able to control it."

"Come on, come on," McMicking said impatiently, eyeing the Spider as we arrived at the door. "You really want to bother with that thing?"

"Might come in handy," I said. "Let's swivel him around."

A minute later we had the Spider turned around so that it was resting on the top of the stretcher, its legs pointed forward. "Okay, open up," I told McMicking. "Let's see what we've got."

I'd fully expected to find the crowd of walkers waiting in this, the last passenger coach before the baggage cars, ready to charge us the second we stepped inside. It was with a definite feeling of anticlimax that the door opened to show nothing but rows of empty third-class seats.

"Too easy," McMicking muttered, eyeing the apparently deserted car. "He's planning something."

"I know," I said. "Check the washrooms."

He stepped to one of the doors and yanked it open. A quick look inside, and he closed that door and opened the other. "Clear."

"No choice but to go for it," I told him. "You first—watch yourself. Bayta, have the Saarix ready."

McMicking started down the aisle, again checking each row as he passed. I kept us a couple of paces behind him, not wanting to let any of our group get too far ahead or behind.

We were halfway down the car when two Halkas suddenly leaped up from the row just ahead of McMicking and hurled themselves at him. McMicking staggered the first one back with a nunchaku blow across the top of his head, then danced back a step and turned to the second.

And as he did, the entire rear of the car erupted with Modhran walkers, three crammed into each side of each row. Each group had a piece of broken Spider; and in their usual perfect unison, they hurled them at us.

Their primary target was McMicking, who was instantly buried beneath a pile of debris. Reflexively, I grabbed Bayta's arm and yanked her down behind the partial protection of the stretcher, stifling a curse as a section of Spider leg flew past and caught me squarely across the back. "Do it!" I snapped.

I didn't have to give the order twice. Even as another round of flying objects slammed into the chairs all around us, I heard the sizzle-*pop* as she triggered the second carry-bag handle. I held her tightly to me, hoping that McMicking had managed to keep his mask on.

The missiles stopped flying, and the commotion stilled. Cautiously, I looked up.

Once again, the Saarix had done the trick. The walkers were dead.

And our last trump card had now been played.

"Don't just stand there," McMicking's muffled voice called from beneath a pile of twisted metal. "Get me out of here."

Bayta and I squeezed around the stretcher and got to work, and a minute later we had him free. "You all right?" I asked as I helped him to his feet.

"I'm fine," he grunted, shaking his arms experimentally as he bent down to retrieve his nunchaku. "That second Halka was kind enough to take some of the impact for me."

"Nice of him," I said, looking back. Losutu was just coming down the aisle toward us, his eyes frowning over his mask. "Come on, Losutu, shake a leg."

"I was checking the medical kit," he said, his voice tight. "The oxygen tank and mask are gone."

"Terrific," I said, my stomach tightening as I did a quick survey of the bodies draped across the seats and lying in the aisles. Other than ours, there were no masks in sight.

"We didn't get around to checking the kit in the last car, either," McMicking reminded me. "That means they could have two of them."

"Three, if there's one in the Peerage car," I said. "I wonder what he's done with them."

"Nothing good," McMicking growled. "The sooner we're out of here, the better."

"Definitely," I agreed. "You want me to take point for a change?"

"No, I've got it," he said, setting his nunchaku into fighting position again and moving ahead. "You might need to ditch the stretcher, though."

I studied the narrow aisle and the mass of bodies lying in our path. He had a point. "Bayta, is our Spider still alive?"

"Yes, barely," she said.

"You and Director Losutu grab it," I said, manhandling

the big oxygen cylinder off its rack and hoisting it up on the seat back next to me where I could get into the straps. "McMicking?"

"Looks clear," he called from the rear door.

"Okay." I got my arms into the straps and settled the cylinder onto my back. "Go."

There was no one waiting for us in the baggage car. At least, not visibly. "Stay sharp," I warned the others as I looked around.

"I'm on it," McMicking said, moving forward and peering between the stacks of safety-webbed crates. "Where exactly are these hatches?"

"There," Bayta said, pointing upward as she and Losutu eased the Spider onto the floor. "We might have to move some of the crates to make steps."

"Or we could climb the webbing," I suggested, craning my neck to look at the hatch. It was pretty big, and Bayta had already said it was heavy. "Any idea how we're going to get it open?"

"Maybe we can use this," Losutu suggested, lifting the pointed end of one of the Spider's legs.

"Might work," I agreed. "If we can get it up there—"

"Compton?" someone called from the far end of the car. "Frank Compton?"

I spun around. That voice . . . "*Falc* Rastra?"

"Yes," Rastra called. "Please—I'm unarmed. I just want to talk."

"No," McMicking said before I could answer.

"Absolutely not," Losutu seconded. "It's a trick."

He was almost certainly right, I knew. Still . . . "Come out where we can see you," I called.

There was a moment's pause, and then Rastra stepped out from between two stacks of crates at the far end of the car. "I'm unarmed," he said again, holding his hands out as he took a step toward us. "You're making a big mistake."

"I do that all the time," I assured him. "I'm used to it."

"No, I mean it," he insisted, taking another step forward.

"The Modhri isn't the evil, villainous creature you seem to think."

"And all this comes from personal experience?" I asked, slipping the oxygen tank off my back and setting it down on the floor.

"Actually, it does," he said, taking another step forward. "I've lived with part of him inside me ever since I was promoted to *Falc*."

"What a coincidence," I said, walking up behind McMicking. "*I've* lived with a whole bunch of him for the past hour myself. Can't say I recommend the experience."

"What did you expect?" Rastra countered. "You're siding with people who are trying to destroy him."

I reached McMicking's side. "Go back to the others," I ordered him quietly. Behind his back, out of Rastra's sight, I slipped my multitool from my pocket and extended the blade. "If this is a diversion, that's where the main attack will come."

"You want me to just take him out and be done with it?" he murmured back.

"No, I don't want you getting that far away," I said, transferring the multitool to my right hand and covering the blade with my fingers. "I can handle him if there's trouble."

McMicking nodded and backed away. "They're trying to destroy him because he's trying to take over the galaxy," I called to Rastra, lifting my right hand and resting it casually against the nearest stack of crates. Just around the corner where Rastra couldn't see, I slipped the blade beneath the safety webbing and started to cut. "On a more personal level, he was trying to take over *me*."

Rastra clicked his beak reprovingly. "He was trying to help you become part of a community," he corrected. "Be honest, Compton—how long has it been since you truly felt yourself to be part of anything important?"

"That's beside the point," I said, sliding my hand casually up the corner of the boxes, slicing through the webbing as I went. I cut the strands as far up as I could conveniently reach, then shifted the knife to point down and started working on the lower ones. "Besides, I've never thought of slavery as much of a social club."

"It's not slavery," he insisted, his voice calm and persuasive. "I'm sure the Spiders and Bellidos told you differently, but it really isn't. The Modhri never interferes with your actions except when absolutely necessary. Like on the Kerfsis transfer station—remember? That was him calling to the soldiers, reacting faster than I could, telling them not to kill you."

"I remember," I said. "I believe 'don't kill *it*' were his precise words. Shows you how highly we stand in his estimation."

"He was rattled," Rastra said, some frustration starting to creep into his voice. "Are you going to base your judgment on a single hasty word? Especially a word that saved your life?"

"So what *should* I base it on?" I countered, feeling fresh sweat starting to gather beneath my collar. We needed to get moving, but we couldn't very well start climbing to the ceiling with Rastra standing there watching us. The second the Modhri realized what we were doing, he would throw everything he had left against us.

"Base it on what he can give you," Rastra said. "Insights you couldn't get anywhere else. Information your peers don't have, courtesy of a mind that is everywhere and sees everything. Most importantly, base it on the promise of ultimate peace."

I frowned. "Peace?"

"What need will there be for conflict when friends of the Modhri sit across every boardroom table and diplomatic pedestal across the galaxy?" he said. "Finally, and forever, we'll all be in true harmony with each other."

"Sounds like heaven on earth," I agreed. "And all due to our mutual cooperation with the Modhri?"

He clicked his beak again. "Exactly."

I shook my head in mock amazement. "You're good," I told him. "You're very good. Every other time I've heard you, you've sounded like the gloating would-be conqueror from some dit rec drama. I see now that you can also play the Earnest Friend Of Mankind role."

"What are you talking about?" Rastra said, the scales around his beak creasing. "This is *me,* your old friend, *Falc* Rastra."

"My old friend was *Tas* Rastra, Modhri," I corrected. "And as far as I can see, all that's left of that friend is his body."

A look of consternation flashed across Rastra's face. "Compton—Frank—*listen* to me."

And in that instant, the Modhri sprang his trap.

From behind me came the sudden rustle of cloth against plastic, and I spun to see JhanKla's guard-assistant Yir-TukOo roll off the top of one of the stacks and drop to the floor between Losutu and Bayta, one of the missing oxygen masks covering the lower half of his face. His left hand slapped Losutu across the side of his head, dropping him to the floor, while his right went the other direction, backhanding Bayta across her face as well and sending her staggering backward. He stepped over Losutu's crumpled form as McMicking leaped to the attack—

There was a scuffle of movement behind me, and I twisted around to see Rastra charging toward me, fastening a mask of his own over his beak as he ran. Swearing under my breath, I slashed my knife at the remaining strands of mesh and then jabbed the blade solidly into the side of one of the crates.

And as Rastra finished sealing his mask and stretched out his hands, I got a firm grip on the multitool and threw my full weight to my left.

The crate I was pulling on shifted partway out through the hole I'd cut in the mesh; and with the crates above it suddenly unbalanced, the entire stack collapsed, sending the boxes tumbling out into the aisle. I got a glimpse of startled Jurian eyes as Rastra was buried under the avalanche, then wiggled my knife free and headed back to the others.

Up to now I hadn't seen McMicking have any real trouble

with anything the Modhri had thrown at him. But either fatigue had taken its toll, or else the metal hailstorm in the previous car had shaken him up more than either of us had realized. Even as I sprinted back to help, YirTukOo ducked beneath the swinging nunchaku and slapped his closed right hand hard across McMicking's face. McMicking staggered two steps backward and tripped over the broken Spider, his nunchaku clattering against the nearest stack of boxes as it fell from his hand. Clenching my teeth, I shifted my knife around into stabbing position and picked up my pace. YirTukOo saw me coming and lifted his hands into combat stance, and I could imagine a smug smile beneath his mask as he waited for me to reach him.

Only in that frozen moment of time I saw something he didn't. Filling my lungs, I sent a bellow of challenge through my oxygen mask to echo off the ceiling.

A bellow that covered up any noise Bayta might have made as she came up behind the Halka and threw herself onto his shoulders. Wrapping her arms tightly around his neck, she dug both knees hard into his back and pulled.

It was probably the last thing YirTukOo had expected, that someone he'd hit that hard would already be back on her feet, and the shock of it paralyzed him a fatal half second too long. He started to grab for her arms, realized that I was already too close, and tried to get his hands back into a defensive posture.

Before he could, I was on him.

There were very few weak spots in Halkan physiology, and even fewer that could be reached by a knife as short as mine. Unfortunately for him, I knew all of them. Two quick and precise jabs, and it was over.

"You okay?" I asked Bayta as I shoved the Halka's body off her and lifted her to her feet. The whole right side of her face above her mask, I saw, was a solid red mass where the back of his hand had connected.

"I think so," she said, a little shakily. "What about the others?"

"I'm all right," Losutu grunted from the floor behind her.

He started to pull himself to his feet; and then, abruptly, he froze. "Oh, no," he breathed. "Look."

I followed his pointing finger to YirTukOo's right hand. In it, still held loosely by the dead fingers, was a small lump of coral.

I felt my stomach tighten as I replayed the fight through my mind's eye. He'd hit Losutu with his left hand—no danger there. With his right he'd hit Bayta, but with a back-handed blow that should have kept her clear.

And then he'd hit McMicking.

There was a muffled groan from behind me, and I turned to see McMicking push himself to his feet. "Cheap shot," he muttered, rubbing the back of his head as he retrieved his nunchaku. "Cheap damn lucky shot. What happened?"

"Bayta and I got him," I said, peering at his face. There was a touch of red just above the left side of his mask, right at the end of a long scratch across the mask itself.

"Looks like most of it hit the mask," Bayta murmured hopefully from beside me.

"Yeah," I said heavily. "But not all of it."

"What are you talking about?" McMicking demanded, reaching up a finger to touch his cheek. He pulled it away, his eyes going flat as he saw the smear of blood. "Hell," he said, very quietly. "Is this what I think it is?"

"I don't know," I said. "It could have been just his hand that got you."

"I doubt it," he said with a sigh. "Well, that's it. You'd better get going. Want me to help you get the hatch open first?"

"You're not staying behind," Losutu said firmly. "I won't have it."

"You don't have a choice," McMicking said, just as firmly. "I'm one of them now. Or I will be soon enough."

"But not for days or weeks," Losutu said. "Isn't that right, Compton? We've got time to get him to a hospital."

"A hospital won't do him any good," Bayta said, her voice tinged with sadness. "The doctors wouldn't even know what to look for."

"What about your Spider friends?" I asked, wondering

why I even cared. McMicking was nothing more than an employee of someone I also happened to be working for, after all. "Would *they* know how to help him?"

She hesitated. Just a split second, but long enough. "No," she said. "I'm sorry."

"But he still has those days or weeks, right?" I persisted. "Even if we can't help him, we can take him back with us."

"And then what?" McMicking demanded. "You'll still have to kill me eventually."

"I was thinking that an actual specimen might help prove our story," I said.

Losutu looked at me, his eyes hard and disbelieving above his mask. "Compton, you are the most callous, heartless—"

"Save it," McMicking cut him off. "He's right. Fine, I'll go. Can we get this hatch open now?"

"We can try," I said. "Bayta, can you—"

I was interrupted by a clunk from above and a sudden swirling of air whipping around me. I looked up to see a section of the roof sliding down like a rolltop desk. "Bayta?" I called over the hurricane.

"The Spider," Bayta called back, her voice barely audible as the air rushed out of the compartment.

My ears popped once, painfully, then seemed to settle down. Apparently, seven centuries of leakage from ten thousand Quadrail stations had left the Tube with at least enough air pressure to keep our eardrums from blowing. "I'll take the tank," I shouted to them, stepping back to where I'd left it. "McMicking, Losutu—you take the Spider."

It took all of us to get the Spider up the sides of the stacked crates and through the hatch. Losutu and McMicking scrambled up after it, and I helped Bayta up behind them.

I had made it to the top and had a hand on the hatch when something made me pause and look down.

Rastra's body was still pinioned beneath the crates I'd pulled over on him. But his face was visible, and his eyes as he stared up at me were burning with impotent fury above his oxygen mask. I could see his beak moving, but the air in the compartment was too thin for whatever he was saying to carry that distance.

"I'm sorry," I said aloud, knowing that he wouldn't be able to hear me, either. Knowing, too, that the *Tas* Rastra who I'd once known and liked and respected wasn't the one who was staring hatred at me. What I had done had been necessary, but that didn't diminish the pain and guilt whispering through me.

And even then, it occurred to me, the Modhri had missed a bet. He should have released Rastra to talk to me now, to plead in honest bewilderment for me to help him.

I might even have been tempted to do so.

But I had more pressing matters on my mind than the mourning of an old acquaintance. Turning my back on the thing lying dying on the floor, I made my way the rest of the way onto the roof.

It wasn't nearly as bad as I'd feared it would be. The coach roofs were reasonably flat, and while there weren't any lips or other guardrails at the edges, there were plenty of built-in hooks and anchor points for Spiders and maintenance cranes to attach to. The low air pressure meant only a gentle breeze would be brushing against our faces, and unlike the dazzling light show the Coreline typically put out at Quadrail stations, here it was giving off only a gently undulating glow behind its loose wire mesh, a glow not much brighter than a nice harvest moon.

"I'll go first," I instructed the others. "Bayta will come next, then McMicking and Losutu. Bayta can drive this thing if she has to, so if you can't get the Spider across without risking a fall, leave it." Bayta stirred at that, but remained silent. "Ready? Let's do it."

I set off across the top of the baggage car in an elbows-and-knees commando crawl, moving as quickly as I dared. Bayta had said it was impossible to open the doors outside a station, but I didn't trust the Modhri not to find a way to do it. I reached the front of the car and eased myself down onto the slightly lower and more flexible top of the vestibule, then crawled across it and up the other side. Checking over my shoulder once to make sure the others were following, I continued on.

I had passed over that car and was just coming up out of the vestibule onto the next when I tilted a little too far to the side and the tank on my back began to roll off.

I stopped instantly, spread-eagling my arms and legs to the sides. The tank was better than half my own weight, and it wouldn't take much movement on its part to pull me up onto my side and possibly roll me off the train altogether. I held that posture, feeling the rhythmic vibration of the train beneath me, until I was sure the tank had stopped moving. Then, carefully, I pushed up on that side with shoulder and hip to try to shift it back into position over my spine. It started to move, but a few centimeters shy of its proper position it froze up again. I tried jiggling it, but it wouldn't budge; hung up, most likely, on one of its own straps.

Briefly, I thought about waiting for Bayta to catch up and seeing if she could straighten it out. But there was still the Modhri to worry about, and I didn't want to waste the time. Besides, there was more than one way to skin a cat. Bracing myself, I hunched my back sharply upward, throwing the cylinder into the air and breaking it loose from its snag. With that much weight in motion my body bounced up with it, and I felt myself lift a fraction of a centimeter off the roof.

And suddenly I found myself skidding helplessly along the top of the car.

I flattened out again, grabbing futilely for the handholds as they whizzed past, fighting to slow down even as I tried to figure out what the hell had happened. My first, horrifying thought was that the Modhri had managed to take control of the engine and had hit the brakes. My second, even more horrible thought was that we'd hit something. Either way, unless I could stop myself, I was going to keep sliding until I ran out of train and tumbled onto the tracks ahead.

Abruptly, the roof dropped out from beneath me. I braced myself for the worst, and had just enough time to realize I had dipped into the next vestibule before I slammed head-first against the edge of the next car forward.

I lay there for the next couple of minutes, watching the stars bouncing around my vision and wondering if I'd broken my neck, split my skull, or both. Fortunately, I'd done neither. The pain subsided to a less pervasive level, allowing my brain to get back to the question of what the hell had happened. There had been no squealing or thudding of brakes, nor had there been the flash or sound of an impact. As far as I could tell, in fact, the Quadrail was still trundling merrily along its way.

I puzzled at it for another minute, but it was clear I wasn't going to figure it out lying here. Meanwhile, there was still a trainload of walkers to get away from. Giving my neck one last experimental rotation, I pulled myself up onto the next car.

And got the shock of my life. Directly ahead, one car past the one I was on, was the Quadrail's engine.

I stared at it, wondering if the shimmering glow from the Coreline was playing tricks on my eyes. But it was the engine, all right, all bright and shiny and pulling us through the Tube at its steady pace of one light-year per minute.

Only that was impossible. I'd been on the back of the coach two cars forward from our baggage car, nine back from where I now suddenly found myself. Had I blacked out somehow? Could I have done all those intervening cars in my sleep?

Or could my blackout have had a little help?

My mouth felt suddenly dry behind my mask. A blackout, an attempt to run across the cars instead of crawling across them—yes, it could all fit with a Modhran colony weaving its little spells through my body.

But in that case why was I still alive? Surely the Modhri wouldn't have tried to run me off the train and then had second thoughts about it. Would he? I stared at the engine chugging along ahead of me . . .

And then, suddenly, I had it. It hadn't been the Modhri, after all.

It had been something far worse.

I don't know how long I laid there. Long enough to start thinking again, anyway, and to remember my priorities. Rubbing my neck, I crawled up onto the car and made my way to the front.

The engine didn't have a convenient vestibule to crawl down onto, but there was a wide connector fastening it to the rest of the Quadrail with plenty of hand- and footholds along the way. Moving carefully, I climbed down, stepped across the connector, and made it onto the back of the engine itself. The cab door, fortunately, faced the rear. I tried it, found it unlocked, and went inside.

I was waiting there, the big oxygen tank set up and ready to go in one of the front corners, when Bayta arrived.

"Whew!" she said as she climbed inside the cab and collapsed onto the floor beside the tank. "I've never been on top of one of these before. Not nearly as bad as I was afraid it would be. Don't open that tank yet—the compartment doesn't have an airlock."

"Yes, I know," I said. "You okay?"

"Yes, I'm fine," she assured me. "Why, don't I sound all right?"

"You sound nervous," I told her. "You're talking a blue streak, and you never do that."

"I'm just tired," she said quickly. Too quickly. "Too many emotional tumbles in the past hour."

"Uh-huh," I said. "As long as we have this moment alone together, let me ask you something. Back in the baggage car, after McMicking got hit by the coral, you said you couldn't do anything to help him."

Her eyes skittered guiltily away from mine. "I'm sorry."

"Don't be sorry yet," I warned. "To be precise, what you said was that the *Spiders* couldn't do anything. You never said whether or not *you* could."

"I don't know what you mean," she said carefully.

"Yes, you do," I said. "You recovered from YirTukOo's attack a lot faster than any of us expected. Including him."

Her eyes had gone very still above her mask. "I'm not a Modhran walker, Frank," she said, her voice steady.

"No, you're not," I agreed. "You're one of the ones *fighting* the Modhri, as well as controlling the Spiders and the Quadrail and, apparently, pretty much the whole galaxy." I lifted my eyebrows. "And I'm guessing both you and the Modhri came from something of the same stock. Tell me I'm wrong."

For a long minute she just gazed at me. Fleetingly, I wished I could have waited until we'd had a room full of air, when I could have seen more of her face and maybe had a clue as to what she was thinking. But the cab was too small to provide any privacy, and I definitely didn't want McMicking and Losutu in on this conversation. "What do you want?" she asked at last.

"I want your people to clean the polyps out of McMicking," I said. "And I want to talk to one of your leaders and get the whole story about what's going on here."

She shook her head. "I can't do that."

"You have to," I said, letting my voice harden. "Because I know your secret, Bayta. I know what you've been doing. And I think I know why, but I want to hear it from someone in charge."

The lines around her eyes crinkled, and I pictured a wan smile beneath the mask. "You ask an awful lot, Frank Compton."

"That's because I have a lot to give," I said. "Because I also know the secret the Modhri just killed a trainful of people to protect."

She straightened up. "You know where his new homeland is?"

"I know where it is, how it got there, and maybe even how to destroy it." I ducked my head to look out the viewport set into the cab door. "And you've got until the others get here to make your decision," I added. "Yes, or no?"

She turned to look out the viewport, too. "All right," she said at last. "But we can't take the whole train there."

"Then cut it loose," I said. "Everyone aboard is dead anyway, remember? It might even be easier for the Spiders if the thing just disappears, with no bodies around to ask unpleasant questions about."

She gave me a sharp look. But the sharpness faded, and she nodded reluctantly. "You're right," she said with a sigh. "What about Losutu and McMicking? What are you going to tell them?"

"Nothing," I assured her. "Don't worry, I can handle them. Where are you planning to take us?"

"You've asked to speak to the Chahwyn," she said, bowing her head formally. "I'll take you to our home."

"Oh. Good," I said, suppressing a shiver. So I'd been right about her. I'd rather hoped I'd been wrong. "They just better not be clear across the galaxy. I don't think either McMicking or the facilities here are geared up for a long trip."

"They're very close," she assured me, getting to her feet. "Let's see if the others need any help."

Losutu and McMicking were pretty worn out by the time we helped them maneuver the Spider into the cab. But their mood brightened considerably once we got the area pressurized and they could finally take their masks off.

It brightened even more when I told them where we were going.

"But I thought Bayta said there wasn't anything they could do for me," McMicking said, eyeing her suspiciously. "If this is some sort of soothey-smiley game, forget it."

"It's no game," I assured him. "But it comes with a promise of secrecy." I looked at Losutu. "On both your parts. The Spiders insist on it."

"Understood, and promise given," Losutu said gravely. "What about you?"

"Bayta and I have some strategy sessions to attend," I said. "Among other things, there's going to be hell to pay when that train out there vanishes into the mists with all aboard."

"What do you mean?" Losutu asked, stiffening. "You can't just—"

"They're all dead, Director," McMicking said.

Losutu's lips compressed, but he just nodded. "Of course," he murmured. "How will you do it?"

"It's already done," I said, glancing out the viewport at the rest of the train, decoupled now and falling slowly away behind us. Something about that glance belatedly caught my attention, and I turned back for a second look.

There, on top of the first car, was the lone figure of a Halka, standing straight and tall as he watched us pull away. His flat face was half covered by his oxygen mask, but his red/orange/purple Peerage robes were unmistakable as they flapped gently in the breeze.

And as I watched, I saw him lift his fist defiantly in our direction. JhanKla, High Commissioner of the Halkas, Modhran walker, and undisputed master of the engineless train that was even now coasting its way toward a silent, lonely death between the stars.

I wished him the joy of his victory.

TWENTY-THREE :

We never actually made it to Homshil Station. Bayta took us onto a siding that had been shown on her private map, and from there onto another line that was definitively *not* on the map.

The hours passed slowly. The engine cab hadn't been designed to hold more than a couple of Spiders at a time, and four human bodies pretty much filled the available space. Fortunately, after what we'd just been through, none of us felt much like exercise anyway. Mostly we sat or lay around, dozing when we could, conversing only occasionally.

Sometime in the first three hours, our rescued Spider quietly died. Bayta sat silently after that, wrapped in her own thoughts, not speaking to anyone even when spoken to.

I was just starting to worry about such things as food, water, and bathroom facilities when we arrived.

"Mr. McMicking will be taken to a facility here in the station for treatment," Bayta informed us as the engine rolled to a stop in what I was coming to recognize as a standard Quadrail siding. "Director Losutu will accompany him. You will stay with him at all times, and not attempt to leave," she added, leveling a gaze at Losutu. "Is that understood?"

"Yes," he said calmly. "Am I permitted to ask any questions?"

"Ask as many as you wish," she said. "Most of them won't be answered. Mr. Compton: Come with me."

She turned and opened the cab door, and I felt a small twinge. *Mr. Compton.* After all the hell and fury we'd just been through, it was suddenly back to *Mr. Compton.* A not-so-subtle signal that I shouldn't have forced her to bring us here?

Maybe. Still, her people couldn't afford to kill me. Not yet.

There were eight Spiders waiting outside, two of them drudges and the rest the unknown class I'd first seen when Bayta took me to see Hermod. Two of the latter detached themselves from the group and led us fifty meters across the siding to a red-rimmed hatchway. It opened as we reached it, and Bayta led the way down the steps into a small shuttle.

"Do I get to know where we are?" I asked as we took seats in front of a bank of displays, labeled with markings consisting mostly of nested curves. There were no actual controls I could see; Spiders and Chahwyn alike apparently ran their various gadgets via telepathy.

"Would the system's name tell you anything?" Bayta countered as the hatchway above us closed and we dropped away from the Tube.

"Probably not," I conceded. There was a click, and all around us cabin panels irised open into viewports.

It was a typical starscape, the kind you could see from any of a thousand systems across the galaxy. In the center of our view was a small star, mostly white but with a strange greenish tinge. "Welcome to Viccai," Bayta said, pointing toward a dark circle with a bright edge directly ahead. "It means 'hope' in our language."

"I take it this isn't your people's original home?"

"No, we moved here after the Great Revolt, after we and the Spiders built the Tube," she said. "There was no other life here, and no worlds anyone could ever want or use. It was the safest place we could be."

"You might be surprised at what Humans want," I said. "Whether or not we can actually use it."

She shrugged. "Perhaps."

"Trust me," I assured her. "How long ago was this Great Revolt?"

"Sixteen hundred years," she said. "But that's a subject better left to the Elders."

"I suppose," I said, frowning as another piece fell into place. "The messenger who brought me my Quadrail ticket was another one like you, wasn't he?"

"Yes," she said, and I could hear the quiet pain in her voice. "We were sent to Earth to bring you to Hermod. He went off to meet you, while I made preparations at the skyport. We were supposed to all ride out to the Quadrail together." She closed her eyes briefly. "And then you showed up at the skyport alone, and I didn't have time to try to find him before I had to leave with you."

"I'm sorry," I said. "If it helps any, there was probably nothing you could have done to save him. If you'd been there, it would have been two of you dead instead of one."

"I know that." She took a deep breath, let it out tiredly. "But all the logic and reason in the world doesn't help when someone was your friend."

I turned away. "I'll take your word for it."

I could feel her eyes on me. "You have friends, Frank," she said. "Or at least, they're there if you want them."

"I'll take your word for it," I said again, a little more brusquely this time. I didn't need her sympathy. "So how exactly does the Modhri fit into all this?"

"The Elders will explain," she said. "They're the ones who best know the history." She hesitated. "And they're the only ones who can make bargains with you," she added. "*If* they choose to do so."

The planet Viccai, when we reached it, was every bit as cold and dark and cheerless as it had looked from a distance. If this was the Chahwyn's idea of hope, I decided as we flew over the bleak landscape, I'd hate to see what they considered depressing.

But like Bayta herself, things here were not exactly as they seemed. We touched down, and even before Bayta had finished shutting off the systems the landing area began to sink into the ground. Within a few minutes we'd reached a subterranean city filled with lights and music and strange but pleasant aromas. Bayta led me to a nearby building and into a small room with sculpted walls and a ceiling designed to look like a normal daytime sky, complete with drifting clouds and a bright yellow sun. In the center of the room were nine chairs arranged in an inward-facing triangle.

"Sit there," Bayta told me, pointing to one of the corner chairs as she sat down in one of the others. "The Elder who will speak to you is coming."

The words were barely out of her mouth when a door I hadn't noticed opened in the wall behind the third corner of the triangle and a single figure wearing soft shoes and an elaborately draped toga sort of robe strode in to join us.

I had been expecting some sort of alien being, something never before seen by mortal man. To my surprise and vague disappointment, the Elder was as human as the kid next door. He was of average height and build, with brown hair and eyes and a calm, almost beatific expression. "Good day, Frank Compton," he said, inclining his head as he stepped into the triangle and seated himself in the third corner. His voice was as melodious as that of a trained Shakespearean actor. "Welcome to Viccai."

"Thank you," I said. Very Human . . . but not quite Human enough. Now, with a more careful look, I could see the vagueness of the details around his lips and ears, the false way the wrinkles at his eyes and mouth fell into place, the slight misjointedness of his wrists and fingers as he settled his hands into his lap. "But please," I added. "Don't go to all this trouble just for me."

The Elder inclined his head. "Hermod was right," he said. "You were indeed an excellent choice." He smiled; and as he did so his skin seemed to melt, the facial features smoothing out, the fingers and arms thinning and lengthening. Most of the brown hair flattened and slid back out of sight beneath the flesh, while a handful of the tufts above the eyes stretched out into clusters of catlike whiskers.

And when the transformation was finished, he was every bit as alien as I had first expected.

"Thank you," he said. Oddly enough, his voice was still melodious. Probably he'd decided to keep whatever adjustments he'd made to his vocal system. "It is so very difficult to maintain an unfamiliar form." He gestured two bony fingers toward Bayta. "Which is why it was necessary to have genuine Humans to walk among you."

"Bayta said you would tell me about the Modhri," I said, deciding to let that one pass for the moment.

The Elder nodded. "The story begins four thousand years ago, with the rise of a race called the Shonkla-raa," he said. "It was they who first discovered the secret of interstellar travel and began expanding their influence across the galaxy. Within fourteen hundred years they had mapped out the locations of all inhabited and inhabitable systems and begun a thousand years of conquest." He paused. "I'm told you claim to know their secret."

"I know *your* secret," I told him. "I can only assume it's the same as theirs."

The Elder inclined his head. "Tell me."

They couldn't afford to kill me, I reminded myself firmly. "In a nutshell, your glorious Quadrail is a fraud," I said. "The whole thing: the trains with their intriguingly mysterious fourth rail, the fancy laser connections bouncing off the front bumpers, even the big light show from the Coreline. It's nothing but a carefully arranged set of window dressing designed to misdirect and obscure what's really going on."

The Elder had gone very still. "Which is?"

"That it's nothing but the Coreline," I said. "There's something inside that fancy packaging that makes the whole thing work. Some kind of quantum thread, I'd guess—I don't know enough physics to even take a stab as to what kind. The point is that once you're in motion, the closer you get to the Coreline the faster you move. Quadrails move at a light-year per minute; information cylinders, which I gather get somehow kicked up onto that mesh framework around the Coreline, go a hell of a lot faster."

I looked at Bayta. "You saw it, didn't you? My accidental hop, when I was briefly disconnected from direct contact with the Quadrail. Even a fraction of a centimeter closer to the Coreline sent me leapfrogging nine cars ahead before I came back down."

She nodded soberly. "I was hoping you wouldn't realize what had happened."

"So it's true," the Elder said, a strange melancholy in his voice. "The secret is lost."

"Well, no, not necessarily," I cautioned him. "There's no reason that information has to leave this room. Because I think I also know *why* you went to all this trouble in the first place." I waved a hand out toward the stars. "Back on the Quadrail, the Modhri tried to spin me a nice little spindrift about how he wanted peace for the galaxy. You Chahwyn, on the other hand, have actually done something to create it."

"We had no choice," the Elder said in a low voice. "We'd seen what uncontrolled access to the Thread led to. The Shonkla-raa were conquerors, arrogant and violent. Once they gained control of the Thread and learned how to ravel bits of it off to other star systems, there was no stopping them. They built huge warships and sent them rushing between worlds, dominating or destroying all other life."

"So what finally stopped them?" I frowned as a sudden thought struck me. "Or is the *Modhri* the Shonkla-raa?"

The Elder's eye-ridge tufts quivered. "Not at all," he said. "The Modhri was merely the Shonkla-raa's final weapon."

Weapon. The word hung in the air for a moment like a scattering of black dust. I looked at Bayta, back at the Elder. "Maybe we'd better take this from the top."

The Elder nodded. "Sixteen hundred years ago, after a thousand years of slavery, there was a carefully coordinated uprising of the other races of the galaxy, a revolt long planned and long concealed. It ultimately cost the lives of many, including at least five entire races, and in the end all races had lost the capability to travel even within their own star systems. But the victory was worth the price, for our oppressors were finally and utterly destroyed."

"You sound like you were there," I suggested.

His alien face twitched. A smile? Or a grimace? "The Chahwyn were there, certainly," he said. "But we were merely one of many servant races, genetically created by the Shonkla-raa to be their technical laborers. We had been made incapable of aggression or combat, and thus were necessarily kept in the background during the war. As a result, our people survived better than most.

"But as I say, all peoples were beaten back to pre-space-flight levels, some to even preindustrial levels. So matters remained for three hundred years. The Thread still existed, but no one had the capability to reach it. Indeed, for most peoples even the rumor of its existence was lost." He paused. "Then, by chance, the Chahwyn discovered a cache of Shonkla-raa technology that had been hidden before war's end. With it we were able to reach again into space; and with access to the Thread, we gained the stars."

"Only the Shonkla-raa had made sure to breed all the fight out of you," I said. "Which meant that anyone you ran across could beat you silly if they had a mind to and take all the goodies for themselves."

"And the whole cycle would begin again," the Elder said. "We knew that before we approached the other peoples of the galaxy, we had to find a way to make interstellar war and conquest impossible."

"And so you built the Tube."

"And so we built the Tube," he said. "But we needed assistance, so first we created the Spiders. For that we used the Shonkla-raa's genetic equipment and our own flesh. We didn't dare mingle with other races ourselves—there was too much risk that our weakness would be discovered and that we would again be enslaved."

"Couldn't you have used the equipment to eliminate your

passiveness?" I suggested. "Then you could at least defend yourselves if necessary."

"Or we could become a second Shonkla-raa," he countered darkly. "No. Even if we knew how and where to draw such a delicate line, we would not dare take the risk."

"Very noble of you," I said. The words came out with less sarcasm, somehow, than I'd actually intended. "So you and the Spiders built the Tube. How long did it take?"

"Very long," he said. "Even with the spatial distortion near the Thread working in our favor, it still took six hundred years to complete."

"At which point you set up Quadrail service and invited the rest of the galaxy to come out and play," I said. "Which brings us back to the Modhri."

The Elder's face quivered in yet another unreadable expression. "He was to be the Shonkla-raa's final weapon against the Grand Alliance," he said. "Genetically engineered to be a group mind that could infiltrate, subvert, and ultimately control the leaders of the forces arrayed against them." A doglike shake ran briefly through his body. "Fortunately for us all, the war ended before he could be properly deployed, and for centuries he lay dormant within the coral formations of Modhra I.

"Then, two hundred years ago, the Spiders opened a station for the Halkas in the Sistarrko system. We know now that during their explorations the Halkas discovered the coral, and with that the silent war began. Within sixty years, we believe, the Modhri had spread his tendrils throughout the Halkavisti Empire and taken partial control of its leaders. At that point he turned his attention outward, sending Halkan walkers out into the galaxy to sell Modhran coral to the other species."

"Pricing it out of reach of everyone except the upper business and governmental echelons, naturally."

"Yes," he agreed. "Though at this point his expansion seems to have been more for information-gathering than conquest. He established outposts for future use, but still seemed interested mainly in bringing the Halkavisti Empire more firmly under his control.

"Within the next thirty years, though, the Spiders began to notice his influence among the Halkas, though they as yet had no idea what it was or where it came from. Growing increasingly concerned, they approached the Juriani, themselves relative newcomers to the galactic community, and asked if they could discover what was happening to their neighbors."

"And bang go the Juriani," I murmured.

"Yes," the Elder said grimly. "Their investigation was detected and the investigators infected. And because the team members were part of a military chain of command, the Modhri was able to use thought viruses to quickly leap himself up those contact lines to the very top of the government."

He gestured with his long fingers. "We hadn't known about this particular Shonkla-raa weapons program, but when we saw the same subtle influence now spreading among the Juriani we suspected some such evil was involved. We redoubled our efforts to search Shonkla-raa archives, trying to learn what it might be."

"Why didn't you just close down the Sistarrko Station?" I asked.

"At that point we had no idea where the Modhri was located," he said. "Nor did we know the mechanism of the attack, particularly how emotional connections allowed him to spread so quickly among a society's elite. Even more worrisome was the fact that he seemed to be increasing the pace of his conquests. It had taken nearly sixty years to conquer the Halkas, but only fifteen to reach the same level of control of the Juriani."

"Do you want anything to eat or drink?" Bayta put in suddenly. "I'm sorry; we should have offered that sooner."

To my surprise, I realized that I was in fact ravenously hungry. But this was far too interesting to interrupt even for food. "No, I'm okay," I told her. "Please, continue."

"Over the next sixty years the Spiders tried again and again to learn who and what this enemy was," the Elder said.

"They were able to get four other races interested in the problem, each taking a turn at solving it. All four ultimately fell, and it finally dawned on us that our actions were actually facilitating the invasions. The Modhri was also spreading out on his own, but we learned too late that these official investigation teams were probably the fastest and simplest route to high government levels."

"And even after all this, you still had no idea where the attacks were coming from?" I asked.

"Actually, by then we *had* narrowed it to one of the worlds along the Grakla Spur," he said. "Sistarrko was considered the most likely system."

"So again, why didn't you shut down the station?"

His eye-ridge tufts vibrated again. "We tried," he said ruefully. "Citing economic reasons, we closed down the entire Spur. But the pressure from the other empires was enormous, and not only from those controlled by the Modhri. We didn't dare take the chance that someone might become angry enough to storm the Tube itself, possibly destroying a section and thereby learning the secret of the Thread. So after a few weeks, we reopened the line."

"And business returned to normal."

"Except that now the Modhri knew who it was who'd been behind the various probes launched against him over the years." The Elder shivered again. "And with that, the Spiders themselves became targets for conquest."

I felt my throat tighten. Passengers, cargo, and mail, I remembered thinking rather resentfully back at Terra Station. If the Spiders were conquered, that ultimate hat trick would pass to the last-ditch weapon of an all-powerful tyranny. "I hope you've taken some precautions."

"The very nature of the Spiders and their armor makes a normal Modhri attack impossible," he assured me. "Still, with enough walkers in hand, other methods would become possible." His eyes flicked to Bayta. "One of which you have already seen. I will admit that we began to wonder if there was still any hope for us, or whether we and the galaxy had instead begun the long dark path to defeat.

"And then, thirty years ago, you Humans burst upon the scene."

He paused, his eyes again shifting to Bayta. "You were a wild race, full of confidence and energy and cleverness. The Shonkla-raa had either failed to notice you or else had decided your world had nothing worth stealing and had passed you by. But you were certainly a shock to the rest of us. Nothing quite like you had ever been seen in the galaxy, and I will admit that many of us were somewhat taken aback. But others saw you as perhaps our last, best hope for victory against the Modhri."

I felt my throat tighten. "Are you saying there isn't anyone else left?"

His eye-ridge tufts bristled. "At that point neither the Bellidos nor the Cimmaheem had shown signs of Modhran influence," he said. "And we think the Filiaelians, at the far end of the galaxy, may yet be untouched. Their routine manipulation of their own genetic code provides a natural barrier to Modhran intrusion."

Which was probably why Hermod had pointed me toward the Fillies in the first place. Watching a Spider agent go charging off to one of the last remaining bastions of independence would have pretty much guaranteed the Modhri's attention.

"But you were the ones with the drive and the curiosity that gave you a unique edge," the Elder continued. "We needed only to wait until you were acclimated to the cultures around you and ready to act."

"And meanwhile, the Bellidos decided to take their own crack at the Modhri," I said, remembering our conversations with Fayr aboard the Quadrail.

"And failed like all the others," the Elder said grimly. "Still, it was their effort that finally solved the mystery of the thought-virus mechanism."

"So when Fayr decided to try it on his own, he had the whole story available to him," I said, nodding. "And as an extra bonus, you even provided him with a nice little diversion."

The Elder ducked his head, the gesture looking very

strange the way his neck was jointed. "For that I apologize," he said. "But Fayr was in motion, and while we had no details of his plan or timetable, we nevertheless deemed his attempt had a good chance of success. We further judged that Humans were not yet ready to make a serious effort against the Modhri on their own. So we did what we could to help the Bellidos, while at the same time not jeopardizing the possibility of a future Human attack."

"And it worked pretty well," I had to admit. "I didn't divert the Modhri quite the way you planned, but my presence at least muddied the water a little. And Fayr was good enough that none of it made much of a difference to his plan anyway."

"Yes," the Elder murmured. "Except that it seems his plan was only a partial success."

"Unfortunately," I said. "My guess is that once the Modhri figured out that you were the ones behind all these attacks, he decided he'd better pull up stakes and get out of town. He picked a new homeland and started shipping his coral there as fast as he could."

"So that by the time Fayr destroyed the Modhran coral beds, enough of him had already made the transfer to begin again," the Elder said heavily. "But now Bayta tells us you know where this new homeland is."

"Yes, I do," I said, folding my arms across my chest. "Now all you have to do is convince me that I should tell you."

He stared, his eye-ridge tufts going suddenly rigid. "What do you mean?" he asked.

"I mean that from where I sit, you and the Modhri are looking way too much like fraternal twins," I said evenly. "You both communicate telepathically, you both like to be in control"—I hesitated, but this was no time to worry about a little hypocrisy—"and you both play fast and loose with the truth when it suits you."

I looked squarely at Bayta. "*And* you both invade people's bodies."

"It's nothing like that," she insisted. Unlike the Elder, her human face carried emotional cues I could read, and it was clear she was stunned by my abrupt refusal to spill my guts on cue. "The Modhri is a parasite, emotionally as well as physically, a creature who seeks to manipulate and control others for his own ends. I, on the other hand, am a true synthesis, with the Human and Chahwyn parts of me forming a genuine partnership."

"And how much say did the Human half of you have in the arrangement of this partnership?"

A flicker of something crossed her face. "She was a foundling," she said, her voice low. "A baby born aboard a Quadrail, then abandoned."

I felt my skin crawling. That sort of thing wasn't supposed to happen anymore, certainly not among the rich and powerful who could afford to travel among the stars. "Did you try to find her mother?"

"Yes, they found her," Bayta said. She was trying hard to sound like she was just reciting facts, but I could hear the pain beneath the words. "But she didn't want me. Or so she insisted."

"We, on the other hand, had great need of her," the Elder said. "We had the Spiders bring her here and . . . the two were melded."

A shiver ran up my back. "At least the Modhri has the courtesy to wait until someone's full-grown before taking over."

"We had no choice," Bayta snapped, glaring at me. "You saw Hermod, how big and fat and ungainly he was. That's what happens if you try to meld a Human and Chahwyn later in life. We had no *choice*."

She swallowed, her glare fading. "We were fighting for our survival," she said. "*And* for yours."

"We're not talking about me," I said. "We're talking about you, and how you've cheated an innocent Human being of her right to live. How exactly was this so-called melding done?"

"It was simple enough, at least from a technical standpoint," the Elder said. "Though despite what you say, we *did* think long and hard over the ethical questions. But as Bayta has said, we had no choice. So we took the Human foundling and introduced a newly born Chahwyn into her body."

So they'd done the same thing to a baby of their own, too. "Just like that?"

"Just like that," he agreed uncomfortably. He extended a finger, stretching it out toward Bayta like an invisible hand pulling taffy. "Our bodies, as you've already seen, are far more malleable than yours," he said, withdrawing the finger to its original size. "It didn't hurt either of them, I assure you."

"The Modhri within a walker is always a separate entity lurking in the background, looking for advantages for himself," Bayta said. "With me, though the Human and Chahwyn parts are in some ways separate, we are at the same time truly one person. We are partners, companions, friends. We are stronger than the sum of our parts."

"If you say so," I said, looking back at the Elder. "What about the one who brought me my Quadrail ticket? Another foundling?"

The Elder hesitated. "He, too, was unwanted."

"Was he another foundling?" I repeated.

He sighed. "He was purchased," he admitted. "Another child whose mother didn't want him. In his case, we worked through Hermod and an agency to obtain him."

"So there you have it," I said, the ashes of defeat in my mouth. I hadn't really wanted to prove the worst about the Chahwyn. But it seemed I'd done so anyway. "You buy and sell and use people like commodities, just like the Modhri. So you tell me: Why should I even bother to pick sides?"

"We've kept the galaxy at peace for seven hundred years," the Elder said, his voice tight as his hoped-for victory began to slip between his malleable fingers. "We don't interfere with politics or commerce or—"

"Do you want the woman back?" Bayta asked abruptly.

I blinked. "What do you mean, do I want her back?"

"You said we'd cheated an innocent Human being of her right to live," Bayta said. Her face was pale, but her voice was steady. "We can't change what has been for the past twenty-two years. But if the Chahwyn part of me is willing to die and return the rest of her life to her, will that make sufficient amends for our injustice?"

I shot a glance at the Elder. He seemed as flabbergasted by the offer as I was. "I don't know," I said. "What would that do to her?"

Bayta took a deep breath. "It would return her to what she would have been," she said. "She would be fully Human once more."

"And?"

Bayta hesitated. "She would be fully Human," she repeated. "Would that be sufficient amends?"

I studied her face. If there was any duplicity in her offer, I couldn't see it. "Let me think about it. What's happening with McMicking?"

"The work will take a few hours more," the Elder said, floundering a little as he tried to get back on track again. "Fortunately, he was brought here while the Modhran infection was still small and localized. Do you—?" He shot a look at Bayta. "Bayta reminds me you still need food and rest. Perhaps you will allow her to show you to a place where you may obtain both."

"Thank you," I said, studying Bayta's face. Two beings, separate yet one. I didn't understand it, but it seemed clear that she found the arrangement both reasonable and comfortable.

Perhaps more than just comfortable. *Partners, companions, friends,* she had said.

Friends.

She had told me flatly that she wasn't my friend. Yet for the sake of her people, she was willing to give up the closest friend she had . . . and that closest of friends was in turn willing to die.

If I demanded it.

I flipped my mental coin and watched it land where I knew it had to. No, the Chahwyn weren't perfect. But then, which of us was? "Yes, I'd like something to eat," I continued. "But let's first get the matter of the Modhri's new homeland out of the way."

The Elder's eye-ridge tufts fluttered. "I thought—"

"I know," I said. "But in the end, I guess, everyone eventually has no choice but to pick sides. And like you said, you *have* kept the galaxy at peace." I looked at Bayta. "Besides, Bayta has all the same clues I do. She could put it together if she wanted to. Question: What does the Modhri need in a homeland?"

"Cold and liquid water," the Elder said. "The polyps can survive in many other environments, but only in cold water can they create more coral and expand his mind."

"Okay, but you can get cold water almost anywhere," I said. "What I meant was that he needs a place where he can avoid the kind of attack Fayr used against him."

"I understand," Bayta said, her forehead suddenly wrinkled in concentration. "He needs a place where you can't bring in trade goods and buy weapons. Because there are no weapons to buy?"

"Exactly," I said, nodding. "But at the same time, obviously, it has to be a place with Quadrail service. In other words, a primitive colony."

"There must be a hundred such places in the galaxy," the Elder murmured.

"At the very least," I agreed. "Fortunately for us, the Modhri was kind enough to point us directly at it. Bayta, you told me Human society and government hadn't been infiltrated yet, correct?"

"That was what we thought," she said, her eyes gazing unblinkingly at me. "Yet we know now that Applegate *was* a walker."

"So the Modhri *has* infiltrated," I concluded. "Only he *hasn't* infiltrated the top levels. Losutu, for instance, would have been an obvious target, yet he clearly hasn't been touched. Why not? Answer one: The Modhri knew you were watching the people at the top level and would pick up on any moves he made. Answer two: He had more urgent fish to fry."

"It's on a *Human* colony!" the Elder exclaimed suddenly. "And you have only four of them."

"Narrows the field considerably, doesn't it?" I agreed.

"But I can narrow it even further. Tell me, Bayta: When exactly did we suddenly become the focus of Modhran attention? Was it when that drudge grabbed my luggage at Terra Station in front of everybody? Applegate was there, and that incident would certainly connect me to the Spiders in the Modhri's mind. Did it seem to bother him at all?"

"No," she said slowly. "At least, nothing obvious happened there."

"What about after you split off my car from the train and we had our chat with Hermod?" I continued. "That was what caught Fayr's attention. Did the Modhri seem to notice?"

"Again, no."

"And after we left New Tigris we went to the bar where Applegate was right across the room entertaining a couple of Cimmaheem," I reminded her. "Yet he didn't even bother to catch my eye and wave. Clearly, he didn't care what I was doing or who I was doing it with."

She caught her breath. "*Yandro,*" she breathed.

"Yandro," I confirmed, feeling the heavy irony of having come full circle. "A useless, empty world that certain people behind the scenes were nevertheless hell-bent on colonizing. A useless world that I was fired over, in fact, when I tried to rock the boat. And a world where you set off red flags all across the local Modhran mind segment when you made that hurried visit to the stationmaster during a fifteen-minute stopover."

"Yes," she said, and there was suddenly no doubt in her voice. "That has to be it."

"But what can we do?" the Elder asked. "If the system is as empty as you say, the Bellidos' approach won't work."

"Which is precisely why the Modhri moved there," I agreed. "Unfortunately for him, I have an idea."

The Elder eyed me. "And the cost for this will be?"

Right on cue, my stomach growled. "Right now, all it will cost is dinner," I said. "After that . . . we'll need to talk."

TWENTY-FOUR :

"This is certainly a pleasant surprise," Larry Hardin commented as McMicking and I walked between the palm trees flanking the doorway that led into the formal solarium of his New Pallas Towers apartment. "When the news about that missing Quadrail hit the net I assumed you were both lost. Does this mean the Spiders have found it, after all?"

"I don't think so," I told him. In actual fact, they *had* gone into the Tube and retrieved the derelict train. But since the Modhri had already killed everyone aboard, I doubted that would ever be announced. "Fortunately, we'd switched trains."

"Lucky indeed," Hardin agreed, gesturing toward a bench across from him set between a pair of lilac bushes. "As McMicking may have mentioned, I've had some second thoughts about your employment."

"Yes, he did," I confirmed, sitting down on the bench and sniffing appreciatively at the delicate scent of the lilacs. McMicking, for his part, went and stood at the back corner of Hardin's bench, watching me closely. "Unfortunately, I'm afraid that you were right the first time."

Hardin's eyebrows lifted. "Excuse me?" he asked ominously.

"I'm afraid I'm not going to be able to deliver, after all," I told him.

"You're giving up?"

"I give up when a job is finished or I'm convinced it's not possible," I said. "In this case, it's the latter."

"I see." Hardin leaned back against his bench. "Speaking of unfinished jobs, I've been having my people do a little investigating of your, shall we say, unaccounted-for funding. Oddly enough, it's also been impossible to track."

"And what do you conclude from that?"

"Possibly that some governmental agency is involved," he said. "I understand that a UN deputy director, who was also supposed to have been aboard that vanished Quadrail, has also returned alive and well. I further understand that you and he came back on the same torchliner *and* that you spent a great deal of the trip in his cabin."

"You're very well informed," I said.

"I try to be," he said. "You realize, of course, that our agreement has an exclusivity clause in it."

"I haven't told Director Losutu anything about this that I haven't told you," I assured him. "Our discussion was on other topics."

"In that case, the only other possibility is that you were suborned by the Spiders themselves." Hardin's already cool gaze went a few degrees chillier. "And *that* wouldn't be simply an exclusivity violation. It would be contract malfeasance and fraud, both of which are felonies."

"You could certainly file charges and launch an official investigation," I agreed. "Of course, that would mean letting the rest of the world know what you were planning to do. You really want that?"

"Not particularly," he said. "But one way or another, I think we can agree that your actions have voided our contract. As such, according to Paragraph Ten, you owe me all the monies you spent over the past two months."

"I understand," I said. "Actually, as long as we're on the subject anyway, money is the main reason I came here today. I'm afraid I'm going to need a little more of it."

An amused smile touched Hardin's lips. "You have chutz-pah, Compton, I'll give you that. Fine, I'll bite. How much?"

"A trillion dollars ought to do it."

His smile vanished. "You *are* joking."

"Maybe a little less," I added. "We'll have to see how it all shakes out."

"How it shakes out is that you've outstayed your welcome," he said tartly, signaling for the guards standing in the shade of the door palms. "My accountant will contact you when he's finished totaling up what you owe me."

"I'm sure he will," I said, making no move to stand up. "Interesting thing about that young man who died outside the New Pallas the night I left New York. You *do* remember him, don't you?"

Hardin's forehead creased slightly. "What about him?"

"He'd been shot six times," I said. "Three of those shots being snoozers. Yet apparently he was still able to made it from my apartment all the way here to the New Pallas Towers."

"Must have had a very strong constitution."

"Indeed," I said, lifting my eyebrows. "You don't seem surprised to hear that he'd come here from my apartment."

The guards had arrived at my bench now. "Yes, sir?" one of them asked.

Hardin hesitated, then shook his head. "Never mind."

"Yes, sir," the guard said. He gestured to his companion, and the two of them headed back through the foliage toward their posts.

"You see, I got to thinking about him during the trip back to Earth," I continued when they were out of earshot again. "There are really only three possibilities as to who might have killed him." I held up three fingers and started ticking them off. "It wasn't your average mugger, because your average mugger carries snoozers or thudwumpers but usually not both. It also wasn't the man's enemies—never mind who they are—because his presence here would have alerted them to my relationship with you and they would certainly have moved to exploit that. Which leaves only the third possibility."

I ticked off the third finger. "You."

I saw the muscles in his throat tighten briefly. "I was in here with you when it happened," he reminded me.

"Oh, I don't mean you personally," I said. "But you were certainly involved. The way I read it, your people reported there was someone hanging around my apartment, which got you wondering if our deal maybe wasn't as secret as you'd hoped. You told them to bring him in for a chat, but they weren't able to do that. So you told them to get rid of him."

Hardin snorted. But it was a desperate, blustering sort of snort. "This is nonsense," he insisted.

"Only he wasn't as easy to kill as they thought," I continued. "So when they hopped into their car and headed back here to report, he pulled himself up off the pavement, grabbed an autocab, and followed them. That's the only way he could have been waiting for me when I came out that night."

I gestured toward McMicking. "And it's the only way to explain how McMicking was on the scene so fast. He'd gotten the frantic report that the target was not only alive, but was standing on your doorstep, and had gone down to finish the job. Unfortunately for you, I got there first."

"Ridiculous," Hardin murmured. But the denial was pure reflex, without any real emotion behind it.

"That was the real reason you made a point of coming to see me at Jurskala, wasn't it?" I asked. "You'd figured out that the dead man and I were connected, and you needed to find out if I knew you'd been involved."

Hardin took a deep breath; and with that, he was on balance again. "Interesting theory," he said. "Completely unprovable, of course."

"Oh, I don't know," I said. "We could subpoena all the personnel who were on duty in Manhattan that night. Unless the messenger gave someone time to change clips, the presence of both snoozers and thudwumpers implies two shooters. I'd bet at least one of them would be willing to skid on you to save his own skin."

"I'd take that bet, actually," he said with a touch of grim

humor. "But I'm forgetting—you don't have anything left to bet with anymore, do you?"

"You really think your people will fall on their swords for you?"

"No falling necessary," he said calmly. "All you've got is conjecture. There's absolutely no proof of any of it."

"And the courts are open to the highest bidder?"

He shrugged. "I wouldn't go quite *that* far," he said. "But you'd be surprised what the right legal representation can do."

"What about the court of public opinion?" I persisted. "This kind of accusation splashed across the media would make you look pretty bad. And you have plenty of enemies ready to fan the flames."

He smiled tightly. "You, of all people, should know how fickle public opinion is," he said. "A couple of months, and whatever fire you managed to kindle would quietly burn it-self out."

I glanced up at McMicking. He was looking back at me, his face completely neutral. "So you're not afraid of me, the courts, or public opinion," I said, looking back at Hardin. "Is there anything you *are* afraid of?"

"Nothing that's worth a trillion dollars in hush money," he said. "And now you really *have* outstayed your welcome." He started to get up.

"How about the Spiders?" I asked.

He paused halfway up. "What do you mean?"

"Oh, that's right—you didn't know," I said, as if the thought had only now occurred to me. "The man your people killed was an agent for the Spiders. The way I hear it, the Spiders are very unhappy about his death."

Slowly, Hardin sat down again. "It wasn't the way you think," he insisted, his voice tight. "*Yes,* I was concerned about this stranger hanging around; and *yes,* I wanted him out of the picture. But I never wanted him dead. That was a completely unauthorized overreaction."

"I'm not sure that the Spiders would understand that kind of subtlety," I said. "And I'd bet you'd lose an awful lot of money if they embargoed you from shipping anything through the Quadrail. Probably a lot more than a measly trillion dollars."

His eyes hardened. "This is blackmail."

"This is business," I corrected. "Can I expect your credit authorization in a timely fashion? Or do you need the Spiders to cut off all your shipments for a month or two to prove you can't slide anything past them?"

For a dozen heartbeats he continued to glare at me. Then the corner of his mouth curled in surrender. "The money will be messengered to you by tomorrow afternoon," he said, his voice as dark-edged as a death notice.

"Thank you," I said. "If it helps any, the money will be going to a very worthy cause."

"I'm sure it will," he ground out. "Once you leave this apartment, you're to stay out of my way. *Far* out of my way."

"Understood," I said, getting to my feet. I looked again at McMicking, got a microscopic nod of confirmation in return. Hardin would pay up, all right, and he wouldn't make trouble. McMicking would see to that.

And in paying up, Hardin would save the Spiders, the Quadrail, and the entire galaxy. Just one more bit of irony for my new collection. "Thank you, Mr. Hardin. I'll see myself out."

Six months later, I stood at the edge of the icecap that covered Yandro's Great Polar Sea and waited for the enemy to appear.

He came in the form of a dumpy little man in a polar suit who emerged from a small meteorological station perched on the Polar Sea's rocky shore. "Hello," he called as he walked toward me. "Can I help you?"

"Hello, Modhri," I said. "Remember me?"

For a moment the man just stared. Then his eyes seemed to go blank, his face sagged briefly, and he nodded. "Compton," he said, his voice subtly changed. "You who disappeared, only to return from the dead."

"Which is more than can be said for that particular segment of your mind, of course," I said. "My condolences."

"A great mystery, still unsolved," the Modhri said. "Would you care to tell me the story?"

"There's not much to tell," I said. "The mind segment tried to kill me. I killed him instead."

"And now you face me here," the Modhri said, his eyes glittering with anticipation. "A very accommodating Human, saving me the trouble of preparing a suitable death for you in the far reaches of the galaxy."

"I'm afraid you have it backwards," I told him mildly. "It's *you* who's about to die."

"Really," he said, his eyes still glittering as he took a step toward me. "You against me, as it was aboard the Quadrail?"

"Actually, this time it's going to be a little more one-sided." I gestured to my right at the torchcruiser squatting on the rocks, its hatchway sitting open. "Recognize it?"

He glanced in that direction, turned his eyes back to me. "No," he said, taking another step forward. "Should I?"

"I would think so," I said. "I would assume you'd keep track of every vehicle in the entire Yandro system."

He paused, a frown creasing his forehead as he took a longer look at the torchcruiser. The frown deepened as he looked back at me. "You've repainted and renumbered one of them," he accused.

I shook my head. "No. It's a brand-new vehicle, never before seen in this system."

I pointed upward. "So are the three Chafta 201 ground-assault bombers that are currently mapping out the extent of your coral beds."

The walker stiffened, throwing an involuntary glance at the darkening sky. "Impossible!" he hissed. "No vehicle parts or weapons systems have come into this system in over a year."

"Not through your Quadrail station, anyway," I agreed. "Not through the station you've built up such careful defenses around. But then, you didn't know, did you?"

"Know what?"

I smiled. "That Yandro now has *two* Quadrail stations."

He stared at me, his breath coming in quick puffs of white frost. "No," he whispered.

"It's more of a siding than a full-service station, actually," I continued. "Very small, with no amenities whatsoever. But it has a parking area, unloading cranes, a couple of cargo hatchways, and enough Spiders to unpack and assemble four spacecraft and all the weaponry that go with them. Only half a trillion for the whole collection, plus another half trillion for the siding itself. A bargain all around."

"You lie," he insisted, his voice taking on a vicious edge. "I would have known if such money was missing. I have many walkers among the lesser beings at the United Nations."

"Yes, the same behind-the-scenes people who helped push through the Yandro colonization in the first place," I said, nodding. "That's why we did the whole thing with private money, with no trail for your walkers to follow."

"I see," the Modhri said, his voice as bitter as the air temperature. "I should have killed you two years ago instead of merely having you fired."

"You probably should have," I agreed. "But then, you couldn't really do that, could you? Any more than you could haul me into JhanKla's Quadrail compartment or over to the resort casino waterfall and just rake me bodily across the coral. You didn't know who else might be watching, and you absolutely couldn't risk doing anything so blatant that it would draw attention to Humans and the Terran Confederation. You had to play it exactly as you always did, and hope you could either infect me just like any other walker or else find a way to use me against Fayr's commandos."

I inclined my head at him. "Unfortunately for you, both attempts failed."

"I underestimated you," he murmured. "Very well. What are my options?"

I lifted my eyebrows. "Options?"

"You wouldn't have come here merely to gloat," he said. The anger and shock were gone now, replaced with something cold and calculating. "What do you want? Wealth? Power?"

"Ah, so we're going with the three wishes thing," I said, pulling out a comm.

"As many wishes as you choose," he said, his voice smooth and seductive and utterly sincere. "I can give you anything you want."

"I'll settle for a promise," I said, my finger poised over the comm's power switch. "That you'll bring all the rest of your outposts back here, and that you'll let the colonies inside your walkers die. You can live here in peace, but that's all you can do."

He hesitated, then sighed. "Very well," he said. "If there is no other way."

"There isn't." I gestured to the man. "You can start by releasing this one."

The walker's eyes narrowed slightly. Then, with another sigh, he nodded. "As you wish." He took a deep breath, and suddenly the man gave a violent twitch, blinking in obvious confusion. "What—?" he said, glancing around and then looking back at me. "Did you—I'm sorry; were you saying something?"

"No," I assured him. "It's all right now." Nodding, I turned to go.

Hooking his gloved hands into talons, he leaped.

I jumped away, but not far enough. His outstretched hand slapped hard, knocking the comm out of my hand. "You fool," he bit out savagely, grabbing my wrist with one hand and yanking me toward him with unexpected strength. "And now you *will* die."

He was reaching his other hand toward my throat when the thundercrack of a gun came from the open door of my torchcruiser, the impact of the shot throwing him flat onto his back. He skidded a meter across the ice and lay still.

I staggered a bit as I stepped over to him, trying to avoid the bright blood spreading out over the whiteness, my ears ringing with the sound of the gunshot. "Thank you," I said to the Modhri inside him. "That was what I needed to know."

McMicking had joined me by the time I retrieved my comm. "I thought we agreed to use snoozers," I said.

"*You* agreed to use snoozers," he corrected me calmly. "I didn't think it would be smart to take that chance. Besides, the Modhri would have had to kill him anyway once he'd used him to murder you."

"I suppose," I conceded, grimacing down at the dead man.

"Casualty of war," McMicking said. "You ready?"

I nodded, and keyed on the comm. "This is Grounder," I said. "Alpha code beta code omicron. Commence attack."

"Acknowledged," a terse voice came back.

McMicking and I were back in the torchcruiser and starting to lift off when the fire began raining onto the ice and the hidden coral below.

TWENTY-FIVE :

Bayta was waiting for me when I arrived at our agreed-upon Terra Station restaurant. "Well?" she asked anxiously as I sat down across the table from her.

"It's done," I told her. "They hit it, did a second scan, hit it again, and did one final scan. It's all gone."

She took a deep breath. "Thank you."

"No thanks needed," I assured her. "So what happens now?"

She gave me a wistful smile. "I fulfill my part of the bargain, of course."

"No, I meant what happens with the rest of the Modhran mind," I said. "The outposts and the walkers. What are you going to do about them?"

"I don't know," she said. "If the mind goes dormant, we can probably leave everything as it is. If not—if what's left continues trying to grow and spread his influence—I suppose we'll have to try to stop it." Her lip twitched. "I mean . . . *they'll* have to try to stop it."

"You won't be helping?"

"I doubt I'll be of much use to them anymore," she said, her gaze dropping to the table. "I'm not even sure how much will be . . . you know. How much of me will be left."

"You're very close, aren't you?" I asked quietly. "I mean, the two of you."

She gave a little shrug. "I don't know how to describe it," she said. "The goal of the Modhri was to bring all things into himself. The goal with me was to create someone composed of two separate beings who could yet genuinely act as one. It's going to be like losing half of what I am."

"Then why do it?" I asked. "You've gotten what you wanted from me. If this melding and this combined person are so important, why not just renege on your promise?"

"Because this person is only one of my friends," she said, looking up at me again. "You're my friend, too. And friends don't do that to each other."

I felt a lump forming in my throat. "You told me once I wasn't your friend."

She winced. "I couldn't afford to be, then."

"Couldn't *afford* to be?"

"That's why I couldn't tell you everything the night before the raid," she said tiredly. "I couldn't let you trust me. Not completely. If I did, or if I'd allowed even a spark of friendship between us—" Her throat tightened. "That Saarix in your carrybags wasn't for you, Frank. The Spiders hid it there because it was safer than hiding it in mine. But it wasn't for you. It was for me."

"I see," I said, a creepy feeling whispering through me. That possibility had never even crossed my mind. "So you were willing to give up your life for your people."

She nodded. "For my people, and for the rest of the galaxy."

"And now you're willing to do the same for me?" I persisted. "Even now that the biggest danger is gone?"

"To make amends, yes."

"Even though you don't think the woman is worse off than she would have been without your interference?"

"I made a promise," she said simply.

"Suppose I released you from that promise?"

The stiffness of her expression cracked, a flicker of hope peeping through. "What do you mean?"

"I mean that I've thought it through a little since then," I said, leaning back in my chair. "Like I said, you could have reneged, laughed in my face, and walked off onto the next Quadrail. But you didn't."

"Because you're my friend."

"Because you have integrity," I corrected. I wasn't entirely ready to accept her friendship. Not yet. "Besides, what's left of the Modhri may not be considerate enough to simply roll over and die. If he doesn't, we'll need all the resources we can get to defeat him."

"*We?*"

"I still have my Quadrail pass," I reminded her. "And with Hardin still steaming, the less time I spend in the Terran Confederation, the better." I consulted my watch. "The next Quadrail to the Bellidosh Estates-General will be hitting the platform in fifteen minutes. This morning's news said another coral display on Bellis had been mysteriously vandalized, so I presume Fayr and his commandos are still alive and kicking. I thought I might head over there and try to reestablish contact with him."

"Good idea," she said, getting to her feet. "Would you—I mean—"

"Like a little companionship?" I finished for her as I stood up as well. "I thought you'd never ask."

She paid the bill, and we headed for the platform. "There's something I never got around to asking you," she said as we skirted around a drudge carrying a piece of oversized luggage toward one of the other platforms. "Back on the Quadrail, McMicking said something about Mr. Hardin protecting his investments. What did he mean by that?"

"He meant me," I told her. "Hardin had hired me for a private job. *Just* hired me, in fact—we'd only just finalized the details when your messenger showed up with that Quadrail ticket."

"I didn't know that," she said, her voice suddenly sounding wary. "You never said anything to Hermod about another job."

"I thought it might have been a little awkward," I said with a shrug. "You know these ultra-rich people—always looking for new challenges, new vistas, new business conquests. And always in dead secret, of course, lest some competitor get wind of the plan and beat them to it."

"I suppose," she said doubtfully. "What were you supposed to do for him?"

I smiled as I gazed down the Tube. In a universe awash in irony, this was the best one of them all. "He wanted me to find a way for him to take over the Quadrail system," I told her. "I think that's our train coming now."

ABOUT THE AUTHOR

Timothy Zahn is the author of more than thirty original science fiction novels, including the very popular Cobra and Blackcollar series. His recent novels include *Angelmass, Manta's Gift, The Green and the Gray,* and the Dragonback young-adult adventures *Dragon and Thief,* an A.L.A. Best Book for Young Adults; *Dragon and Soldier;* and *Dragon and Slave.* He has had many short works published in the major SF magazines, including "Cascade Point," which won the Hugo Award for best novella in 1984. Among other works, he is the author of the bestselling Star Wars novel *Heir to the Empire, The Hand of Thrawn* duology, as well as other Star Wars novels. He currently resides in Oregon.